P9-CRI-875

Maisey Yates is a *New York Times* bestselling author of over one hundred romance novels. Whether she's writing strong, hardworking cowboys, dissolute princes or multigenerational family stories, she loves getting lost in fictional worlds. An avid knitter with a dangerous yarn addiction and an aversion to housework, Maisey lives with her husband and three kids in rural Oregon. Check out her website, maiseyyates.com, or find her on Facebook.

Published since 2009, *USA TODAY* bestselling author **Naima Simone** loves writing sizzling romances with heart, a touch of humor and snark. Her books have been featured in the *Washington Post*, and *Entertainment Weekly* has described them as balancing "crackling, electric love scenes with exquisitely rendered characters caught in emotional turmoil." She is wife to her own real-life superhero and mother to the most awesome kids ever. They all live in perfect, sometimes domestically challenged bliss in the southern United States.

New York Times **Bestselling Author**

MAISEY YATES

THE RANCHER'S WAGER

**HARLEQUIN
BESTSELLING
AUTHOR
COLLECTION**

**HARLEQUIN®
BESTSELLING
AUTHOR
COLLECTION**

Recycling programs
for this product may
not exist in your area.

ISBN-13: 978-1-335-47389-9

The Rancher's Wager
First published in 2021. This edition published in 2023.
Copyright © 2021 by Maisey Yates

Ruthless Pride
First published in 2020. This edition published in 2023.
Copyright © 2020 by Harlequin Enterprises ULC

For questions and comments about the quality of this book, please contact us at CustomerService@Harlequin.com.

Harlequin Enterprises ULC
22 Adelaide St. West, 41st Floor
Toronto, Ontario M5H 4E3, Canada
www.Harlequin.com

Printed in U.S.A.

CONTENTS

THE RANCHER'S WAGER

Maisey Yates

Chapter 1

Cricket Maxfield had won any number of specious prizes in the game of life. From being born youngest in her family, barely rating a passing glance from either of her parents and being left to essentially do as she pleased, to being the only Maxfield sister born with both pigeon feet *and* buck teeth.

The latter was largely solved by braces, the former was mostly dealt with by casts on her feet when she was a baby.

She hardly walked turned in at all anymore.

All the way to a decrepit ranch that had been buried in her father's portfolio, discovered after his disgrace, and unwanted by anyone else in her family.

She had a feeling, though, that she was about to win the strangest prize of all—six feet and four inches of big, rock solid cowboy.

She couldn't have planned it better if she'd tried.

Oh, *he* didn't think he was going to lose. She knew he didn't. Because he had been betting like a fool all the way through this hand, and he had no idea that she had just gotten the absolute best hand possible.

No. He was playing like a man with a full house or a straight flush.

But she was a woman with a *royal* flush.

This final hand was always the most interesting part of this charity fundraiser, and it was the first year that Cricket had ever been in the hot seat for Battle of the Gold Valley Stars charity poker tournament.

This was the grudge game. This was the game for spectators.

Huge amounts of money had already been counted and distributed in previous rounds, all of it donated by businesses as each player had fought tooth and nail against each other, pouring cash into a pot for the sole purpose of giving back to the community. Now came the part where things got interesting.

Rivals tried to get back bits of their own, as hotly contested items that had been tussled over at rummage sales, and family heirlooms that had gone back and forth in this game for decades, were all put in the pot.

Cricket was currently wearing an oversized black leather jacket with fringes—won in the previous round from Elliott Johns, the guy who ran a water filtration company in the area. She also had an oversized black cowboy hat that she had already won from her current target. It was resting low on her head, and smelled vaguely of sweat, which was unnerving, since smelling Jackson's sweat made her feel strange. Just the idea of it.

It was a bit like that feeling she'd gotten when she

was a child, and had been tempted to do something she knew she shouldn't. A strange tingling low in her stomach, that then went lower and spread down her thighs, making her feel restless and strange. She shifted in her chair, her dress slippery on the material of the seat. Another specious prize. A hand-me-down red gown originally worn by her sister Emerson to this event.

Cricket's fidgeting was just anticipation. And being so close to Jackson Cooper.

A man she usually avoided.

From afar, she had made a study of the Cooper family over the years. Something she was embarrassed to admit.

She had gotten to know Jackson's brother, Creed, a little better over the past few months, since he'd become her brother-in-law. She'd acted shocked and appalled and said any number of things about her sister Wren when she found herself involved with a Cooper. It had gone way past involved now, and they were married with a baby. And Cricket had sworn to Wren, up and down, that hardheaded, irritating, stubborn cowboys would never ever be her type.

Cricket was a liar.

Jackson made her feel strange…but he was also the only one of the Coopers who could answer the questions she needed answered.

Because of Wren, she couldn't really talk to Creed. And she didn't really want to talk to the youngest Cooper either, even though Honey was closer to Cricket's age. She'd never found the other girl approachable.

In some ways, Cricket was jealous of her.

Honey was a country girl. A tough cowgirl. And

she just seemed to fit with her family. In a way Cricket did not.

Case in point, Cricket had never really had much of anything to do with the family winery. But she was a fantastic card player. And with their father officially out of commission—having been exiled in disgrace, and for good reason—Cricket had been nominated by her sisters to take his place.

And Cricket was about to take it all.

"I'll raise you," she said.

Oh yes, it was time. In that pot were a great many things she was interested in. Jackson's cufflinks. His watch. A pony from his ranch.

She'd only had to offer a diamond bracelet—wasn't hers anyway—a case of Maxfield reserve wines, and the dollar from her father's very first sale, which still hung in his vacant office, framed on the wall. Something that Jackson said he was going to give to his father.

The Maxfield and Cooper families were rivals from way back, though that rivalry had been dented some by her sister marrying Creed.

Still, sitting here across from a Cooper brought out her competitive spirit. Especially because right along with that competitive spirit, Jackson also brought out that complicated sensation she could honestly say she wasn't a fan of.

And now it was right down to the final bet.

"I bet myself," she said.

"Excuse me?"

"I bet myself. I will work for Cowboy Wines for free for thirty days."

His brows shot upward. "That's pretty rich."

"You afraid?"

He snorted. "I'll see you. And raise you. I'll work at Maxfield Vineyards for thirty days."

"No," she said. "The winery doesn't need you. You'll work at my ranch for thirty days. And sleep in the bunkhouse." She desperately needed a ranch hand. And she knew that Jackson Cooper knew what he was doing when it came to horses.

Cricket wanted as far away from the uppity confines of her upbringing as possible. And this ranch was her one way to get there.

"And if I lose…"

"You'll work at Cowboy Wines, in the tasting room. Dressed up in cowgirl boots and a miniskirt and serving our guests."

He was trying to scare her or humiliate her. But she'd grown up with James Maxfield. She'd been made to feel small and sad and unwanted for years. It was only recently she'd started to suspect why her father had treated her that way. But after a lifetime of humiliation, a miniskirt and waiting tables wouldn't defeat her. "Deal."

And she wouldn't lose. She wanted his forfeit and wasn't worried at all about her own.

She needed Jackson on her ranch. Unfortunately, she was all stalled out. Didn't quite know where to begin. That's where Jackson would come in handy.

And then there was that *other* matter.

And so she waited.

"You look awfully confident," he said.

"Oh I am."

He laid down his cards, that handsome mouth turning upward into a smile.

The smile of a man who had never lost much of anything in his life.

Oh how she would enjoy showing him what a foolish mistake that smile was.

Because not only had he lost. He had lost to her. A woman at least ten years younger than him, a woman she knew he didn't think of as wise. A woman she knew he thought of as not much of anything special.

He'd made that clear the few times they'd seen each other since they'd become kind of, sort of family.

Dismissive. Obnoxious.

"I hate to be a cliché. But read 'em and weep, cowboy."

Cricket Maxfield had a hell of a hand. And her confidence made that clear. Poor little thing didn't think she needed a poker face if she had a hand that could win.

But he knew better.

She was sitting there with his hat on her head, oversized and over her eyes, and an unlit cigar in her mouth.

A mouth that was disconcertingly red tonight, as she had clearly conceded to allowing her sister Emerson to make her up for the occasion. That bulky, fringed leather jacket should have looked ridiculous, but over that red dress, cut scandalously low, giving a tantalizing wedge of scarlet along with pale, creamy cleavage, she was looking not ridiculous at all.

And right now, she was looking like *far* too much of a winner.

Lucky for him, around the time he'd escalated the betting, he'd been sure she would win.

He'd *wanted* her to win.

"I guess that makes you my ranch hand," she said. "Don't worry. I'm a very good boss."

Now, Jackson did not want a boss. Not at his job,

and not in his bedroom. But her words sent a streak of fire through his blood. Not because he wanted her in charge. But because he wanted to show her what a boss looked like.

Cricket was…

A nuisance. If anything.

That he had any awareness of her at all was problematic enough. Much less that he had any awareness of her as a woman. But that was just because of what she was wearing. The truth of the matter was, Cricket would turn back into the little pumpkin she usually was once this evening was over and he could forget all about the fact that he had ever been tempted to look down her dress during a game of cards.

"Oh, I'm sure you are, sugar."

"I'm your boss. Not your *sugar*."

"I wasn't aware that you winning me in a game of cards gave you the right to tell me how to talk."

"If I'm your boss, then I definitely have the right to tell you how to talk."

"Seems like a gray area to me." He waited for a moment, let the word roll around on his tongue, savoring it so he could really, really give himself all the anticipation he was due. "Sugar."

"We're going to have to work on your attitude. You're insubordinate."

"Again," he said, offering her a smile. "I don't recall promising a specific attitude."

There was activity going on around him. The small crowd watching the game was cheering, enjoying the way this rivalry was playing out in front of them. He couldn't blame them. If the situation wasn't at his expense, then he would have probably been smirking and enjoying himself along with the rest of the audience, watching the idiot who had lost to the little girl with the cigar.

He might have lost the hand, but he had a feeling he'd win the game.

And it was hardly dirty poker. Cricket had started it, after all.

She was in over her head, and he knew it.

When he'd heard that James Maxfield owned the property next to his, Jackson had figured he'd swoop in and buy it now that ownership of the man's properties had reverted to his family. But then Cricket had grandly taken control of the land—with great proclamation, per Jackson's brother, that she was going to be a rancher.

But Jackson knew there was no way in hell Cricket had the chops to start and run a ranch. It was hard enough when you had experience. She had none. And he knew she had some of her dad's money, but it wasn't going to be an endless well.

She was out of her league.

And a month spent as her ranch hand was more than enough time to show her that.

"Also, you should bring my pony," she said.

She was placated by the pony. He was going to end up getting that pony back. He knew it down in his bones. Because in the end, Cricket had not one idea of the amount of work that went into having animals. No idea the amount of work that went into working a ranch. Working the land.

She was stubborn and obstinate, and different than her sisters.

Their families might be big rivals, but they all worked in the same industry. He'd watched Cricket grow up. He had a fair idea of her personality. And he also had a fair idea of just how privileged the Maxfield family was.

They had a massive spread, worked by employees.

Any vision she had of ranching was bound to be romanticized.

He knew better.

He knew people looked at him and figured he was just another guy who'd grown up with a silver spoon in his mouth. Well, not literally. They didn't look at him and think that. He looked like a cowboy. But the fact was, he had grown up in a family that was well-off. At least, for most of his life. He was still old enough to remember when they had struggled.

He knew his younger brother didn't remember much of that time, and their youngest sister, Honey, didn't remember it at all. But Jackson did. He also knew Cricket had never known a moment of financial struggle in all her life. It wasn't that he thought she was stupid. She wasn't. She was bright and sharp, and a bit fierce.

He had always found her fascinating, especially in contrast with the rest of her family. Even before it had turned out her father was a criminal and a sexual predator, Jackson had always found the Maxfields to be a strange and fascinating family. So different from his own. There had always been tension between James Maxfield and his wife. Wren and Emerson had always seemed like perfect Stepford children from an extremely warped, upper-class neighborhood, cookies from the same cutter.

But not Cricket.

She had never been at the forefront of any of the events they had put on at the winery. And though Maxfield Vineyards and Cowboy Wines might have been rivals, they often attended each other's events. Professional courtesy, and all of that. And scoping out the competition. So he'd seen Cricket many times over the years. Usually skulking in the background, but then, when she got older, not there at all. One time, three years ago or so—she must've been eighteen—she'd been out on a swing in the yard, wearing a white dress he was almost certain she didn't want to be wearing. It had been dark out there, and inside, the Maxfield event room had been all lit up.

She was just lit up by the moon.

She had looked completely separate. Alone. And he'd felt some kind of sympathy for her. It was strange, and a foreign feeling for him. Because he wasn't an overly sympathetic kind of guy. But the girl was a square peg, no denying it. And in his opinion—particularly at the time—it wasn't round holes she needed to fit into. Just a family of assholes.

Now, he had changed his opinion on Wren and Emerson in the time since.

But his general opinion of Cricket's family, of her father, had certainly been correct. And just because he now thought Wren and Emerson were decent people… they were still so different from their sister. So different—it was the strangest thing.

But Cricket wasn't so different from her family that she would simply be able to step into ranching life. And he'd be right on hand to show her just how much work it was. He wouldn't have to do anything. Wouldn't have to sabotage her in any way.

She just needed a dose of reality.

And then she'd be willing to sell him that property.

He'd bought his own ranch and transitioned from working the one at Cowboy Wines after his mother died. And yes, he had people who helped him, so they would cover the slack of him not being there.

And that was the thing. Ranching never took time off. That was something he understood, and well.

"Report for work first thing on Monday," Cricket said. "And bring a sleeping bag. I don't have any extra and the bunkhouse gets cold."

She did not shake his hand. Instead, she clamped down on that unlit cigar, scrunched up her nose, grabbed the brim of the black cowboy hat and tipped it.

And right then, he vowed that no matter that Cricket had won the pot, he was going to win the whole damn thing.

Whatever that looked like.

"You *what*?"

Cricket looked at Emerson, keeping her expression as sanguine as possible. She wasn't going to get into the details of any of this with her sisters. Not now. Not just yet.

"Well, you would have known if you would have gone."

"I'm a whale," Emerson said, gesturing to her nine-months-pregnant stomach. "And my ankles were so swollen, I couldn't get my shoes on. So I didn't go."

"And I didn't tell her," Wren said, grinning. "Because I wanted her to hear it directly from Cricket's mouth."

"I won him in a poker game," Cricket said. "I won him fair and square, and now he has to come work on my ranch."

Triumph surged through her again. Her plan was

working out perfectly, and she had a handle on it. All of it.

"Your ranch."

"And I won a pony," Cricket said, grinning with glee. "Why are you looking at me like that?"

"Because," Emerson said. "Jackson Cooper is a tool."

"So is Creed Cooper, but Wren married him." Cricket's teeth ground together as she said that. The whole thing with Wren and Creed had come as a shock, and like with all things Cooper-related, Cricket had kept that shock completely to herself, but she was still struggling with it a bit. "Come to that, your husband is kind of a tool," Cricket said to Emerson. "Just not to you. Also, I'm not *marrying* Jackson, I'm just having him work for me. For free."

She was practiced at pretending she didn't think much of Jackson. But this conversation pushed her thoughts in strange directions. Directions she'd been actively avoiding for months now.

"All right, I have to hand it to you, it's a little bit brilliant."

"I'm just happy to see you're doing something," Wren said. "Unfortunate double entendres aside. We've been worried about you."

"I know you have. For more than a year now. But you are both too afraid to say anything to me."

They didn't know how to talk to her. That was the truth. They might never admit it, but Cricket knew it. Fair enough, she often didn't know how to talk to them either.

"We never know what's going to make you run further and faster," Emerson said. "I'm sorry. But you know... You're not a little kid anymore. But I think it's easy for us to think of you that way. There's no reason for that."

"Glad to know that I'm finally getting a little respect."

"I did question your sanity when you asked to take on the ranch."

"It's paid for. I mean, there's definitely a lot of work to be done on it, but there was no reason to just let it sit there going to seed. And this is something I've always wanted. My own place. Wine isn't my thing and it never has been. I know you're shocked to hear that."

"Yeah, not so much," Emerson said.

"We're just different," Cricket said.

Honestly, she and her sisters couldn't be any more different if they tried. Emerson was curvy—though sporting an extra curve right now—and absolutely beautiful, like a bombshell. Wren was sleek and sophisticated. Cricket had always felt extremely out of place at Maxfield events. It was like her sisters just knew something. Innately. Like being beautiful was part of their intrinsic makeup in a way it would never be for Cricket. And she had never really cared about being beautiful, which was another thing that had made her feel like the cuckoo in the nest.

So she just hadn't tried. Emerson and Wren had. They'd tried so hard to earn Jameson Maxfield's approval. Cricket had hidden instead. Had flown under the radar straight into obscurity.

She could remember, far too clearly, asking her father about college four years ago.

"You didn't particularly apply yourself in school, did you?"

"I..."

"What would you want to do?"

She'd been stumped by that. *"I don't know. I need to go so that I can figure it out..."*

"Emerson and Wren contributed to the winery with their degrees. Is that what you plan to do?"

There had been no college for Cricket.

She knew her dad could afford it. It wasn't about the expense. It was about her value.

Both of her parents had always been so distant to her. And it wasn't until later that she'd started to understand why.

Started to suspect she was not James Maxfield's daughter...

Well, the suspicion had made her feel like she made some sense. That her differences made sense. There were things that hurt about the idea, and badly. But she'd put those things in their place.

She'd had no choice.

"I appreciate it. I do."

"And whatever you think about our husbands," Emerson said, "they're both cowboys, and they would be happy to help you with the ranch."

"I know that. And when I've exhausted my free Cooper labor, I may take them up on it. But for now, I'll solve my own problem."

"Well done, Cricket," Emerson said, sounding slightly defeated. "I can't even see my toes."

"You're not supposed to," Wren said.

Wren's baby was three months old now, and of course, her slim figure had already gone right back into place. But even slightly built Wren had been distressed about the size of her stomach at this stage in her pregnancy.

It was weird to see her sisters so settled in domesticity. Having babies and all of that. They had never seemed particularly domesticated to Cricket, but they had fallen in love, and that had changed them both. Not in a bad way. In fact, they both seemed happier. Steadier and more sure of themselves. But that didn't make any of that racket seem appealing to Cricket.

Who just wanted…to be free.

To not feel any of the overwhelming pressure to fit into anything other than the life she chose for herself.

Maybe she'd wanted something else when she'd been young and silly and hadn't understood herself or her life.

She was the awkward sister. The ugly sister, really. She didn't mind at all about her looks. She was tall, and she was thin, and her curves weren't anything to write home about. But while that seemed elegant and refined on Wren, with her somewhat bony shoulders and knees, Cricket had always just thought her thinness seemed unfortunate on her. Her cheekbones were sharp, and she had freckles. Her top lip was just a little bit more full than the bottom one, and even though she'd had braces to solve the buck teeth situation, the gap between her two front teeth hadn't closed entirely, and it remained.

Her features were… Well, they were strong. And like everything else about her, kind of a love or hate situation.

Cricket didn't much care how she looked. She cared about what she could do. She was good at riding horses. She could run fast; she was strong. Her hair was a little bit wild, but she didn't much mind. No, she didn't mind at all. Because it made her look like she was moving. Made her look like she was busy. And that was what she liked.

That was the thing. As much as the Coopers were supposed to be rivals of her family, in some ways, she could identify a little bit more closely with them than she did with the Maxfields. They had country roots and sensibilities. That was what she understood.

It was what she connected with.

Country strong was hard to break. And that was what Cricket wanted to be.

It was what she was.

"I plan on making good use of Mr. Jackson Cooper," Cricket said triumphantly, immediately picturing the man, his broad shoulders and large hands.

Good for work.

And a good place to start when it came to figuring out how to…how to broach the topic of what she thought might be true between them.

"Yes indeed," she said to herself.

Her sisters exchanged a glance. "Just be careful."

"Why?"

"The Coopers are a whole thing," Wren said.

Cricket blinked. "I don't understand what you mean."

"You start talking about making full use of Cooper men, and I'll tell you, it gives me ideas," Wren said.

Cricket still didn't get it.

"Sex, Cricket," Wren said. "Some people might think you mean sex."

Cricket was suddenly made of heat and horror. "No! No. Not at all. Never. How could you… Look, Wren, I'm not you. When I finally do decide to take on a man, and I'm going to need to get my actual life in order a whole hell of a lot better before I do, it is not going to be… He's *old*."

Among other things.

Wren laughed. "Right. So old. Like two whole years older than my husband."

Cricket sniffed. "And I'm several years younger than you."

Wren seem to take that as a square insult, her lips snapping shut.

Fine. Cricket wasn't old enough to take age commentary as that deep of a wound yet.

"This is strictly a business arrangement," she said. A fluttering grew and expanded in her chest. Evidence of her dishonesty. "He's going to help me with my ranch. And that's it."

"If you say so."

"I absolutely do."

"The one thing I know about you, Cricket. When you set your mind to something, you do see it done."

And what she had her mind set to, was finding out for sure if she wasn't a Maxfield at all...

And hiring Jackson Cooper was the best way to do that.

Chapter 2

The place was a mess.

To call it a ranch was a stretch. The house was... It was damn near falling apart. The porch was sloping on one side. He didn't want the place for its current assets, though.

He wanted it for the location.

This property was the best and only way for him to increase his spread, and that was what he needed to do. He wasn't going to spend his life working on his father's legacy.

He wasn't his father.

And when that screen door opened, and Cricket came out, she looked like the feral pirate queen of a sinking ship.

She had a hat on over frizzy blond curls, and a tight white tank top and denim shorts. She also had on cowgirl boots. She was quite unintentionally the very image of a sexy, tousled cowgirl, and he knew that she hadn't done that on purpose. Not at all.

Her legs were long, endless. Her curves were slight, but they were ripe. She had no makeup on her face, but she was damn pretty. Unique looking, that was for sure. But he liked her look, he found. At least, he had been liking it more and more lately, which he didn't really care to dive into.

He wasn't here to look. He was here to educate.

In such a way that she might realize the subject matter was not for her.

"Reporting for duty," he said.

"Excellent," she responded, grinning.

"So what is it you had in mind, because this is way more than a month's worth of work, I can already tell."

She looked immediately crestfallen and he had to wonder if she was going to make it easy for him. "Why? What do you see?"

"You're liable to fall right through that porch if somebody doesn't get in there and reinforce it. I have some concerns. Are you living in this heap?"

"Yes," she said. "It's fine. I just avoid the saggy boards over there."

"Cricket," he said. "You're about to slide through the whole damn thing."

"I won't."

"Okay. Maybe you won't, because you probably don't weigh a buck and a quarter soaking wet. Somebody like me is going to fall right through."

"Well, sounds basically like the equivalent of a cowboy moat to me. And I may be okay with that."

"You got something against cowboys? Because it

seems to me that you need one to get this place going." He looked around and affected an expression he hoped looked something like overwhelmed.

He'd never been overwhelmed a day in his life.

"You might need more than one cowboy, realistically," he added.

"Nothing *against*. Just don't need one in my house."

"I also suspect that isn't true. Because I'm thinking you probably need some things fixed in there."

She looked stubborn for a moment. But under that he could see…she was wary and he wasn't sure why. He'd never given her a reason to be wary. "Well, maybe a few things. But I can call someone else out for that."

"Why?" he asked. "You've got me."

Her eyes narrowed. "You know how to repair things?"

"I sure as hell do."

"Well… All right. I'll let you come take a look then."

"Lead the way. Point out the mushy boards."

He walked up the steps and through the front door, into the tiny, shabby entryway.

Cricket held her arms out. "Well, this is it." She smiled. "What do you think? Just kidding. I don't care."

He looked around, turning in a circle. "It's…something, Cricket."

To tell the truth, the little farmhouse wasn't so bad. It was worn with years, and a bit shabby, but it was definitely repairable.

What he couldn't imagine was a girl like Cricket— who'd grown up in a monstrosity of a mansion that was doing a poor imitation of a Tuscan villa—settling into it.

"I thought so. It's a ranch. I feel like… That's what I feel like I want to do. Wine's not really for me."

"Yeah, I noticed you were never all that into any of the Maxfield events."

But there was a lot of ground between not wanting to be part of the winery and wanting to run a ranch. She might not know it yet, but he did.

He'd spent years working the ranch at Cowboy Wines. Years. Pouring blood and sweat into his father's land. His father's legacy.

Until he'd found out the truth about Cash Cooper. And then he'd just...

He'd wanted his own.

Now, he still worked at the winery. He wouldn't cause a rift. His mother wouldn't have wanted that. She'd spent years working to make sure she kept the family together at the expense of her own happiness and he wouldn't be the one to wreck that.

But he didn't have to make his father's life his own.

"No, I was really not," she said. "And this has always been kind of my dream. So..."

"Why ranching?"

Her expression suddenly went shy, then sharp. "I don't know. I feel like it's in my blood. Which is weird, because my family doesn't do it. Is that how you feel? Like ranching is in your blood?"

He shifted. Shrugged. "Can't say as I know. It's just something I do. I can't see doing any different."

"Yeah. That's exactly it. Except, it wasn't just right there for me, so I had to figure out what that meant. What it might mean for me that I dreamed about having my own little house out in the middle of... Well, just like this. A field all around. I want horses."

"How are you going to make money? Are you breeding horses?"

"Well…"

"Cattle?" He didn't wait for her to respond. "Dairy or meat? Have you thought about dealing with slaughtering cows? With getting to the nearest USDA station and the cost of it all?"

"I…"

"If you decide to do horses are you going to keep studs or have sperm brought in?"

"Well," she sputtered again.

"Doing produce? More of a farm? Have you thought about CBD? That's a growing industry."

"The thing is," she sputtered, her manner that of a wet hen. "I haven't exactly decided. I don't really know what I want to do with the place. But I kind of feel like until I get a bit more… Until I get it into shape, I'm not going to know."

"I don't know how that's going to work," he said, like he was honestly doing her a favor. The girl had no idea what she was getting herself into. She'd be in water five feet high and rising. Before she knew it, she'd be in over her pretty head.

This was practically a rescue mission.

Yeah, don't go that far. You're being a dick. Own it.

Sure, he'd own it.

Like he'd own this ranch in the end.

But Cricket suffered from the overconfidence of the young and inexperienced. Jackson Cooper hadn't been young or inexperienced for a long time. The problem with someone like Cricket was she was sure she knew exactly what was happening, exactly what she was doing, and she was also certain no one could possibly know better than her.

"I mean, I'll be honest," she said. "I don't know if

I have the fortitude to do beef. But it seems to me that the overhead with horses is really high."

"Horses are expensive. Getting into good ones... That's pricey. But it might be more what you're looking for. Breeding good horses."

"Maybe that's it." That she seemed to be considering anything he said shocked him. "I'll think about it. I'll spend some time reading." She sighed. "Fundamentally, I have time. This place is paid for. And I have some reserves."

"From your dad's estate?"

"Pretty much. I sold my stake in the winery. I wanted out. I wanted to...follow my own path, and I knew I wanted out. So... I sold my stake. I got some cash."

"And you're using me for slave labor."

"Well, since I had the opportunity, that just seems like good business. Why pay for something when you can get it for free?"

"Let's start with the house," he said, walking from the little sitting room into the kitchen. There were spiderwebs in the corner. "Have you cleaned?"

"A little," she said.

He said nothing, he just kept on looking. At the dust, the peeling paint.

She wrinkled her nose. "Okay. I'm not really used to doing any of my own cleaning. I'm not opposed to it. There's nothing wrong with being prepared. It's just... I haven't really done it, so I don't really think of everything. And I hate that, because I don't feel like I'm a spoiled rich girl, but I guess to an extent I am. I feel like I *can* do all these things, but I never have. It's all based on... Well, basically nothing. Just my feelings about the fact that I can do this. But that has to mean something. Right?"

Granted, he was here to try and give her advice. Advice that would discourage her from all this. The truth. He was here to give her the truth, but she was suddenly looking at him like he might contain the answers to the mysteries of the universe, and he had no idea why.

He didn't like it either.

"I don't know," he said. "But I do know that it is always a good time to learn to take care of your own damn self. So go get a broom and clear your cobwebs. I'm going to evaluate." He began to walk the perimeter of the room, making note of places where it felt like there might be water damage. Right by the sink. He wasn't surprised. It was an old farmhouse, and it was easy to believe it hadn't been worked on at all, judging by the rest of the place.

He was surprised when Cricket did what he asked, and went into the small pantry, grabbed a broom and began to harass the spiders in the corners.

"Granted," she said. "I can keep the spiders."

"I would've thought you and spiders were natural enemies."

"Why?"

"Don't they eat crickets?"

She rolled her eyes. "Funny."

Her name was just another thing that didn't quite fit with the rest of the Maxfields. A name with bounce and humor. And he didn't think anyone in her family had an ounce of either. "Why did they name you Cricket?"

"Why is your sister named *Honey*?"

"Well, that's easy. Mom picked it, and my dad agreed because it was so sweet to finally have a girl."

She frowned. "He sounds nice."

That was the problem. Cash Cooper was nice. A good father in many ways. It would have been easier if he was an out-and-out asshole. He wasn't. Jackson resented him plenty sometimes, carried a lot of anger toward him.

But Honey adored him. Creed had been so mired in his own issues he'd never gotten to know their mother as an adult the way Jackson had, and she'd certainly never confided in Creed.

Jackson was the only one who knew.

"He has his moments," he said. "I mean, he's a crusty old man."

"Yeah, well, James Maxfield is a little more than crusty."

James Maxfield had been unveiled as an unrepentant sexual predator. One who'd gotten a girl pregnant and cast her aside, left her a shell of herself after a mental breakdown. A man who'd blackmailed any number of employees who'd felt harassed by him. A serial cheater, liar and all-around asshole.

Cash might have his flaws, but he wasn't that.

"Right. Sorry." Then, he did feel bad, because she looked so lost.

And the way she looked reminded him of how he'd felt when his mother had died. It had been…a hell of a thing to lose her. The entire family had done what they could to stay strong in the aftermath and they had each other. But he remembered that feeling. Cricket was hollow-eyed, and he had to wonder if James's behavior was as shocking to her as it had been to her sisters. It hadn't shocked him. The way his father had always carried a grudge against James Maxfield had made Jackson suspect there was a very serious reason for it. Of course, there would be. His father wasn't the kind of man who disliked somebody just because.

"It's okay. So, how did your dad get interested in wine? You know, since he was a cowboy first."

Jackson peeked under the sink, frowning when he saw water. Then he turned on the water so that he could try and figure out the exact source of the leak. "Well, he didn't like your dad. And I think his aim was more or less to try and prove that he could do exactly what your dad did. But better."

"That's a pretty powerful dislike. To do something just to prove you can. I mean, I respect it. That's exactly the kind of thing I can understand. Needing to prove yourself that much. It makes perfect sense to me."

"A little bit vindictive, are you, Cricket?"

She shrugged. "I think so. I mean, in seventh grade Billy O'Connor made fun of my buck teeth, and then I got braces, and two years later I made him think I wanted to go to a school dance with him, only so I could turn him down."

"That's pretty stone cold."

"He shouldn't of made fun of my teeth. Did you have buck teeth?"

He frowned. "No."

"Did Honey?"

"If so, I don't recall."

"Oh. Well, I do. And no one else in my family does. I think that's kind of weird."

"Families are different."

"Of course. I'm not saying they aren't. I'm just... I dunno. Sometimes I try to see something in common with my sisters, and I just can't. But I don't know. That feeling kind of goes away here. Spiders or not."

"Well, good to know." He knelt down, had a good look at the pipe. "I have some plumber's tape in the truck. But I'm going to need to go get a part from town to actually fix this."

"Can I go with you?"

"Sure," he said.

"Great." He headed back out toward the truck, and he could practically hear her holding something back. "Yes?"

"It just occurred to me that maybe I should go out to the bunkhouse with you. Show you around."

"Okay." He looked at her. "Are you really going to make me sleep in the bunkhouse?"

If he were another kind of man he'd sneak across the field and into his own house. But he was honorable with his dishonor. They'd had a bet.

He was sticking to it.

"Absolutely. It was part of our bet. You're going to be my ranch hand."

She didn't elaborate. Didn't offer any sort of reasoning behind why she needed him here. He just had a feeling it amused her.

Cricket was a bloodthirsty little thing.

He had to grudgingly respect that.

She led the way down a trail that had been worn into the grass, and he followed. And groaned when the very rustic-looking house came into view. "You're not serious."

"I am absolutely serious. What's wrong with it?"

"If the house is dilapidated, how bad is this going to be?"

She kicked open the door, and inside was... Well, pretty much nothing. There were bunks, but they looked like they were moldier than not.

"Cricket," he said.

He'd slept in worse, that was for damn sure. But not for as long as a month.

"Okay," she relented. "All right, I have a better idea. You can sleep in the house."

The look he gave her was full of skepticism, but his skepticism wasn't her problem. She was enjoying talking to him. Trying to get a sense of what he thought. What he knew. If they were *alike*.

And when he had talked about his dad...

She had wanted to know more. She was jealous. Because her own father had never cared for her at all. What would it have been like to grow up on the ranch? To have a place where she belonged. It had actually become something of a cherished fantasy.

The idea that James Maxfield wasn't her father. The idea that she made sense.

"Sleep in the house."

"Yes. There's an extra bedroom."

"Great."

They went back toward the house, him with his sleeping bag in tow.

"There's a quilt," she said.

"Is it full of dust?"

"Don't be silly." She waved her hand. "I beat the blankets out. I looked that up online. I've got this, I really do."

"Right."

"This place wasn't totally unoccupied until recently.

The older lady who lived in it passed away. I don't really know why my dad owned it. He wasn't charging her very much in rent, which honestly doesn't seem like him. It leads me to believe that one of his business managers must've bought it and he didn't remember. Or even know. That does sound like my dad. He doesn't really notice people."

It was weird to call James Maxfield her dad. She had suspected he wasn't for at least six months. Not since she found out that the reason for the feud between the Coopers and the Maxfields was that her mother had once been in love with Cash Cooper.

It had all made so much sense then.

Her mother hadn't felt like she could get married to Cash, because he was penniless. And so, she had chosen to marry James Maxfield, and signed on for a life of misery. But Cricket had long suspected that the reason *she* existed, the reason she was a late-in-life child, was not because her parents had suddenly found a way to rekindle their romance ten years after her sisters were born. No.

It made much more sense to her that her mother had gone straight back into the arms of Cash.

It was just Cricket wanted to tread lightly in finding out the truth. Because his wife had passed away not that long ago, and she imagined it would be very painful for Creed, Jackson or Honey to accept that their father had had an affair.

From her point of view, it was pretty romantic. But then, her father wasn't heroic to her. Cash seemed much nicer. Though, she knew the Coopers loved their mother very much, and she'd seemed like a nice woman.

Cricket didn't like the idea that Cash might have done her wrong.

For all that Cricket could see the affair as a forbidden romance, she imagined the Cooper children wouldn't view it in quite the same way.

So she had to tread carefully. Treading carefully wasn't her strong point. Never had been.

She tramped up the steps again. And Jackson cursed sharply. She turned just in time to see his foot go through the second step.

The only problem with all of her theories had been Jackson. And the way she'd felt about him for the last ten years. And the way her suspicions had forced her to…

Well it was a relief, really. She'd *always* hated how Jackson made her feel. Like her heart was too big for her chest and her breath was too big for her lungs. She'd felt connected to him, from the first moment she'd laid eyes on him, and she'd hated it. Especially as she'd gotten older and seen how badly a relationship could hurt a woman. Her parents' marriage was toxic. She'd never wanted anything like that, but her heart had attached itself to Jackson all the same.

That connection had made a strange, dizzying sort of sense when she'd realized. When she'd figured it out. Because, of course.

Of course she wasn't so foolish as to fall in love with him.

Of course love at first sight wasn't real, especially not as a kid.

Of course that connection was something else.

Of course.

Cricket didn't trade in uncertainty. And for years,

the intensity of the emotions she'd felt around Jackson Cooper had felt *uncertain*.

It was a relief to find certainty.

It was.

"I've never had that problem," she said.

"Like I said. Not more than a buck twenty-five soaking wet."

"Can't help it." She scampered the rest of the way up the steps and into the house. He followed her, and she noticed that he didn't lighten his footsteps at all to make allowances for the fact that some of the boards were iffy. He got what he got. If he ended up severing a tendon it wasn't her fault.

"Thank you for the wild goose chase around your property."

"No, that wasn't a goose chase. We'll goose chase later. There's a pond."

"Do geese favor a pond?" he asked.

"Mine do."

"You have geese?"

"A few domestic. One Canada goose. He has a broken wing. It's flipped kind of upside down. He can't fly."

He frowned. "You have a Canada goose?"

"I do. His name is Goose."

"Creative."

She arched a brow. "Do you have a problem with a Canada goose?"

"No. Not at all. But you can't exactly make a ranch off of them."

"I'm not suggesting that it be a *goose ranch*. But my point is that tomorrow we'll go on an actual tour. No drama. This was just a walkabout."

"I can't believe you were going to throw me in the bunkhouse without ever having looked at it."

She shrugged. "I figured you're tough. And you can take it."

"I could sleep there."

"This will be more comfortable," she said. "Just down the hall."

She didn't really want to alienate him. She also didn't quite know how to wrangle him. She had a feeling that if she suddenly started being extra nice to him, he would only be more suspicious than not. So she was trying to be measured in her interactions with him. She had to… get to a place where she could talk to him. Where they had a little bit of trust. Perhaps like training a dog. She'd done that. That she understood. She might not have any experience with men, but she did know animals pretty well. Her dad might have spent a lot of years ignoring her, but she also hadn't been denied much. And when she'd asked for animals, she'd gotten them. She'd had several dogs growing up, and still had her favorite old ranch dog, Pete.

Perhaps Jackson would be like Pete.

If only she knew how to cook. Then she could feed him. Dogs really responded well to food as an incentive. Perhaps men did too.

She'd heard that. That old-fashioned saying about the way to a man's heart being through his stomach. Not that she wanted Jackson's heart.

Well, she sort of did. She needed him to feel *something* for her. Some sort of connection. Without that, he would just think she was crazy and reject everything she had to say. Without that, he might just think she was trying to ruin his family. And that wasn't it.

Not at all. She had no designs on causing any kind of trouble in his family.

But her own family was broken. Smashed all to pieces. And her place, it had never been secure. She wanted to find her place.

She pushed the door open to the small bedroom. The bed was tiny, shoved into a corner, brass rails surrounding a thin mattress that might just as likely be stuffed with corn husks as anything. The quilt that was placed over the top of it was threadbare and worn.

"It's simple," she said. "But hopefully adequate."

"Adequate." He set his sleeping bag down, and looked around. "It'll do just fine."

"Yeah. I suppose." He looked absurd, too tall and too broad for the space. His feet were going to stick through the rails at the end of the bed. And the little lace curtains behind him… Well, they seemed absolutely ridiculous.

The sun shone through the window, catching his face, highlighting the stubble on his jaw. His hair was dark, his eyes a startling blue. The same color as the bluebonnets on the quilt fabric. She didn't look like him. Not even a little bit. Her eyes were somewhere between pine cone brown and green, depending on how the sun shone. Her hair was light. But his sister had lighter hair. He was so tall. Cricket was fairly tall for a woman. About an inch above average. He was…massive. His hands were bigger, his shoulders muscular. His chest broad. He looked like a man who did hard labor all day, every day.

She felt a strange sort of cracking expansion happening in her chest.

Then he turned and looked out the window, squinting

against the sun, and something in her stomach leaped. And fear gripped her.

He was just very handsome.

Of course he was. It was one of those things that was indisputable. And her feeling about that was…pride. She could see that now.

She was…proud of him.

When she was twelve years old, she'd realized it. The girls in her class were all giggling over Ryan Anderson and his floppy blond hair and she'd been fixed on Jackson Cooper. She'd been a little embarrassed about it. She'd told no one.

She knew she was a girl and he was a man and there was no way they could ever…

She'd never been silly enough or brave enough to write about him in her diary. To have a diary *at all*. But she'd thought of him every night and wove stories where they could be together, on a ranch.

Him all rugged and handsome and her riding a horse right alongside him. There had been freedom in those fantasies. In this idea that her place in the world, her real and rightful place, was alongside this forbidden man whose family her father hated.

She'd never let on how much it bothered her that Wren had swooped in and taken up with Creed. Cricket had been the one full of forbidden desire for years and years.

Wren had gone and made a Cooper and a Maxfield hooking up a thing of no particular consequence.

But now Cricket knew there was consequence after all. And anyway, she'd been twelve when she'd imagined her place by Jackson. When she'd imagined fitting into a life with him.

And it made sense now. That mystical feeling of connection, the idea that she would fit in with his life, with his family... He was her half brother. Of course. Their connection finally made sense.

A twelve-year-old couldn't be in love. The truth was just that the connection she'd felt to him had gotten muddled because she hadn't known.

It was pride she felt for him. That was all. A desperate longing for a place where she fit.

That was all it was.

That was all it could be. All it could ever be.

Get a grip, Cricket.

"Well."

"Did you still want to go to the store?"

"You know. I was actually thinking I might whip up some food. Some dinner. So why don't you go to the plumber, and I'll handle all that here."

"You cook?"

"Of course I do," she lied.

She had either been going down to town and getting a burger for dinner or eating frozen pizza for weeks now. But he didn't need to know that.

"All right. I'll see you in a bit."

"See you in a bit," she repeated decisively. He walked out, and suddenly it was easier to breathe. He walked out, and suddenly, everything inside her chest eased.

She scurried back into the kitchen, and opened up the fridge. Wren had brought her some groceries, and she'd been ignoring them. But now, staring at the leafy greens and wrapped steaks, she felt that she had to figure something out. She picked up the phone and called her sister.

"How do you cook?"

"That is a broad question," Wren said.

"Well. You gave me all this food. And I don't know what to do with any of it. And I just told Jackson that I would cook dinner."

"You're going to cook him dinner? Honestly, Cricket, are you sure you don't have some kind of crush on him?"

That would have been a horrifying thing for her sister to ask six months ago.

It was worse now.

"I do not," she said ferociously, ignoring the tightening in her stomach. "I don't. That would be…ridiculous."

"All right. I'll walk you through… What were you thinking you were going to do?"

"Make steak."

"Right. Fantastic. What else did I get you?"

"I don't know. Green stuff. Green beans."

"Okay. I will walk you through very simple pan-fried steak and green beans. Do you have potatoes? I'm pretty sure I brought you potatoes."

"Meat and potatoes," Cricket said. "Perfect."

And in the end, she barely broke a sweat over the whole thing and managed to put together something that smelled pretty darn decent.

"Thank you," she said to her sister.

"Seriously. Are you okay? Because I feel like this is the most we've talked in…ever."

"I don't know," Cricket said. "I mean, I know I'm okay. I just don't really know how to explain us not talking. Except… I spent a lot of years hiding. Running as fast as I could through childhood. Through that house. I hated it there. I always did. I never felt at home. I never felt like one of you. I don't want to be mean, but nothing with James really surprised me." She couldn't quite bring herself to call him Dad. "He wasn't cruel to me, nothing like that. It's just that he didn't care about me at all, and there was something in that way that he dismissed everything I was that… Nobody ever saw me—and it wasn't your job to. I was a kid and you were teenagers, and then you were having lives. You went off to school. I didn't do that."

"You could have."

"Maybe," Cricket said. "But I didn't know what I wanted anyway. I guess that's the thing. I've never fit. And I've been searching for the place where I do. I think I might've found it."

She might have found her family.

"And now it feels… I don't know, I feel more like talking."

Because even if Cash Cooper was her real father, her mother, Wren and Emerson were still her family. But if her suspicions were right, Cricket could finally disavow that piece of herself that had never really fit. It would all suddenly make sense.

"I can understand that. I always felt like I was being wedged into a life that I didn't fully want. I embraced it, and I care about the winery—I'm happy to work on it now—but, you know, I'm working toward my architectural engineering degree because it's something I always wanted. But I always knew I couldn't because Dad didn't want me to do it, because it wasn't useful to him."

"Believe me," Cricket said. "I do understand that being in his sights wasn't necessarily better. I really do."

"I know. It's not a competition. A tough childhood is a tough childhood. Whether you're in a nice house, whether your dad pays attention to you... Doesn't really matter. It is what it is. I mean, we were better off than a lot of people. But it doesn't take away the things that weren't great."

"I know. Anyway. I... I think I'm going to be happier."

"I'm happier," Wren said. "I think Emerson and I weren't really that much different than you, when you think about it. We started our own lives. Really and truly. And even though we are still maintaining our stakes in the wineries, we have more than that. We *are* more than that. The winery was never for you. And it's a good thing that you're finding the thing that you want."

Cricket nodded, and then after exchanging farewells, hung up the phone. Just in time for Jackson to return with a whole bag full of supplies. He had his cowboy hat on, his jacket. He was such a striking figure. Because he was an emblem. Of what she wanted. Of the life she was hoping to find.

Because he represented something that fit. That was it. That was all it could be, and she had to really know that, understand it.

Had to understand what the extra thump of her heart meant. The jitter in her stomach.

She had to.

She had no choice.

"Smells good," he said.

Deep pride swelled in her chest. "Really?" She cleared her throat. "I mean. Sure. Impossible to mess up a decent steak."

Except she had a feeling it was very possible and if she hadn't been receiving instructions the entire time, she would've definitely done so.

"Well, I didn't realize I would be receiving payment in the form of steak."

"I do try. Food first," she said. "Then you can get to the plumbing." She served their plates and sat across from him. In the tiny kitchen, it felt incredibly…domestic.

It was such a world apart from the life she usually lived. She'd grown up with a grand banquet hall set for every dinner. Her dad all the way down at one end away from the rest of them. This little square table with peeling red paint felt homey in a way dinners never had. And Jackson smelled like soap and skin, close enough for her to get the scent. It was simple. Down-home and perfect in a way she'd always wanted things to be.

There had been a time when she'd dreamed of this. Sitting at a table with Jackson. Asking about his day, having him ask about hers.

Her Jackson fantasies had run the gamut over the years, but they'd always led to one conclusion. The only place for her was beside him.

That had terrified her before six months ago, because—as she'd gotten older—she'd realized what her feelings must mean, and she'd been unhappy with them. Ready to perform an exorcism, in all honesty.

She didn't want to get married and be miserable like her mother was.

It had been a relief to discover the real truth behind her feelings.

"What were your dinners like growing up?" she asked.

She was hungry. But not for steak. She wanted to know him. His family. What his life was like, and how hers might have been.

"Well, something like this. I mean, we started with a house that was pretty similar to this. It expanded as time went on."

"And that changed things? I mean, for all of you?"

"I guess so. I'm probably the only one who really remembers the change. Who really remembers what it was like before. Or... I don't know. Creed probably does to an extent. Not Honey, though."

"Right." So that wouldn't have been different. If she had grown up with them, she would have been like Honey. She wouldn't have known what it was like to have normal family meals around the table. She knew that being wealthy was a privilege. It wasn't that. It was easy to romanticize things you didn't have. Easy to look at them in a simple way. She knew that too.

She wasn't stupid.

She'd spent a lot of time by herself. And as a result, she'd spent a lot of time thinking. She thought a lot about the way other people lived. The way families looked on TV. And while she knew there were other struggles involved in their lives, she also knew that some of the good things they showed on sitcoms were real.

"So you got a big table, probably then," she said.

"What does the size of the table have to do with anything?"

"You know, on TV," Cricket said. "When everybody sits around this little, cheerful table. Just like this. And they have some kind of casserole. It's always casserole. And I don't even know anyone who's ever eaten a casserole."

"Yeah, can't say as I've had a lot of casserole experience myself."

"Well, there's always a casserole, and they're all sitting together, and reaching for the dishes, and talking. And we didn't have a table like that. It was big and long, this banquet hall. As if there were fifty of us, but there wasn't. And my dad would always sit down at his end, miles away. And that's just… It's a metaphor. Really. For my family. All spread out, all engaged in their own thing and not paying attention to each other. Oftentimes we would even have different food. We had a chef. And we could basically put in an order for whatever we wanted at the beginning of the week. We would sit there in the same room and basically all be…separate. And sometimes I just wanted a small table. Because I thought that would fix things."

"Well, we might've gotten a bigger table, but we all sat down at one together."

"Oh," she said, feeling wistful. "You all really love each other."

"You love your sisters," he said, and she noticed he skimmed over her question.

"I do," she said. She looked up at him, taking a chance at meeting his gaze. "My siblings are the most important people in my life."

His lips curved upward, and something in her stomach shivered. She didn't like it. She didn't like the feeling at all.

"Well, I… Anyway. I don't know. I'm just curious. About how other people grew up."

"Did you go over to anyone's house when you were a kid?"

"Not really. My sisters went to private school. They were away from home a lot. They sent me away for a while, but I hated it. I wanted a family, and being at school with strangers didn't help at all. Dorm rooms and formal dining halls and all of that. I just ended up walking the grounds alone. They brought me back. They enrolled me in a school in Gold Valley. But they didn't really want me associating with any of the local people. So I had friends. But only at school. My parents didn't let them come over. They didn't let me go over there. The stupid thing is, I'm not sure my dad would have actually known what I was doing if I hadn't asked for permission. But I've never really known how to live."

Except, she was deceiving Jackson a little bit. And that made her feel... Well, that made her feel marginally guilty. It wasn't the most honorable thing, but her deception was all in service to something bigger.

She looked at him, and the sense of intensity, of longing, grew. She couldn't feel bad. Not now. She wanted him here. She needed him here. And some part of her knew that. On a deep, cellular level. She knew that.

"Anyway. I'm just kind of making up for lost time. For things I didn't have."

"So, you got yourself a little kitchen table."

"Yeah. And you're the first person to sit with me here."

He looked a little uncomfortable with that statement. Cleared his throat. She blinked, wondering what he thought she meant. And then she realized her words could be misconstrued.

"Only that..."

She must've sounded panicked, because he held her gaze, his expression steady then. "No drama."

"Right." His words made her feel immediately soothed and she didn't really know why.

She'd first felt this weird sort of connection to him

years ago. He hadn't been as broad then as he was now. He'd been lean and rangy, and very different from his brother, Creed, who was often at winery events, fulfilling much the same job as her sister. Jackson wasn't a salesman. He wasn't the kind of guy who was in the front of the house. Much like her. He was behind the scenes. It was also very clear that Jackson was an integral part of his family in a way that Cricket had never felt like she was.

Jackson very clearly had a firm hand in everything.

He wore his authority with ease. It was so different from the way her father was. James blustered about, ordering employees around. All Jackson had to do was walk into a room. She had seen him helping with setup at different community parties on more than one occasion. He was a man who led by example. He was a man, she had always thought, to be admired.

And she had. She admired him greatly.

Wherever Jackson was, her eyes seemed to find him.

It was hard to explain how it had felt to find out there was a high probability he was her half brother.

It had been the death of a dream she'd told herself had never been real.

But it had felt like a real, actual death. Before, she might have pretended she knew he was off limits, but apparently part of her had always secretly hoped...

That connection was so powerful. That sense of need she felt when she saw him.

And the connection had only grown and intensified as she had gotten older.

As she began to realize just how much of a misfit she was with her family.

So really, finding out about her mother and his father…it made sense. And she shouldn't be sad.

"I'll help clean up," he said.

"You don't have to do that."

"You said yourself you don't know how to clean. Anyway, there's no dishwasher here."

He took her plate, which was empty, went over to the sink and started running water. She could only stare at his broad back, at the way he worked, smoothly and capably.

And then she realized she was staring at the back of him while he washed dishes with her mouth dropped open. Like he was performing some kind of Herculean effort, rather than just scrubbing a couple of dinner plates and a pan.

She scrambled to her feet and looked around the tidy kitchen. There wasn't really much to do. Not after the spiders had already been chased away and the cobwebs had been dealt with. She grabbed the broom again and began to sweep the floor, even though there was no dirt on it.

But she needed to do something, and she wasn't going to go stand over by the sink.

"Cricket," he said. "Why don't you dry?"

Well, apparently, she was going to go stand by him.

She moved over to the sink, and he thrust a dish towel in her direction. She grabbed it, her fingertips brushing his. His hands were rough.

She'd never touched him before.

She'd dreamed about it.

About his hands.

She hadn't known just how rough they would be.

She felt the lingering echo of that touch and she did

her best to try and ignore it. He was warm too. She could feel heat radiating from his body as she stood beside him. Her shoulder vibrating with it as they stood with just an inch between them while she dried the dishes that he set on the side of the sink.

She looked over at him, and he turned his head. Then she immediately looked back down at the dish in her hand. She was acting weird. And he must realize that. He must know that things were weird. But she imagined he had no idea why.

She could tell him. She could tell him right now.

You don't even know why. Do you get what you're doing?

This wasn't the reaction a woman should have to her half brother.

A pit of despair grew in her stomach.

She was supposed to know better. She was supposed to have fixed this.

No. She couldn't tell him her suspicions yet. It would only cause problems. It would only... It would ruin things. Everything. She couldn't take a chance on springing all this on him too soon.

So instead, she cleared her throat, mirroring the same gesture he'd done only a moment before, and carried the plates to their rightful spot in the kitchen.

"Well, I'm going to head to bed," he said, turning and gripping the edge of the counter. The muscles in his forearms flexed, and she made a study of the red paint on the tabletop. Of all the places that it was chipping and wrinkling.

"It's early," she said.

"Not really."

Then he brushed past her and left her standing in the

kitchen. The room suddenly felt much larger without him standing in it. And that left her with a whole lot of questions she couldn't quite form. And even if she could, she wasn't sure she wanted to know the answers.

Chapter 3

This was Jackson's favorite part of the day. When the sun hadn't risen yet, and he put the coffee on. As strong as he could make it. When the world outside was quiet, and still. When the whole day had a wealth of possibilities in it.

Once upon a time, he'd spent mornings like this with his mother at the kitchen table. His father wasn't one to enjoy mornings. A rancher he was, but he also was always half stumbling out the door after the first rays of light had begun to filter over the mountains, his coffee in a to-go cup, his eyes bleary.

Not Jackson. And not his mom. Four o'clock had been his wake-up time for as long as he could remember. Plenty of time to get a jump on the day. To plan everything that needed to be done. To do it without all the damn people cluttering up the world. Let them sleep.

Those times had become especially precious when his mother had been ill.

He had lived in his own place at that point. But he still worked the family ranch. He got up, he drove over, he sat with his mother and had coffee. And then he went out to work the ranch.

In the years since, he had begun to exclusively work his own place. His father had enough hands on deck to handle the family place without Jackson. And anyway, once his mother had been gone, there had been no real reason to stay. There had been no one to have coffee with in the morning.

Jackson had realized at that time that the only reason he had stayed was that he was hanging on to something in his past that he had known wouldn't last forever.

And once she was gone, it had been time for him to move on too.

Anyway. His father was still barely dragging his ass out of bed and making it out to work on time.

Jackson didn't mind having coffee alone.

He walked down the hall, taking note of each squeaking board as he went into the kitchen and started the pot of coffee. This was not the kind of coffee maker he was accustomed to. But in truth, he could make coffee anytime, anywhere. He could MacGyver coffee with nothing but a tin can, a cheesecloth and a campfire. He could do what needed to be done. He could make this little plastic job work. But he preferred his programmable machine at home. Which had everything waiting for him as soon as his feet hit the ground.

He might enjoy this hour of the day, but there was nothing wrong with wanting everything to be in its place, and as easy as possible. At least, not to his mind.

He thanked the good Lord that Cricket had coffee, and got it all started, his mood lifting immediately as the sound of the water beginning to heat filled the room, as the scent of the freshly ground beans hit him.

He really did love mornings.

He had a feeling Cricket didn't. Because she wasn't up. That actually suited him just fine.

He still couldn't figure out what the hell she actually wanted.

For a woman who said she couldn't wait to run a ranch, she really didn't seem to have a concept of what it took. And then there had been the way she'd behaved last night.

Like you don't know what it is?

Dammit. It really wasn't worth examining. He had been sure that when she wasn't in that dress, when she was back to being the Cricket he had known since she was awkward and had those buck teeth she'd been talking about earlier—which he did remember—those feelings of lust that he'd felt the night of the poker game would vanish.

But the problem was, now he'd seen the potential in Cricket. And he didn't much like it.

He wasn't a man for relationships. He had arrangements. Satisfying, adult relationships with women his age who, for whatever reason, didn't want relationships either. Divorcées, single mothers, busy women who traveled through in a group of friends, or with a bachelorette party. City girls looking for flings with a cowboy.

Yeah, he was down for all that.

But not young, earnest looking girls who had roots in this valley as deep as it was possible to have, who had already been wounded by her father, and who clearly had issues. Daddy issues.

That made him grimace. He supposed being a bit more than a decade older than her put him squarely in the territory of daddy issues.

And what did that make him?

Just a man, he had a feeling. Men were basic. And while he prided himself on maybe not being as basic as some of them, the fact of the matter was... He wasn't any different. He liked arrangements because he liked sex. And he didn't go without.

Come to think of it, though, he'd been without for a while.

He'd had to increasingly spend more time at the vineyard. Their father hadn't really gotten better since their mother had died, he'd only gotten worse. He was withdrawn. And he wasn't functioning in quite the same way that he used to.

Which pissed off Jackson, since he wasn't quite sure why his dad had fallen apart so much, all things considered. But the blowback was hitting the vineyard, and it was hitting Honey, and Jackson didn't want that to happen.

He had no idea how to fix it. Not when he had never really reconciled his own grief, or the accompanying anger at his dad.

His mother had been the single most important person in his life.

She had been a strong woman. And she'd sacrificed everything for Jackson. Everything. He hadn't realized just how much until he'd gotten older. And he'd never had the chance to repay her. He'd been planning on it.

But there hadn't been enough time.

Grief about all that was always close at hand. But here in the silence of the morning, he could remember his mother as she'd been.

And he felt a little closer to her, instead of impossibly far.

He waited until he had his first sip of coffee. A smile touched his lips and he looked out into the yard. Everything was quiet. There were still stars in the sky. Then, once the caffeine had begun to do its work, he decided it was time to make his move. He went down the hall, doing nothing to modify the sound of his steps, and threw open the door to Cricket's bedroom.

"Get up, princess. There's chorin' to do."

"Mfffmmmmmmgh."

"What's that?"

The indignant figure in the bed moved, then sat up. It was dark, but he could see that her pajamas consisted of a white T-shirt. And he wondered if there was anything else. Or if she was bare underneath that thing. Then he quickly turned his focus away from that.

"Go away!"

"It's time to start doing work."

"It's…" She whipped her head around to look out the window. "It's midnight."

"It is 4:30."

"Basically midnight."

"Not in my world. And not in your world either. Not if you want to be a rancher. I thought this was in your blood?"

He couldn't see her face. Obscured as it was by the fact that the light was off. And she was lucky. Because if he'd been in a really mean mood, he might have turned it on. But while he enjoyed harassing Cricket, there was no real reason to poke at her quite that much.

"I think sleep might be in my blood at this hour of the day."

"Too bad. If you have animals, you're going to have to get up and take care of them."

"I…"

"Sorry. That's how it works. You gotta get up early to be ready to work."

"That seems obscene."

"I grant you, I like an earlier morning than most."

"Go away. Morning people are suspicious."

"I made coffee."

She made a rumbling sound again.

"I'm going to go into the kitchen and pour you a cup. Don't make me come back in here and wake you up."

He turned around and walked down the hall. He did not need to see her get out of bed. He did not need to answer any of the questions he had about what she was or wasn't wearing under that T-shirt.

He didn't like the whole thing. This whole sudden, errant attraction to Cricket. It could definitely be argued that it would be a fine enough thing in theory. Because it wasn't like they weren't both adult people, even if he was a bit older. But he couldn't give her anything. And that… That didn't seem fair. She was young and scrappy and trying to make it on her own, and the last thing he wanted to do was…

Well, none of it bore thinking about because he was a grown man. And thinking a woman was pretty didn't mean acting on anything.

He wouldn't do it. Most especially because he was here to talk her out of her ranch. He had his limits.

He got a small, chipped mug out of the cupboard and poured some coffee in it. Just in time for Cricket to appear, in what he thought might be the same T-shirt, her blond hair resting on top of her head in a messy knot, jeans and a pair of boots.

"Good morning," she groused.

"You said you wanted to be a cowgirl."

He handed the coffee mug over to her.

"I was unaware that being my own boss would involve being woken up at a specific time. Hey. I'm your boss. You're not my boss."

"Yes. But the land waits for no one, Cricket. That's your first lesson in being a real, bona fide rancher."

"I don't like it."

"Doesn't matter. Why do you love the idea of being a rancher?"

"I don't know," she said.

"You have to do better than that."

"I feel… I don't know. I feel weird and wrong most of the time. I feel like I don't fit. But outdoors, I always felt like maybe I belonged. You know, I was better at riding horses, at dealing with bugs and dirt and all of that kind of stuff than my sisters. It was something I was just naturally more comfortable with. And maybe that's not right or fair. Maybe that's a little bit smug. To like something simply because I was better at it, when I couldn't be better at school, or being pretty."

"Better at being pretty?"

"Oh, come on. Wren and Emerson are naturally elegant and completely and totally perfect in every way."

"They're perfect when it comes to their particular kind of pretty, I'll give them that. And I'm not going to say people don't tend to have their favorite kind of flower. But all flowers are pretty."

"Surely not all of them."

"You're messing with my metaphor."

"It's too early for metaphors."

"It's never too early. Drink your coffee."

He didn't know why he felt the need to be nice to her. It was just that she seemed…utterly lost. He related to the feeling. He supposed that in some ways, losing whatever connection with her father that she'd had—though she claimed that it wasn't a very deep one—was a lot like a death.

And he knew what it was like to lose a parent. It was hard. It had left him feeling… Honestly, he hadn't known what to do after his mother had died. He hadn't been ready for it. No one was ever ready. But he had felt deeply and profoundly unprepared for the way the grief had rocked his life. For all the things he'd left unsolved and unsaid. For all the regret he felt on her behalf.

He knew she'd felt stuck in a loveless marriage. Even though she'd loved their family. Loved the kids.

Sometimes he felt…responsible for her unhappiness.

His dad was mired in grief, as if she'd been the love of his life, but sometimes Jackson thought the real reason his dad was mired in grief was that he'd known they *weren't* the loves of each other's lives and they'd trapped each other.

Sometimes, as a family they'd been so happy…

It didn't matter. All he knew was there was something in Cricket that he recognized. Didn't matter that she was a completely different creature than him. He knew what she was feeling.

And he might resent the position he found himself

in, but honor prevented him from backing out. Anyway, now that he was here, he wanted to help her.

She sat at the table, her shoulders hunched up by her ears, and sipped her coffee a bit too slowly for his taste. He liked a leisurely morning, but you needed to get yourself out of bed a bit earlier if you were going to be that sluggish with it. Granted, they didn't actually have specific chores. But this was her lesson. Her lesson in ranching. And if she really thought she was going to do it… Well, then she had better get used to this.

He didn't think she would, though.

In fact, he had a feeling he was a step closer to being able to make his move than he'd thought he'd be at this point.

"Come on, little Cricket," he said as soon as she had drained the last drop of her coffee.

"I'm not little," she said.

"You are to me."

"I'm quite tall," she sniffed.

He looked down at the top of her head. "Again. Not to me."

"Well, you're ridiculous. Height runs in your family," she commented.

"Honey is short."

"But you and Creed are very tall."

"Yes," he agreed.

She seemed suddenly renewed, and he opened the front door and held it for her, and she went past him, going straight down the steps. "What are we going to do?"

"Well, why don't we start by looking at your pastures and your fencing. Then we're going to take a look at the barns and see what kind of shape they're in."

"That's all a very good idea," she said.

"Well, that is why you hired me. Or rather, won me."

"Yes," she said, frowning. "I suppose you are the expert."

"Say that again?"

"You're the expert," she said, but this time angrily.

"Just remember that."

He opened the door to his truck.

"What are you doing?"

"I figured we'd drive."

She got in, grumbling the whole way. They started driving out on one of the access roads that went toward the back end of the property. They would start there, and work their way back. At that point, the sky was beginning to lighten, and turn a bluish gray. The mountains were like sloping ink spills bleeding down into the fields. It was a beautiful piece of land. Hell, if Cricket didn't want to keep it, he'd be happy to add it to his own portfolio.

"Except," she said. "You do kind of have to admit that there is no actual reason for us to be up this early since there are no animals."

"Again," he said. "Practice. And also to give you a little dose of reality."

"You think I need a dose of reality?"

"Before you go committing to having lots of animals, I do think you probably need to have an understanding of what you might be in for."

"Bully for me."

"Yeah, well. You chose me to be your consultant."

"Ranch hand," she corrected.

"Yeah, who's calling the shots?"

She sputtered. But at that point, he put the truck in

Park and got out. "Oh boy," he said, going up to the edge of one of the fences. It was light enough to see now, now that the sun was rising, the sunlight spilling rapidly over the landscape. "This fence is a mess. You're going to have a lot of work ahead of you."

"Well, we need a crew."

"We're going to have to figure out your budget."

"Don't talk to me like I'm a child. I do understand that. I know I haven't lived on my own, and I know that I come from money, but I also know there has to be money. Don't worry. Like I said, I sold my stake in the vineyard. So I have a bit of cash."

"Great. You're going to need quite a lot of cash."

"I'm sure you have an idea of how much a winery like Maxfield Vineyards is worth."

"True." Cricket was probably a fairly rich woman at this point. Even selling a quarter stake would've probably netted her quite a lot. "But it still wouldn't hurt you to have training. There may be an emergency, and you may not be able to get someone out here in time. What's going to happen if part of your fence comes down and you've got horses everywhere? You're going to have to know how to solve some of your own problems. Fortunately, I have tools. This," he said, indicating the whole fence line, "is going to be a hassle. And you're right. We're going to need to get a crew out here. But we can start it together."

"That sounds unpleasant."

"No, sweetheart. It's ranch work." He handed her a hammer and a pair of wire cutters. "Living the dream."

Cricket was exhausted and sore by noon. But at least then Jackson produced beer and sandwiches, and she found herself sitting happily on the tailgate of his truck, eating and watching as he continued to work. He never stopped.

"All right," he said, "let's head to the barn."

"We're not done?"

"Nope. And this is ranch work when you haven't got any animals. I'm just letting you know what you're in for."

"I feel like you're trying to actively discourage me."

He lifted a shoulder. "If you can be discouraged from being a rancher, then you should be."

"What does that mean?"

"That it's a hard life that often produces very little profit. And if you don't love it, you should do something else."

"Why would you say that?"

"Because it's the kind of thing that needs to be said, Cricket. If the work doesn't deter you… Then it doesn't. But you know, you could still live here without being a rancher. You could lease the fields to someone. Or you could sell up, get yourself a nice farmhouse and a couple of chickens."

"I don't want to do that," she said, feeling resolute. "I want to have my own life. My own land."

That statement was clarifying.

Because honestly, he had worked her ragged enough today that she had begun to question some things. And yeah, she was having to admit that she was a little sheltered. That she hadn't done all that much work in her life. She had done a lot of running around in the country, and she had managed to equate that with doing this kind of work. But it wasn't the same.

She just wished that she could do things half as effortlessly as he could. His body was a machine. Every muscle, every movement contributing to the other. She felt like she was all thumbs. That it took her five hits of the hammer to create the same kind of movement he got out of one. He was more efficient, more precise... It was frustrating. Maddening, even.

Though watching him was...

Well, she was learning a lot. She felt her cheeks get prickly. But she chose not to think too much about that and got into the cab of the truck with him as they drove to the barn.

He parked in front of the old, run-down building, and the two of them got out.

He walked over and pushed the door open, muscles straining. And yet again, she realized she was standing there gaping at the back of Jackson Cooper.

She mobilized herself, scampering through the open doorway as soon as it was wide enough for her to get through.

He came in behind her, and she could feel him. It was the strangest thing. Like there was energy crackling between them. It was more than just his body heat; it was something else.

She turned, and was looking up underneath his jaw. At the square line there, the stubble on his chin, his lips.

His lips were really very compelling. They were turned down slightly, naturally, which gave him a bit of a grim look. An intensity. That was one of the things that had always fascinated her about him. That quiet, brooding intensity. Something she did not have in common with him at all, because there was very little about her that was brooding. She wasn't quiet, she just avoided things by choice.

She took a step away from him and moved deeper into the barn. "Well," she said. "This is it."

He made an amused sound. "Not much," he said. "Is it?"

"No. I mean, all of it can be revamped." She looked at him sharply. "I know that it costs money."

"I know you do."

"Well, you do a lot of lecturing. So I can't exactly be sure."

He walked past her, and she noticed, not for the first time, that he had a very particular scent to him. His skin and soap and the wild. The pine from the trees, and a bit of the earth. "This could be a decent facility, with some upkeep. Don't get me wrong. I'm not trying to discourage you. I promise."

"Well, that's good to know," she said.

"There is a whole lot of moldy hay in here, though. We need to get it cleaned out. Why don't you grab a shovel?"

"More chores?"

"Yes," he said. "Actually, thinking of it as chores is kind of counterproductive. It's part of the gig. Part of life. Everything in life that you care about, whether it's your house or the land, has to be taken care of by somebody. I understand on the Maxfield family spread that somebody else does a lot of the caretaking. At our place, the Coopers do the caretaking."

"And you're currently caretaking your own ranch?"

"Obviously I have help," he said. "Which is good for you. Because if I didn't, I wouldn't be here."

"Right, right."

"Grab a shovel."

That was how she found herself feeling sweaty and

indignant, moving great piles of moldy hay out into the bed of his truck.

"It will make decent enough compost. But you don't want it in here," he said.

"It smells," she said.

"A whole lot of things about ranch life smell."

"I don't mind it," she said, resolute.

"Sure."

"I really don't. I was just saying."

He arched a brow, half of his lips curving up into a smile. "You do a lot of questioning for somebody who just knows, and is fine with everything."

Her cheeks burned. She didn't really know why. "I'm fine," she said, stepping into the corner and grabbing another shovelful of that vile hay.

"Yeah, you seem totally fine."

"It's just a lot to learn. I'm happy to. I want to. That really is why I…" Except that would be a lie. She was about to finish the sentence with *it was why I wanted you here*. But it wasn't why. The words caught in her throat, and then her gaze caught his and held. She couldn't seem to look away. And he didn't look away either. He was close.

Closer than she had realized a moment ago. Or maybe the space around them had shrunk. She didn't know which. Except, of course that was impossible. But there was something about his nearness that felt impossible all on its own. Like she had been dropped onto an alien planet, into an alien body.

But there was no guide for how this should feel. Living with this man who had captivated her for the better part of a decade. This man who was so unlike anyone she'd ever known, and who she didn't really know, but who felt like he might be the answer to *something* all the same.

This was not what she'd dreamed about. But...she had to make what she was feeling something else because the only other option was for everything she'd suspected to be nothing and she couldn't bear that either.

To have her life just be the same.

To have her whole self just be the same as she'd always been.

His gaze flickered downward, and she realized that he was looking at her mouth. And that was when the tension in her stomach twisted, making her organs roll. Causing her heart to stutter.

And suddenly, her mouth felt like it was on fire. She was just so very aware of it. Had never, in all her life, been quite so conscious of the fact that she had lips.

But she was now.

Because he had looked at them. Because he was standing there, so close. Because they were sharing this space, sharing the air. Because he fascinated her in a way no one else had.

Because he had the answers.

Her heart started racing.

No.

No.

She had never been this close to him. And last night his hands had brushed hers and now he was standing right there. She knew she had to think of him differently now, and not as a man, like she'd always seen him. But she couldn't make him that. She just couldn't. Couldn't force her body to acknowledge what her brain suspected, no matter what she'd tried to tell herself about their connection.

He was there. And she *wanted*.

It couldn't be.

But then the light went on in those eyes, and even she could recognize the expression there, because she'd eaten dinner with the man last night.

Hunger.

And she felt it. She felt an answering appetite low and deep.

He moved, and she didn't know if it was toward her or away from her, because she dropped her shovel and ran out of the barn.

Ran.

Like the devil and all of hell was coming after her. Ran and didn't look back. Ran past his truck, through the fence, and out into the middle of the field. She stopped, panting, her forehead damp with sweat. She planted her hands on her knees, and only then did she realize what she'd done.

She had run from him.

He must think she was insane. She was acting insane. Except...

Why?

The word was more a groan in her soul than a real, actual word. A deep, enduring sadness that made her feel like she might be crushed with it.

It wasn't fair. It just wasn't fair. How in all the world was he...

The one man, the *only* man, that she had ever felt this for?

She was sick. There was something wrong with her. *You always knew there was something wrong with you.*

Yes, but she hadn't thought *this*.

She made a rough sound of distress. Out loud, and she didn't care if it carried all the way back to the barn. She couldn't care.

She looked around suddenly, wildly, to see if he was behind her. He wasn't.

Why was this happening to her? She had thought she had finally been on her way to finding her place. She had been resolute in winning over Jackson, in getting to know him so she could approach him about their potential connection...

And what if he had been moving toward her? What if he had been about to kiss her?

Well, then everything was ruined. Absolutely everything.

Cricket wasn't one to cry. She wasn't one to give in to despair. But she wanted to now. Yes, she did. She wanted to now because she had thought she'd found a way out. She had thought she'd found a way to change her life. To change everything. But she hadn't. She was just weird, awkward Cricket, who would never find a place that felt comfortable.

Because this certainly wasn't comfortable. This was an abomination.

And you're not a baby. You're going to figure out how to face him, apologize and get your head on straight.

Yes, but she couldn't face him now. So she spent about an hour picking through the field and ignoring the fact that she was going to have to face him eventually. And when she finally went back to the barn, his truck was gone, and so was he.

And it left Cricket to wonder if she had hallucinated the whole thing.

Chapter 4

Jackson had decided to go to town to get some things for the ranch, and check on his own spread. Anyway, a drive to town was good for a little bit of self castigation. Obviously, he had terrified Cricket earlier when he'd moved in on her. He could pretend that he hadn't been about to kiss her. But he had been. And he knew better. Earlier, he had decided that he wouldn't. But for a minute there, she had seemed like she wanted him to, and his reasoning had gotten lost.

He hadn't felt like an ass for having ulterior motives for agreeing to the bet, knowing he'd lose. Knowing it would put him in a prime position to convince her to sell. Until now.

Because one thing he wouldn't do was get into a personal relationship with her while trying to get her land.

That was a step too far.

He had thought about going after her, but he had figured it would only create more problems. She had run for a reason, after all. It was pretty clear she didn't want him to go after her.

Now, of all the reactions he'd had from women he'd made a move on, running full tilt the other direction wasn't one of them. Sure, sometimes they might decide they weren't into it, and then all it took was a simple no thanks. He wasn't a man to push himself on anyone. And anyway, he didn't have to.

But Cricket had run like he might. And that made him wonder things about her. And he didn't want to wonder about her. Not any more than he already did.

He also figured that while he was out, he should go and check in on his father. Honey still lived at the ranch, and he knew she took on a fair amount of responsibility. Probably more than she should. It suited him that she was relatively sheltered, he had to admit.

And that got him right back into guilty thoughts and feelings about Cricket. She and Honey were roughly the same age. And if a man his age made a move on Honey, she wouldn't be the one running away. *He* would, with Jackson right after him.

He maneuvered his truck down the driveway, up to the winery show room. The place was no less grand to him now than it had been when he was a boy. It always would be. But he would also always picture his mother standing there, waiting with a smile. No matter how many years she was gone, that's what he would see.

But she wasn't there. It was Honey.

"What brings you around?" his sister asked, pushing the door open to the tasting room. "Aren't you in indentured servitude to Cricket Maxfield currently?"

"Currently."

"Honestly, I'm glad you lost the bet. I can't imagine having her working the tasting room."

"What do you have against Cricket?"

Honey shrugged. "I just don't really know her. Anyway, she's not all that friendly."

He frowned. "She's not particularly unfriendly."

"I don't know. She's weird. Don't you think?"

He thought about all the things Cricket had said. About feeling out of place. And that his sister's take, that she was weird, made him feel...

Sorry for her, he supposed.

"That's not a very nice thing to say."

"Since when do you care?"

"I don't."

"You must, a little."

He shrugged. "She's a nice kid. Anyway, I feel bad for all of them."

"Maybe someday I'll get there. I still can't believe Creed married Wren."

"You like Wren."

"I know. But... Isn't it weird? Switching allegiance like that."

"The problem was James."

"I don't know. I think it's deeper than that. Dad really..."

"Dad's not perfect," he said. "Dad's feelings on something don't have to be the final say."

"I know that."

Poor Honey had only been a teenager when their mother had died. And Jackson felt like she had thrown herself in a relationship with their dad even deeper, trying to please him much more than she would have if that hadn't happened. There was no gray area with Honey when it came to Cash Cooper. While Jackson's relationship with him came with about fifty shades of it.

"Speaking of Dad," Jackson said. "Is he around?"

"Yeah, he's just back in the office."

The main office for the winery was at the back of the tasting room.

"You have any groups coming today?"

"A couple. Stick around, it's a bachelorette party."

And he found he had no interest at all. He found he was soured on the thought of it. Maybe his reaction had something to do with a woman running flat away from him not that long ago.

Or maybe it had something to do with Cricket herself, and her deep, seeking eyes. And that pretty mouth of hers.

Well.

He waved a hand toward his sister, then walked back to the office, his boots making a hard sound against the reclaimed barn wood floor. He knocked once, then opened the door without waiting for his dad to respond.

"The prodigal has returned," Cash said.

"Just to check in," Jackson grunted.

"Jericho came by yesterday and made it sound like you are pretty busy with your new boss."

"Yeah," Jackson said. "Jericho can shut it." Jericho was basically another brother to Jackson. They had grown up thick as thieves, and had started their own ranches about the same time. Like a brother, Jericho could also be a spectacular pain in his butt.

"Why exactly are you here?"

"I came to check in on you. I don't like being away for so long."

"You don't sound happy about it."

"What's going on, Dad? Look, I've never called you out. Not once. Not in front of Creed, and not in front of Honey, and I won't. Not even in front of Jericho. You might not be his dad, but he looks up to you. But I was closer to Mom, and I know that… I know that you're grieving. I believe that. But I don't get exactly what you're grieving. Because I don't think she was the love of your life."

"Jackson…"

"I know that things weren't always great with you."

"I loved your mother."

Jackson paused, a muscle jumping in his jaw. He wasn't going to argue with his dad about what he felt or didn't. "I'm sure you did. But enough that you're still nonfunctional five years later?"

He sighed. "It's complicated."

"I'm sure it is."

"You've never loved a woman in all your life, Jackson, let alone two. So what would you know about the kinds of things that I've been through?"

Jackson's senses sharpened. "Two?"

"I'm not going to discuss it with you. All I can tell you is nothing in my life has been right since I lost your mother. There are a variety of reasons for it. And maybe you're right, but to me it's not so simple. And maybe you don't think I deserve to have the grief and regret that I do. But I do. You know what's worse than grieving the love of your life? I think it might be grieving a person you wronged."

"What exactly…"

"Not up for discussion. Why don't you get on back

to the Maxfield property? Used to be you were all so against them."

"*You* were against them," Jackson said.

His father cleared his throat. "Yeah. I was."

"Not anymore?"

"James was the problem."

"I figured as much."

"Turns out he was a problem for everyone."

"Again, not a surprise."

Though, Jackson wondered if her dad's problems had been a bigger surprise to Cricket than she let on, and if that was maybe part of *her* problem.

He had no idea what his problem was. Why was he overthinking every interaction with Cricket? He didn't overthink anything. If anything, he tended to under-think. He was a man of action. If there was something to be done, he liked to get it done. But maybe that was the problem. He couldn't quite figure out Cricket's aim in having him work at the ranch. Yes, she needed some guidance, but she often seemed to bristle beneath it, and she seemed more interested in him as a person then she did in his ranching expertise half the time.

But then, when he'd nearly kissed her, she'd run away. He would have thought that if there was a motivation, her having a crush would make sense.

Still, he preferred to take his chances with Cricket than trying to stand here and reason with his father. Trying to understand his father. "I'll see you around. Just... Why don't you go to the bar tonight or something? Do something. Honey shouldn't have to cook you dinner every night."

"She doesn't have to. I could easily get food from the winery."

"She doesn't want you to do that. She wants you to take better care of yourself. And you not doing it is keeping her here."

"Didn't keep you here."

"Yeah, well, I don't feel responsible for a stubborn old man. And she does."

He put his hat on his head and walked out of his dad's office. Honey was standing in the middle of the room, and Jericho was there too.

"Don't you have your own place?" he asked his friend.

Jericho grinned. That particular grin of his, the one he got when he wasn't being genuinely friendly. "Yeah. I do. Just came to see how everyone was faring. Saw your truck, and thought I'd see how you were doing with your life as a ranch hand."

"What is it exactly that you find that so funny?"

"Because long as I've known you, you've never taken orders from anyone. And I hear you're taking orders from her."

"Not exactly."

"And sleeping in a bunkhouse," Honey said. "If I recall the terms of the bet correctly."

"Turns out the bunkhouse was in disrepair. I'm sleeping inside."

That earned him openmouthed stares from both Jericho and Honey.

"Really?" Jericho asked, a dark brow lifting.

"Really," he said, giving his friend a flat look.

Jericho frowned. "I didn't take you for a cradle robber."

"I'm not." He shoved his discomfort aside, shoved

the memory of a couple hours ago aside. "Anyway, I didn't take you for a busybody."

"Well, it's not every day my best friend is suitably lowered to such a position. I'd be lying if I said I wasn't enjoying it."

"Some friend."

"I never claimed to be a *good* friend, just the best one you have."

"No kidding," Honey said. "Just an exasperating one. Anyway, I have work to do, unlike you two lazy cowboys. I actually still work here."

"And the place is hopping," Jericho said, looking around the empty space.

"I have a bachelorette party coming in twenty minutes. And no, I've decided neither of you can stay. I can't bear watching you go for the low-hanging fruit. I'd like to have more respect for you."

"I never pick low-hanging fruit," Jericho said. "The sweetest ones are at the top of the tree."

"Well, put up your ladder somewhere else, cowboy. Because you're not picking off this one." She made a shooing motion with her hands. "The ladies deserve to have a party in peace."

Both he and Jericho allowed Honey to kick them out of the room, and he walked out toward his truck with his friend. "What were you really doing here?"

"I… I have a meeting with your dad."

"You have a meeting with my dad?"

"Yes. About the vineyard."

"Really?"

"You and Creed are silent partners. At least, more or less these days. Your dad is… Well, he's not enjoying this as much as he used to. He wants to get out of it."

"Are you buying my dad out?"

"Talking about it."

For some reason, that bothered Jackson. "You didn't think to talk to me about it?"

"It's a business deal, Jackson. I don't have to talk to you about my business."

Jackson knew that Jericho had been very successful with investments. His friend was a rancher, but he was a great deal more than that. Successful, extremely so, and not because he sat on his hands, or did things with caution.

"No. But you are my friend."

"Yes. I'm talking to you now. But I figured I would have a conversation with your father before I did that. I haven't finalized anything yet."

"What's the deal?"

"I'm buying half. And I'm going to transition to running the day-to-day."

"That means you're buying Honey's portion."

"She hasn't come into it yet. Because of her age. So yes."

"She's going to be…"

"She should be free of this. Don't you think?"

"Now you're going to tell me that you have nothing but my sister's best interest at heart?"

Jericho shook his head. "No. But I care about her too. I'm not just acting without thought."

Jackson shook his head. "She's going to kick you in the nuts."

"She might. Like I said. It's business. It's not personal."

"It kind of has to be personal. Given that our relationship is personal."

"If it were personal, I would be buying him out for a good deal. I'm not. I'm overpaying."

"Well, at least there's that."

His dad hadn't told Jackson, of course. Bottom line, there had been a wedge between his parents whether his dad was ever going to address it or not, and by default Jackson had ended up on his mother's team. They had all rallied when they'd needed to. His dad had been there for his mom. He couldn't fault him for that. No. If only it were more straightforward. If only things had been toxic. Because if they had been toxic then Jackson could have disavowed his dad. If his father hadn't been there for his mother, then Jackson could easily cut his father out of his life.

But it was never going to be that simple. His dad wasn't a bad man. But as far as Jackson could tell he'd been a bad husband.

He'd also been there when it had counted.

"Look, I gotta get back to work. I'll see you around."

Jackson got into his truck, leaving Jericho standing there, leaving his conflicted feelings there at Cowboy Wines, because it was easier than staying and confronting them. Honestly, dealing with Cricket was much easier than all of this.

Chapter 5

Cricket was bound and determined to pretend that nothing had happened earlier. Though, when Jackson arrived in his truck, she was a little bit chagrined. She had hoped that she might get a small reprieve. After all, he hadn't said why he'd left, and it was entirely possible that he figured, since she had run away from him like someone not thinking straight, he had every right to back out of their agreement. But no, he was back.

She flung open the door to the house, and stood there with a grin fixed permanently on her face. A grin that dared him to comment.

He got a couple of paper bags out of the truck, and held them. Standing there staring at her.

"Glad you're back," she said.

"Yeah," he said. "I'm ready to fix the sink."

"Well great," she said.

"Yeah, I said I would."

He slammed the door of the truck shut and began to walk toward her. She scampered back through the entryway, but still stood there, with her hand on the door. She didn't want to look like she was running scared. Not again. She needed to get a grip. That was the thing. She needed to stop acting this way.

"I really appreciate it."

"Yeah, I mean, you said."

He brushed past her, and she held her breath. Because she didn't want to smell him. Didn't want to get the impression of his scent again, because it did weird things to her insides and she heavily resented all the weird things Jackson did to her insides. She couldn't think about it right now though. Because she had to act… She had to act like everything was okay. She just really desperately needed to pretend like everything that happened earlier hadn't happened.

He set the bags on the table and she stood in the doorway, watching as he got out pipes and tape and tools.

"Do you want to learn something?"

"Well, you are ever the teacher."

They had found a way back to their earlier rapport, so there was that.

"That I am."

"Where's the water shut off, Cricket?"

"I don't know that," she said.

He shook his head. "Well, we're going to have to turn the water off or we're going to end up with a flood."

"Okay. Maybe it's… Maybe it's in one of the cabinets."

"The water shut off is in the cabinet."

"No, I mean the instructions. There's some paperwork that has information on the house. In this cabinet." She walked past him and reached up into a cabinet that was full of papers. She didn't have enough dishes or utensils to bother moving them. She had plenty of space in the kitchen that they could stay right there. She pulled out the paperwork and spread it out on the table, rifling through the sheets, but he had already walked out of the room. She heard the door shut, and a few moments later he was back.

"Found it."

"How?"

"Logic. Experience," he said. "Anyway. It's fine now."

"I should probably know where the water shut off is," she said, still standing there holding the papers.

"I'll show you afterward." He got down underneath the sink, tools in hand, and began to dismember things.

"Can I hand you stuff?"

"Sure."

They set up an assembly line, where he asked for things, and she handed them to him. When he was done, he would give it back, and she would put it on the table.

Things felt not quite so fraught. And it was easy for her to forget that earlier today had gone so horribly wrong.

"Come down here," he said.

She started. "What?"

"I want to show you something."

Slowly, cautiously, she knelt down beside him. It wasn't him she was afraid of. It was herself. He wasn't the one who knew why earlier was such a disaster, and he probably didn't even…well, she hadn't stayed to find out if he'd even been leaning in toward her. It was all in her head, that was the thing. So she resolutely got down next to him and made a valiant attempt at not breathing the same air, since that had caused her some serious problems earlier.

"What are you showing me?"

"I'm going to have you fit the pipe."

"Oh…okay."

He handed her a wrench. "Lean in and tighten it right here."

She leaned in and she couldn't help but breathe. And when she did…

When she did, she was overwhelmed by him.

Why did he have to smell so good? Why was he so compelling? She looked at the square line of his jaw, the straight blade of his nose. The intensity in those eyes. Those eyes that had always been so fascinating to her.

It *had been* a crush but now it *couldn't* be.

It couldn't be.

It couldn't be.

She still couldn't breathe.

She looked down. But then… She could feel him looking at her, and she couldn't keep herself from looking back.

And when she did, he was so close. His eyes were so intent on hers. She had run away earlier. And she had been smart to do that. She had needed to do that.

She should run. She should run. She should move away. Because this was wrong. And it was crazy. *She* was crazy.

And for some reason—anger, rebellion against what she was feeling—she didn't run. Instead, she leaned forward.

Instead, she closed the distance between them.

She was going to prove, once and for all, that she did not want him.

This would disgust her.

It would burn all those feelings to the ground.

And for the first time in her life, Cricket's lips touched another person's.

Because she was sure she'd find that once she kissed him, once she took the mystery out of it all she'd be disgusted. She had to be, right? Because surely, *surely*, nature would take care of this and she'd recoil in horror when their mouths met.

As soon as her lips touched his, though, she knew she was wrong.

It was like a flash bomb had gone off inside of her stomach.

And Cricket ignited.

He moved, large, rough hands cupping her face, holding her steady as he consumed her. His whiskers were rough, his mouth hot. He smelled like heaven.

She was shaking. Guilt warred with desire as her mind went blank of everything. Of what she should be doing. Of who he was. Who she was. And what she suspected. It was all gone. There was nothing left but the intense sensation of being touched by him, kissed by him.

How had this happened?

How had she… How had she ended up desiring him?

You don't know? As if it hasn't been halfway to a crush all this time?

She'd been fascinated by him but she'd never called it that. She'd been interested in him, intrigued by him, but she'd never…

And then she'd found out about their parents and…

and…she'd thought what she'd been feeling was something else.

She didn't know anything.

She'd moved to this ranch convinced that she was
finally figuring things out. Finally making a move toward having a life that she wanted. But here she was,
drowning in confusion. Drowning in desire. A desire
she had no business feeling. Not at all. Here she was,
making the biggest mess of everything that she could
possibly make.

She was less certain now than she'd been before. Less
of anything, less of everything. And more too.

Jackson Cooper. This is Jackson Cooper.

And he's probably your half brother.

She jerked herself away from him, gasping. "No."

"Cricket, it's okay," he said. "You don't have to run
away."

"No," she said. "I might."

"You don't need to be afraid of me."

"It's not you I'm afraid of."

"What?"

"It's me," she said. And much to her horror, tears
sprang to her eyes. And they started to fall before she
could even consider holding them back. Cricket didn't
cry. And here she was, weeping like an inconsolable
child in front of Jackson. He must think she was insane.
She thought she was insane.

"What is it?"

"It's us," she said. "Jackson," she said. "I think you
might be my brother."

Chapter 6

Jackson was on his feet and halfway across the room as soon as that last word came out of Cricket's mouth.

He didn't know what the hell she was on, but she was wrong.

He knew that down to his soul.

He had a sister. He knew what that felt like. This did not feel brotherly at all. Not in the least. Absolutely nothing about what he felt for Cricket could fall under the heading of familial. She was a beguiling little minx who had essentially been a source of irritation for him for the last several years, and then had turned into a wholly irritating, and far too attractive, woman.

Then she'd kissed him. And now she was telling him that she thought she was his sister.

"You better explain yourself, and quick."

"I just… I found out something about our parents.

My mother and your father... They used to be... Did you ever wonder why your father hated mine so much? I mean, beyond the fact that James is a real piece of work, there had to be something else. And I knew there had to be. Well, my mother started talking about it more. And since she and my father got divorced... Well, she told us. She told us that she used to be with your father. She was in love with him, but he was poor, and she chose to marry James instead. Why am I so much younger than my sisters? It doesn't make any sense. I don't fit with them. I fit with you."

"Cricket," he said. "You are not my sister."

"I pretty much have to be," she said.

"You pretty much don't," he said. "There is no way, no way in hell, that you could possibly be my sister."

"Why not? I think it makes plenty of sense. Seems to me that it's reasonable enough."

"There is nothing reasonable about any of this."

"I have always...thought that I didn't fit. And I think this is why."

"So why did you psychotically decide to kiss me?"

"To prove it would be gross!"

The way his blood was burning through his veins made a mockery of that statement. He just stared at her.

"Hey," she groused. "*You* almost kissed me earlier. Why do you think I ran away? It's wrong, Jackson. And I was just trying to make it right and now I messed it all up!"

"Get in the truck."

"What?" she squeaked.

"Get in the truck. There's one person who can settle this."

"I mean," she said, using that same arch, certain tone

she'd used many times she'd been certain, but wrong, in the time he'd known her, "there are DNA tests that can settle it. Many men in labs could settle it…"

"We're talking to my father."

"Oh…"

"I'm going to have him tell you, once and for all, you couldn't be his daughter."

"I…"

"Did you talk to your mother?" he asked.

"I… No. I didn't ask her directly. But you have to understand that she… It took her so long to tell me any of the specifics about her life. About her relationship with your dad. We're not really all that close. And I just didn't… Talking to her won't mean a lot to me. I won't believe that it's true."

"I'm sure that if you told her you were considering jumping my bones, she might give you the straight answer."

"Don't say that. Anyway, I never said I wanted to do that. I just kissed you."

"You're not in high school, Cricket, when does it end with just a kiss?"

"Well." She didn't know what to say to that, and it was clear. And he was being mean, but he…

Hell. His father had cheated on his mother…

Would it really surprise you?

He didn't think Cricket was his sister. End of story. He knew too much about women and chemistry to think it, even for a moment.

His certainty in his libido was sound.

His certainty in his father? Less so. And even though he knew Cricket had the wrong end of the stick here, he was worried that one piece of it might be true.

He had enough of a hard time with his old man without having to believe he'd been unfaithful to his mother.

"Get in the truck," he said. "I'm not repeating myself again."

They marched out to the truck, and he jerked the passenger side door open for her.

"Thank you," she said softly.

"No problem."

He started the truck and pulled out of the driveway much faster than necessary. "Why didn't you tell me? Why didn't you tell me right away when you had a suspicion?"

"Because. Because I knew that... It doesn't bother me to think about my mom cheating on my dad. I wouldn't blame her. I think she loved your dad, and she made a terrible mistake. And I can see how... When someone gets under your skin, Jackson, it's not that easy to get rid of them. I can understand that."

"Can you?"

"Yes," she said, filled with fury. "I can. I don't judge my mom. Except... Except on behalf of yours. Because I know how much you love your mom. And she was a lovely woman from what I remember. And she's gone, and I just didn't want to... I wanted to get to know you better first. I wanted to figure out the whole situation."

"Why didn't you just ask Creed?"

"I'm not even that close with Wren and Emerson. I'd like to be closer. But... That's the thing. We're not a normal family, and we never have been. They're close with each other because they're close in age. Because they had more in common in their upbringing. I'm different. I always have been. So I'm not just magically close with Creed because he married my sister. I'm not even magically close to my sister."

"What? You thought you'd become magically close to me?"

She made a sputtering sound. "I've always… I… I don't know. Forget it."

He thought back to how she'd trailed after him. Like a damn puppy when she'd been young. Had she thought he was her brother even then? No, she'd said that it only occurred to her recently. And all his thoughts, all his intentions toward buying her ranch, everything…just kind of faded away.

Because handling this was what mattered.

Settling it was what mattered.

He pulled up to the winery and saw that there was still a light on in the tasting room. He was sure that his dad was still in there.

"Come on."

"Okay," she said, clearly filled with trepidation.

He gripped her arm, and propelled her forward.

"Can you not touch me?" she said, jerking her arm out of his hold. She was as disgusted by the whole thing as he was.

Except.

Except, the problem was his body wasn't all that disgusted.

His blood was on fire from that kiss. And while there had been a momentary dampening caused by the shock of what she'd said, it had not created in him an instant disgust.

They needed to get this settled.

He needed her to be as sure as he was that there wasn't any truth to her suspicions at all.

Fact was, he was sure he had more experience than Cricket when it came to sex. So maybe she was naive enough to think they could be related, but he was not confused about connections, chemistry and attraction.

And he knew what was happening here.

None of it was familial.

He opened the door to the tasting room and walked in. Cash Cooper was standing at the back of the room, examining the stock.

"Dad," he said. "We need to talk."

His father turned, shock registering on his face when he saw Cricket standing there. "What can I do for you?"

"Oh…" Cricket started to fidget. "I just had a question to ask."

"What's that, young lady?"

"Well, I kind of need to know if I'm… If I'm your daughter."

It had happened. *It had happened.*

She was standing there in front of Cash Cooper, and she was asking him if she was his daughter. Except now… She hoped that it wasn't true.

Because Jackson was in her blood. And she…she wanted him. And she had been so sure she could overcome that. That she could put all these feelings in their proper place, but she hadn't managed to do it. She didn't know if she ever could. She just didn't know. She had tried. She had tried, and it had ended with her kissing him on the floor of her kitchen.

Everything was a disaster. It was an absolute and total disaster. But then it had been from moment one, hadn't it? Because there were only two scenarios here.

One, she was hopelessly and utterly attracted to Jackson Cooper who was unobtainable in every way, who would never want her, and who would never keep her even if he enjoyed kissing her, and she was just out of place in her family because she was.

Or the second one, which was that she was unforgivably, irrevocably attracted to her half brother.

No, she couldn't win.

"What made you think that, young lady?" Cash asked.

And he was so kind, it made her heart ache. It made her chest feel like it was being cracked in two, because James certainly wouldn't have been this nice. She wanted Cash to be her father, but she did not want Jackson to be her brother, and she didn't think that there was...

There was just nothing.

"My mother told me. She told me she was in love with you. She told me that she married James Maxfield and it was the wrong choice. And I've just never felt like I belonged. I've never felt like I fit. When she said that it all made a lot of sense. That... That maybe I'm not a Maxfield, and that's why I don't fit. That maybe I was supposed to be here the whole time. Because I want to be a rancher. I don't want to spend my life in a stuffy winery. Because I want different things and I look different and I act different and I... I just thought maybe that was why."

"Cricket," Cash said, and his voice was so kind and gentle she thought she might break apart. "I'm not your father."

She wanted to cry. In despair, with relief.

Jackson wasn't her brother.

He wasn't her brother. So that was... There was that.

Beside her, she heard him let out a huge sigh of relief. And that brought a skeptical look from Cash, but he didn't say anything. Then he looked back at Cricket. "I did love your mother." Then he turned to Jackson. "I… That was the problem, Jackson," he said. "I loved Lucinda. And I never quite got over it. You know… You know that your mother and I got married because she was pregnant with you. I acted rashly because I was heartbroken. She and I both paid for it for years. We tried. And we love you kids. With everything. I cared for her. I cared for her a whole hell of a lot. But you know what makes me the most sorry? That I could never be the husband she needed. That she died being with someone who always had feelings for someone else. That's what kills me."

Cricket felt guilty. Standing there listening to this.

It was clearly a private conversation, one that needed to happen without her presence. But here she was.

All because she had been…

Because she had been so desperate to fix this thing inside of her.

What was wrong with her? Something was wrong with her. And there always had been something wrong, and this was just further evidence of it.

A tear slid down her cheek and she felt horrified. Horrified to be displaying this kind of emotion in front of not just Jackson but Cash. This man who wasn't her father, who should feel nothing for her at all.

"You look like your mother," he said softly.

She hadn't expected that. It was like an arrow to the heart.

"No, I don't," Cricket said. "My mom is elegant. And

pretty. And her hair never…does this," she said, gesturing to her curls.

"She used to be like you, Cricket. And she was my first love. Just like I was hers. But love wasn't enough. Not for her. That's fine."

"It wasn't fine though, was it? She was miserable. She was absolutely miserable being married to him. I hope you weren't miserable."

"I wasn't miserable," he said. "I think I might've made my wife miserable. But I wasn't. Still, I have a lot of regrets."

"My father doesn't have any. His only regret is that he's lost everything. He doesn't care about anything or anyone else. When I say everything, I don't mean us. James Maxfield never cared about a damn thing. And he's…he's my father."

Sadness settled deep in her stomach. Because for just a little while she had hoped. She had really, genuinely hoped…

"Did you ever cheat on Mom?" Jackson's voice was granite.

"No," Cash said, addressing his son. "I swear it. I swear to you I never did."

"Well then. I guess that answers all those questions."

"I'm not sure if I should apologize or not," Cash said.

Cricket shook her head. "I should. I assumed something about you that wasn't fair. And I did it because I… I'm not happy with my family. I'm not happy with my place in it. But that's just the way it is. There's no answer for it. So… So. That's it."

Then, she turned and ran out of the tasting room, back to the truck. She leaned against the door, breathing hard.

She was doing so much running.

And all she could think was—what a mess she'd made out of everything. She'd revealed to Jackson that she was interested in him, revealed that she had suspected he was her half brother... Every single thing that she'd been so bound and determined to have control over, she had gone and just made a huge mess of. He was never supposed to know that she was attracted to him. And she was supposed to time this whole thing... better. But did it even matter?

He came out a few moments later, looking like thunder. And she knew that the truth didn't matter. She had managed to absolutely and totally... She felt stupid. And small. And wrong.

Every bad thing she had ever felt, it was magnified now.

"I can walk..."

"You cannot walk. Get in the damn truck."

She didn't even argue, because she felt too guilty. Too bad. So she got into the truck, and they made the drive back to the ranch in total silence.

She was going to send him away. Send him back to his place, because there was just no... There was no point in anything. She wasn't a rancher. It wasn't in her blood. She had spun herself all manner of fantasies about Jackson Cooper when she was a girl, when she didn't know anything about anything. And then, when her family had imploded, she had spun different fantasies altogether. She had watched her beautiful, elegant sisters win over handsome cowboys, and Cricket had realized that her own darkest, most cherished secret— the thing that she had lied about for years—would never come true. Because Wren had gotten the interest of Creed, and Wren was…well, she was beautiful.

Elegant and sophisticated and refined and everything Cricket could never be.

And not only was Cricket too young for Jackson to ever evince an interest in, she was also just… She was just her. And so yes, it had been convenient to weave a new fantasy. About all the reasons why she might feel wrong. All the reasons why she might have felt connected to Jackson, ways that explained away the feelings that she had, but that would still mean he mattered.

She stumbled out of the truck when they got to the house.

"Jackson…"

He rounded the front of the truck quickly, his eyes filled with liquid fire. "First things first," he said.

And before she could react, before she could open her mouth or say anything, his lips were on hers. And he was kissing her again. Deep and hard and longer than the first time. There was rage in this kiss. An intensity that she had never known a kiss could possess.

Wrong.

Small.

Ugly.

All the words that she felt inside—all the words she had used to describe herself—slowly began to fall away, each pass of his mouth over hers stripping them back. Creating something new inside of her. Something different. Something she had never experienced before. Like an avalanche. One of need and desire and hope.

It was the hope that stunned her. Suddenly that yawning, cavernous thing in her chest was filled with light.

Suddenly it was lifting her, propelling her forward. Up on her toes and more firmly into his arms.

He angled his head, his tongue passing over hers.

And she felt right.

Because this had been the feeling all along. That first connection that she'd felt to him. When she had first known what it meant that she would be a woman some day, and that she would want to be in the arms of a man, and that she was certain that man was Jackson Cooper. In that one blinding moment he had taken everything that felt wrong and turned it around.

Because he had kissed her.

She wasn't wrong about that. He was kissing her, and he was doing it with just as much passion as she felt inside of her for him. And if he felt that, then she wasn't wrong.

She hadn't been wrong.

Life had been wrong.

And she had altered her expectations, changed what she felt to make it easier to digest. She had been trying to create a story that was easier to live with.

One where her father didn't love her because she wasn't his.

One where her mother found her difficult because Cricket was a reminder of sins.

One where she was so different from her sisters because they were only half of each other.

And one where Jackson mattered not because she had an unobtainable crush, but because he was her long-lost brother.

One where she wanted to be a rancher because she came from a family of them, not just because she did.

But this was proof.

That she had her own dreams just because.

That she was herself, wholly and singularly, for better or for worse. That she wanted him, maybe because—like ranching—he was too big, too unobtainable and too impossible to have.

Maybe that's who she was.

A pioneer. A person who saw what was possible and asked for that little bit more.

A person who looked around and said this doesn't have to be just enough, I can have more, I can have better.

Maybe that was who she was.

It was a revelation. Just like his arms, just like his mouth.

But then, just as suddenly as he kissed her, he was pulling away.

"That had to happen. Because I had to... I couldn't leave it at that last one. Not with what you said."

Cricket launched herself back into his arms. Because she didn't want to be anywhere else. Because she wanted to feel. All these things that he and he alone had made her feel for all these years.

It was done. That was the beauty of it. The beauty of having made such a damn fool of herself already. There was no going back. There was nothing to protect.

The crushing reality was that James Maxfield might be her father. Or he might not be. But the one thing that mattered most was that Jackson *wasn't* her brother.

Her long-held crush had no doubt been revealed by her earlier actions, but that was freedom in many ways. She had wanted him—she had wanted this—for so long, and there was no reason to not simply...take it now. None at all.

So she did. She drank deeply from his mouth like she was a dying woman and he was the source of life-giving water.

His whiskers were rough beneath her palms, where she grabbed hold of his face and stretched up as hard as she could, on her toes, kissing him with all the breath she had in her.

"What exactly do you want?" he said, large hands grabbing her hips and setting her back on the ground. "Because you've got to know, little Cricket, that you're playing with fire here. I don't want you to get burned."

She scoffed. "I'm not afraid of fire."

"You're not?"

She tilted her face upward. "I'm not afraid of anything."

"You're trembling."

"Yeah, that happens sometimes, when a woman is turned on, didn't you know?" She spoke with a bravado she didn't necessarily feel.

"You might have to educate me on the subject."

"I'm not afraid of anything, do you know why? Because… I already can't have the approval of my family. And you know, I was really scared of what it meant that I wanted you, suspecting what I did. I was really scared to look foolish, but you know what? I did. I do. So where is there to go from here? I guess I could fear for my own physical safety, but I don't. Not when you hold me. I spent my whole life wanting things I couldn't have. Wanting my parents to care about me in a way that they didn't. Wanting to fit in a way that I couldn't. Wanting to be part of a family that I wasn't." She felt like it was the better part of valor to maybe not mention that wanting him was part of what she'd been denied for all this time. She might not have a whole lot of pride, but she had a little, and she was going to protect it.

"I'm tired of that. No, I'm not afraid of this. I'm not afraid of you. I'm just afraid of living more of the same."

"Marriage is not for me," he said. "Just right up front. Relationships aren't for me."

"That's real flattering, cowboy, but did I propose?"

"I'm just getting that out there, Cricket, because I can't ignore the fact that you had a hell of a day, and from the sounds of things, a hell of a few weeks. On top of that, you are younger than me. And I just need to make sure that we are both completely aware of what this is."

"I want you. I'm very tired of not having the things I want."

"Seems fair."

It was deeper than that. But it wasn't really his business. She had a feeling, though, that Jackson Cooper was a mountain she had to climb if she was ever going to figure out what lay on the other side of him. On the other side of this. Because honestly, the weirdness of the last few months was all bound up in him, and before that, years of a crush that had quite overtaken her life.

So, there was no magical, mystical connection to the Cooper family.

But Jackson was still a thing. And that needed to be sorted out before she could be the new Cricket. This woman who was going to make a way apart from her family. This woman she wanted desperately to be. Needed to be.

He was so tall and strong and beautiful. And she had no idea what he was getting out of this. But that wasn't her concern. Her concern was...*her*.

It didn't matter what anybody else thought. Didn't matter what anybody else wanted from her, what they thought of her. It didn't matter what he thought. She had been dragged into Cash Cooper's very own tasting room, and she had accused him of cheating on his wife. Had asked if *he was her father*. She had reached the height of humiliation. So she was all in on this, because there was nothing left to protect or destroy.

She was Cricket, reduced.

And she wanted to build herself back up again.

"I'm tired of talking," she said.

Talking wasn't her thing. She had spent so many years just off on her own, daydreaming about the life she might have someday. She had done more talking with him over the last week than she had ever done with anyone, really. She didn't want to talk. She just wanted him.

"Suit yourself."

That was how she found herself being lifted off the ground, his large hand on her ass, around her back, as he picked her up and kissed her, hard and deep. She could feel his body, firm and insistent against hers, evidence of his arousal. And it thrilled her. Thrilled her down to her soul. To know that he wanted her the same as she wanted him. To know that, of all the mistakes she'd made, and all the things she might have done wrong today, she hadn't dampened his desire for her.

He did want her.

He did.

His kiss was wild now, far beyond anything she'd ever fantasized about. She'd done a lot of fantasizing about Jackson Cooper, but it had been gauzy, and it hadn't been half so physical. She hadn't really known about the heat of another person's body pressed against hers, the rough feeling of his whiskers, the firmness of his mouth. That slick friction of his tongue against hers. The way their breaths would mingle, the way she could feel his heart raging through his chest and against hers. Those rough hands, moving over the fabric of her T-shirt, and then under it, against her skin. His body was so very hard.

No, she hadn't counted on this. The intensity of it. The reality of it. It was blindingly brilliant and beautiful, and was making her into a version of herself she hadn't known was possible—a wild creature, which in many ways she'd always been, but with aim, with purpose.

Because her wildness was pouring out of her and over him. She didn't feel embarrassed. Didn't feel nervous.

There was no inhibition at all. She bit his bottom lip and he growled. And she didn't know why she'd done it, only that it had felt right. And she didn't question it. Didn't question anything. This felt natural. This felt right in a way that nothing else ever had in her entire life. He felt right, fitted against her, the softness of her body seemingly made for the hardness of his, and she couldn't recall a time when she had ever felt so…right. So real. So complete.

So certain that the things about her that were different were what made it all so good.

For all her life she'd felt like the lone misfit toy on an island of beauties, and now, she didn't feel misfit at all.

No, she fit just right.

He carried her up the front steps, stumbled slightly on a board, then braced her hard against the door, and she gasped. His erection pressed firmly between her thighs, hitting her right where she was the neediest for him. At the place where she was desperate with longing.

He rocked against her, growling as he took the kiss deeper. She gasped, letting her head fall back, arching into him, rubbing her breasts against his chest, reveling in how sensitive she was.

She had been so ashamed, so embarrassed of her every desire for a great many years—to feel a total lack of that shame was a revelation she hadn't known she'd been waiting for.

He pushed the door open, then propelled them both down the hall and toward his bedroom. Toward the little twin bed there.

She doubted he fit on it by himself, she had no idea how the two of them were going to fit. But her bed wasn't any larger.

He didn't seem concerned at all. Just like a loose board hadn't caused him to make a false move, the bed size didn't do it either.

With knowing, competent hands, he pulled her top off over her head, and with one deft motion took her bra with it.

She was standing there, totally topless in a pair of jeans, and mesmerized by the look of abject hunger in his eyes.

He wanted her. More than a little. He wanted her, and it was obvious.

And she, with all her slight curves and frizzy hair, felt desired. Felt beautiful.

She closed the space between them, pushing her hands beneath his shirt, loving the feel of his hard muscles, the rough hair that covered his hot skin. She'd never thought much about sex in general. Only sex with *him*. But he was far and beyond anything she'd ever fantasized about. Far and beyond anything she'd ever dreamed she might have.

She pushed his shirt up and over his head, revealing his body. So much more beautiful and perfect than she could have ever imagined. That broad chest, lean waist and perfectly defined muscles. He was all things masculine and glorious, and everything feminine within her bloomed with glee.

And suddenly, she wanted to cry. Because Cricket Maxfield never got what she wanted. Cricket Maxfield never got the best or the brightest. She had the leftovers of her family's gene pool. She wasn't brilliant or beautiful, particularly ambitious. She wasn't the one the sun shined down on with favor.

But she had wanted Jackson Cooper for as long as she'd known what it meant to want, and she was getting him.

Whatever happened after this didn't really matter.

Because this was the most perfect moment she'd ever felt. Ever experienced.

Oh, she'd tried to pretend that her feelings for him could be something other than this, but they couldn't be. This was the connection. For her, this was what it was. What it always would be.

"What?" he asked.

"You are just stunning," she said.

He laughed. Honest to God. A chuckle rumbling in his chest. And then she found herself caught up in those big, strong arms, her bare breasts brushing against his hot, rough skin.

"Well I'm glad you think so."

She found herself being kissed again, and all the while his hands worked on getting rid of her jeans, her panties, socks and shoes.

Until she found herself stretched across the bed with his big body over the top of hers. She completely naked, he still in his jeans. The denim was rough between her thighs, the delicate skin there scraped by the raw material. And she could feel him, right there, so hard and insistent and…

She ached.

And he just kept on kissing her. And kissing her. He shifted slightly, putting one hand between her thighs, finding her slick and wet, each pass of his fingertips over that sensitized bundle of nerves creating a white, electric heat that nearly left her blinded.

She had never felt anything like this before. And yes, she'd put her own hand between her legs plenty of times, but it wasn't like this. His skin was rough, and she had no control over how fast he worked, how slow. How much time he took. And when he pushed a finger inside of her before drawing her wetness back out over the source of her desire, she gasped. He did it again, and again, adding a second finger to the first, until she was sobbing. Until she was begging. For what, she didn't even know.

She fumbled for the front of his pants, tried to get his jeans open.

He chuckled. Husky and knowing.

"Not yet," he said. "I'm not done with you."

He dropped off the bed and she found herself being dragged to the edge of the mattress. Her thighs draped over his shoulders, the heart of her completely open to him.

"Jackson," she said, her voice trembling.

She might be a virgin, but she wasn't innocent. In that she fully knew all the things men and women did to each other. Her sisters had never been particularly shy about their sex lives, or their desires. And beyond that, she hadn't kept herself sheltered in terms of what she watched or read.

But having a man right there, looking at her, with no way to hide herself, that was a different proposition altogether than simply knowing. And when his mouth touched her, she jumped back, only to find herself pinned firmly against his face, his strong arms wrapped around her thighs, holding her there.

She wiggled as he lapped at her, as he tasted her like she was a decadent dessert.

"Jackson," she said, a feeling like flying building in her stomach, making her certain that she was no longer being held to the bed, but somewhere among the stars.

She couldn't breathe.

She didn't want to. She just wanted this. Forever.

Him. His hands. His strength. His mouth.

The pleasure she felt wove around all those things and created the magic tapestry that wrapped itself around her, cocooning her, making her feel safe even as she was brought to the edge of an intensity like she had never known before.

She rocked her hips in time with the motion, and when he pushed two fingers inside of her again, she broke apart. Her internal muscles squeezing around his fingers as he worked them in and out of her body. As he continued to tease her with the flat of his tongue.

She was left desperate and panting, begging for more.

"There's more," he said, his voice rough. "Don't worry."

He stood, and she watched transfixed as he undid his jeans, lowering the zipper slowly, the strong column of his arousal coming into view.

And he was... Well, much larger than she had imagined. Not that she had a great frame of reference. Or a very good idea of scale. But he was as beautiful as he was intimidating. And he was a lot of both.

Everything about his body was glorious. Strong and well defined and damn near miraculous.

And she didn't have time to cling to her worry, because then he was positioning himself at the edge of the bed again, wrapping his arms around her thighs, this time lifting her hips up off the mattress as he positioned himself at the entrance of her body, and thrust home.

The pain nearly blinded her.

She cried out, hand scrabbling for purchase, but she couldn't reach any part of him. And she wanted to hold on to him, wanted to dig her nails into his skin to keep herself from crawling out of her own.

His eyes widened, and for the first time, he looked truly at sea.

He adjusted their positions, bringing her legs around so that her feet were pointed toward the end of the bed, bringing himself onto the mattress the right way, still inside of her, but over her now, and she gripped his shoulders, squeezing her eyes shut tight.

"Cricket," he growled.

"Don't stop," she begged. "It's already done."

"Cricket..."

"Just please don't stop." And then, she opened her eyes, grabbed his face and kissed him.

And that seemed to work.

She could feel his control begin to unravel as he

started to move slowly at first, gently even, until the pain began to recede. Until it was replaced with a full, complicated pleasure that made her want to cry as well as scream with desire.

She began to move her hips in time with his, as they found a rhythm that pleased them both. As they found each other.

And then, he took control, his movements no longer measured, his skin slapping against hers. The primal edge to their joining so much more than she had ever imagined it could be. So much better.

Desire built inside of her until she was trembling again, like she had done outside, like she had done after their kiss. He reached between their bodies, moved his fingers along the sides of where they joined, then back upward, pinching her gently as he thrust in, and light— bright and brilliant—flashed behind her eyes, pleasure breaking over her like a wave.

It was unlike any reality she'd ever known. Deep and unending as she pulsed around him. And he thrust inside of her, once, twice more, and on a growl gave himself up to his own pleasure.

She felt rocked. Stunned. The aftershocks of everything that had just happened continuing to move through her, little tremors of need that caused her to cling to him with each passing ripple.

"Well," he said. "You should've told me."

"Oh, about being a virgin?"

"Hell yes," he said.

"I figured that was pretty evident."

"Not evident enough, Cricket," he said.

"Well. It wasn't really any of your business."

"It was exactly my business."

"I didn't want it to be. I just wanted it for me. Please don't ruin it by lecturing me or scolding me or yelling at me, because I just don't care about your opinion, okay? It was good." She let herself fall backward onto the bed, her head resting against the pillow. "It was good, and that's all I care about."

"Cricket... I shouldn't stay."

"Why?" She scrambled into a seated position, leaving herself completely uncovered. She didn't know why she was so at ease being naked in front of him. It felt right though. Natural. In a way that being clothed in many other situations never had. She felt... Well, she felt essentially Cricket. Like the baseline nature of who she was was completely and totally reinforced by this. Like the essence that made her her, that had always felt wrong and out of place, suddenly fit. In this house, in this bed. With this man. And, she didn't see any point in feeling regretful or shy. In apologizing to him for the fact that she'd been a virgin.

Really, if it didn't bother her, it shouldn't bother him.

"Because there are things you don't know about why I agreed to come and work here."

"You lost a bet, cowboy. Seems pretty straightforward to me. Though, the bet had nothing to do with this, so don't go and try to cheapen it now."

"I'm not going to," he said, his eyes level. "Cricket, why do you think I bet myself as your ranch hand?"

"You thought you were going to win."

"No. I thought I was going to lose. I *knew* I was going to lose. Your level of bravado was not that of a woman who had an iffy hand."

"How..." She felt utterly aghast. "How can that be?"

"It just is, sweetheart. I knew for a fact that you were

going to win, and I agreed to these terms because I wanted to be here. Because I wanted to… I wanted to show you that you didn't have the chops to be a rancher."

"You what?"

"I wanted to talk you out of it. Because I wanted to buy this place."

She frowned. "You… You were tricking me?"

"Yes. Though, in fairness, I never lied to you, not once. I never lied about how much work it takes to run a place like this. Everything I said to you was the absolute truth. The morning wake-up time was real. The amount of work and money and time that is going to be needed for this place is all real. And nothing I said to you was off base there. But I certainly didn't do anything to encourage you. Not really. Because what I wanted was for you to give up and throw in the towel, and for me to be there ready to buy you out."

"Jackson…"

"Yeah. And now I feel like an ass. Because I didn't know that all this was going on. That you thought we might be related. And I…"

"So wait a minute, were you going to…seduce me to try to get the ranch away from me?"

"No."

"Just please tell me this was real. If nothing else, Jackson, just tell me this was real."

"It was real. But that doesn't mean it can be anything but tonight."

"Why not?"

"Because it's a disaster. Because I'm not the kind of man who can give you what you want. You've already been hurt by too many people in your life, Cricket, and I don't want to be another one."

"Well, too bad. Because this is hurtful."

"I'm sorry about that. I didn't want to hurt you."

"No. You just wanted to crush my dreams and make me think that I wasn't up to them, and then buy my dream piece of property out from under me. Jackson, you did want to hurt me. It was just that you didn't know me, so you didn't particularly care. And if you feel guilty now, it's only because you've seen what a pathetic human being I am, and I was a virgin on top of it."

"I don't pity you."

"Then what is it?"

"Having seen you naked, having been inside of you, I can't take advantage of you. Okay? Because yeah, I can stand here and justify my actions, and say that I didn't lie to you like that makes it all okay, but I know it's not, Cricket. I know it was a shady thing to do. And the fact of the matter is, I could ignore what a shady thing it was when I wasn't personally involved with you, but after tonight I think it's pretty safe to say that personal involvement has happened. From dragging you in front of my dad to getting into bed with you."

"Well, then how can you stand there and say it can't be anything else? If we are already personally involved…"

"It's a mess."

"Oh, no argument here. Believe me. I've been pretty much mired in the mess this whole time." She let out an exasperated sigh. "Don't you know that I have had a crush on you the size of the Willamette River for… I don't know, years? So finding out that you were possibly my brother was about the worst thing I could think of. Do you have any idea what it's like to spend years lusting after somebody, and then find that you might share a dad? It was horrifying. I'm sorry, but I needed to know, and then once I did know… I needed to be with you. Because I felt so wrong, in so many ways, for so many years—I think this had to happen for me to…get over it. To start feeling some things that are…a little bit more normal. Like, believe me, none of this was how I saw…the hookup between us going. But that whole trying to get my ranch thing… That was pretty awful. And, you know, not something I thought you would do."

"Cricket, I didn't know you had a crush on me. But I'd venture to say that you might have a slightly better view of me than is realistic. I'm just who I am. I'm not a particularly bad man, but I'm not a really great one either."

"Why my ranch?"

"I'm right next door. It just makes sense. If I want to expand…"

"Why do you need to expand?"

"It's what people do."

"I mean, to what end? For more money?"

"No," he said. "For more of something that's mine."

"Oh. Well, I mean I understand that. Wanting something that's yours. But this ranch is mine. And you can't have it. And I don't really care how hard it's going to be to make it work. It's going to be mine. You underestimated me. You had no idea about everything that was going on in here." She tapped her temple. "Honestly, it's been a wasteland of horror for the past…six months at least. So, don't go trying to scare me away."

"I'm going back to my place tonight. Let's just… cool off."

She sputtered. "I don't want to cool off."

"I need to."

She stared at him. "We had a deal," she said. "And none of that's changed because of what just happened tonight. Are you the kind of man who backs out of the deal?"

"Things have…"

"Changed for you. Because you were lying to me. But I was never lying. I was always being honest, and…"

"Except for the part where you thought that I was your brother, and you figured that you needed to… I don't know, what were you trying to do exactly?"

"Get close to you, enough that I could say, 'Do you suppose it's possible your father cheated on your late mother, and he is perhaps my dad?'" He barely moved, but a muscle in his cheek flinched. "Yeah," she said. "Exactly. It's awful. And there's really no good way to approach it. At least, not one I could think of. And believe me, I tried. I tried to think of something better than that. So yes, I guess I had ulterior motives too, but I also just want to run my ranch. And I need your help. And you promised me thirty days. Staying here. Free labor."

"You're in my bed."

"So, you have a couple options. You get back in bed with me, you go to the bunkhouse with the spiders, or you go to my bed, where I may just end up."

He sighed heavily, then came back down onto the mattress. "You don't know what you're playing with here, little Cricket."

"There's only one way I'm going to find out, though, isn't there? By continuing to play."

She took a deep breath, focusing on the tenderness in her chest. "In all honesty, Jackson, I am just really sick to death of feeling like I'm fundamentally wrong. And this felt right. So…why don't we just keep on?"

"I lied to you," he said.

"Yeah. But so what? I mean, we're not friends. You lost a bet. End of story. You're not my family, so we don't have some kind of mystical connection like I thought we might. We are not...anything. So what does it matter? Your plan would've only worked if you could have talked me out of my dream, and quite frankly, if you could have talked me out of it, I would've deserved what I got."

"Is that really what you think?"

"Yes. As it is, you were never even close to making me second-guess it. Because you know what's harder than figuring out how to do chores and work a ranch? Growing up in a mausoleum. An altar to your father, when you don't even like or respect the man. Being made to feel like you have to fit in, when you don't particularly want to, or see the benefit of it. Yeah. That's hard. And, well... I decided not to do it. I decided to figure this out. So I did. So I took it upon myself to figure this out. A few early mornings weren't going to scare me off."

"You're a whole thing, aren't you, Cricket?"

"Not by choice. It just kind of seems to be the way I am."

He lay down next to her, and gathered her up against his body. She put her hand on his chest, tracing shapes over the broad expanse of muscle. "You seem like a man who might be able to handle a whole thing. And you kinda make me feel like less of one. Or at least like... this might be the place for it."

"Sure, if you want to play... You know I'm here to play. But playing is all I got."

"That's okay. I'm trying to figure out my life. I'm

trying to figure out what I want to be. Who I am. What it means… James is my father, most likely."

"Are you going to ask your mother directly about it?"

She nodded. "I am. Because I need to know the truth. I'm afraid this is probably it."

"Sometimes, you have to contend with things you don't like about your parents. And I grant you, your dad is a hell of a lot worse than mine."

"Your dad seems… Well, I mean, to me he really seems not bad at all."

"He's not, I suppose. But his relationship with my mom… I wouldn't have been surprised if he'd cheated."

"I'm sorry."

"None of it's your fault."

"Well. I kind of put you in an awkward situation tonight."

He shrugged. "My dad's own behavior actually put him in that situation."

"For what it's worth… I used to look at your family and think… Well, I really wished that I could be part of it."

"I guess that's the thing, then. I never wished that I was part of your family. I suppose that's the difference."

"Yeah, there is imperfect, and there's dysfunctional. Believe me, there's kind of an important distinction between the two."

"We might be skirting the edge of dysfunctional, here," he said.

"Yeah, but I think we can both handle it. And we're not dragging anyone else into it."

He huffed. "True."

"Might as well enjoy this. I have twenty-one days left of indentured servitude from you."

And then suddenly she found herself pinned to the mattress, his large body over hers, his eyes glittering. "Might as well," he growled.

And then, they were done talking for the rest of the night.

Chapter 7

Jackson felt like an ass. He should have left last night when he'd said that he would, but Cricket had looked at him like she was a wounded puppy, and he couldn't bring himself to do it. Still, there hadn't been much of an excuse to stay. Except that he was weak. And human, and basically just a man. And she had presented a temptation he couldn't turn away from.

Though it wasn't just being a man, that was the thing, because if it was, then it would've been about her just being a woman, and fundamentally, he could have turned down any other woman. It was Cricket that was the problem. Cricket was a damn problem.

He was marinating on that as he drove into town for more lumber the next day. She had been up early, at the crack of dawn, without so much as a complaint, while he had been the one who'd had a hell of a time getting his ass out of bed. He was driving back out toward Cricket's spread when he noticed his brother's truck in the oncoming traffic lane. Creed waved his hand, and Jackson found the nearest turnaround and followed his brother, both of them parking by the side of the road. It wasn't extraordinarily unusual to randomly run into his brother about town. Gold Valley was a small enough place. And they were off running similar errands, considering they were both ranchers. They had the same haunts, the same basic routines.

"Fancy meeting you here," he said.

"Likewise," Creed said. "I was figuring on coming out to see you today anyway."

"Oh?"

"Yeah. My wife has been after me to check in on you."

"Why?" Jackson asked.

"Just to make sure nothing untoward is happening between you and her little sister."

Jackson kept his face flat and immovable as stone. "Is that so?"

"Yeah. She told me that Cricket called her the other night inquiring about how to make steak. Because she was cooking for you. And that got Wren stirred up."

"I fail to see what your wife's feelings have to do with me."

"Well, the funny thing is, then I went by the winery this morning, and I talked to Dad, he said that you and Cricket stormed the place last night, and she demanded to know if he was her father."

"Oh."

"And that you said it was really important to know for sure."

"Look, she had a valid suspicion."

"Why? Dad was crazy about Mom. He would never have cheated on her."

Jackson's frustration finally boiled over. Maybe it was Cricket and all the nonsense with her, or just the vast unfairness of his brother's complete and total obliviousness over something Jackson had borne the weight of for years. Whatever the reason, he was at the end of his patience.

"Are you blind, Creed? Dad was not crazy about Mom."

"The hell you talking about? He's been deep in the throes of grief for her for…five years. Completely messed up. Not right at all. You can't tell me that's a man who was not crazy about his wife."

"He's a man who was crazy with guilt." Jackson let out a harsh breath. "Look, I was closer to Mom than you."

"I…feel bad about that. But I was pretty deep in some of my own stuff there for a while."

"I know. It wasn't a criticism. I'm just saying… Believe me, what Cricket thought was valid enough. Did you ever wonder why Dad hated James Maxfield so much? Not just because he's a prick."

"Yeah, I mean it crossed my mind a time or two."

"Dad was in love with *his* wife. Always. And I think, whatever he felt for Mom never overshadowed what he felt for her. It wasn't… It was never fair. Ever. It's not just grief that has Dad a mess. He has a mountain of regret. And he should."

Creed huffed out a breath. "That doesn't make any sense. Why would Mom… Why would she be with him?"

"Why do you think? They stayed together for the kids." He looked at his brother. "That would be us."

"Why did they get married in the first place?"

Jackson sighed and shifted his weight. "Me. She was pregnant with me. Haven't you ever done that math? I have. And anyway, I don't have to rely on math. She told me. I thought… Damn, you know, I thought we had this great, happy family. And then I found out… Not so much. A forced family, and then they tried to… Honey was their attempt at making things better. But that doesn't work. Or at least, it rarely does. Anyway. That's what everything was about with Cricket. She suspected, given that she, like our sister, is a late in life baby… That maybe she was the product of an affair. An affair her mother had always wanted to have. But no. Dad said no."

"Oh. Well, that is entirely different from what Wren was afraid was going on. And I can't say I could really figure out what I thought was happening…" Creed stared past him, off at the thick grove of pine trees that lined the highway. "I don't know what to make of any of this. I… I didn't know that Mom and Dad…"

"They didn't want us to know."

"Why did Mom tell you?" Creed sounded hurt. Jackson didn't have the capacity to deal with his brother's hurt. Not now.

"She had to tell someone. She was lonely. And…"

"Dad was there for her though. He was. He didn't leave. And if he didn't have an affair…"

"You're a married man, Creed, don't tell me you wouldn't feel a difference between being the love of your wife's life, or knowing there was someone else out there that she wanted first."

"Right. But you know…" Creed chuckled. "Wren and I got married because of her pregnancy."

"Given your background, I understand that."

He nodded. "But it's not why we stayed together."

"Yeah, but I think it was why Mom and Dad stayed together."

"Well, I just pulled you over to give you a hard time, I didn't figure you'd give me this depressing as hell story."

"I'm just explaining the last twenty-four hours, which believe me, have been a little weird for me too."

"Well, be careful with her. Wren is really worried."

It was Jackson's turn to stare at the trees.

He could feel his brother's eyes burning into the side of his face. "If you're sleeping with my sister-in-law… I might have to punch you. I'd rather not."

"I'll be careful with her."

"That's not a denial."

"Can't give you a denial."

"Really? Really. *Really? Cricket. Really.*"

He shot his brother a look. "Say it one more time."

"So…she thought you were her half brother, and somehow you ended up… You know what. I don't want to know." Creed lifted his hands and took a step back. "The less I know the better, because I'm going to have to explain it to Wren. And I don't want to be the keeper of that information, because God knows I love my wife, but she is the kind of woman to shoot the messenger. And I like all my body parts where they are."

"So do I."

"And *really* don't let Holden find out." Creed's brother-in-law, married to Emerson, the middle Maxfield sister.

"Why is that?"

"My loyalty is torn. You're my brother. Holden… Well, his loyalty is in one place firmly. And, also, I get the feeling he's done some things."

"Look, nothing happened that Cricket didn't want."

"I'm confident in that. I'm still confident it won't matter to Wren."

"Just let us sort it out."

"I can't keep secrets from her. But I can keep her busy." Creed grinned.

"Great. Do that. And keep this to yourself. What's going on with me and Cricket is nobody's business but ours."

"I just don't get why. I mean, she's cute enough, sure. But…"

Jackson felt a violent surge of…protectiveness? He didn't even know. Just something primal and overly irritable. He couldn't explain what appealed about Cricket. It was not simple. But… She was special, and when he saw her as something other than an adversary to be defeated, he could truly see that. She was tough. And beautiful. Naive in some ways, sure, but in others… Like a person outside age or time. Not like anyone or anything he'd ever known. He came back to that vision he'd had of her the first time he'd rolled up to the ranch.

When he thought of her as a feral pirate queen on the deck of her ship. And he should have known then. She wasn't a woman to take prisoners, and neither would she be one to negotiate. She wasn't going to give up on what she wanted half so easily as he had hoped. And now, he didn't even want her to. Because somewhere in all of this, he'd begun to root for her. He wanted her to win. That vulnerable, delicate piece of herself only he'd seen was something he wanted to protect now, not exploit.

"Don't worry about me. And don't worry about Cricket. She can more than handle herself."

And he was…well, dammit all, he was going to help her.

* * *

Jackson had been gone for most of the day, and it was probably for the best, Cricket had to concede. She wished he was in bed with her instead of seeing to ranch chores. But the ranch chores were important and all. It was kind of the whole point of having him on the property. But now she wanted the point to be more of him in her bed, and honestly, who could blame her? Having an orgasm was a lot more fun than doing chores.

But…she also needed to do something other than chores today. Which was how she found herself driving to Maxfield Vineyards.

She usually avoided the place as much as humanly possible. But it was weird. Today, with a bit of distance from her family, from everything that they were, and all the pain and isolation she had experienced growing up here… She was not feeling trapped by it. It felt…better. She felt able to appreciate the beauty of it. The rolling vineyards, the vast, Tuscan-style villa. The elaborate pavilions and tasting rooms. It was a beautiful facility, when she wasn't a prisoner.

"Prisoner" wasn't really fair. But she had felt trapped in her circumstances, that was for sure. And now that she had another place to be, now that she had…

Honestly, had a night with Jackson changed her so much? She looked the same. She had checked herself over in the mirror this morning just to see if this change was visible, that shift that had taken place inside of her last night. But as far as she could tell it wasn't. She took a breath, and put her car in Park, right in the circular drive just in front of the massive entry to her family home. A place that had never, ever felt like home to her. But she didn't have the same knot of dread that she used to have when James was in residence, didn't have the same feeling of discomfort. So there was that.

She knocked, because she didn't live here anymore, and when one of the members of the staff opened the door, she was led in as politely as if she were a guest.

She stood in the foyer, waiting for her mother to appear.

When she did, Cricket could only stare. Her mom was still every inch the lady of the manor, even though the circumstances at the manor had changed pretty drastically.

"Cricket," Lucinda said, smiling brightly. "What brings you by?"

"I… I really need to talk to you. About…" She took a breath. "I spoke to Cash Cooper last night."

"Oh," her mom said, faltering.

"I asked him if he was… If he was my father."

"Cricket…"

"I know that you are in love with him. And I know that he was in love with you. And I know you didn't marry him because you chose money over love. I just thought that maybe…"

"He's not your father."

"That's what he said."

Her mom looked…embarrassed. "Was he…"

"He wasn't mad. I mean, not much. Jackson was kind of mad, but… I don't know. I was just embarrassed. But I really thought… There's something wrong with me? I think? Because I'm not like anyone in this family, and I just thought that maybe I would fit better with the Coopers. And I thought that after I found out that you were in love with him…"

"I was always in love with him. I always will be. I

gave things up, Cricket. For a life that I thought would make me happy. But I was very foolish. I was very wrong. And it has taken me all this time to be able to admit it. All this time to be able to understand. Just how… Just how wrong I was. I thought this house could take the place of love. I thought money could do it. And then I thought social standing, because Cash managed to go and make all that money, just to show me what I was missing. I won't tell you I wasn't tempted by him. I won't tell you *we* never were. There were times… We had opportunity, and it was hard. Because I remembered what it was like with him. And it wasn't… I shouldn't tell you all of this. You don't want to know about my love affairs, I'm sure."

Cricket didn't really, it was true. But she could be a whole lot more understanding about them now that she'd experienced a bit of it herself. Would it be like that with Jackson? Forever and ever? Staring at him from across crowded rooms and knowing how it was? If he married someone else… Would she still always remember what it was like to have his hands on her body? What if she married another man?

Frankly, she couldn't imagine it. She didn't really have dreams of being a wife and mother. She had always had dreams about him.

"But you didn't. That's the important part."

"No."

"And did you… With anyone else?"

"No."

"So James Maxfield is my father." It wasn't a question, but a heavy confirmation.

"Yes."

"Okay." Cricket turned, her chest feeling weighted

with answers. The fact was, she hadn't wanted to ask
her mother before because she had been afraid that this
was the answer. And it turned out…it was. There was
nothing half so romantic as a hidden family out there
waiting for her. Nothing half so wonderful as an explanation for why she was the way she was.

She just was.

And she was going to have to find a way to cope with
that, to understand herself.

To be okay with that.

"He said that…" She took a breath. "Cash said that
I looked like you." She turned around again to face her
mother, looked at her smooth, unlined skin, her sleek
blond hair. "I don't see how. He said I reminded him
of you."

Her mother's expression became soft. Wistful. "Because back then I did. You're probably the most like
me, Cricket, of any of the girls. I was wild, and I was
headstrong, and I couldn't be told a damn thing. I made
a sport out of daring him. Of pushing him. I felt like I
was meant for bigger and better things than I could get
in Gold Valley. Bigger and better things than he could
give me. And I would yell that at him. I would tell him
that if he really wanted me, if he really loved me, then
he would figure out a way to give me the kinds of things
I wanted. Because you see… I really believed that the
man who would make me happy would come with all
the things I wanted, and I didn't think about the kinds
of things I would give to him. And that was how I ended
up in a one-sided marriage where I didn't ask any questions, and I just took everything that came my way. I
didn't have dreams of my own. Not beyond what I could
have. And when I realized that I was stuck with a man

who didn't love me, with a man who wasn't faithful to me... I had you girls. And I wouldn't do anything that might jeopardize my having you. And he used the three of you to threaten me." She closed her eyes. "I'll be completely honest, half the time the only thing that kept me away from Cash Cooper was knowing that if your father found out he would do his best to make sure I never saw you again."

"I'm sorry, Mom," Cricket said. "And I'm sorry I never realized how unhappy you were here."

"Yes, well. I'm the one who made this place." She looked around. "It was my prison. And I built it for myself, and locked myself inside. And you right with me. I never felt like I had a right to offer you any comfort."

Cricket didn't know what to say. Except... She remembered what Jackson had asked her, that first day he had come to her house. "Can I ask... Why did you name me Cricket?"

Her mom smiled. "Because it reminded me of who I used to be. A hot summer night sitting outside and listening to the crickets. Of simpler things and simpler times. And by then I knew... I knew I wasn't ever going to find happiness here. The only happiness I had was you girls, and I didn't... I was distant, because I let my guilt and my fears determine how we connected. I'm sorry for that. I really am. The divorce—this has been like a slow waking up. I'm not liking everything that I'm seeing around me. My own flaws. My own...failings in all of this."

"James Maxfield is kind of an evil bastard."

"Well, there was a time when I was suited to him. And that doesn't fill me with any great joy."

"I don't understand how you could... I don't want

to pile anything on, Mom, and for the most part, I just think… We were all victims of his. But one thing I don't understand is how you could marry him knowing that you loved Cash."

"Cash didn't come after me. He let me marry him. And up until the wedding I imagined him riding up on a white horse and taking me away from it all. I really did. I thought he would rescue me. And he didn't. Instead he found someone else, and they had children right away. Much faster than your father and I did. And I threw myself into loving the money. If Cash hadn't gotten married, I don't think my marriage to your father would've lasted. But my other option was gone."

"Have you ever thought that…now it might not be?"

She smiled sadly. "He's a proud man. I don't think he would have me. I can't say that I blame him."

"I don't think you can know that. Unless you try. And don't you think we all deserve a chance at being happy? Whatever that looks like?"

"I know that you do. I think for me it might be too late."

Cricket left her mom's house with a lot to think about. And she wasn't sure that she liked any of it. It sounded to her like her mother's relationship with Cash had been more than a little dysfunctional. And she couldn't deny that her mom had a decent sized stake in the way things had gone. But she also didn't see the point in the two of them continuing to be sad forever. They both clearly had feelings for each other that they hadn't resolved. But one thing Cricket couldn't imagine was…

She could never marry another man.

The conversation with her mom had solidified that thought. Not after Jackson. She couldn't have another man's children. Chances were, she would grow old with her ranch. But at least she would have her own dreams.

When she pulled up to the house, he was on the porch, hammering boards in place. Each swing of his hammer was hard and decisive, every muscle and tendon in his body working harmoniously toward its goal. He was a thing of beauty. And the porch was... It was practically brand-new. In the few hours since she'd left, he had transformed the place. It was no longer sinking, no longer looking dilapidated. It was incredible. And it was all him.

He was incredible.

Her heart lifted in her chest, and she felt... She didn't really know. Renewed in some ways. Her mother's story was tragic, but it was also a reminder that there was no circumstance Cricket could simply sit back and accept.

She was James Maxfield's daughter. That hadn't been her choice. But everything she did with her life... that was her choice. James didn't own her. Didn't have a claim on her. She was Cricket. Named after the simple summer nights her mother loved and remembered. After a time in her life that had been special to her. After memories that had mattered. And Cricket was made of those things as much as she was her father's DNA.

It made her feel rooted, grounded to this place, and certain of her decisions. Much more so than she had ever been before.

"Horses," she said as soon as she got out of the truck.

"Excuse me?" Jackson looked up, his gaze meeting hers, sending her stomach into a freefall.

"Horses," she reiterated. "I want to breed horses. That's what this ranch is going to be. I've decided. I want to start right away."

"We're going to have to build stables."

"Then let's work out a budget. And I can find a contractor. I know it might take some time, but I'm willing. Because my life is going to be what I want it to be. It doesn't matter what my DNA is. I talked to my mother today. James is my father. For sure and for certain. But that's not even really the biggest thing. My mom lived a life that she didn't love for years because she felt trapped in it. Because she felt like she didn't have a choice. I never want to feel like I don't have a choice. I'm not one determined thing because I'm James's daughter, and not Cash's. I'm not anything but what I decide to be."

"Good for you."

She pointed her index finger at him. "But you can't have my ranch."

"That's okay."

"And you still have to finish out the terms of the bet. I'm not going to have you back out early, just because you can't do your whole secret…thing. I have nothing but your own honor as a man to hold you to it."

"You got me."

"And I want to keep sleeping with you," she said, suddenly resolute in that decision too. "Until this is over."

"You sure?"

"I'm sure. I'm building my life. And this is who I am. I don't sit back having crushes on men and not saying anything. I don't just dream about having a ranch. I'm going to have all those things."

"And then at the end of the thirty days?"

That made her chest feel sore. But she was resolute either way.

"You go your way. I'll go mine."

And she wasn't going to worry about all the things he could and couldn't give her. She was going to focus on what she could do. Who she could be. What she could give to herself.

Because she would never be her mother. A passive participant in her own life.

No.

She was the one who decided.

Nobody else. She would have a ranch, and a man. And sure, it would be temporary. But it would be hers. The start of something.

And she was so very ready for her life to begin.

Chapter 8

The crew had started work on Cricket's stables. It was weird, now that his focus had shifted. He actually wanted her enterprise to be a success. And that meant looking at things from an entirely different point of view. That meant teaching her about ranching, rather than just making overarching statements and watching her stumble around. It meant bringing her alongside him for repairs, not just to show her how hard it was, but to show her that she could. And with each improvement on the property, he saw her become more firmly rooted in her sense of who she was, and there was a great sense of accomplishment inside of him that he couldn't quite explain. Except that... Except that he'd felt useless to fix the sadness that he saw inside of his mother, and being able to do something to give Cricket a better life did something to help heal that sense of failure.

Somewhere in the back of his mind, he always

thought that if his mother had gotten better, maybe he would have helped her leave his father. Given her a place to stay, proved to her that it didn't matter whether they were together like a traditional family. What really mattered was her happiness. She didn't need to stay. Not for him. But he'd never said it to her. She'd died before he ever could. Before he'd gotten his own place up and running. And maybe part of him had still been working toward that with wanting to expand to Cricket's property. But he didn't need to do that now. What he could do was help Cricket find her way to a dream.

And then maybe that would help put something to rights in his own life. Cricket wasn't out with him today, she was off bustling around the house. He told her he would check in on the building site, and then he was going to drive up to the upper pasture, and get the lay of things. It really was a beautiful property.

He thought back to what she'd asked, if ranching was in his blood, as he stood out in the middle of the bright, patchwork field, filled with brilliant green mixed with patches of dark olive and backed by rich pine. As he looked at the sprigs of yellow that clustered around the perimeter interwoven with waving fire-colored Indian paintbrush and dappled orange fritillaria, at the pale blue sky that would be a richer blue come the height of summer, he knew the answer was... It was deeper than blood. It was down in his bones. He was part of the land, and it was part of him. Something that went further than want.

And he'd never thought about it that way before. Only when Cricket had asked, did that thought grow into a feeling.

And he understood. He understood why she wanted

this. Why she was here. It was true. When it was part of you, it simply was. Nothing you could do about it.

He heard the sound of a truck engine and turned, and there was Cricket, rumbling up the dirt road, driving that big beast of hers.

That was another thing that was getting down into his blood. Because he hadn't just been helping her on the property.

No.

They'd spent long nights in beds that were too small, exploring, tasting, and he loved to say that he was teaching her there as much as he was around the ranch, but it was more than that. Because Cricket was a whole new landscape, one he'd never seen or explored or imagined before. She was strong, and she was energetic.

She had no limit as far as he could tell. Nothing embarrassed her.

Rather, she touched and tasted with full enthusiasm, never shying away from anything. That wild girl he'd seen out on the swing at the Maxfield Vineyards brought that sense of the unrestrained into the bedroom, and there were no lessons involved in any of it. No. He was just on the ride. At the mercy of it. And he loved every minute.

He gritted his teeth. There was no getting attached to it.

Why not?

He pushed that thought aside. Cricket got out of the truck, wearing a white tank top and tight jeans, holding a blanket and a picnic basket. And she looked like far too much of a temptation for him to handle.

And hell, she wasn't a temptation he had to resist over the last couple of weeks, so why should he start now? He crossed the distance between them, and wrapped his arms around her slender waist, pulled her into his arms and planted a kiss on her lips.

"What are you doing?"

"I brought lunch," she said, a pleased smile curving her lips. "I've been practicing being a good pioneer woman. I made bread, I cooked a ham and I've made sandwiches."

"You really made bread?"

"Yes," she said, her face shining with triumph. "And two of the four loaves turned out. So, you have sandwiches."

"Cricket, that was awfully nice of you."

"I know," she said. "And often I'm not very nice, so it surprised me too."

"You're plenty nice."

Or at least, her particular brand of sharpness was nice for him. Didn't really matter either way.

She spread the blanket out in the meadow and took a seat, and he stared at her, the golden glow of the sun shining on her face. And he couldn't figure out quite why she'd done it. Quite why she'd given him this. He couldn't recall anyone else doing similar for him. Sure, his mom cooked for them. But... She was his mom. Family.

Cricket wasn't family.

She wasn't beholden to him in any way. He'd lost a bet to her. That was why he was here. And his education hadn't included cooking. She had just done this. Just because.

And it did something to his chest that made him want to growl, because he wasn't a sentimental man. And he didn't concern himself much with things like this.

But it was…unexpected, and it was a hell of a lot more than he'd ever wanted or gotten from another person.

It shocked him how good everything she made was. Though he supposed it probably shouldn't surprise him. Everything Cricket set her mind to she did with her whole self. And it didn't mean she couldn't fail, but she was determined enough that he had a feeling she would have baked ten loaves of bread in order to present him with just one. Because what she wanted, she went and got. And that was something. It was really something.

He liked to watch Cricket eat, among the many things he enjoyed about her. Because she did that with the same level of ferocity and intensity she did everything else. She was sitting on the blanket with her elbows propped up on her knees, her sandwich gripped tightly in her hands. She had brought cans of Coke for the two of them, and when she had eaten about half of her sandwich, she brushed her hands off and picked up the Coke, tipping it back like a beer.

She looked over at him. "What?"

"What?" he repeated.

"You're staring at me."

"You're pretty." That made him sound like a dumb high school boy. Come to that, he kind of felt like one.

But Cricket blushed. Cricket, tough little thing that she was, blushed, and he found that was all the payment he needed for the worse moment of feeling like an idiot. Something he wasn't accustomed to.

"Well," Cricket said. "So are you."

"Really?"

"Yeah. I mean, I've always thought so."

"Yeah," he said. "You mentioned something about that." He wasn't sure he wanted to know. Because al-

ready he felt some kind of strange obligation to her.
Deeper than his obligation to any other woman he'd ever
had a physical relationship with. And he wasn't sure
he wanted to dig in any deeper, but sitting there under
that brilliant blue sky, eating her homemade bread and
ham sandwich, he didn't know if there was any other
option but to dig in. He didn't know how *not* to be involved with her, and it was absurd. It had started with
a bet, an assumption on her part that they might be related, a nefarious plan on his part to talk her into selling him her ranch...

But maybe that was it. The whole thing was so bi-
zarre—how could they come away from it with neutral
feelings about each other? Maybe it was impossible.
Maybe the only option in a situation like this was to
develop some kind of attachment. Maybe it was the
only way.

"I'm pretty sneaky," Cricket said. "I mean, I'm used
to hiding what I feel from people. And you were no ex-
ception. I mean, the way that I felt about you. I would
just tell my sisters that I thought cowboys were annoying. And that I didn't want anything to do with any of
them. It was a pretty convincing ruse, if I say so myself. Plus, I knew you were way off limits. A thousand
years older than me."

"Hey. Not a thousand."

"Well, it seemed like it at the time. The gap feels a lot
smaller now." She smiled. "Oh, I didn't like any of the
boys at school. None of them. But how could I, when I
already liked a man? And a Cooper at that. I knew nobody would understand. But nobody understood me,
so that didn't really bother me. And so I just...kept it a
secret. And then I was so mad when Wren hooked up

with your brother, because I felt for so long that being attracted to you was this great, impossible thing, another sort of deeply rooted difference in who I was. In my genetic makeup versus the rest of my family. And then she got to Creed before I could get to you. Honestly. It was an insult. But still, when she told me that I would maybe find my own cowboy... I played it off. I told her no. That I didn't want anything to do with a man like Creed, and I didn't. I just wanted you. So it feels right, you know? To start this new phase of my life with you... Though I'm not asking you for anything. I promise."

"Well, happy to help."

Except it made him feel... He didn't even know. It kind of made him angry, because she was the younger one. She was the one without experience, and she made him feel like he had no idea what he was doing. It didn't seem right. That was all.

He should be the one who knew what he was doing. He should be the one who had total confidence in everything taking place between them. But he couldn't say that he did. He couldn't give a reason. Couldn't give a speech about what he was doing here. He had written it off as being male and basic and taking the sex that was on offer, but he knew that wasn't true. It wasn't how he did things. It wasn't how he looked at women. And he had been telling himself a story, all this time. Cricket's story made a lot more sense, and had a purpose behind it. And he just... He just wanted to touch her. It was a hell of a thing.

"You know, the way you were talking to your dad that day... Tell me about your mom. I mean, tell me

about all that. Because you know about my dad, and
you know all about my mom…"

"They were obligated to be together. And it was pri-
marily because of me," he said. Because he might as
well tell her. She was right. He'd had a front row seat to
all of her issues. He'd talked to Creed about it, sure. But
Cricket? She could hear it all. Because she didn't have
a connection to the family, so why not? It was a safer
place. This moment out here in the meadow.

"One day when I was sixteen, she was crying. Then
I asked her what was wrong. We were the two that got
up early. And we used to spend mornings together. I
loved that. So I would have all this extra time with her.
And one morning, I asked her what was wrong. And it
was like everything I ever thought about my life broke
to pieces. My father married her because she was pregnant. My father was in love with another woman. He'd
told my mother that. Before they got married. He was
honest, if nothing else. And she thought that he'd fall in
love with her. But instead, it had just become years of
the two of them stuck. Because they had a family. Because they had a business. Because they had all these
things that were obligated to come before having feelings. Before love.

"And you know, I'm not over-bothered by my dad
anymore. I think that was enough for him. He couldn't
have your mom, so he made himself a life he enjoyed.
But I'm not sure my mother ever got to fall in love with
anyone. Not for real. Not and have them love her back.
She was just stuck. With a partner, sure. And when
she was sick… I can't fault my dad for how he was. He
was a partner. He cared for her. And he stayed with her.
And you know, plenty of marriages that are founded on

love, they don't end up that way. Somebody gets sick and they go through a years-long battle, and the other person leaps. It's too much for them. And sometimes I wonder if maybe my dad not being in love with her made him more able to take care of her during that time. It's complicated as hell. Because there was a very real partnership between the two of them, but sometimes it made my mother feel broken, and I will never not feel responsible for that. Like I should've found some way to fix it."

"They made their choices," Cricket said. "That's what I'm realizing about my mother. For all her own misery, for all that I feel bad for her sometimes, for all that my father was an unforgivable asshole, my mom made her choices. She wanted money. And she thought that would be enough. She wanted to have things, and thought that would transcend love, but it didn't. And then she didn't leave. She stayed. Because she was afraid. And all her reasons, they were real enough, but they were still excuses. Even if they were pretty valid ones. My mom stayed with James for us. Because she was afraid that he would find a way to take us from her. But she also could've had the fight. She weighed her options. And she chose."

"I have some sympathy for that," he said. "If she thought she couldn't win…"

"It was still a choice. Just like your mother had one. It's not like it was the 1800s. They could've gotten a divorce. They could have. Nobody had to be unhappy. They sat there in rules they made for themselves, and lived lives they made for themselves, prison walls they decided were okay. That isn't your fault, and it isn't mine."

"Yeah, but on the other side, now your mom has a chance to make something new. Mine doesn't. It's a hell of a thing."

"I know." She shook her head. "I'm not saying it would've been easy. I'm just saying you can't take their choices and blame yourself for them."

"You're twenty-two years old."

"Yeah. And you're what? Thirty-four? Thirty-five? So what? I'm not stupid. I've had a lot of time to think. That's what comes of being the isolated, odd one out in your family. You have way too much time to think. And believe me, I've had tons. I don't need experience to have figured that out."

"So you have the whole world all figured out, do you?"

"I mean, I'm not gonna say the whole world. But maybe my piece of it."

This girl. This woman. She didn't know when to question or doubt. She dove headlong into everything. Bets at a poker table, wild conclusions and into his bed. And he just…he liked that about her.

"Bold claim, little Cricket."

"I don't know, things make more sense now than they ever have. I didn't think that was possible. I just walked through the messiest, weirdest time of my life. And it's really not so bad. And yeah, I basically do have it all sorted out."

He wrapped his arms around her, and pulled her on top of him, laying them both back on the blanket. He looked into her earnest face, and desire stirred in his body. "You have everything figured out, is that it?"

"Basically. The mysteries of sex are even solved."

"Every last one?" he pressed.

He didn't know why he needed this right now, but he

did. It was deeper than lust, that was the problem. He couldn't write it off as simply basic desire. He'd wanted to. He'd tried to. But it was so much more than that. That was the thing. With her, it always would be. And whatever was happening between the two of them, she didn't have to be here. They didn't have to be here. They were choosing it, out here under the unending sky. With the land and the ranch in their blood, and his need for her pumping hot and insistent through his body.

"Bet you can't teach me anything," he said, his voice rough.

And Cricket, true to form, sat up, her thighs on either side of him, and stripped her white tank top up over her head without pause. She was wearing a plain, matching bra, her lean, athletic body a sight to behold. "Is that a *bet* bet, cowboy?"

"Sure."

"You know, historically, you lose bets with me."

"Yeah. I feel like a real loser right now." With her sweet ass perched on top of him, and all her beauty blocking out the sun.

"Well."

"Just remember that there are some bets I lose on purpose." He gripped her hips, sliding his hands up to her slim waist, then up further still, brushing his thumbs over her breasts. Then he reached around and unhooked her bra, flinging it off somewhere in the grass.

She made a small sound that might have been indignant, but he didn't much care. Because she was bare and gorgeous and perfect and he was dying for a taste.

He pressed his palm firmly against the center of her back and brought her down toward him, toward his mouth. He sucked one perfect, ripe bud between his lips, and the cry that escaped her lips wasn't indignant this time. Not at all. It was one of pleasure, one of desire, and he reveled in it. She wrenched his shirt over his head, wiggling away from him as she did. And he pinned her down on her back, her arms up over her head, and kissed her deep.

"Little Crickets with smart mouths get themselves in trouble," he said.

A challenge glimmered in her eyes. "Do we? I sure hope so."

"Do you?"

"Yes. I lack discipline."

"Is that so?"

"I've mostly been neglected. I need a firm hand."

"I could probably provide you with one."

"So many promises. And yet…"

He growled, unsnapped her jeans, unzipped them and pushed them down her thighs, and she helped eagerly. Then she wiggled downward, kissing his chest, his stomach, still on her back beneath him as she undid his pants and freed him. She peered up at him, squeezing his length and making a sound of purely feminine satisfaction.

"You're really kind of a work of art," she said, leaning forward and rubbing her cheek against him. He could honestly say a woman had never done that. And the look on her face made him so hard he thought he might burst.

She shoved lightly, and he moved, going onto his back as she bit her lip and looked down at him. Then she knelt over him, taking him slowly into her mouth, the sweet, wet heat an assault on his senses. She tortured him. And she wasn't practiced or knowing or anything like that. Didn't have a parade of well coordinated tricks, but she made up for it with enthusiasm. Pure and simple. She was a woman in full enjoyment of his body, and he didn't think he'd ever experienced anything quite like that. And hell, looking at her, at the elegant line of her spine, her ass up in the air as she pleasured him, was something more powerful than he'd ever experienced.

This moment was free of obligation. Something in his chest began to unravel, as if each pass of her tongue, each movement of her mouth over his body, was working to loosen something inside him, unraveling something he hadn't been aware was there.

Who knew that sandwiches and a blow job out in the middle of a field would be enough to make a man almost believe in romance? He sure as hell hadn't. But it was something. *She* was something. Far and away beyond anything he'd ever known or experienced or figured he might want to understand.

Cricket.

She pleasured him until he thought he couldn't take it anymore. Then he reached in his back pocket, grabbed his wallet and took out the condom, tearing it open and guiding her up his body as he sheathed himself with one practiced hand.

She seated herself on top of him and took him inside of her slowly, achingly so, her mouth dropping open, her head falling back. She flexed her hips, a ragged sound on her lips, and then she began to move, slowly at first. Then more quickly. But it still wasn't enough for him. He grabbed on to her hips, moved her up and down over his body, driving them both crazy. Pushing them both until she cried out her pleasure. And then he reversed their positions, pounding into her, unable to hold himself back any longer. It was primal and urgent, and exactly what he needed to compound that strange unraveling in his chest. Only then, she opened her eyes and met his.

And he couldn't breathe. Not then. Just as his climax took him over, he was lost. In Cricket. In the look of wonder on her face, the absolute trust there. He was her first lover. The only man who had ever touched her like this. He was bound up in all of the strange things she'd been going through for all this time, and he didn't want to be even more turned on by that, but he was. And he lost himself then, just went over the edge, growling out her name as she cried out his and convulsed around him. As she stared up at him, the look of absolute contentment in her eyes undid him. She didn't know better. Didn't know a different man.

He had taken her crush and used it to his advantage.

He had taken her inexperience as a rancher, as a poker player, and had used it to his advantage there too.

He felt... Well, he felt like shit, actually. Because there was something in him that knew instinctively he could never answer the depth of longing in her eyes. There was something in him that knew he had bound her to him. Her childish feelings, her awakening desire—she would feel connected to him in a way she shouldn't. That was a fact. That was the problem. And he would... He would what? Take her away from this place that she was turning into her own? Away from this life she was making and into his? He would just be another man taking a woman's dreams and putting them underneath his own.

They would be done at the end of the month. That

was the deal. And whatever possibilities he felt out here in the wilderness… They just weren't to be.

That was good. It was right that he knew that, felt that. Everything would go back to the way it had been, when all this was said and done. That was for the best. Because he wouldn't be able to give Cricket what she wanted. Not really. And when she realized that, then they would both be trapped in the exact same hell their parents had been trapped in.

And he wouldn't have that.

Not ever.

But he didn't say anything. Instead, he kissed her forehead, and she snuggled against him. And right out there in the open, completely naked, the two of them fell asleep.

What happened at the end of the wager was a problem for their future selves. Because right now, they had this.

And Jackson's last thought before he drifted out of consciousness was that he couldn't remember the last time he'd felt quite this content.

Chapter 9

It was the thirtieth day.

Cricket hadn't had the heart to ask if he would be staying the entire day, or leaving right away, or... She didn't know. And she was afraid to find out exactly what the answer was.

She was a coward.

She desperately wanted this to keep on going. She desperately wanted him to stay with her.

Right. So you're going to beg him to stay in your little ranch house? And for what? You're trying to find your own way...

No. She couldn't beg him to stay.

But they woke up the morning of the thirtieth day in the same bed just as they had every morning since they'd begun sleeping together, and he had gone out to work the same as he had from the beginning.

And so when he returned that evening, dirty and disheveled, she breathed out a sigh of relief.

Maybe he wasn't ready for things to change either. Maybe things wouldn't change. Maybe it would all stay the same, just for a little while. Maybe they could put off all the hard conversations for another time. They could say goodbye another day. She had cooked. Just in case. And she had been rewarded. It was funny, how much she enjoyed cooking. And she would have been more annoyed about the fact that she liked such a traditionally feminine pursuit, except that he seemed to enjoy it so much, and he appreciated it. She thought back to the day she'd made bread and brought out ham sandwiches. Oh yes, he'd appreciated that a whole lot. She felt a dreamy smile cross her face when she thought about it. These times with Jackson had been… Well, they'd been everything.

He'd been everything she'd ever fantasized about.

She knew this moment was supposed to be about moving on. About moving into the next phase of her life, but…

No. It doesn't bear thinking about.

Except, he was here.

And she kept thinking that, even as they each built hamburgers out of the ingredients she had laid out.

"Jackson," she said softly as they finished eating. "How was your day?"

"Good. And yours?"

"Good and—"

She cut herself off. Because she didn't care. She didn't want to have this conversation. She really didn't. She didn't want to talk at all. Because her insides were jumbled up and everything hurt. Because this was the last day, and she didn't know how to ask him if he would stay. She didn't know how to explain to herself, in a way that made her not feel silly, why she might ask him to stay.

Because I want to marry him.

And I want to have his children.

Because I would be his ranch wife in this house or any house.

Because he was her dream. And that was the bottom line.

She was young, and she was supposed to go out and live. She knew that. She wasn't supposed to want a man she had been completely hopeless over since she was twelve. She was supposed to experience more. Have more lovers. Travel. Something.

But she just didn't want to.

And she had the sick, terrible feeling that—much like her mother—there was really only one man for her, and there would never be anything that would take away her feelings. So she didn't want to waste time talking.

She flung herself into his arms, climbing up on the same chair as him, her legs on either side of his, the heart of her right up against where he was rapidly growing hard. And she kissed him. Kissed him until she thought she might die. Kissed him because she thought if she *didn't* she might die.

He stole her oxygen and became it all at once, and she couldn't have explained that feeling if she'd been put before a firing squad. She had never thought in terms of fate. She had always believed she was a pragmatist. But he felt like fate. This moment felt like fate. And she really couldn't deny it. Didn't really want to. Didn't want it to end.

He stood up from the chair, and he swept their plates to the side, breaking them on the floor. "I owe you a set of dishes," he said roughly.

"I don't care," she said.

Oh she *really* didn't care. Because she just wanted him, wanted this. And nothing else mattered. Not plates, not anything. And she gave thanks that she had worn a dress, which she so rarely did, because it made everything easily accessible for him. Because then he had his hands at her hips. Had his fingers between her thighs, stroking her, stoking the fires of her desire. This was like madness. This was like every fantasy she'd ever had.

And she had a terrible feeling that it had been love she'd been feeling from the very beginning. Love and fate—and that was why. That was why it had been him from the time she was twelve years old. And it didn't matter how much she wanted to deny it. It simply was. It simply, simply was. But he was here. He was here.

And he had broken dishes and cleared the table and was kissing her on top of it.

This table that had been an emblem of everything she'd been missing.

And she'd thought what she'd wanted had been some generic idea of a sitcom family. And she'd tried to shoehorn Jackson into that picture. But that wasn't what she'd wanted. It hadn't been quiet dinners that she was missing. It had been him. Just him. It wasn't an aching for domesticity that she felt that first night they'd sat down to dinner together, it was a life spent with him. It had been things shared with this man that had called to her from the very first time she'd ever seen him.

It didn't matter if the idea was crazy. It didn't matter

if she was younger than he was. It didn't matter if she was just starting out. Because she knew.

He'd made fun of her the other day, when she'd said she'd understood all these things, but she did. She understood this. Now, suddenly, in his arms—she understood.

She loved him.

And that was all there was to it.

She loved him and she wanted to be with him. And whatever else she needed to experience, it didn't matter. Because this was the one thing her heart and her body had known from the beginning. A lifetime spent feeling like she might always have to be second best, not quite so spectacular as her sisters, had seen her trying to find another explanation for how she felt. To find a way to protect her heart. But there was no protecting it, not now. She felt exposed. Cut open. She couldn't hide or protect herself even if she wanted to. So she didn't try. She surrendered to this madness between them.

And then he was inside of her, the table hitting up against the wall with each and every thrust. And he was amazing. In every way. And she let herself feel it. All of it. The love she felt for him expanding, growing in her chest, so much so that she thought she might burst. So much so that she nearly wept, and when her orgasm finally broke over her, she did. She shook and cried and held him, as his own release took him over.

And when it was done, he stood, and she just lay there, wrecked. The dishes on the floor a metaphor for her body.

"I..."

"Jackson," she said, at the same time.

"Cricket, this has been... It's been... The bet's over."

She just lay there, frozen, her arms spread wide, like a butterfly that had been pinned in place in a collection, unable to move, her back against the table.

"Are you leaving?"

"It's the end of the bet," he said again.

"Day thirty," she said. "You almost left me that first night too. Why don't you just…not."

His eyes looked tormented then, pained. "I should have left you then. That's the thing. Better late than never."

"No…"

"But it has to be some time. I've got a ranch. I've got a life, and so do you."

"Well, maybe don't leave me with my fucking dinner plates on the floor, you asshole," she said.

He didn't flinch. Instead, he righted his clothing and went over to the corner, grabbed the broom and the dustpan. His actions reminded her so much of the first night he'd been here, when he had fixed things and she had swept, that she nearly cried. And she just lay there, naked, while he swept up the glass on the floor, but left all the pieces of her heart.

"If you ever need anything—if, when the horses come, you need something… You just let me know, Cricket."

"No," she said.

Because what she wanted from him, he wasn't going to give.

The words were lumped in her throat, and she couldn't bring herself to ask for them. And when he left her house, and she was there, nothing but misery, she had to wonder if she had changed at all.

Because she hadn't said what needed to be said. She

hadn't. She'd just left it all there, in her chest, afraid of rejection.

What was the point? What was the point of any of it if she hadn't gotten strong enough to say what she needed?

What was the damn point?

But she didn't go after him. And for the next several days, she did nothing at all. Until she started to realize that something wasn't right. Not just the loneliness or her heart. She was pretty upset by Jackson leaving, and by his not coming back, but not enough to screw with her cycle. And when she showed up at her sister Emerson's house, practically shivering from the cold and clutching a bag that contained a pregnancy test, she was in a daze.

"What are you doing here?"

"I couldn't go to Wren. Because she is married to Creed."

"Yes," Emerson said, stepping back away from the door. "She is."

Cricket stepped inside, and held up the test.

Emerson touched her stomach. "I'm actually good. But is there something you need to tell me?"

"Yes," Cricket said. "I mean, maybe. I need to use your bathroom."

"You know you can."

"Please don't tell anybody," Cricket said.

"I won't."

She went into the bathroom, and didn't come out for way longer than the prescribed number of minutes. It didn't take long for Emerson to knock.

"I feel like your lack of communication indicates

the test results were not what you wanted." Her sister's voice was soft through the door.

"No," Cricket said. But even as she said that, she didn't feel like it was true. She wasn't devastated. She wasn't even sad. It felt…right somehow. That there was no way she was going to get out of a relationship with Jackson without keeping something of him.

Without being changed.

"Honey," Emerson said. "Open the door."

And Cricket did, knowing she must look every inch the bedraggled insect her name suggested she might be.

"Whatever you need. I'm not here to judge. If you need a ride to anywhere, if you need me to provide you with an alibi while you collect a weapon to go kill someone…"

"No," Cricket said.

"No to…"

"Any of those things. I'm fine. I mean, I will be. I've just got to…tell him."

"And by him, do I take it you mean Jackson Cooper?"

"The very same. And I didn't want Wren to tell Creed to kill him."

"Well, I'm fixing to tell Holden to kill him, so all you're really doing is sparing Creed's conscience."

"Please don't kill him. I've got to tell him."

"Sure."

"I'm not upset."

"You look upset."

"Well we're not really…together anymore. So that kind of sucks."

"Well, you don't need him. You've got us. Whatever you want to do, you've got us."

"I want to have a baby," Cricket said. "And I didn't

think I did. But now that it's happening... I mean, I guess it's not a bad thing that I'm not horrendously un-happy about it."

"Yeah," Emerson said. "I guess so."

"I just need...to see him. Before anything else."

Emerson had been protective, but Cricket managed to extricate herself from her sister and get herself on her way to Jackson's place. She had never been there before, and she was stunned by how impressive the modern ranch house was. All black windows, reddish wood siding and charcoal paint. An extraordinary col-lection of shapes and angles. So very different from the classic little farmhouse she had.

They were so different.

But...

At their core, they had plenty in common.

There was a reason they were in this situation, after all. Chemistry, for sure, but more than that.

She would never forget that day they had spent out on the picnic blanket. He might have been stern and cold the last time they made love. The last time she'd seen him, but that wasn't the sum total of what they were as a couple.

A couple.

But they had never been that, had they? They'd been two people bonded together by a bed, by her pain and...

And glimmers of his. Which he had shared, but so sparingly. And she knew there was more to him. She did. Knew there was more to who he was and every-thing that he carried around inside of him, even if she didn't know quite all what it was.

But this was the time, she supposed. This was where

the rubber met the road and the…well, the positive pregnancy test met with their present reality.

She took a deep breath and got out of her truck, making her way up the paved walk that led to the large, flat entryway. The door was huge, and it made Cricket feel tiny. She stood there and took a breath, trying not to be reminded of feeling tiny in other circumstances. Standing outside the door to her father's office. Sitting way down at the end of a long banquet table, feeling lost in the family villa.

No, this was different. Because she was standing there a changed woman from who she'd been back then. When she'd just been a girl. When she hadn't known who she was or what she wanted. When he called her little Cricket, it wasn't a bad thing. And she didn't mind. When he said it, it somehow made her feel special, protected. And right now, she was protecting a life inside of her. And that made her feel strangely powerful. Renewed and changed.

She'd never really thought about being a mother. And in fact, in passing, had thought she wouldn't be. After all, her own experiences with family hadn't been any good. But she didn't feel tied to that. Not now. Not anymore. Whatever the Maxfields were, it didn't make Cricket Maxfield one of them. It didn't mean she had to repeat their legacy over and over again. Somehow, that little inner boosting helped buoy her on, and she raised her hand and knocked on the solid oak door. She shook her hand out, because it hurt. And she wasn't even sure it had made a sound in the gigantic space.

But then, the door opened, and she jumped back. Because there he was, standing in the doorway wearing a tight black T-shirt, jeans and a black cowboy hat. And he looked…well, amazing.

"Hi," she said.

"Cricket," he responded. "What are you doing here?"

"Well, that's not the friendliest greeting."

"Sorry. Do you want to come in?"

"Probably should."

He opened the door, and let her into the room made of the same wood as the exterior of the house, glossy black details punctuating the rustic look, making it feel somehow modern. The room was huge, square, with a ceiling so tall it brought her back to that place of smallness.

Of course, Jackson and all his height contributed to that, as well.

"We need to talk," she said. "The way you left me… I wanted you to stay."

"Yes, and I explained that I couldn't." His jaw was tight, his expression firm.

"Yeah, and you didn't give me a good reason. So I'd like to hear it. I really would."

Before she told him what she had to say, she wanted to know what he might say to her without that information.

"It's complicated."

"No. Complicated is having a crush on a man for years, then finding out he might be your half brother, then wanting to sleep with him anyway. Then finding out he's not your half brother and sleeping with him for the duration of a thirty-day wager. That's complicated. So, we've been through complicated already, so whatever else you have on your mind, whatever else you have to tell me, is not going to touch that. I think we can figure it out. Trust me when I say I'm pretty resilient."

"All right, Cricket," he said. "You really want to have this conversation?"

"Yes. I do."

"I don't want to get married. I mean, what's the point? It just two people being tied together for no particular reason that I can see."

"So, why does there have to be marriage? Why can't we just be together?"

"I would never want to be responsible for not loving someone enough. For doing to them what my father did to my mother. And at the end of the day, whether I admire or look up to him or not, I'm Cash Cooper's son."

"And I'm James Maxfield's daughter, but I'm not going to sexually harass anyone. I'm not going to treat my kids like an afterthought and my wife…well, husband, like a trophy. It doesn't matter whose son you are. What matters is what kind of man you are. And that's your choice."

"Okay then, it's my choice not to put myself in a position where I could hurt someone that way."

"So you don't think you could love me."

She stared at him, willing herself not to break his gaze. Not to be a wimp. She would brazen this out. She just would.

"It's not you."

"Oh, it's not you, it's me. Very original. You know, Jackson, I expected better from you. Better from us. For us. We are not like anyone else. So don't be a cliché now."

"I'm not trying to hurt you…"

"Another good one. Who writes your dialogue? Because it's not very good."

"I'm sorry."

"And I'm pregnant."

Chapter 10

Jackson felt like a bomb had been dropped in the middle of his living room. It was like watching a horror movie. Looking back on the last few weeks. Sitting there, wanting to tell the idiot not to go into that house, but he'd gone in anyway. And now here he was. Exactly the thing he'd been trying to avoid.

She was pregnant.

That was absolutely everything that he hadn't wanted to happen.

"When did you find out?"

"Literally an hour ago? I went to my sister's house—not the one who is married to your brother—and then I came straight here."

"What the hell are we going to do?"

"Well, the unfortunate thing is I was kinda hoping

you would have something better to say than what you just did."

"You understand that we can't get married."

"Well, fantastic," Cricket said. "I figure I'll just find another man to marry, then."

"You damn well will not."

"But you don't want to marry me. Then maybe somebody should. Because maybe I care about that kind of thing." She took a big, deep breath. "Maybe I care about tradition and I don't want my child to be a bastard. Did you ever think about that?"

"Well, do you?"

"No. What I care about is the fact that you're being ridiculous. We are good together."

"And this is exactly the kind of thing I wanted to avoid. This obligation. This idea that two people have to be together. For the sake of the child. Do you know what it does to a child, Cricket? I was worried about you. About what I might do to you if I couldn't be what you needed... But a kid. Dammit, that kid is basically me. You know what it's like to find out you're the unhappy glue that held your parents together for better or for worse? Mostly worse?"

"We already talked about this. It's all about choices and—"

"But I've seen what it does. If I committed to that, if I committed to you... I would never let you leave."

"Great. I don't want to leave," she said. "I want to be with you. I want to stay with you. Why is that bad? Why would it be so wrong?"

"I don't love you," he said, the words scraping his throat raw, and he knew they felt wrong. He knew they *were* wrong. But he couldn't find any other words.

Couldn't figure out what else to say, what else might come from that hammering feeling in his chest.

"What if I said I loved you?"

"That's what we can't do, Cricket. We cannot have that. We would make each other miserable. I would make you miserable."

"I want to be with you. I'm choosing that. What about my choice? Maybe I want to be with you even if I would be sorry that you didn't love me. Maybe I'd rather be with you than not."

"Cricket…"

"No. Be honest. Be honest about what you want and what you don't want, Jackson. But don't blame it on me, and don't blame it on your need to protect me. Because that's not what's happening here. You're not protecting me. You're…protecting yourself. I'm standing here, and I'm not scared. I'm not scared to love you. I'm not scared to have this baby. And you know what? I'm not scared to do it alone, either. I would rather not. I mean, flat out, I'd rather not. But that's just because I'd rather share my life with you. Because I have never felt so happy as I did living in that farmhouse with you. And so I would weather anything to figure out how we could work. You're the one who doesn't want to. And I can't quite figure out why.

"You think because I'm young, because I was inexperienced, that I can't understand what I want. But I do, Jackson. I do. I have always known what I wanted. A place in this world where I fit, and to be with you. It seems to me that what you're after is a life where you won't regret anything. And I don't think anyone can guarantee you that, Jackson, I really don't. We could be together, for better or worse, like you said. And maybe sometimes it would be worse. But I think it would still be a better kind of worse than being apart."

"Because you don't know what that looks like. Not really. I do. I watched my mom… I watched her wish for another life. And I was the cause of her not having it."

"So, we can get married. And if you were miserable, we could get divorced."

"Cricket…"

"No, really, what's your problem? You're afraid of what? You're afraid of failing? Because we're not trapped. We wouldn't be. It would be up to us. But you're afraid of something. Otherwise…this would be a different conversation. You're acting like I didn't grow up around a dysfunctional marriage. So why don't you stop hiding behind the one you grew up around. I thought cowboys were supposed to be brave."

Her words were like a dagger through his heart. He did feel like a coward. He felt like the worst kind of coward, standing there and offering her absolutely nothing. Standing there and failing her, except…

He knew what he knew.

He knew what it was to be a child who had been part of a marriage of obligation. More than that, he knew what it was to be the child who'd caused it. And maybe Creed had been willing to do that to be with his kid, but his brother had been through something entirely different. His brother had been barred from seeing his child.

His child.

So Jackson was going to live in a different house than his kid?

This was why they'd done it. He could understand it. That was the thing. Standing there staring at her, and the enticement of the future they could have…

But Cricket hadn't said she loved him.

She was standing there, asking for something that would make their lives easier on a surface level. The thing that so many people did. To try and make a family for a child.

But he knew that beneath the surface of the happiest-looking nuclear family there could be rot and decay. A kind of desperate sadness that nobody saw but the people on the inside of the arrangement.

And whatever he was, he didn't want to be her obligation. Whatever he was, he didn't want to be her regret.

You're protecting yourself...

How? He didn't feel protected. Not now. What he felt was angry. Infuriated and just damn helpless.

He hadn't done any different than his parents. And that was a galling thing. But he would do different now. He would. He would do better, for them both.

"Do you even want to be this baby's father?"

"I'll be a father. If I made a kid, I'm going to take care of the kid."

"It's a shame you can't feel a little bit of that for me."

"Whether you see it or not, Cricket, this is me caring."

"No, I don't see it," she said, her tone as icy as her expression.

"We'll find a way through this."

"To what? Coparenting? Sharing custody? Will we trade our kid back and forth in the parking lot of the grocery store?"

He didn't like anything about the future she painted with those words. He didn't like any of this. What he wanted to do was grab her and pull her up against him, pick her up in his arms and carry her upstairs and make her his.

He wanted to keep her.

And she would stay.

For the child.

And he would still be that obligation he'd always been.

He gritted his teeth, shoved that aside. "Whatever you need."

"Except a husband."

"It's better."

"Well, if you say so. But if I were you, I don't know that I'd lay a bet on it. Since you'd only lose. Because you know what, I got the better hand." She stopped and looked at him, her expression almost pitying. "The thing is, Jackson. You keep thinking that you know exactly how this is going to play out. You keep thinking that you know better than me. Even from the beginning. When I won, you felt like you had another plan, and so you didn't really lose. But you did, though, didn't you? I got my way. So if I were you, I would maybe try to figure out what all I know that you don't."

And then Cricket left.

Turned and left him there, driving off in her great truck down the hill, taking some piece of him with her. But she didn't understand. She didn't understand that this was how it had to be. Because in her mind she could will all these things into fitting together, and he knew better. He'd spent his life as an obligation.

But now he was standing there, feeling like he'd cut his own heart out of his chest, and he knew he was a liar.

He couldn't love her…

He already did.

And he was every bit the coward she had accused him of being.

* * *

Cricket didn't go back to the ranch. She couldn't. Instead, she went to Emerson's. And it didn't take long for Wren to show up. At this point, there was no protecting Jackson from the wrath of her brothers-in-law. And Cricket didn't intend to try. She was too angry at him. He was being…ridiculous.

He didn't have a damn good reason for any of this.

Cricket had never sulked so hard in her life. But she was doing her best to work a groove into her sister's overstuffed, white fluffy beanbag chair with the weight of her indignant sighs.

"So, when do we get the whole story?" Emerson asked.

It all came pouring out of Cricket, from her lifelong crush to their love affair, to the half brother thing, and all the way to what had just happened at his place.

"Well," Wren said. "Creed is going to kill him."

"I know," Cricket said. "It's why I went to Emerson first. Because I didn't really want him to die. I'm feeling more flexible on that subject right at the moment."

"So he said he can't love you?"

"Yes. He did. And you know what, if I believed it… then maybe I would think he was doing the right thing. But I don't believe it. I do think he can love me. I really do. I think he might love me already. And I think he's being afraid."

"Well," Wren said, "love makes fools out of men. Trust me."

"Even Creed?"

"Oh, Creed was the *worst*," Wren said.

"No," Emerson said, "I think Holden was the worst. I told him that I loved him and he lost his mind."

"Yeah, Creed was not exactly receptive to me loving him either."

"Oh," Cricket said, frowning.

"What?" Wren asked.

"I didn't exactly tell him that I loved him."

"Really?" Emerson asked. "But you do, right? I mean, you have for years."

"I... Yes. But I...wanted to see what he would say, and I didn't want to..."

"Cricket," Wren said gently. "I'd like to kill him. With my bare hands. If he didn't think that he could give you something real he never should've touched you."

"No. I told him it was okay. He was honest with me. He was upfront. He was. He never lied to me. It's just... I thought I could be with him and then move on. I thought I could be with him and then make it part of a phase that I moved past. But I couldn't. I was lying to myself. He was never a phase. He was always fate."

"Then you need to tell him."

"He *humiliated me*."

"Yeah. And...sometimes we have to be fools for love."

"I don't like that at all."

"I don't either," Wren said. "But I love my husband. And I would debase myself for him a thousand times to keep him. But he doesn't make me. Maybe the real problem is that Jackson needs to know how you feel. The Coopers are... They're hard men. And I don't know all of Jackson's issues. But I do know what it looks like when a Cooper runs scared."

"So what? I don't wait for him to come to me? I don't…wait for him to say it first?"

"You can. But I think you have a good head on your shoulders, Cricket. And you always have," Emerson said. "You know who you are. And it would be great if relationships could be fifty-fifty, but they can't be. Everybody has to give everything they've got all the time, and sometimes you're going to have to be the one carrying your partner. No, it should never look like Mom and Dad's marriage. Where one of them dies emotionally, without any kind of love or support. But sometimes you have to be the first one who's willing to break. The first one who's willing to be vulnerable. And it might be tough, but it's best. Because otherwise you end up in a stalemate forever, and nobody wins."

"Maybe it's just a bad hand. All around."

"No. Don't say that. Look, he's a good man, and you're a good woman. And I don't believe for a minute that the two of you can't find a way to make something together."

"But…"

"It sucks," Emerson said, "but anything that matters is tough sometimes. The only person who ever has it easy in a relationship is someone like Dad. Someone who doesn't care enough to be hurt. Who doesn't care enough about someone else's feelings."

Those words resonated inside of Cricket and sank down deep. She had always wanted to be protected, but being part of her family, in the way that she had wanted to be…it had been a bigger risk than she was willing to take. It hadn't mattered enough. It hadn't mattered enough because she hadn't aspired to the kind of life her mother and father had anyway. So contorting herself to become part of it had seemed the opposite of a good idea. But Jackson… He was different. The life they could have—she could see it. She ached for it. A life together, one with their child. And that hadn't been her fantasy. She had thought about Jackson, about having him. Not about domestic bliss or anything of that kind. But she wanted it. It was a future that burned bright and hot in her mind. A future that mattered.

Because she loved him.

And where in the world did pride fit in with love? She *couldn't* protect herself.

That was what he was doing. Whether he would admit it or not, that was what he was doing. And she wasn't going to do that. She wasn't going to sacrifice love on the altar of her own pride. Because this was deeper than that. It was in her bones, in her blood. Like the land. Like ranching.

Some things simply were.

And for her, loving Jackson was one of those things. And she was going to fight for it. Fight for him.

Because her life mattered too much to let someone like James Maxfield twist her sense of who she was enough to prevent her from being happy even when he wasn't around. And it was the same for Jackson, whether he knew it or not. His parents' mistakes didn't get to decide what he was.

She burrowed out from the large poof she'd been sitting on. "All right," she said. "I'm going to tell him that I love him."

"A good idea. Maybe not at nine o'clock at night, though," Emerson said.

"Why not?"

"Formulate a plan. You got this. But it wouldn't hurt to take some time with it."

Cricket nodded. "Okay. Time."

And that was when she did start to form a plan.

"I'm going to need to borrow your dress again," she said to Emerson.

"Whatever you need."

Chapter 11

Jackson was no stranger to grief. But what surprised him this time was that the situation with Cricket felt more like death than he'd anticipated anything like this could feel. He had reached the end of his rope and he knew he had two options. Reach for the bottle of whiskey, or reach for his car keys. He opted for the car keys, and found himself driving down from the ranch and heading to where his father was, at the tasting room, and that was how Jackson ended up pounding on the door. He knew he'd woken up the old man, but he didn't really care.

"Jackson? Is everything all right?" Cash asked, tying his robe hastily as he pulled open the door.

"Cricket is pregnant," Jackson said.

"Well hell," Cash said. "You really did need to know who her father was."

"I told you I did."

"You didn't waste any time."

"It was inevitable. But it doesn't matter. I need to know something else from you, and I need to know it now. Why did you marry Mom if you couldn't love her? Why did you do it for me? Because you know what, it doesn't feel very good to be the reason your parents are miserable. To be the reason that they're together. To know that you're why they are not happy."

"You were never why we weren't happy," Cash said. Then he sighed wearily. "Come in."

Jackson stepped inside, enveloped by the sense of strangeness he always felt when he entered his childhood home. He had sat at the dining table countless times with his mother. He had opened Christmas presents in the corner, right there by the fireplace where the tree always was. He had read to his mother while she lay on the couch, while she wasn't well. While he was losing her, watching as she slipped away.

He couldn't be in here and not...feel.

"You need to understand that we weren't unhappy," Cash said. "Not always. Just like we weren't happy always. And look, the pain that your mother felt, that was my fault. We had a bad fight. Must've been...fifteen, sixteen years in, and she told me how much she hated the winery, and at that point, it had made us so much money, it felt like the best thing I'd ever done. But she said it just reminded her that my whole life was built on the foundation of trying to win back another woman."

Cash shook his head. "And I... I let that sit inside me. I let that fester. And I figured... It would've been a lot easier to be married to Lucinda Maxfield. But I know better than that. I mean, I know better than to believe that being with Lucinda would've fixed all my problems. Because you can't compare a childish infatuation to a marriage that spans decades. You just can't do it. Every what-if supposition your mother and I ever had about if we hadn't been together... We were never with anyone else for all those years. I didn't have children with anyone else. The stresses and pressures that time in a family put on you can't be compared to anything else. We grew up with each other, for better or worse. We changed together, in sickness and health. We were part of each other."

"You were together because you felt obligated," Jackson said.

"Is that a bad thing?"

"Yes. You should be with someone because...hell, because you love them."

"Where the hell did you get the idea that love didn't come with obligation? Loving a child is full of obligation. A marriage is filled with obligation. *Obligation* is not a bad word. It's bad people that turn away from it, don't you think?"

"I can't say that I ever thought of it that way."

"We weren't perfect. We weren't blissfully, perfectly happy. And I carry so much guilt for all my feelings. For the kind of husband I wasn't. It's not that I couldn't have loved her, it's that I chose—*we* chose—to let certain things affect what we believed. To let certain feelings grow rotten and determine how much and how little we could feel and forgive."

"When she told me that you only got married because she was pregnant with me—"

"Maybe," his dad said. "Maybe that's true. But she doesn't know that. Not even I know that. We could say that, shout it at each other at the worst of times, and we certainly did. But that doesn't make it true. That doesn't make it a sure thing that we can know. We loved each other then."

"Well, you were only with mom because Lucinda Maxfield married James."

"This is the problem," Cash said. "I don't know the way things would've gone, or could've gone if we'd done things differently. If we'd been less stubborn. Less self-righteous. But we weren't. And that's my burden. It's not yours or anyone else's, and she shouldn't have put it on you. But there's a lot of things I shouldn't have put on her... You shouldn't have been the person she had to talk to. But the problem is—this is all 'should have,' 'could have.' And you drive yourself crazy with it, Jackson. Believe me. I've done it. For years and years, I've done it. And most of all since she passed."

"Why since then?"

"I told you. Guilt. And regret. Because at the end of the day, I loved your mother very much. And what I didn't do was show it. Because I kept expecting it to feel the same as something I felt when I was young, something I felt that was impossible and painful, and wonderful in its way..." He shook his head. "And then, I wonder what could have been between us now and that makes the regret even worse. Because I can hear her in my head, saying I was just waiting for her to die so I could be with the person I really wanted. But that's not the truth of it. It just isn't."

Jackson let out a long, slow breath and rocked back on his heels. He didn't know what the hell to do with any of this. Cricket looked at him and talked about fate. She had talked about him and her as if they were something preordained. And his dad was making this all sound a lot like choice. And a whole collection of hard ones at that.

But something else Cricket said burned bright inside of him.

They weren't their parents.

And they weren't. It was true.

Because Jackson didn't feel conflicted or confused about whether or not he should be with Cricket because he had feelings for someone else. He'd never had feelings for anyone like he did for Cricket. And he wasn't young and naive. But what he was, was damn tired of feeling like a sacrifice. And if he was truly honest with himself, he was angry at his mother. Because she'd made him feel that way. Whether she'd meant to or not. And hearing his dad say he wished she hadn't dumped that on Jackson gave voice to all these things he'd tried not to think about.

"You know, son," Cash said. "She was sick, not a saint. A wonderful woman to be sure, but flawed like any of us. I know she didn't mean to hurt you. But the fact of the matter is…she did. Doesn't mean she didn't love you."

"I know," Jackson said.

"For what it's worth, she would've walked into fire for you. Marrying me was only a hardship for part of the time."

"Do you regret the way things happened?"

"I regret the way I handled them. I regret that I didn't find a way to be a better husband. I've never regretted you. I've never regretted the life your mother and I built together. But I didn't let go of the past the way I should have, because your vows say you forsake all others. And

I never cheated, but I kept that desire and those memories in a special place inside myself. You make choices every day, Jackson. And I don't know that you'll ever be able to live a life with no regrets, but you should make sure you live a life that's honest. Those games we all played, they were games. And games don't amount to much. Nothing more than needless heartache, anyway."

"I don't want to feel like she has to marry me."

"She seems like a modern enough girl."

"I told her I wouldn't marry her."

"Well hell, boy," Cash said. "I didn't raise you to wimp out on your responsibilities."

"I'm not. I'm trying to make sure she doesn't see me as another responsibility."

"Well, ask her if she does. Don't just try to protect yourself. Ask her how she feels."

"How will she know?"

"How will she know?" Cash repeated. "You want too much. You're going to have to trust her. You're going to have to believe her. Trust would've gone a long way in fixing my marriage. Trust, faith and honesty. If I could do more of any three things, it would be those. And we would've had a different life."

Jackson loved Cricket. He did. He was sure of that, standing there in this house filled with all these memories. All those weighted, hurtful memories that had seen him silently carrying around a whole lot of baggage he hadn't realized was there.

And she had been right. He was protecting himself. Because the burden of feeling like an obligation to his mother, a debt that he'd never been able to repay, haunted him. And the last thing he wanted was to be that burden for Cricket.

But he would have to ask. And he would have to trust.

And he would have to hope that...well, that Cricket really did know everything. And that she had faith in all those things she'd shouted at him before she left.

She was right. He'd lost the bet.

But it was one he was glad to lose.

The next morning, when Cricket opened her door wearing that red dress from the poker tournament, that oversized leather jacket, cowboy hat, but no cigar, Jackson was standing there. He looked haunted, like a man possessed. Like a man who hadn't slept all night.

"What are you doing here?"

"What are *you* doing?"

"Well, obviously I was on my way to stage a very serious scheme."

"Very obviously. Do you have a pistol on you?"

"No pistol." Her heart hammered, hard, as she looked up at him. As she tried not to hope what his presence meant.

"I fold," he said.

"You...what?"

"I fold, Cricket. I'm done. I surrender to this, to you. And you're right. I was afraid. I was a coward. A damn coward. Because I didn't want to face the fact that I wasn't really afraid of being my father, I was afraid of being my mother. Sitting all bitter and hollow at my kitchen table and telling my teenage child I was only in a marriage for their sake. That there was no love. No, the real thing I was afraid of was being the one who felt unloved. Because I have to tell you, when my mom said all that to me, that's how I felt. Like a burden and an obligation that she should never have had to take on. And I couldn't stand being that for the rest of my life. Not with you. But I love you, Cricket. And I'm willing to be that. I'm willing to do anything if it means being with you, having you. I'm willing to be an obligation, and to earn your love later. I know you want to be free. I know you want to start a life, and I know that having a child right now, and settling down with me, doesn't have much of anything to do with that. But I think… this is fate. And far be it from me to go against her."

"Jackson," she whispered, her heart expanding in her chest. "You're not a burden to me. I went to my sister's house last night and I complained to her about how you rejected me. And then they asked me if I told you that I loved you, and I realized that I hadn't. That was me protecting myself. I wanted to know what you felt, what you thought, before I put myself out there. It was easy to talk about marriage, and so much harder to talk about my heart. Because I've never done it. I've never seriously talked to anyone about how I felt. Except for you. And I've done more of that over the past month than ever in my life. Told you more about who I am, what hurt me, and what made me who I am. The bottom line is, above all else, and with everything else shoved aside, I love you. I have loved you for years. And I would want to be with you, pregnant or not. It was just the thing that got me up the mountain. It was just the thing that forced me to be as brave as I was, and even then, I wasn't all that brave. So I didn't really have a right to yell at you."

"You had plenty of right."

"Jackson," she whispered. "I really, really love you. And I have never wanted much of anything in my whole life enough to fight for it. Except for you. Only you. I can't imagine another person, another feeling, another anything that would ever be worth all this hassle. You're not an obligation. You're my inevitability."

"Cricket Maxfield," he said, wrapping his arms around her waist and looking at her, square in the eye. "You're the surprise I didn't see coming. Little Cricket, you're the thing I've been missing. I didn't know the right place to look to fill the hole in my heart. But you've known all along. You are wiser than me. Smarter than me. Braver than me. And I am going to love you today, and every day after. I don't care if some days are hard. I don't care if there are sleepless nights, or if I have to move out of my house and into your farmhouse. Because nothing matters but you. And that's... My dad said to me, that obligation and love often go together, and I expect that he's right. Love is what makes you want to fulfill that obligation. But this is different. Everything else feels like an obligation. You feel like breathing. And that's as deep as I can explain it."

"Is it in your blood?" she asked, her voice a whisper.

"Yes," he responded. "It's in my blood. My bones. My heart."

"Mine too."

And then he kissed her, and she couldn't think anymore. Couldn't breathe. She could only feel. And somehow, she knew she felt the same thing he did. Somehow, she knew that in this moment they were one. And it wasn't a pregnancy or marriage vows that would make it so. They could never have parted even if they'd wanted to. Because it was too late. The chips had already gone down. The game was over.

And in the end, they had both won.

Cricket Maxfield had won any number of specious prizes in her life. And she had often felt uncertain about her place in the world. But the biggest and best prize she'd ever won was loving Jackson Cooper and having him love her back. And if all the years of feeling misfit and frizzy and gap-toothed and like she didn't belong was what it had taken for her to get here, then she counted them all worth it.

She wouldn't change a single thing, not about herself, not about anything. Because it had brought her here. To this man, to his arms.

And that was truly the greatest prize of all.

* * * * *

RUTHLESS PRIDE

Naima Simone

To Gary. 143.

Chapter 1

"If your success was earned through hard work and honesty never apologize for it."

Joshua Lowell silently repeated the Frank Sonnenberg quote that had been a favorite of his father's. He pinched the bridge of his nose, a low, dark growl rumbling in the back of his throat. Too bad Vernon Lowell hadn't believed in the "practice what you preach" school of thought. According to that quote, his father had a ton of apologizing to do. Wherever he was—hell or a bungalow in some country without extradition policies.

Dropping his head, he refocused his attention to the spreadsheets displaying the previous month's profit-and-loss numbers for Black Crescent Hedge Fund's investment in stock of a telecommunication company. Compared with this time last year, the investment was doing very well. Their clients would earn more than a modest return, and Black Crescent would receive a substantial management and performance fee...

Unlike his father, Joshua had stuck to the more traditional investments such as stocks, bonds, commodities and real estate. Vernon had been a daredevil in business, which initially had made him one of the richest men in the tristate area of New York, New Jersey and Connecticut. That fearless and adventurous spirit had also increased the millions his very select clients had invested with him into high-yielding portfolios, and grew his boutique business into one of most successful in the area.

It'd also cost those select clients millions. It'd devastated them.

So no, while some might call Joshua's business decisions rigid and even too conservative, he refused to do anything different. Too many people's livelihoods and futures depended on him making those safe choices. He refused to be another Lowell who betrayed their trust. Who destroyed them.

He'd been the last man standing when Vernon Lowell disappeared—for both the company and his family. Because he'd left with not only his clients' money, but the majority of his family's, as well. So even though the last man sometimes wanted to yell and rage at the unfairness of it all, at the grief and shame that often pounded within him like a second heartbeat—at the death of his own dreams—one thing the last man *couldn't* do was slip up or falter.

He couldn't afford to. Literally.

"Josh, did you hear what I said? Of course you didn't." Haley Shaw, his executive assistant, snorted, answering her own question before he could respond.

"Or you're just ignoring me, which you should know by now doesn't work. Whatever you're doing now can be put aside for just a few moments. This is important," she insisted, an edge invading her tone.

"Haley. Not now," he said without glancing up from his spreadsheet.

"Well, I'm sorry to interrupt," a brisk, husky but very feminine voice that carried zero hint of apology interjected, "but I'm afraid it's going to have to be now."

Two small hands with slender, unadorned fingers flattened on either side of his computer monitor. Surprised, all he could do for several long seconds was stare at those delicate hands. At the short, unpolished nails, the thin map of light blue veins under sun-kissed skin. Why did he have the odd but strong urge to place his mouth right on the joint where hand met wrist—and sip?

Hell. They were fucking hands.

The mental but mocking admonishment didn't stop him from traveling up the lengths of her arms clad in white sleeves to slim shoulders partially hidden by light brown and gold-streaked hair, past a graceful neck and slightly pointed but stubborn chin with its slight indent to a face that—*goddamn*.

Deliberately, he eased back in his office chair, careful to control all the muscles in his face. He forced himself to maintain the cold, aloof expression that he'd adopted and mastered fifteen years ago as a defense. But inside…inside, lust slammed into him like a hurricane intent on leveling every structure in its path. And right now he was the only thing remaining, and *Christ*, he was shaking right down to his foundation.

Thickly lashed silver eyes that gleamed with barely suppressed anger. Striking cheekbones that lent a bold strength to otherwise ethereal features. A gently sloped nose and a mouth that had him gripping the arms of his chair like they were the last lifeboat that kept him from drowning. Thing was, he wanted to leap from the safety of the raft and dive into that wide, full-lipped mouth. Teach it what it was created for. Show it how it could give both of them the filthiest of pleasures...

His heartbeat echoed its thundering rhythm in his cock, pounding out a need that ricocheted through him.

Unsettled by his visceral reaction to this stranger—a stranger who had barged into his corporate office uninvited—he narrowed his eyes on her, allowing the corners of his mouth to curl in a derisive snarl.

Haley heaved a sigh. "Joshua, let me introduce you to Sophie Armstrong," she said, a thick coat of resignation painting her words.

"I don't know a Sophie Armstrong," he stated coldly to his assistant, although he didn't remove his gaze from the woman in front of him. Maybe some instinctual part of him recognized that she was the biggest threat in the room—a threat to his schedule, his carefully laid-out day...his control.

"The name would be familiar if you bothered to answer any one of my phone calls or emails." She snorted, cocking a dark eyebrow. "I've been trying to contact you, Mr. Lowell, and you've ducked and dodged every attempt."

He frowned. Yes, he'd been busier than usual lately, but he would've remembered if she'd reached out to him. "I've never ducked or dodged anyone." Not even when he'd desperately longed to. "Especially someone who doesn't have enough manners or sense to not force herself into a place of business where she wasn't invited or wanted without an appointment. Now that you're here, you have exactly thirty seconds—twenty-nine more seconds than I would give anyone else—to explain what the hell you're talking about."

Others would've—had—recoiled and backed down from the hard, ice-cold fury in his voice. But Sophie Armstrong didn't even flinch. Instead, she met his glare with one of her own. A quicksilver flash of surprise flickered within him. He wasn't arrogant, but he also acknowledged his appeal to the opposite sex. Understanding his money proved just as much of a lure as the appearance he'd inherited from his handsome father, he never lacked for female attention. Or sex.

But to this woman, he might as well be Quasimodo taking a break from his Notre Dame tower to hang out in the Black Crescent offices. Sophie Armstrong didn't bother to employ any advantage her beauty might press—not that it would. But she didn't know that.

No, unless antagonism passed for charm these days, she was confrontational and contemptuous.

And goddamn, if it wasn't hot.

She reached into the bag over her shoulder, withdrew a stack of papers and slapped the pile on his desk. "That's what I'm talking about. All the emails I've sent you. And I can pull out my phone and scroll through and play every voice mail—there are fifteen of them. All asking you to reply in a timely manner. Apparently, your idea of timely and mine don't coincide because I meant at least a couple of days and yours apparently runs along the line of seasons in Narnia."

The snort slipped from him before he could contain it. He shouldn't be amused. And he certainly shouldn't let her see it.

"You have five seconds left," he informed her, leaning forward and with a will that had been forged in the fires of desperation, humiliation and pride over a decade ago, he shifted his attention back to his screen. "I suggest you make the most of it."

A soft, feminine growl filled the air, and the reverberation of it rolled in his gut, clenching the muscles there so hard he nearly grunted in pain. With the wrenching came the dark but HD-clear image of her, head thrown back, all that hair sprawled across black sheets, beads of sweat dotting the slender column of her throat. And that same, rumbling growl vibrating from her. Only it sounded hungrier, needier...

Christ, he needed her out of his office.

"I'm assuming that king-of-the-manor-got-no-time-for-peasants thing intimidates other people, but I hate to break it to you. It does nothing for me." She crossed her arms over her chest, and if Jesus had come down at that moment and warned him against giving in to his baser needs, Joshua still wouldn't have been able to stop his gaze from dipping to the slightly less-than-a-handful but firm breasts that pushed against the plain white dress shirt. Guilt streaked through him, slick and dirty. He wasn't his father; he didn't ogle women or treat them like eye candy, there for his pleasure. Even women who made his dick hard but he didn't particularly like. "I'm telling you now—like I did in my last voice message and two emails—I'll be writing my story with or without you. But it would be a better one *with* you."

Story. What *story*?

A sense of foreboding wormed its way into his chest, hollowing it out. Making room for the churning unease.

"I repeat," he stated, the flat tone revealing none of

the steadily encroaching panic that crept into his vision, that squeezed his rib cage like a steadily tightening vise. "What are you talking about?"

"The anniversary piece on the Black Crescent fiasco that I'm writing for the *Falling Brook Chronicle*. And unlike all of the articles written about that time period, I would like to include an interview with the company's current CEO."

Anger crystallized within him, hard and diamond bright. And sharp enough to cut glass. The "get out" burned on his tongue, singeing him. But he extinguished the words before they could escape him, refusing to betray any emotion to this woman who sought to rip open the seams of the past, to expose old but unhealed wounds for public consumption. To relive the nightmare of his father emptying the family bank accounts as well as embezzling millions from his clients and disappearing, abandoning him, his mother and brothers to the wolves. The abrasive rub of judging eyes and not-so-hushed whispers. The smothering guilt that ten families were left devastated and destitute because of his father's actions. The agonizing pain from being deceived and abandoned by the man who'd raised him, who'd loved him and who he'd respected.

This woman had no clue about the pressure from the weight of that guilt, that responsibility. How they straddled his shoulders to the point of suffocation at times. How dealing had become second nature to him. There'd been no one to lean on when his father disappeared, when he'd taken on the responsibility of repaying the families so they wouldn't sue for the remaining money his father hadn't disappeared with. When his mother withdrew from the exclusive community of Fall-

ing Brook, New Jersey. When his twin brother, Jacob,
fled to Europe to backpack his problems away, and his
youngest brother, Oliver, dropped out of college and
become the poster child for professional playboy, complete with a nasty cocaine habit.

Nothing in his Ivy League education—not even the
economic courses he'd taken at his father's insistence—
had prepared him for being alone, grieving and terrified with the fate of not just his family but ten others on
his still-young shoulders. Of having to make the bitter
decision of burying his own dreams so he could repair
those of others.

He'd grown up fast. Too fast.

And damn if he needed an article written by an ambitious reporter—no matter if she possessed the face of a
fairy queen and the body of a Victoria's Secret Angel—
to drag him back to those desolate, black times when
he'd breathed fear as much as he did air.

"No."

Joshua gave her credit—she didn't flinch at the flat,
blunt answer.

Instead, she tilted her head to the side, that fall of
thick caramel-and-sunlight hair sliding over her shoulder, and studied him as if he were a problem to solve.
Or an opponent to wrestle and pin into submission.

"I can understand why you would initially be reluc-
tant to speak with me—"

"Oh, you can?" he interrupted, trying but failing to
keep the bite from his voice. Silently, he cursed himself
for revealing even that much. The last fifteen years had
taught him that he couldn't afford to betray the slightest weakness of character lest he be accused of being
just like his father. Other people were allowed room for

mistakes. He was not offered that courtesy. While others could trip up in private, his missteps were splashed across newspapers and online columns for fodder. Including *her* paper. "So you've had a—how did you so eloquently put it?—fiasco in your life and had every paper in the country report on it? Including the *Falling Brook Chronicle*? Which, if I remember correctly, was one of the harshest and most critical? Well, good," he continued, not granting her the opportunity to answer. "Since you have experienced it, you'll understand why I'm ending this conversation."

"I've read the past articles from the *Chronicle*, and you're right, they did cover it…punitively," she conceded. In the small pause that followed, the "can you blame them?" seemed to echo in the office. "But those reporters aren't me. You don't know me, but I graduated from Northwestern University with a BS and MS in journalism. While there, I worked with the Medill Justice Project that helped free an unjustly convicted man from a life sentence in prison. I've also won the Walter S. and Syrena M. Howell competition, was a recipient of the NJLA's journalism award and was a member of the journalistic team who won the Stuart and Beverly Awbrey Award last year, all well-respected awards. I don't intend to do a hatchet job on you or Black Crescent. As a matter of fact, I would like to write this article from a different angle—the artist submerged. From my research, I discovered you were once a very accomplished artist—"

"We're done," he ground out, rising to his feet, flattening his palms on the desk.

Hell, no. Pain, like crushed glass, scraped his throat and chest raw.

He hadn't been called an artist in fifteen long years. And hadn't picked up a camera or paintbrush in just as long. Once, his trademark had been oversize, mixed-media collages that provided cultural commentary on war and human rights. He'd poured his being into those pieces, falling into endless pockets of time where nothing had mattered but losing himself in photographs, oils and whatever elements captured what swirled inside him—metal, newspapers, books, even bits of clothing. But when his father had vanished, Joshua had put aside childish things. At least that was what Vernon had called Joshua's passion—a childish hobby.

It'd been like performing a lobotomy on his soul. But now, instead of channeling his anger, grief and pain into art, he suppressed it. And when that didn't work, he funneled it into making Black Crescent solvent and powerful again. Or took it out on a punching bag at the gym.

The whole shitfest with the hedge fund had left him with precious little—the death of his art career, the eradication of his relationships with his brothers, a ghost of a mother, an overabundance of shame and a ruined family company. But they'd been *his* choices.

All that had remained in the ashes after the firestorm were the ragged tatters of his pride because he'd had the strength, the character, to make those choices.

And now Sophie Armstrong sought to steal that dignity away from him, too.

No. She couldn't have it.

"Mr. Lowell," she began again with a short shake of her head.

But again, he cut her off. "I have a busy day, and you've had more than the thirty seconds I allotted. We're through talking. You need to go," he ordered, knowing his mother would cringe at the lack of the manners she'd drilled into him since birth. Not that he gave a damn. Not when this woman stood here prying into an area of his life that wasn't open for public consumption.

"Fine, I'll leave," she said, but nothing in the firm, almost combative tone said she'd conceded. She drew her shoulders back, hiking her chin in the air. Though she stood at least a foot shorter than him, she still managed to peer down at him with a glint of battle in her silver eyes. "You can try to erase the past, but certain things don't go away no matter how hard you try to bury them. The truth always finds a way of resurrecting itself."

"Especially if there are reporters always armed with a shovel, ready to dig up anything that will sell papers," he drawled.

The curves of her full mouth flattened, and her eyes went molten. He waited, his body stilling except for the heavy thud of his heart against his rib cage. And the rush of hot anticipation in his veins.

It'd been years since anyone had challenged him. Not since he'd proved he was his father's son in business and, at times, in ruthlessness. But Sophie Armstrong... She must not have received the memo, because she glared at him, slashes of red painting her high cheekbones, as if even now, she longed to go for his throat. Was it perverse that part of him hoped she did? That he wanted that tight, petite, almost fragile body pressed to his larger frame with those delicate but capable-looking hands wrapped around his neck...exerting pressure even as he took her mouth as she attempted to take his breath?

Yeah, that might make him a little sick. And a hell of a lot dirty.

Still… He could picture it easily. Could feel the phantom tightening of her grip now. And he wanted it. Craved it.

But not enough to rip open old, barely scarred-over wounds so she could have a byline.

"Thank you for your time, Mr. Lowell," she finally said, and disappointment at her retreat surged through him.

God, what was wrong with him? He wanted—no, needed—her to drop this "artist submerged" bullshit and get the hell out of his office.

She whirled around on her boring nude heels and stalked across the room to his office door. Without a backward glance, she exited. He half expected her to slam it shut, but somehow the quiet, definite snick of the lock engaging seemed much more ominous.

Like a booming warning shot across his bow.

Chapter 2

"The Black Crescent Scandal: Fifteen Years Later."

Joshua gripped the Monday issue of the *Falling Brook Chronicle* so tightly, it should've been torn down the middle. She'd done it. Sophie Armstrong had run with the story, placing his family's sordid and ugly history on the front page as fodder for an always scandal-hungry public.

He lifted his gaze to stare out the windshield of his Mercedes-Benz at the Black Crescent building. He knew every railing, every angle, every stone inch of the modern midcentury building built into a cliff. His father's aim had been for the headquarters of his hedge fund to stand out in the more traditional architecture of Falling Brook. And he'd succeeded. The building was as famous—or infamous—as its owner.

And his infamy had made page one of the local paper. Again.

Studying the imposing structure offered the briefest of respites. Almost against his will, he returned his attention to the newspaper crinkling under his fists. He'd already read the article twice, but he scanned it again. It recounted his father's rise in the financial industry, his seemingly perfect life—marriage to Eve Evans-Janson, the pedigreed society daughter and darling whose connections further installed Vernon as a reigning king of Falling Brook; his three sons, who'd shown great promise with their Ivy League educations and fast-track career goals; the meteoric success of his business. And then his epic fall. Millions of dollars missing from the hedge fund's accounts. The death of Everett Reardon, his father's best friend and CFO of Black Crescent, who'd crashed his car while trying to elude capture. Vernon's disappearance.

The ten clients his father had stolen money from plunged into a nightmare of bankruptcy and destitution. The company's—Joshua's—agreement to pay back the families so they wouldn't file a lawsuit. How some of them still hadn't recovered from Vernon's selfish, unforgivable and criminal actions.

And then Joshua.

The artist turned CEO who had stepped into the vacant shoes of his father to save Black Crescent. Yes, it shared how he'd left his promising art career and turned the company around, saving it from ruin, but it also painted him as Vernon's puppet, coached and raised to take over for him since Joshua's birth. Which was bullshit. At one time, his path had been different. Had been his.

The article also cited that no one had heard from Vernon in a decade and a half, but despite rumors that he'd been killed in retribution for his crimes, there was also the long-held belief that his father was alive and well. And that his family was secretly in contact with him. That Vernon still pulled the strings, running Black Crescent from some remote location. Which was ridiculous. After his father initially vanished, his mother had hired a team of private detectives to locate him. Not to mention the FBI had searched for him, as well.

Fuck. He gritted his teeth against releasing the roar in his throat, but his head echoed with it. What did he have to do to redeem himself? What more did he have to sacrifice? He'd stayed, facing judgment, scorn and suspicion to rebuild the company, to restore even some of the money lost. He'd stayed, doing his best in the last fifteen years to repay those affected clients at least part of the fortune they'd lost to his father as promised. He'd stayed, enduring his brothers' ridicule and disdain for following in dear old Dad's footsteps. He'd stayed, caring for their mother, who'd become something of a recluse.

He'd stayed when all he'd wanted to do was quit and run away, too.

But he hadn't gallivanted off to Europe or found sweet oblivion in drugs and parties. Pride and loyalty had chained him there. Fatherless. Brotherless. Friendless.

And Sophie Armstrong dared insinuate he hadn't busted his ass all these years? That his father had done all the soul-destroying work.

His sharp bark of laughter rebounded against the interior of the vehicle. Its serrated edges scraped over his skin.

A part of him that could never utter the sacrilegious

words aloud secretly hoped Vernon was dead. Just thinking it caused shame, thick and oily, to slide down his throat and smear his chest in a grimy coat. But it was true. He hoped his father no longer lived, because the alternative... God, the alternative—that he'd abandoned his family and emptied their bank accounts without the slightest shred of remorse and never looked back—sat in his gut, curdling it. If Vernon wasn't dead, then that would mean the man he'd loved and had once admired and respected had truly never existed. And with everything else Joshua had endured these past few years, that...that might be his breaking point.

His cell phone rang, and a swift glance at the screen revealed Oliver's number. On the heels of his past staring him in the face this morning, his chest tightened. He and his younger brother's relationship was...complicated. Oliver lived in Falling Brook, but he might as well be across the Hudson River or even farther away.

Once, they'd been close. But that had been before Joshua had stepped in to head Black Crescent in place of their father. He'd lost some respect in Jacob's and Oliver's eyes that day. And a part of Joshua mourned that loss. Mourned what had been.

Briefly closing his eyes, Joshua slid his thumb across the screen and lifted the phone to his ear.

"Hello."

"I'm assuming you've seen today's paper," his brother said in lieu of a greeting.

"Yes." Joshua stared across the parking lot, no longer seeing the building that had been the blessing and curse on his family. In front of him wavered an image of a perfect family. Of a lie. "I've seen it."

A sound between an angry growl and a heavy sigh

reached him. "This shit again. Why can't people just let it die?" Oliver snapped.

"Because it makes for good copy apparently," Joshua drawled. "We'll ride this one out like we always do."

He uttered the assurance, and it tasted like bitter ashes on his tongue. He was tired of weathering storms. And more so of being the stalwart helm in it.

Oliver scoffed. "Right. Because that's what Lowells do." Joshua could easily picture his brother dragging his hand through his hair, a slight sneer twisting his mouth. "Do you know if Mom has seen the article?"

"I don't think so." Joshua shook his head as the stone of another burden settled on his shoulders. "I've sent Haley over to make sure the paper isn't delivered."

Thank God for Haley. She was more than his assistant. She was his taskmaster. Right-hand woman. And the bossy little sister he'd never had.

When the scandal around Black Crescent had broken fifteen years ago, and employees as well as friends had abandoned the company and the Lowell family, Haley— a college intern at the time—had remained. Even forgoing a salary to stay. Through the last decade and a half when Joshua had given up his own dreams and passion to step into the gaping, still-hemorrhaging hole his father had left, she'd been loyal. And invaluable. He couldn't have dragged Black Crescent from the brink of financial ruin and rebuilt it without her at his side.

The woman could be a pain in his ass, but she'd proved her loyalty hundreds of times over to his family. Because she was family.

"Since Mom doesn't leave the house too often, I'm not concerned with her mistakenly seeing it," Joshua continued.

Eve had become something of a hermit since her husband's crime and disappearance. Unfortunately, that option hadn't been available to Joshua.

"Good. I don't even want to imagine what this would do to her. Probably send her spiraling into a depression," Oliver said, and while Joshua and his brothers might not agree on much, this one thing they did—their mother's emotional health and protecting her. "I'll go by and see her this evening just to check in."

"That sounds good. Thanks," Joshua replied.

A snort echoed in Joshua's ear. "She's my mother, too. No need to thank me. Talk to you later."

The connection ended, and for a long second, Joshua continued to hold the phone to his ear before lowering it and picking up the newspaper again. He zeroed in on one line that had caught his attention before.

But is Joshua Lowell that different from his father? Appearances, as we know, are often deceiving. Who knows the secrets the Lowell family could still be hiding?

The sentences—no, not so thinly veiled accusations—leaped out at him. What the hell was that supposed to mean? Every skeleton in their closets had been bleached and hung out for everyone to view and tear apart. They didn't have secrets.

And where had she uncovered the photos included in the article? He scrutinized the black-and-white images. A few of his art pieces. His father as he remembered him with his mother on his arm. God, he hadn't seen her smile like that in years. Fifteen of them, to be exact. Him and Jake on their college graduation day, hugging Oliver between them. A family portrait taken at their annual Christmas party. The ones of him and Jake on campus. The snapshots of him painting in art class. The concentration and…joy darkening and lightening his face. He analyzed that image longer, hardly recognizing the young, *hopeful* man in the photo.

Well, Sophie had done her grave-robbing expedition well. He'd accused her of using her shovel to dig up old news. To acquire these photographs, she must've found a fucking backhoe.

Where had she gotten her information? She shouldn't have had access to those pictures, so who'd provided them to her?

There was only one way to find out.

Joshua tossed the paper to the passenger seat and pressed the ignition button to start the car.

He would go directly to the source.

"Great article, Sophie," Rob Jensen, the entertainment columnist, congratulated with a short rap on the wall of her cubicle.

"Thanks, Rob," she said, smiling. "I appreciate it."

"You did do an excellent job," Marie Coswell added when Rob strode away. She rolled in her desk chair to the edge of her cubicle, directly across from Sophie's. "But wow, woman," she tsk-tsked, shaking her head and sending the blunt edges of her red bob swinging against her jaw. "You didn't hold anything back. Aren't you even the least bit concerned the Lowells will retaliate? I mean, yes, their names were persona non grata around here for a while, but that was a long time ago. They have serious pull and power. Makes me real thankful that I'm over in fashion. No way in hell would I want to tangle with a Lowell, especially Joshua Lowell. Well, hold on. I take that back." She grinned, comically wriggling her perfectly arched eyebrows. "I'd love to tangle with that man—but nekkid."

Sophie laughed at her friend's outrageousness even as heat streamed up her chest and throat and poured into her face. Times like these, she cursed her father's Irish roots. Even her Italian heritage, inherited from her mother, couldn't combat the fair skin that emblazoned every emotion on her face. Good God. She was twenty-eight and blushing like a hormonal teenager.

"Holy shit. Are you blushing, Sophie? At what? The thought of Mr. Tall-Insanely-Rich-and-Hot-as-Hell?" Marie gave an exaggerated gasp. "Oh, you *so* are. All right, give. What happened when you stormed over to his office like it was the Alamo? Did you rip something else besides a strip off his hide? Like his clothes? What aren't you telling me?"

Sophie groaned, closing her eyes at her friend's exuberance and the *volume* of it. She loved the other woman, but she really should've been the gossip editor with her sheer adoration for it.

"Nothing happened. Clothes remained intact. The only thing stripped away was my pride." She winced, just remembering her ill-conceived decision to charge into Joshua Lowell's office and the ensuing confrontation.

That definitely hadn't been one of her finer moments. Thank goodness the front desk receptionist at the main level had been away from her desk. Otherwise security would've probably been called on her. Wouldn't Althea Granger, the editor in chief, have loved to receive that call about one of her investigative reporters needing to be bailed out for trespassing?

Why Joshua hadn't had her escorted out still nagged at her. Just as memories of the CEO did.

She shook her head, as if she could dislodge the question and the man from her mind with the gesture. As if it were that simple.

"Sophie." Althea Granger appeared next to her cubicle, as if her thoughts had conjured the older woman. With thick dark hair, smooth, unlined brown skin and beautiful features, she could've easily been mistaken for a retired model rather than the editor in chief of the exclusive bedroom community of Falling Brook's newspaper. But after stints in major papers across the country, she'd run the *Chronicle* with a steel hand, judicious eye and the political acumen of a seasoned senator for years. And she was Sophie's mentor and idol. "Could you join me in the conference room, please?"

"Absolutely." Sophie rose from her desk chair, ignoring Marie's concerned glance. Too bad she couldn't do the same for the kernel of trepidation that lodged between her ribs. Usually, if Althea wanted to speak with her, it was in her office. Not the more formal conference room.

Could this be about her article? No, it couldn't be. She instantly rejected the thought. Althea had personally read and approved the story before it'd run in this morning's paper. If she'd thought Sophie had gone too far, hadn't been professional or objective in her reporting, the other woman would've had no problem in calling her on it.

Then what could it…possibly…be… *Oh God.*

She almost jolted to a halt in the doorway of the room where most of their editorial meetings were held. Somehow, she managed not to grab on to the jamb to steady her suddenly precarious balance.

Joshua Lowell.

He stood at the head of the long, rectangular table, hands in the pockets of his perfectly tailored, probably ridiculously expensive navy blue suit, those unnervingly sharp and beautiful hazel eyes fixed on her.

How wrong that eyes so lovely—light brown with vivid brushes of emerald green—were wasted on such a hard, cold...gorgeous...face.

Okay. So, she hadn't fabricated how unjustly stunning the man was. It seemed unfair, really. Joshua Lowell, a millionaire, CEO, son of a powerful if notorious family, educated and sophisticated, and then God had deemed fit to top that sundae of privilege with a face and body that belonged pressed on an ancient coin or forever immortalized in marble for some art collector's pleasure.

She tried and failed not to stare at the angular face with its jut of cheekbones and stone-hewn jaw—the stark lines should've been severe, made him appear harsh. But the beauty of those eyes and the lushness of his too-sensual-for-her-comfort mouth with its fuller bottom lip softened the severity, making him a fascinating study of contrasts. Cruelty and tenderness. Coldness and warmth. Carnality and virtue.

Her gaze reluctantly drifted from his face to his broad shoulders, the wide chest that tapered to a narrow waist and hips. She couldn't see his thighs from her still-frozen position in the doorway, but her brain helpfully supplied how the muscular length of them had pressed against his slacks days ago. With his lean but powerful body, the man obviously worked out. Probably unleashed a lot of aggression there.

How else did he release emotion?

Stop it, she snapped at her wayward mind. *We don't care.*

Mentally rolling her eyes at herself, she forced her feet to move forward, carrying her farther into the room. Joshua Lowell might look like he flew down on winged feet from Mount Olympus, but he was still an arrogant ass. One who, most likely, was here either to try to get her fired or threaten a lawsuit. That ought to knock down his hot factor several notches.

Should.

"Sophie, please close the door behind you," Althea instructed. Once Sophie shut the door with a quiet click, the editor in chief nodded toward Joshua. "Mr. Lowell, I'd like to introduce you to Sophie Armstrong, the journalist of the article in today's edition."

Her pulse echoed in her ears as she waited, breath snagged in her throat, for Joshua to out her to her employer. But after a long moment, he only arched a dark blond eyebrow. His gaze didn't waver from her as he smoothly said, "Ms. Armstrong."

Relief flooded her, almost weakening her knees. Above all things, Althea was a professional, and she wouldn't have appreciated finding out Sophie had met him before. No, correction. *How* she'd met him.

But suspicion immediately nipped at relief's heels. *Why* hadn't he told Althea the truth? What did he want? She didn't know him, but she doubted he did anything magnanimously without it benefiting him. And he owed nothing to her, the reporter who had just aired his family's dark past all over the front page.

"Ms. Granger, I would appreciate it if you gave Ms. Armstrong and me a moment alone, please." He'd added *please*, but it wasn't a request.

And Althea didn't take it as one, though she did turn to her and ask, "Sophie?"

No. The answer branded her tongue, but the last time she'd checked, she wasn't a coward. And since she'd crashed Black Crescent's proverbial gates, it would be the height of hypocrisy to claim fear of being alone with him now. Even if her heart thudded against her chest like a bass drum.

"It's fine," she said.

"Okay." She continued to peer at Sophie for several more seconds, and, apparently satisfied with Sophie's poker face, she nodded. "Fine, but, Mr. Lowell," she added, swinging her attention back to Joshua, "I'm going to trust the words *lawsuit* and *libel* won't be thrown around in my absence. If so, I fully advise and expect Sophie to end the conversation so I can introduce you to our legal department."

With a smile that belied she'd just threatened to sic lawyers on him, Althea exited the room, leaving her alone with Joshua. And a table that had provided adequate enough distance before seemed to shrink, leaving her no protection.

"I assume your editor doesn't know about your little excursion to my office," he stated, with that flat note she'd come to associate with him.

"No," she said. "But of course you already figured that out. Why didn't you tell her?"

"Because it doesn't serve me well to do so right now. And—" his voice deepened to a slightly ominous timbre that had trepidation and—*God*—whispers of excitement tripping down her spine "—if anyone is going to deliver trouble to your doorstep, Sophie Armstrong, it's going to be me."

That statement might not have contained *lawsuit* or *libel*, but it was still most definitely a threat.

"I assume you're here about the piece in the *Chronicle*." She switched the subject, not wanting to dwell on what kind of "trouble" he wanted to visit on her. "Why don't you just get to it?"

He studied her, his silence heavy but fairly vibrating with the tension that seemed to crackle beneath his stoic facade. And something—call it a reporter's instinct or a woman's sixth sense—assured her that it was indeed a facade. Which meant more lurked beneath the surface that he didn't want anyone to see, to know. Secrets. The journalist in her, definitely *not* the woman, wanted to ferret out those secrets. Hungered to expose them to the light.

"Yes, why don't we just 'get to it,'" he repeated, making her suggestion sound like something more wicked. "I want to know how you acquired the photographs in the article."

She crossed her arms over her chest and shook her head. "From my sources, and before you issue a demand wrapped up in a request, I can't reveal them."

"Can't," he pressed, "or won't?"

She shrugged a shoulder. "In this case, it's the same difference."

Another long beat where his unwavering, intense gaze scrutinized her. "Do you know what you are, Ms. Armstrong?" he finally murmured.

"Let me guess. A bitch," she supplied, slipping a bored note into her voice. Wouldn't be the first time a

man in his position had called her that name when she'd
pressed too hard, questioned too much or just didn't go
sit behind a desk or on a set and look pretty. Journalism,
especially investigative journalism, wasn't for the weak
of heart or the thin of skin. And that word seemed to be
the go-to to describe a strong woman with an opinion,
a spine and unwillingness to be silenced.

"No." A flash of disgust flickered across his face as
if just hearing that word sickened him. Or maybe the
thought of calling a woman that particular insult did...
"Maybe you would prefer if I called you that. Because
then you could justify my being here as sour grapes and
damaged pride over a story. But I refuse to make it that
easy for you. No, Ms. Armstrong, you are not a bitch,"
he continued, and the disdain that had appeared in his
expression saturated his voice. "You are a vulture. A
scavenger who picks at carrion until there's nothing left
but the bleached, dry bones."

That shouldn't have hurt her. But, God, it did. It
slashed across her chest to burrow deep beneath bone
and marrow to the core of her that believed in fairness
and truth. Never in her reporting had she gone out of the
way to hurt someone. Which had been one reason why
she'd gone to see Joshua in the first place. She'd wanted
his side, to ensure the article hadn't been skewed.

Maybe it was a remnant from being the child of divorced parents. From that hyperawareness that ensured
neither her mother nor her father feel like she loved one
more than the other. That she didn't confide in, call or
lavish attention on one without making sure she gave
the other equal affection. That balance had been stress-
ful as a child who'd felt torn between two warring parents. And now, as an adult, that careful balancing act

had carried over into her job. She ensured she presented both sides of an issue. And for Joshua to attack that vulnerable center of her… It shook her. It *hurt* her.

"In your thirst for a juicy story and a byline, did you even once stop to consider the consequences? Did you pause to ask yourself how it would affect my family? My mother? She's had to deal with the fallout of someone else's actions for years. *Years*," he bit out, true anger melting the ice of his tone. Sunlight streamed through the windows behind him, hitting his dirty-blond hair and setting the gold strands aglow. Like an avenging angel. "She's suffered, and dredging up ancient history for the sake of salacious gossip will only inflict more harm. But, of course, you couldn't be bothered to take into account anyone or anything else but your own ambition."

"My own ambition?" she repeated, grinding the words out between clenched teeth. She lowered her arms and her fingers curled into fists at her thighs, as she almost trembled with the need to defend herself. To tell him that wasn't her at all. But screw that. She hadn't done a hatchet job; she'd simply done her job. Period. And she'd been fair. *Damn fair.* "You don't know the first thing about me, so don't shove your own biases on me. I understand that you might not be able to view the article objectively, but believe me, I showed admirable restraint. I could have included the complete, unvarnished truth about who and what you are. A truth I'm sure the 'hero'—" she sneered the word "—of Black Crescent wouldn't want to get out."

He didn't reply. Didn't react at all. His hazel gaze bored into her, and she refused to flinch under that poker face that reduced hers to an amateurish attempt.

"I have no idea what you're alluding to. I haven't done anything wrong or that I need to be ashamed of. As much to the contrary as your story hinted at, I haven't been my father's puppet. I've done nothing but try to repair the damage he caused. That's all I've ever done."

Joshua probably wasn't aware of the strained note in his voice, the almost silent fervency that stretched from his words. Yes, she couldn't deny the truth of his statement. Even if the possibility existed that Vernon was pulling the strings all these years, it didn't negate the fact that Joshua had abandoned what had appeared to be a very promising art career to take over the family company. To head it and bear all the heat, enmity and distrust as well as the responsibility on his still-young shoulders. His twin, Jake, hadn't been seen in Falling Brook for fifteen years, and the younger brother, Oliver, had fallen into a destructive partying lifestyle. So everything had fallen to him, and Joshua had put aside his own dreams to take up the burden.

No matter how she felt about the man and his actions, she had to respect that sacrifice.

"Anything I've done, it was and is to protect and take care of my family. I have no shame in that," he said, and that air of arrogance, of utter lack of remorse just… Dammit, it just pissed her off.

"Now, that is rich coming from you," she drawled, propping a hip against the conference table.

His aloof expression remained, but he cocked his head to the side. "And what the hell do you mean by that?" he demanded, almost…pleasantly. But the glitter in his eyes belied the tone.

"Oh, I think you know… *Daddy*."

He blinked, continuing to stare at her. And his lack

of response, of reaction, only stirred the anger kindling in her chest.

"Really?" she snapped. "You're going to continue to pretend to not know what I'm talking about?" She chuckled, the sound brittle, jaded and lacking humor. "You only protect and care for the family you decide to acknowledge. But," she chided, tapping a fingertip to the corner of her mouth, "I suppose that a four-year-old daughter would be extremely inconvenient for someone who lives on that high horse you're so afraid to tumble off of."

Joshua slowly leaned forward and, with a deliberate motion, flattened his palms on the table. "I don't know why you seem to believe that I have a child, but I don't. That's crazy," he said, narrowing his eyes on her.

She snorted. "Just because you might claim you don't—and you definitely act like you don't have a daughter—doesn't make it so."

He didn't reply, but that piercing gaze didn't leave her face. His tall, rangy body remained motionless, coiled as if pulled taut by an invisible string—a string that was seconds from snapping.

She frowned, stepping back from her indignation and, okay, yes, battered pride and feelings, to analyze him more closely. Confusion, and, *oh God*, whispers of uncertainty darkened his eyes.

Could it... *Could he really not know?*

"I—I..." She stopped. Inhaled. And started again. "I'm not making this claim casually or lightly. I have very good reason to believe that you do have a daughter."

"I don't know what your reasons are, and I don't care," he said with the barest hint of a rasp. "And if you knew anything about me beyond your so-called research, you would realize how ridiculous your accusation is. Because that's what you telling me I have a child I've neglected is, Ms. Armstrong. An ugly, unfounded and *untrue* accusation."

She should've flinched at his menacing growl, at the blistering curse. She *should not* be electrified by it. Should not be riveted and fascinated by the sign of heat and a loosening of his iron-clad control.

Should not be considering poking more at the bear, to see if he would roar instead of growl. To see if he would…pounce.

Ill-conceived and unwelcomed desire leaped and cavorted in her veins like a naughty, giggling child. One who didn't care one bit for the rules. She steeled her body against the dark urge to draw nearer to him. Against the almost irresistible need to discover if his body warmth seeped through his suit and see if it would touch her. To find out what scent his skin held. Something earthy and raw, or would it be cool and refined? Fire or ice?

She cleared her throat and inched back, her hip bumping one of the chairs flanking the table. *Jesus, woman. He's not the pied piper, and you aren't some glaze-eyed mouse.* And besides, if she decided to follow any man somewhere—which hell would have to fall into a deep freeze and sell snow cones for extra income for that to happen—it wouldn't be this icicle of a man who carried more baggage than a Boeing 747.

"Listen, I received this information from a source—one that I trust. And if you recall, I attempted to reach out numerous times to interview you for the article. If you had bothered replying to any of my calls, voice mails or emails, I would've addressed this with you. But the fact that you refused only lent credence to my suspicions that you had something to hide." She ignored the scoff he uttered and spread her hands wide, palms up. "I know you doubt my credibility, but I thoroughly researched your family to prepare for my article. And the truth is the rumor about an illegitimate child surfaced several times."

"This source you trust," he countered, "would it be the same one who provided those pictures?"

She hesitated but, after a second, nodded. "Yes."

Of the people she'd interviewed, Zane Patterson had proved to be the most helpful…and rich in information. Rich, hell. He'd been a gold strike. And none of what he'd had to share had been flattering. But considering his family had been one of those directly affected by the Black Crescent scandal, Sophie couldn't blame him for his animosity and bitterness. He'd lost everything— his family's financial security, his home and then his family. His parents had divorced a year later. And he blamed it all on the Lowells. The man still harbored a lot of anger toward that family.

Still, just because he hated them didn't mean he hadn't been able to give her plenty of material. Zane had been a year younger than Oliver Lowell, so they'd run in the same circles in high school. Therefore, he'd had the means to supply her with the kind of info that hadn't been available with a Google search as fifteen years ago social media hadn't been as prevalent as it was today. Not only had Zane given her the photos Joshua seemed so fixated on, but he'd also been the first person to mention Joshua having a love child that he refused to acknowledge. But, like she'd assured Joshua, Zane hadn't been the only person to assert the same.

"Fine. Keep your secrets," Joshua said. He turned away from her, studying the just-awakening main street of Falling Brook. The newspaper's offices were located in one of the older brick buildings lining the street, tucked between a women's clothing boutique and a bookstore. As he stared out the window, the sun's rays caressing his sharply hewn profile, he was like a king surveying his realm.

And maybe he was. The insular bedroom community with its two-thousand-strong population of surgeons, CEOs, a few A-list actors and pro athletes had once looked at Vernon Lowell as a ruler, and Joshua's father had gorged on the admiration and reverence. By all appearances, Joshua seemed to be a more benevolent king, but no one could mistake the power, the air of authority and command that clung to him, as tailormade to fit as his suits.

Part of her acknowledged she should be intimidated by that level of influence. In this community where money not just spoke, but screamed at the tops of its lungs, power of the press was a buzz phrase. If he wanted, he could have her fired. Blackballed, even.

So yes, she should be at least a little leery. But fear didn't skip and dance over her skin, leaving pebbled flesh in its wake. Exhilaration did. Being in this man's presence agitated and animated her in a way only burgeoning new stories did. And the why of it—she lurched away from digging deeper, scrabbling away from that particular crumbling, dangerous edge.

When he turned back and pinned her with that magnetic, intense gaze, she barely managed to trap her gasp.

The force of it was nearly physical. The inane image of her holding her hands up, shielding herself from it, popped in her head.

"You're right," he announced.

She blinked, taken aback. Replaying their conversation through her mind, she shook her head, still confused. "About?"

"You offered me the opportunity to give my insight into the story, and I didn't take it. But now I'm offering you a chance no other reporter has been extended. Come spend a day with me at the Black Crescent offices. I'll grant you access to my world, and you can see and decide for yourself whether or not the rumors stated in your article are true. Or you might just discover that I'm just a businessman trying to repair the past while making a way for the future." He arched an eyebrow. "Either way, it will be an exclusive."

It's a trap. The warning blared through her head. And if she had the intelligence God gave a gnat, she would decline. But she was aware enough to recognize that the woman whispered that caution. The reporter's blood hummed with anticipation at this unprecedented opportunity. She could pen a part two to her piece, and maybe it and the first one could possibly be picked up by the *Associated Press*.

Plus you get to spend more time with Joshua Lowell. The sly whisper ghosted across her mind. Spend more time with the enigmatic, sexy man who kindled a need inside her that she resented. A need that, if she wasn't careful, could compromise her objectivity and her job.

And that she absolutely couldn't allow. Nothing could get in the way of her goals, of her independence. Her mother had shelved her dream of becoming an architect to marry her father. And years later, when her marriage ended, she'd had to start from scratch, dependent on the scant alimony her father had grudgingly provided, having to work low-paying jobs to make ends meet while attending college part-time. It'd taken years of dedication and exhausting, backbreaking work, but she'd finally attained her dream job. But Sophie had learned a valuable lesson while witnessing her mother's struggle. She would never become a casualty of a relationship. And never would she prioritize a man above her own needs, giving him everything while he left her with just scraps to remind her of what she could've had but had thrown away.

She had to take only one look at Joshua Lowell, spend one minute in his company, take one glance in those lovely but shuttered eyes to know he could strip her of everything. And not look back.

If she allowed him to. Which she wouldn't.

"I accept your offer," she said, resolve strengthening her voice.

He dipped his head in acknowledgment. "I'll have my assistant contact you to set up an appointment."

With one last, long stare, he strode toward her, heading toward the conference room door. As he brushed past her, she ordered herself not to inhale. Not to find out—

Sandalwood and dark earth after a fresh spring rain. Earthy and raw, it is.

Dammit.

"Ms. Armstrong." She jerked her head in his direction and met the gaze of the ruthless businessman who had dragged a failing company back from the edge of the financial abyss. "Don't mistake this for an olive branch or a truce. When you wrote and published that article, you threatened the peace and well-being of my family, and I don't take that lightly or forget. Use this as a chance for another smear campaign, and I'll ensure you regret it."

Long after he left, his warning—and his scent— remained.

No matter how hard she tried to eradicate both.

Chapter 3

Joshua pulled his car into the parking lot of his gym and stabbed the ignition button a little harder than necessary, shutting the engine off. Restless energy raced through him, and it jangled under his skin. He'd been this way since yesterday and his visit to the *Falling Brook Chronicle*'s offices. Since his confrontation with Sophie.

Tunneling his fingers through his hair, he gripped the short strands and ground his teeth together. Trapping the searing flood of curses that blistered his tongue. He'd gone there to question her about the photographs and her source for them. And he'd been slapped with a paternity accusation.

The *fuck*.

Even now icy fingers of shock continued to tickle his spine, chilling him. Trailing right behind it came the

hot slam of helpless fury. He hated that sense of pow-
erlessness, of—goddammit—self-doubt.

And he resented the hell out of Sophie for planting
it there. For hauling him back to a time when he'd been
drowning in fear, desperately swimming toward the
surface to drag in a life-giving lungful of air. Despair-
ing that he never would again.

Through the years, there'd been plenty of gossip
about his family on top of the ugly truth about his father and his actions. It would be a lie to claim the whispers hadn't hurt him. That he didn't have scars from that
tumultuous period. But he'd survived. He'd always had
pride in the knowledge that he wasn't his father, that he
didn't harm people out of selfishness and greed. He'd
clung to that knowledge.

And in one conversation, Sophie had delivered a
solid blow to that source of honor, causing zigzags to
splinter through it like a cracked windshield.

Had he been a monk? Hell no. He enjoyed sex, but he
still practiced caution. A man in his position and with
his wealth had to. So he chose his partners carefully—
women who understood he didn't want a relationship,
just a temporary arrangement that provided pleasure for
both of them—and ensured he used protection. Still, he
understood that mistakes could happen. Nothing was
infallible. But none of his ex-lovers had ever approached
him about an unexpected pregnancy or a child. Because
if they had, he would've never abandoned the woman
or the baby. *Never.*

For Sophie to suggest—no, to accuse him of being
able to neglect his own flesh and blood…

With a low growl, he shoved open his car door and
stepped out, slamming it shut behind him. Seconds later,

with his duffel bag in hand, he stalked toward the gym, ready to work off some of the anger and tension riding him like a relentless jockey on a punching bag.

An hour later, sweat poured from his face, shoulders and chest in rivulets. Pleasurable weariness born of pushing his body to the limit sang in his muscles. Yanking off his boxing gloves, he picked up his bottle of water and gulped it while inhaling the scent of perspiration, bleach and the musk from bodies that had permanently seeped into the concrete floors and walls. This gym, located in the next town over from Falling Brook, wasn't one of those trendy establishments soccer moms and young CEOs patronized with stylish athletic wear and skin that glistened or, for God's sake, *dewed*.

Fighters grappled and trained in the boxing ring at the far side of the room. Huge tires leaned against a wall and a smattering of paint-flecked, scratched gym equipment hogged one corner while free weights claimed another. Grunts, the smack of rope hitting the concrete floor and rock music permeated the air. People didn't come to this to be seen, but to push their bodies, to beat them into submission or perfect working order.

So what the *fuck* was Sophie Armstrong doing here?

He scowled, studying the petite, frowning woman as she whipped the battle ropes up and down in a steady, furious pace. Even as the familiar anger and suspicion crowded into him at the sight of her in the gym he'd frequented for years—his sanctuary away from the office and home—he couldn't stop his gaze from following the slender but toned lines of her small frame that the purple sports bra and black leggings did nothing to hide. Without the conservative clothes that halted just shy of being plain, he had an unrestricted view of the high thrust of her smallish and utterly perfect breasts that slightly swelled over the rounded edge of her top. Though he ordered himself to look away, to stop visually devouring the enemy, he still lingered over the taut abdomen that gleamed with hard-fought-for sweat and the gently rounded hips and tight, sleekly muscled legs that seemed impossibly long for someone of her stature.

Like a sweaty elf princess who'd momentarily traded her gilded throne for a dusty battlefield. The silly, fanciful thought swept through his head before he could banish it. Thoughts like that belonged to the artist he used to be, not the sensible, pragmatic businessman he was now. Still... Watching her muscles flex, her abs tighten and those strong thighs brace her weight, he was impressed at the power in her tiny frame.

Impressed and hard as hell.

"Goddamn," he growled. Frolicking puppies. Spreadsheets with unbalanced columns.

His mother's shuttered face and devastated eyes when she read Sophie's article.

Yeah, that killed his erection fast.

And maybe it didn't snuff out the hot licks of lust in his gut, but it gave fury one hell of a foothold.

Clenching his jaw, he stalked across the gym toward the woman who had infiltrated his life and cracked open a door he'd hoped, fucking prayed, would remain locked, bolted and welded shut. Just as he reached Sophie, she gave the battle ropes one last flick, then dropped them to the floor with a thud.

"Stalking me, Ms. Armstrong?" he drawled, his fingers gripping his water bottle so tight, the plastic squeaked in protest.

He immediately loosened his hold. Damn, he'd

learned long ago to never betray any weakness of emotion. People were like sharks scenting bloody chum in the water when they sensed a chink in his armor. But when in this woman's presence, his emotions seemed to leak through like a sieve. The impenetrable shield barricading him that had been forged in the fires of pain, loss and humiliation came away dented and scratched after an encounter with Sophie. And that presented as much of a threat, a danger to him as her insatiable need to prove that he was a deadbeat father and puppet to a master thief.

"Stalking you?" she scoffed, bending down to swipe her own bottle of water and a towel off the ground. With a strength that could be described only as Herculean, he didn't drop his gaze to the sweet, firm curve of her ass. He deserved a medal, an award, the key to the city for not giving in to the urge. "Need I remind you, it was you who showed up at my job yesterday, not the other way around. So I guess that makes us even in the showing-up-where-we're-not-wanted department."

"Oh, we're not even close to anything that resembles *even*, Sophie," he said, using her name for the first time aloud. And damn if it didn't taste good on his tongue. If he didn't sound as if he were stroking the two syllables like they were bare, damp flesh.

She didn't immediately reply, instead lifting the clear bottle to her mouth and sipping from it. His gaze dipped to that pursed, wicked mouth, and a primal throb set up in his blood, his dick. *Stand down*, he ordered his unruly flesh. His loose gray basketball shorts wouldn't conceal the effect she had on him. And no way in hell would he give her that to use against him.

"I hate to disappoint you and your dreams of narcissistic grandeur, but I've been a member of this gym for years." She swiped her towel over her throat and upper chest. "I've seen you here, but it's not my fault if you've never noticed me."

"That's bullshit," he snapped. "I would've noticed you."

The words echoed between them, the meaning in them pulsing like a thick, heavy heartbeat in the sudden silence that cocooned them. Her silver eyes flared wide before they flashed with…what? Surprise? Irritation? Desire. A liquid slide of lust prowled through him like a hungry—so goddamn hungry—beast.

The air simmered around them. How could no one else see it shimmer in waves from the concrete floor like steam from a sidewalk after a summer storm?

She was the first to break the visual connection, and when she ducked her head to pat her arms down, the loss of her eyes reverberated in his chest like a physical snapping of tautly strung wire. He fisted his fingers at his sides, refusing to rub the echo of soreness there.

"Do you want me to pull out my membership card to prove that I'm not some kind of stalker?" She tilted her head to the side. "I'm dedicated to my job, but I refuse to cross the line into creepy…or criminal."

He ground his teeth against the apology that shoved at his throat, but after a moment, he jerked his head down in an abrupt nod. "I'm sorry. I shouldn't have jumped to conclusions." And then because he couldn't resist, because it still gnawed at him when he shouldn't have cared what she—a reporter—thought of him or not, he added, "That predilection seems to be in the air."

She narrowed her eyes on him, and a tiny muscle ticked along her delicate but stubborn jaw. Why that sign of temper and forced control fascinated him, he opted not to dwell on. "And what is that supposed to mean?" she asked, the pleasant tone belied by the anger brewing in her eyes like gray storm clouds.

Moments earlier, he'd wondered if fury or desire had heated her gaze. Now he had his answer. Because he now faced her anger, now had confirmation that when she looked like she wanted to knee him in the balls the silver darkened to near black.

But when she looked like she just wanted to go to her knees for him, her eyes were molten, pure hot silver.

God help him, because, masochistic fool that he'd suddenly become, he craved them both.

He wanted her rage, her passion…wanted both to beat at him, heat his skin, touch him. Make him feel.

Mentally, he scrambled away from that, that *need*, like it'd reared up and flashed its fangs at him. The other man he'd been—the man who'd lost himself in passion, paint and life captured on film—had drowned in emotion. Willingly. Joyfully. And when it'd been snatched away—when that passion, that *life*—had been stolen from him by cold, brutal reality, he'd nearly crumbled under the loss, the darkness. Hunger, wanting something so desperately, led only to the pain of eventually losing it.

He'd survived that loss once. Even though it'd been like sawing off his own limbs. He might be an emotional amputee, but dammit, he'd endured. He'd saved his family, their reputation and their business. But he'd managed it by never allowing himself to need again.

And Sophie Armstrong, with her pixie face and warrior spirit, wouldn't undo all that he'd fought and silently screamed to build.

She must've interpreted his silence as an indictment, because her full mouth firmed into an aggravated line, and her shoulders slowly straightened, her posture militant and, yes, defensive. As she should be. "If it makes it easier to look at that pretty face in the mirror, then go ahead and throw verbal punches," she sneered. *Pretty face.* He didn't even pretend to take that for a compliment. Not that way her voice twisted around the words. "But I did the research, and the information I received was solid, and my sources were legitimate."

"Sources," he repeated, leaping on that clue. "So you had more than one?"

She didn't move, but she might as well as have slammed up an invisible door between them. "Yes," she replied after a long moment. "I didn't rely on gossip or groundless rumors."

"Your sources seem to believe they know a lot about not just my family, the inner workings of Black Crescent, but my personal life, as well," he said, drawing closer to her.

The seeds that their earlier conversation in the *Chronicle*'s conference room had planted started to sprout roots. Roots of suspicion and hated mistrust wound their way into his head, threading around his heart. He resented Sophie for planting those kernels of suspicion about the people who existed in his small inner circle. Small for a reason. Trial by fire had taught him he could trust a precious few, and only those precious few had access to his family, the details of his life. Could one of them be the "source" she referred to? As he'd done on the drive back to his office yesterday, he again ran through their faces: Haley, Jake, Oliver.

Haley, no. Never. She'd proved her loyalty hundreds

of times over. But his brothers… Jesus, he wanted to
dismiss any notion that they could've turned on him,
but… He couldn't. They resented him, resented that
he'd become their father, never appreciating the sacri-
fices he'd made so they could live free of the burden of
Black Crescent and the dark shadow it cast. A shadow
he constantly existed in but strove to, if not be free of,
at least lighten.

"I want names, Sophie," he bit out, the dregs of fear,
grief and anger at the possible identities of her sources
swirling in his mind roughening his voice. He stepped
closer until the scent of citrus, velvet, damp blooms
and woman—*her*—filled his nostrils. Ignoring the
lure of that sensual musk, he lowered his head, forcing
her to meet his gaze. "If someone is digging into my
life and giving information about me, then I deserve to
know who they are." *Who I need to protect myself from.*
"Every man has the right to confront their accusers."

She shook her head, her golden-brown ponytail
brushing her bare shoulders. "No. The people who
spoke to me did so on the assurance of confidentiality,
and I won't betray that. And I absolutely refuse to expose them to the wrath of the Lowell family."

The wrath of the Lowell family? What kind of shit
was that? "My wrath?" he murmured, edging closer.
And closer still until one shift of his feet and their chests
would press together. Their sweat-dampened skin would
cling. His cock would find a home nestled against her
taut stomach. "Do you still have your job? Have you
found yourself and that paper you work for served with
a defamation suit? If you went to any of the stores or
restaurants around here, would you still be waited on or
served? No, Sophie." He leaned down, so close his lips

almost grazed her ear. So close, he caught the shiver that worked through her body as his breath hit her lobe. "If I wanted to wage war against someone who came after me, after mine, the first casualty would be you. And since you haven't been shunned or blackballed yet—because believe me, even with the stain on my last name, I have the power to do all I've mentioned—you haven't felt my wrath. Besides," he added, and this time he let his mouth brush the rim of her ear. Let himself get his first feel of her skin, her body even if it was just something as small as that. "I would never include others in the battle between us. This, sweetheart, is personal."

Air, quick and harsh, rushed from her lips, bathing his cheek, stirring the flames already stroking him from the inside out. God, he wanted to... Grinding his molars together so hard he should've tasted dust, he inched back, placing between them the space he'd so foolishly eliminated. As it was, he now fought the impulse to rub his thumb over the spot where his mouth had glanced her ear. Rub that sensation into his flesh as if it wasn't already branded there.

"Is that supposed to scare me? Should I file that under the threat category?" she shot back. And it would've been effective if it hadn't been uttered in a throaty whisper that rasped over his too-sensitive skin.

Damn her.

Damn him.

"No, Sophie. The last thing I want from you is fear." Let her translate that how she wanted. "But make no mistake, I intend to have those names from you. And that's not a threat, but a promise."

Not waiting for her response, he turned and strode away from her. But not for long. They had an appoint-

ment for a day together at his office. And he would see
the vow he'd made come true.

Sophie would divulge the identities of her sources.

One way or another.

And as his blood hummed in his veins, still lit up
like a torch from his interaction with her, it was the
"another" that worried him.

Chapter 4

Back in the lion's den.

Sophie summoned a smile as she gave the first-floor receptionist of the Black Crescent building her name and waited while she called to verify her appointment. Turning, she stared at the large picture window, not really seeing the parking lot or the ring of towering trees beyond that shielded the property like an inner wall in a medieval fiefdom.

No, images of Joshua Lowell from when he'd cornered her at the gym yesterday flickered before her eyes. Flickered, hell. Paraded. Him, his lean but large and powerful body encased in a sweaty white T-shirt that clung to tendon and muscle, and loose gray knee-length basketball shorts. God, those shorts. If the shirt had her itching to climb those wide shoulders as if they were a scratching post and she was a cat in heat, then those shorts had her palm itching to slide beneath the damp waistband, skim over his ridged abdomen and farther down to grasp the long and thick length that she'd glimpsed the imprint of under the nylon.

Joshua freaking Lowell had been hard. *For her.*

And he'd called her sweetheart.

She still couldn't wrap her mind around that. He hated her. Okay, *hate* might be too strong a word, but he very strongly disliked her. Okay, *disliked* might be too soft a word.

Sighing, she shook her head, dispelling the mental picture, but could do nothing for the sensitive spot just under her navel. The spot where his cock had pressed against her as he'd whispered threats—forget *promises*, those had definitely been *threats*—in her ear. Idiot that she was, she should've been furious, or even a little intimidated, but no.

She'd just been turned the hell on.

And all she could think of was whether or not that sandalwood, earth and rain scent would transfer to her skin if his naked, big body covered hers. Would she wear him on her? Or would they create a new fragrance together—one made of him, her and sex?

Stop this. Now. The silent but strident admonishment rang inside her head, and she heeded it. She *had* to. In several very short minutes, she would once again face Joshua on his turf. Only this time she wouldn't have the benefit of surprise. He would have home-court advantage, so to speak, prepared for her, her questions, her preconceived perceptions of him. Joshua Lowell would be ready to battle. And as he'd warned her, he wouldn't lose.

She had to be focused and professional and, above

all, could not think of how that beautiful body would feel moving over her...in her.

Dammit!

"Ms. Armstrong, they're expecting you upstairs. If you'll take the elevator to the second floor, Mr. Lowell's executive assistant, Haley Shaw, will be waiting for you." The woman gave her a polite but friendly smile as she gestured toward the bank of elevators that Sophie was all too familiar with. She'd covertly stole into them to barge into the Black Crescent offices to interview Joshua Lowell.

"Thank you," she murmured, and followed the receptionist's directions.

Moments later, she stepped out onto the executive floor and approached Haley Shaw's large circular desk. The pretty blonde stood in front of it, smiling up at a tall, handsome man with light brown hair and a presence that screamed confidence and an intensity he couldn't mask. It was that intensity that had Sophie frowning slightly as she approached the couple.

Though both of their voices contained a light note of flirtation, and Haley didn't appear uncomfortable, the man seemed to invade the other woman's personal space, dwarfing Haley's not-inconsiderable height. As a woman who'd often encountered inappropriate advances in the workplace, maybe Sophie was extra sensitive, but it didn't stop her from nearing them and stopping at the executive assistant's side, facing the man, whose smile widened to include her.

Yeah, she didn't trust that smile at all.

In her experience, people who grinned that wide and tried hard to appear affable were usually hiding something. Using overt friendliness and charm as a deflection.

Something whispered to her that this guy was no different.

"Good morning, Ms. Armstrong," Haley greeted Sophie, surprising her a little with the warmth emanating from the welcome. The last time Sophie had been here, she hadn't made such a good first impression. "Can I introduce you to Chase Hargrove?"

"Mr. Hargrove." Sophie nodded, and he extended his hand toward her.

"Ms. Armstrong. It's a pleasure to meet you." Giving her another of those too-amicable smiles, he switched his attention back to Haley. "I have to go. I'll talk to you later, Haley. Hopefully see you then, too, beautiful." With a wink and crooked grin that even Sophie had to admit had her wanting to fan herself, he turned and strode toward the elevators.

"Wow," Sophie muttered as soon as the doors slid closed behind him. "He's definitely...not shy." She shook her head, huffing out a laugh. "Were you okay with how strong he seemed to be coming on? If not, you should tell—" *Joshua* hovered on her tongue, but after a brief hesitation, she said, "Mr. Lowell."

She scoffed, waving a hand toward the direction Chase had disappeared. "He's harmless. Believe me, I can handle him." Pushing off the desk, she swept a hand toward the double doors that led to Joshua's office. "He's waiting for you. Did you need anything? Coffee, tea, water?"

"I'm fine, thanks." Sophie would die on the hill of denial before admitting it aloud, but her stomach twisted with nerves and wouldn't be able to handle anything on it.

Haley nodded, and when they approached the door, she gave it a swift knock, then opened it. "Joshua, Ms. Armstrong is here."

Sweat dotted Sophie's palms, and her heart rapped against her sternum, but she managed a smile of thanks and shored up her mental shields as she moved into the office. After his visit to the *Chronicle* and their impromptu meeting at the gym, she didn't even try to delude herself into believing she could prepare herself for coming face-to-face with him again and not be slammed with the intense presence that was Joshua Lowell.

So when he rose from behind his desk, exposing that tall, rangy body to her, she just let herself soak him in. Took in the short, dark blond hair that emphasized the clean but sharp facial features. Met the green-and-light-brown gaze that seemed determined to strip her of all her defenses. Traced the wide, soft-looking mouth with its too-tempting, full bottom lip. Wandered over the muscular strength and animal magnetism that his steel-gray suit accentuated rather than hid in a cloak of civility.

Maybe not resisting the magnetic pull of his utter sexiness but rather immersing herself in it would strengthen her immunity.

Like a freaking flu shot.

"Sophie," he said, rounding the desk with a confident and commanding stride that shouldn't have set her pulse pounding. But God, did it. "I'm glad you could make it."

She arched an eyebrow. "You doubted I would?"

He halted several feet from her. And it reminded her of how close he'd been in the gym. How his scent had engulfed her. How his lips had brushed her ear even as he whispered threats into it. No. Not threats. Promises, he'd assured her.

And how sick did it make her that a part of her wanted him to follow through on them?

Very. Any therapist worth her or his degree would rub their hands in glee at the thought of getting their hands on her.

"Not for a second," he murmured, that gaze skimming over her emerald sheath and nude pumps before returning to her face.

Her skin hummed from the visual contact, and she fought not to rub her palms up and down her bare arms. She wouldn't give him the satisfaction of knowing he affected her.

"Well, thank you again for the opportunity to tour the inner sanctum of Black Crescent Hedge Fund." See? She could be professional around him. "I'm looking forward to this."

He nodded. "If you'll follow me…"

For the next several hours, Joshua granted her an exclusive peek behind the curtain. Not only did he introduce her to his employees and explain what they did, but he also revealed how he'd implemented safeguards and a checks-and-balances system so what'd occurred with his father didn't happen again. In other words, he'd willingly policed himself.

She discovered a side of the company she hadn't known existed. Over the years, Joshua had donated a mind-boggling amount of money and time to local and statewide programs that assisted domestic abuse victims, literacy and the foster-care system, including his assistant Haley Shaw's own nonprofit organization. But not only did he help his community, he also invested in his own employees' futures by helping put the staff and their families through college with scholarships and almost-zero-interest loans.

And then there were the reparations he'd made to the families affected by his father's crimes. Joshua had made good on that agreement to repay the stolen funds.

By the time she followed him back to his office that afternoon, she was convinced Black Crescent wasn't the coldhearted, corrupt organization portrayed in the news and even by some of her sources.

By her.

"What you've done here is remarkable," she said as he closed the office door behind them. She shook her head. "Especially in the last few years. But I've only heard of maybe two of your philanthropic efforts. Why haven't you shared with the public what you've shown me today? I think most people would be amazed and as impressed as I am with all that you do for the community on a local and even national level."

"If someone brags about what should be their privilege and right to do, I question not just their motivations but their hearts. Besides—" he slipped his hands into the front pockets of his pants and a faint smile quirked the corners of his mouth "—I've found that most people, particularly the press, have never been interested in reporting anything positive about my family or the company."

She tried not to wince. And didn't quite manage it. "Touché. But to be fair, my article didn't attack you, personally."

"Fair?" he repeated, sarcasm hardening his voice. "Forgive me if I've never associated *fair* with the media.

And attack? No. But for an article that was supposed to be about the so-called anniversary of the Black Crescent incident, you invaded my personal life in a way that seemed intrusive and unnecessary."

Her chin snapped up and her shoulders back, offended. "Am I supposed to apologize for being good at my job? I can't control what my sources tell me or where my investigation carries me. I *won't* apologize for the truth. Ever." She narrowed her eyes on him. "If anything you should be thanking me for not including the truth about your illegitimate daughter in the article. I can't say the same would've happened if—"

"Don't say it again," he barked. No, growled. And the ominous rumble of it snapped off her words like a branch cracking from a tree. Thunder rolled across his face, shadowing his eyes and pulling the skin taut across his cheekbones. He took a step forward but drew up short the next instant. "I am. Not. My. Father," he snarled. And somehow, that low, dark statement stunned her more than if he'd yelled it at her. "I would never, ever turn my back on my family the way that bas—"

He broke off, but the rest of his sentence might as well as have been shouted in the room, it echoed so loud, momentarily deafening her.

"The way your father did," she whispered, the words rasping her throat.

Joshua's face could've been carved from stone, but his eyes. God, his eyes damn near glowed with fury… and pain. Such deep, bright pain that the breath caught in her throat, and she ached with it. Ached for him.

She crossed her arms over her chest and turned away from him, eyes momentarily closing. Until this moment Vernon Lowell had been a story, a shadowy, almost urban legend–like figure who'd committed an infamous crime, then disappeared into thin air. But now, in his son's eyes, she saw him as a father—a father who had abandoned and hurt his son so deeply with his actions that even years later, that son suffered. Suffered in ways he hid so successfully that no one—least of all Sophie— had suspected.

That emotion—the intensity of it—couldn't be faked. So was Joshua telling the truth about the child? Did he really not know of her existence? Not only did she rely on her investigative skills in her job, but her instincts. And they were screaming like a pissed-off banshee that maybe, just maybe, he didn't.

Pinching the bridge of her nose, she bowed her head. *I can't believe I'm doing this.* But her heart had made the decision seconds before her brain caught on. And she moved toward the laptop bag she'd left on the couch in the sitting area of his office before leaving for the tour of the company.

Moments later, she had her computer removed and booting up on the coffee table. Glancing up at a still stoic and silent Joshua, she waved him over. "I have something to show you, Joshua," she murmured, using his name for the first time. Something had shifted inside her with that glimpse into his eyes. Standing on formality seemed silly now.

After a brief hesitation, he strode over and lowered onto the cushion next to her. Resolutely attempting to ignore the heat that seemed to emanate from his big body, she focused on pulling up a password-protected file. In several clicks, a report filled the screen.

A DNA report.

He stiffened next to her, and his gaze jerked to her.

Silence throbbed in the office, as loud as a heartbeat, as he stared at her. She met his penetrating study evenly, not betraying the wild pounding of her pulse in her ears or the sudden case of dryness that had assaulted her mouth. She couldn't swallow, couldn't move. Common sense railed that she was making a huge mistake, maybe even violating her ethics. But her sense of decency—her soul—insisted that if she could somehow make this right, she should. If she could ease the pain that he would probably deny even existed, she needed to. Whether that was by confirming his daughter's existence or even having a hand in reuniting them... She didn't know. But she had to try.

He turned to her laptop and, leaning forward, scrutinized the report. Taking in his name at the top and the mother's name, which was blacked out. Scanning the results that ended in one determination: Joshua Lowell was a match for a baby girl born four years ago.

Slowly, he straightened. Shock dulled his eyes, flattened the lush curves of his mouth. Only his fists, clenched so tight the knuckles bleached white, betrayed the hint of a stronger current of emotion that could be coursing through him.

Finally, he shifted his gaze to her. "Where did you get this?" he asked, his deep voice like churned-up gravel. It scraped over her skin, abrading her. "Who sent it to you?"

"I can't tell you that."

"Goddammit, Sophie," he snapped. "How can you show me this and then deny me the resources to determine whether it's true or not. Real or not?" he demanded, fury sparking his eyes.

"I can't, Joshua," she insisted. Shaking her head, she

spread her hands wide, palms up, on her thighs. "I wish I could, but I *can't*. I will tell you this, though. I believe the report is authentic. My source… I've held the actual report in my hand. If it's faked, it's a fabulous forgery."

"Dammit." He surged off the couch and stalked across the floor to the floor-to-ceiling window that made up one of the walls of his office. Thrusting the fingers of both hands through his short hair, he uttered a soft "dammit" again, then pressed a fist to the glass and cupped the back of his neck with the other. "How would they even be able to run a DNA test? I've never been asked or consented to giving a sample." He whirled around, his sharp features drawn, taut. "This doesn't make sense. Someone is playing games. They have an endgame that I don't know about and can't figure out."

Sophie stood and ventured a couple of steps in his direction. But didn't travel farther than those steps. Those pinpricks of caution that she'd felt in his presence before now stabbed at her. Warning her to. Back. Off. To retreat and regroup. Because at some point, she'd become too vulnerable to him. Too open.

And that should have her snatching up her belongings and running for the door like he'd just sprouted fur and fangs. Because in her position, vulnerability was a liability. For her and her job. God, she'd already revealed some of her research to him. What next? Ignore a lead? Refuse a story?

End her career?

She'd seen it with her mother.

She'd *been* her mother.

Shame, glittering bright and filthy at the same time, slicked through her like an oil stain. One would think she'd learned her lesson. Because it'd been brutal, but a good one. But those were the best. Or at least, they should be.

Bumping into Laurence Danvers at a local campaign rally four years ago had been an accident, so she'd believed for a long time. She hadn't known then that he'd planned the meeting that had seemed serendipitous. Fated. And she'd fallen so hard for his handsome features, his wide smile, his charm…his lies. She'd allowed her heart to blind her to his true nature. So when he'd first suggested a different perspective on an article she was writing about the city council election candidates, she saw it as his helping her see a different angle. When he'd convinced her that reporting an indiscretion from a candidate's past would be inflammatory and unfair—even though that candidate was running on a family platform—she'd conceded because he was only looking out for her career and reputation as a reputable reporter.

And when he'd demanded that she resign rather than reveal this same candidate had been accused of sexual misconduct by several women, she almost conceded. Almost. Too many times during her relationship with Laurence, she'd ignored her intuition. But that time, she'd listened, done some digging and uncovered that he was a longtime family friend to the candidate whose rally they'd met at. Meeting her, seducing her, making her fall in love… It'd all been so calculated in an effort to use her.

In mere months, she'd almost thrown aside her career, her dreams, her integrity for a man. As Laurence had walked out her apartment door for the final time, she vowed never to be that vulnerable, that *foolish* again.

And as she stared at Joshua, she could feel herself already climbing that slippery slope. One misstep, and it would be a long, painful slide down. Hell, she'd already shown him part of her research. She shuffled back and away from him, both physically and mentally. She had to approach Joshua and this element of her story as a journalist, not a woman who wanted to cradle that strong jaw and massage away the deep crease between his eyebrows. Or soothe the confusion, anger and pain in his eyes.

"Someone is setting me up," Joshua continued, dropping his gaze to his clenched fist. As if disturbed by the outward display of emotion, he stretched his fingers out, splaying them wide and lowering them to the side of his thigh. "Nothing else makes sense. No one has contacted me about possible paternity or approached me for money. Not even threatened blackmail. Logic says that if there was a woman out there with a child I fathered, she would reach out to me for child support."

Sophie couldn't argue with his assumption. Joshua Lowell wasn't only a beautiful man; he was obscenely wealthy and very well connected, even in spite of the scandal. He could more than afford to provide for a child. And a particular kind of woman would use the situation to her advantage and try for more than money. Like forcing a relationship, marriage. Through her research for her article, she'd discovered that from the moment his father disappeared, Joshua had become a choirboy—well, if choirboys had the bodies and faces of Greek gods and exuded sex like a pheromone. But no hint of impropriety had ever been connected to his name in the media. A person didn't need to have a psychology degree to determine the reason behind that. And a woman looking to permanently bind herself to a powerful and rich family would realize that bit of information, as well.

She tapped a finger against her bottom lip. "That is…curious. Especially since the child is four years old now." This was her cue to walk away. To pack up her things, thank him for the opportunity to see the inside of Black Crescent and leave. "I can't give up my sources. But…if you need or want the help, I'll assist in finding out what's going on. Or try to."

Damn.

So much for walking away.

Joshua stared at her for so long, his eyes shuttered, his stony expression indecipherable, that the rescission of her offer hopped on the tip of her tongue. But as she parted her lips, he asked, "Will what you find out end up in the *Chronicle*?"

She extinguished the bright flash of irritation and offense that flared in her chest. Part of her understood his caution and suspicion. But the other half… "I'm not offering my help as part of some tell-all article," she ground out.

God, he really didn't think too much of her.

Which was fair because she didn't trust him, either. From her experience, most men—especially those with something to lose—did everything in their power to protect themselves.

Several more taut seconds passed, but Joshua finally dipped his head in a short, abrupt nod. "I appreciate your offer, then. If there's even the slightest chance that I could be a father, then I owe it to myself—and that little girl—to find out."

A rush of warmth flooded her.

Those aren't the words of a deadbeat father.

Her subconscious taunted like the know-it-all it was.

But her experience with Laurence had hammered home the truth that nothing—or no one—was as it appeared on the surface. Especially someone who had so much to lose like Joshua did—reputation, money and the added burden of a child. Though he managed to keep his private life more contained than others in his position, she'd still gathered images of him and gossip about him with socialites, some A-list actresses and businesswomen.

No middle-class, student-debt-ridden peasants. In other words, no one like you.

Oh, shut it.

Awesome. Now she was arguing with herself. She really needed to get the hell out of this office. This building. This side of town. The more space between her and Joshua right now, the better. If not, she might do something really inane and unforgivable. Like hug him.

Suddenly wary of herself, she turned, retracing the few steps back to the coffee table and couch. Clearing her throat, she sank to the cushion and, tucking a rebellious strand of hair behind her ear, closed her laptop. "I'll start looking into it on my end tonight." With hurried movements, she slid the computer into her bag and stood. Fixing a smile on her lips, she lifted her head and met his impenetrable gaze again. God, the man could give the Sphinx lessons in stoicism. "Thank you for the tour today. I really appreciate it, and I learned more about Black Crescent that I didn't know. That I'm sure many people aren't aware of. If I have your permission, I'd like to share the information in a follow-up article."

"Why?"

She frowned, stilling midprocess of slipping the strap

of her bag over her shoulder. "Because the public deserves to know about your philanthropic programs and generosity to the community. I get your reason for staying mum on the subject, but—"

"No." He cut her off with a hard shake of his head. "When I invited you here I knew it was for a follow-up article. I meant why are you volunteering to help me?"

Because you looked so lost, and I want to bring home what will make you whole.

The explanation lodged in her throat, stuck. And she didn't try to free it. One, he wouldn't appreciate her reason. Wouldn't believe her. Two, she was disgusted with herself for thinking it. For thinking she could give him anything, much less peace and comfort.

Yes, Joshua Lowell had the whole brooding, tortured millionaire thing down pat. His cold mask of reserve had slipped enough times that she glimpsed the dark mass of emotions he concealed. She shivered, unable to restrain the telltale reaction. What would it be like to be on the receiving end of all that unleashed passion? Because she sensed that when or if he finally let it all loose... It would be a thing of wild, raw beauty to witness. Like a roiling, ominous thunderstorm threaded with lightning. And when those bolts struck the earth? Electricity, heat, smoke.

Her pulse thundered in her ears, and she couldn't tear her gaze away from him. She couldn't deny it; she hungered to be that rich, open earth electrified by him. But he would assuredly leave her scorched beyond recognition afterward. And while her body might crave that burning, her scarred heart feared it.

Inhaling a trembling breath past the constriction blocking her throat, she shrugged a shoulder, grabbing for nonchalance and praying she accomplished it. "Because I'm an investigative reporter, and that's what I do. Investigate." Hiking her purse strap up, she again curved her lips into a polite smile that she—please, God—hoped didn't look as fake as it felt. "I need to head out so I can get back in the office to take care of a few things." Dear Lord, she was babbling and couldn't stop. "Thanks again, and I'll be in touch."

Crossing the room, she extended her hand toward him even though her mind screamed, *What the hell are you doing? Don't touch him!*

But her body had a mind of its own. And as his strong, elegant fingers—an artist's fingers—closed around hers, she cursed the voltage that sizzled from their clasped palms up her arm, down her chest and belly to crackle between her legs. If he dipped his eyes, he would catch the hardened tips of her breasts that were probably saluting him from beneath her dress. No more lace bras around this man. Definitely not enough coverage.

Every primal, self-protective instinct within her had her muscles locking in preparation to jerk her hand free. But pride overrode the need, and she met his hazel stare with a steady one of her own. To prove how she refused to let her body's obviously questionable taste rule her, she even squeezed his hand.

But when his nostrils slightly flared and his eyes darkened to an emerald-flecked amber... Oh no, she'd miscalculated. Flames licked at her flesh, and in that instant, she had a vivid premonition of how he would look in the throes of passion. Hooded, but glittering eyes, skin pulled taut over razor-sharp cheekbones, mouth pressed to a flat, almost severe line, and that big, wide-shouldered, powerful frame held rigidly still as he let her adjust to the blazing, overwhelming invasion of him planted deep and firmly inside her.

Pride be damned.

She yanked her hand out of his grip and refused to rub her still-tingling palm against her thigh.

"Why do I think you're lying to me?" he murmured, and after a few seconds of bewilderment, she realized he referred to her weak explanation about her offer of assistance. "What are you hiding, Sophie?"

"I think you're trying to uncover conspiracy theories where there are none," she replied, flippant. "I'm the reporter. That's my job, to be suspicious."

"Where you're concerned, my fail-safe is suspicion." He cocked his head to the side, studying her so closely she sympathized with those butterflies pinned to a corkboard. He wouldn't make her fidget, though. Or make her reveal any of her closely held thoughts regarding him. They were hers, and not his to use to his advantage.

"Then why are you willing to accept my help?" she asked, bristling.

"Maybe for once I'd like to know how it feels to have the press working with me instead of against me. And—" his voice dropped, and an unmistakable growl roughened the tone, causing her flesh to pebble "—I believe in keeping my friends close and my enemies closer. And you, Sophie Armstrong, I plan to be stuck to."

Another threat he would probably call a promise.

A promise that shouldn't have sent waves of molten heat echoing through her.

But it did. They swamped her, and dammit, she wanted to be taken under.

"Like stink on shit, you mean?" she shot back, pouring a bravado she was far from feeling into her tone.

He shifted forward until only scant inches separated them. Like in the gym, his body filled her vision and his warmth reached out for her, surrounding her along with his sandalwood and rain-dampened earth scent. She held her ground, not in the least intimidated as he invaded her personal space. No, not intimidated. She was throbbing. Hungry.

"Closer," he whispered, his breath feathering over her lips in a heavy but light-as-air caress.

Just in time, she caught herself before she tilted her head back, chasing that ephemeral touch.

Okay, screw pride and standing her ground.

Any wise general recognized the wisdom of retreating to fight another day.

And as she pivoted and escaped Joshua's office, she convinced herself she was being wise not running scared.

She almost accomplished the task.

Almost, but not quite.

Chapter 5

Joshua pulled open the door to The Java Hut, Falling Brook's upscale coffeehouse on Main Street. The air from the air conditioner greeted him like a lover, wrapping around him with chilled arms of welcome. It might be only May, but the temperature already crept toward the midseventies. And he silently bemoaned the loss of the cooler spring weather. While many people worshipped summer because of days spent on the beaches, lounging by the pool and less clothing, he loved the dynamic and vivid colors and crisp breezes of fall and the rain-scented air and reawakening of life that spring brought.

But no matter which season reigned, coffee remained a constant. And a must.

The fresh, dark aroma of brewing coffee filled the shop, and he inhaled it with unadulterated pleasure. At nine o'clock on a Saturday morning, he needed caffeine like an addict itching for his next hit. It was his one vice. And yes, he got how pathetic and boring that made him. But considering his father's roaming eye, Jake's wanderlust and Oliver's taste for drugs, he couldn't afford to indulge any. The Lowell men had a proclivity toward addiction, and compared with his father's and brothers', coffee was the least harmful and the only one Joshua could afford.

He glanced down at his watch: 9:11 a.m. Another forty-nine minutes before his mother's doctor's appointment ended, and he had to return to the office and pick her up. Tension tightened his shoulders, and an ache bloomed between them. Deliberately, he inhaled, held the breath and, after ten seconds, released it. The monthly...dammit, not chore. Eve Evans-Janson could never be a chore. Responsibility. As the oldest son, she was his responsibility. But the monthly task of escorting his mother to her doctor always weighed him down like an albatross slung around his neck. Not because he didn't want to be bothered. Never that. He loved Eve, and she'd suffered just as much—if not more—than him and his brothers.

But each visit reminded him of how far she'd deteriorated from the vibrant socialite who'd raised him, loved him and had been his biggest supporter and fan when it'd come to his art. While Vernon hadn't understood and viewed his passion as a passing fancy, his mother had been so proud and celebrated along with him when he'd scored his own gallery show. She'd been his loudest cheerleader.

That woman had disappeared, fifteen years ago, replaced by a quiet, withdrawn recluse who only rarely ventured past the gates of the family's Georgian-style mansion. Her numerous friends had been abandoned and now the butler, maid and chef were her friends. She left the house only for doctor's appointments, the rare appearance at a charity function or the occasions he practically forced her out of the house to go to lunch or dinner with him. Vernon's betrayal had humiliated her. Especially since she'd initially defended him with unshakable faith. When he'd disappeared, she'd believed he might've been kidnapped—or worse. The victim of foul play. But never would he have cheated his clients and friends or stolen from his family and abandoned them to be the recipients of controversy, scorn and pain. Yet, as the days turned into weeks and then months, and the FBI's evidence piled up, Eve had to face the truth—her husband and their father was a criminal who'd bilked millions from those who'd placed their trust in him, then thrown those who'd loved and depended on him the most to the wolves. She'd never recovered.

And now…now he did what he could to ensure she didn't fade away behind the walls that were less her sanctuary and more her prison.

He clenched his fingers into a fist, then purposely relaxed them, exhaling as he did. Dammit, if he had his father here right now, each finger would be wrapped around his neck. Disgust twisted in his chest. If only what he felt toward his father was as simple as anger.

Stepping to the counter, he shoved everything from his mind and focused on ordering. Moments later, with his Americano in hand, he turned toward the entrance, but slammed to a halt.

A petite woman stood next to a table near the huge

window, her back toward him, the ends of her unbound hair grazing the tank top–bared skin below her shoulders. The black top molded to the slim line of her back. Dark blue jeans clung to the gentle flare of her hips, the gorgeous tight ass that could be an eighth wonder of the world and legs that could grace a runway and climb the rocky, tough face of a mountain.

An achingly familiar itch tingled in his palms and hands. Familiar and painful. The need to hold a paintbrush. To capture the beauty and strength before him. To immortalize it. His medium had been mixed-media collages, but he'd also loved to paint. And right now he would use bold, rich colors to portray the golden tones of her skin, the power in that tiny body, the larger-than-life vibrancy of her personality, the thick softness of her hair.

That hair.

The thick golden-brown strands reminded him of a mare his father had doted on when Joshua had been a boy. Like raw umber with lighter strands of deep, burnished sunlight. His father had babied that horse, brushing her coat himself until it shined.

A yearning for a return to those idyllic times yawned so wide and deep, Joshua barely managed to restrain his free hand at his side so he wouldn't rub the knot that had formed just below his rib cage.

He could hate her alone for dragging that memory out of the abyss even as he fought against the need to burrow his hands in the wavy mass up to his wrists, fist it, tug on it… Bury his face in it. He already had personal knowledge of how far he would have to bend to inhale her citrus-and-flowers scent. As small as she was, he could completely surround her. Until he met Sophie Armstrong, tall, statuesque women had been his type. But now...now he got the lure of a petite woman he could cover with his bigger body. She triggered a primal, almost animalistic desire in him to take down and conquer her even as he did everything in his power to drown her in pleasure. Not that Sophie would take anything easily. No, he imagined she gave as good as she got in bed as much as she did out...

Molten heat swarmed through him at the thought of holding those slender, strong arms above her head, pressing his chest to her small, firm breasts, having those toned thighs clasping his waist as he drove inside her. She would be so tight, so perfect, damn near strangling his dick.

As if sensing his scrutiny, Sophie glanced over her shoulder and met his gaze. Surprise flickered over her face, her gray eyes widening slightly. He wanted them to do that when he first pushed into her sex. Hungered to see them darken like they did now as she slid a long glance down his body, and he swore he could feel that perusal as if her fingertips brushed over his collarbone, chest, abs, thighs...cock. Blood rushed to his flesh, thickening it behind the zipper of his pants. Hell yes, he wanted that touch on his bare skin, light then hard. Gentle then bruising. Yeah, he wanted this fairy of a woman to mark him.

A frigid blast of ice skated over his skin, digging farther to muscle and bone so he was chilled from the inside out.

Of all the women he could get hard over, Sophie Armstrong, reporter for the *Falling Brook Chronicle*, was the absolute last. Just this morning hadn't he witnessed the evidence of her recent rehashing of the scandal with his father in the creases on his mother's face and in the slump of her stooped shoulders? Haley might have managed to nab the paper before it was delivered to his mother's home, but Eve had overheard the maid and butler talking about it in hushed tones. And she'd demanded to see the paper. Reading that article had taken a toll on her.

So even with Sophie's offer to help him determine if the paternity accusation was true or not, he could never trust her. Could never believe that he wasn't just the means to another juicy story. Who knew what her follow-up article would contain? Why the fuck did he agree to it?

No. Sophie was a threat to his business, his family…to his sanity.

But he'd never been led around by his dick, and he wouldn't start a new trend now.

Still, as her lush mouth curled into a smile, he had to remind his body of that.

He tossed his still-full cup in the trash and crossed the room toward her, because no way in hell would he run from her. Or the need that strung his body so tight. It was a wonder he didn't snap in two at the slightest movement.

"Sophie," he greeted, for the first time thankful for the avaricious media and eyes that forced him to perfect a mask of indifference. He swept a glance over the laptop bag that hung near her hip. "Working?"

"Yes, but from home today. I'm a creature of habit, though. Every morning I stop in here for a coffee and their cinnamon-and-brown-sugar scones. Have you had them yet? They're God's way of saying He loves us."

She released a throaty hum that had his gut clench-

ing. Hard. He wanted to hear it again even as he longed
to trap the sound inside her...with his mouth.

Goddammit, he needed to get control. And quick.

"No, I can't say I've had the pleasure," he replied.
"I'll take your word for it."

She arched a brow. "Oh, really? That would be a
first between us."

"Sheathe your sword, Sophie," he said.

"So you finally admit that you need every bit of
help you can muster when going up against me?" she
challenged, amusement lighting her eyes like glittering stars.

"I never said I didn't. Only a fool would encounter
you and not be battle ready with everything in his ar-
senal available to him."

She heaved an exaggerated sigh and splayed her fingers wide over her chest. "I do believe that's the nicest
thing you've ever said to me."

His wry chuckle caught him by surprise. The last
thing he'd ever expected to do with Sophie was laugh.
A warning for caution blared in his ears. He couldn't
afford to let down his guard, become too comfortable
around her.

"What are you doing on this side of town? The coffee here is great, but I've had what you keep at your
office and it's pretty good, too."

"I'm not headed to work this morning. I'm waiting
for my mother. She has a doctor's appointment right
down the street."

She frowned and laid a hand on his lower arm. "I'm
sorry. Is she okay?"

For a moment the flare of heat emanating from her
touch seared his voice, rendering it useless. She might

as well have settled her palm over his dick the way he throbbed and ached.

Gritting his teeth, he ignored the lust coursing through him like a swollen river and said, "Yes. It's just a regular checkup."

"Oh, okay." Her frown deepened for a moment, and it seemed as if she was going to probe further, but in the next instant she skated a quick survey up and down his frame. "So you're not going to the office, but *this* is what you wear on a Saturday morning?"

He didn't bother glancing down to take in the white long-sleeved shirt and black slacks. "Problem?"

She snorted, a smirk flirting with the corners of her lips. "Oh no. No problem at all. I'm just wondering what you wear to bed. An Armani suit? Or maybe a tuxedo."

The humor fled from him, chased away by the desire flaring inside him by the mention of "bed." Hell, she'd reduced him to a fourteen-year-old boy who got hard with the switch of the wind. That didn't stop him from cocking his head to the side and murmuring, "You're wondering what I wear to bed, Sophie? All you have to do is ask."

Slashes of red tinted her cheekbones and her eyes turned to liquid silver. Neither of them spoke as the air hummed with tension, pulsed with an unacknowledged lust volleyed between them. God, he wanted her. Why her—a reporter who sought to paint him as a puppet for his deadbeat father? Would she screw him, then riffle through his drawers to find dirt she could use for the follow-up piece on him and his family?

Something deep inside him objected to that, argued that she wasn't that kind of woman, but this time logic ruled. He'd known too many people who would sooner use him than blink. As a Lowell, men and women looked at him and saw money, connections, information and sometimes a good fuck. But never the man. Never the son struggling to make good and be honorable where his father had failed.

Sophie blinked, the desire clearing from her gaze, and at the same time he edged back a step.

"Pass," she rasped, then, clearing her throat, turned back to her table and gathered up her empty coffee cup, paper plate and plastic fork. "Seriously, though, Joshua," she continued in a stronger voice, that hint of humor returning. "Jeans. Ever heard of them?"

"Sounds familiar," he drawled, following her toward the exit. She dropped her trash in the receptacle and pushed through the coffeehouse door. "What is this sudden fascination with my clothes?"

She laughed as they moved out onto the sidewalk, stepping aside as more customers entered the café. He ignored the curious glances shot their way. After fifteen years, he should be immune to them. But he'd never managed it. They still got under his skin.

"Not your clothes. I'm just curious if you ever relax. If you're ever not Joshua Lowell of the Falling Brook Lowells, CEO of Black Crescent Hedge Fund and just Josh. Does anyone call you that?"

"My brothers did. But it's been a long time," he murmured.

Just Josh.

There was no such person. Once upon a time there'd been. Josh had been an artist on the precipice of a promising career. He'd been the older brother to Jake and Oliver, who'd been friends as well as brothers. Back before they'd looked on him with scorn and resentment for following in their father's tainted footsteps. Josh had been carefree, laughed often and pursued his passion.

His family and the company wouldn't survive if he reverted to Just Josh.

If he tasted the joy, the life-giving fire of art again, *he* might not survive.

So no, Joshua Lowell, savior and CEO of Black Crescent, was much safer.

Sophie studied him with narrowed eyes, then, slipping the strap of her laptop bag over her head so it crossed her torso, she grabbed his hand in hers and tugged him forward. The shock of her skin touching his reverberated through his body and stunned him long enough that he didn't resist her leading him down the sidewalk. He should pull away from her, cauterize the connection that bled fire into his veins...

He flipped their hands so he enfolded hers, so soft and delicate, in his.

Minutes later, she paused in front of Henrietta's Creamery, the town's only ice-cream shop. He stared at her, confused and more than a little taken aback.

"Ice cream?" he asked, not bothering to eliminate the skepticism from his voice. "At nine thirty in the morning?"

She shook her head and mockingly patted his arm with the hand he wasn't clasping. "See? This right here is what I mean. When is there ever an inappropriate time for ice cream? Joshua, that stick in your ass. Was it surgically implanted, or did it just grow there naturally?"

The bark of laughter abraded his throat, shocking him as much as her teasing. No one would ever dare to say that to him. Hell, no one would dare to tease him.

But this slip of a woman knew no boundaries or fear. From the first, she hadn't been cowed or intimidated by him. And God, it felt good.

"Naturally. And it required effort and a lot of pruning and nurturing," he deadpanned, causing a grin to spread wide over her face. Jesus, she was gorgeous.

"Well, I volunteer as tribute to help you remove it. Starting with an ice-cream cone for breakfast. C'mon." She didn't brook any disagreement but jerked on the door to the shop and entered, pulling him behind her.

After a brief but spirited debate over the best flavors, they walked out with two waffle cones topped with a double scoop of ice cream—salted caramel for him and butter pecan for her.

Him.

Joshua Lowell.

Walking down the sidewalk lining Main Street. Eating an ice-cream cone.

Jesus, how did he get here?

But as Sophie tipped her head back and smiled at him, the light of it reflecting in her beautiful gray eyes, he embraced the moment. Embraced, hell. Hoarded it. In less than half an hour, he would be returning to pick up his mother, and the mantle of responsibility that he'd prematurely donned would fall back around his shoulders. Weighing them down with a pressure that was at times suffocating. Pressing them down with an anger-rimmed sadness that he'd never been able to completely banish no matter how many times he'd told himself that they didn't need his father. That they were better off without him.

Yeah, he was going to embrace this moment and grab on to it selfishly. Because as Joshua Lowell, Vernon's son, he didn't have many. The cost for that kind of greed was too high. As his father's actions had taught him.

"Now, I don't want to say I told you so..." she said, an impish smile curving her lips. "Oh hell, who am I kidding? I *so* do want to say it. I told you so."

"I think you might have held that in for two minutes and twenty-eight seconds," he drawled. "Congratulations."

She twirled her hand in front of her, dipping slightly at the waist. "Thank you. I'll have you know my restraint was hard fought."

He snorted, swiping his tongue through the cold cream and barely managing to contain a moan. When was the last time he'd indulged like this? Years. It'd been years.

"I don't want to alarm you, but people are staring," Sophie informed him in a stage whisper. As if he hadn't already noticed. "One woman just almost rear-ended the car in front of her at the stoplight." She gave a mocking gasp, splaying the fingers not holding the ice-cream cone wide across her chest. "Whatever do you think it could be that they find so interesting?"

Joshua didn't answer, but some of the peace and joy filtered from his chest, replaced by a slick, grimy stain that was a murky mixture of guilt, anger and helplessness. The sludge tracked its way across his chest, down to his gut, where it churned. He deliberately relaxed his grip on the cone but couldn't prevent the clenching of his jaw. A hint of neon-red pain flared along the edge.

"It must be so tiring," Sophie murmured, all notes of teasing evaporated from her tone. He glanced down at her, and those gray eyes looked back at him, warm and velvet with a sympathy he never believed he'd glimpse. At least not for him.

"What must be tiring?" he ground out.

"Feeling like an animal in a zoo. Always being on display," she replied softly.

Her observation struck too deep...too on point. He hated it that she saw it. Hated more that he'd allowed her to.

"Being fodder for any newspaper or online gossip column," he lashed out with a biting coldness that was meant to burn.

She bent her head over her treat and licked a melting trail of ice cream. In spite of the anger knotting his gut, lust slid through him in a thick glide, flowing straight for his already pulsing flesh. He wanted that delicate pink tongue on him. Trailing over him like he was the most delicious thing she'd ever tasted. He hungered to hear her moans of pleasure in his ears, have it vibrate over his skin.

His control was soaked tissue paper when it came to this woman.

"I left the door wide-open on that one," she said long moments later, voice quiet. "I won't apologize for my job—it's an important one, and I love it. But I will say I'm sorry that it's contributed to making you feel as if you were a fish in a bowl. I can't imagine that kind of scrutiny is easy."

"But deserved, some would say." They continued to walk down the sidewalk in a silence taut with tension. Or more specifically, the roil of emotions tumbling inside him. Shoving against his sternum, his throat, seeking an escape. A release. "There are days I believe I deserve it. Give people their due. They need to watch me and make sure I'm not exhibiting signs of becoming Vernon Lowell. They have the right to that transparency. Even years later. Even though—"

Even though there were times he wanted to yell that he wasn't his father. That it wasn't him that had wronged them. It wasn't his fault.

But he couldn't. Because in the end, the sins of the father were visited upon the sons.

In their eyes, as the head of Black Crescent, as the only one available to direct their anger and mistrust at, it was his fault.

And he couldn't argue with them. Because deep inside, in that place that creaked open only in the darkest part of night when he had no energy left to keep it closed, he agreed with them.

Beside him, Sophie sighed and tunneled her fingers through her hair, dragging the strands away from her face and offering him an even more unencumbered view of her clean, elegant profile. A small frown wrinkled the smooth skin between her eyebrows.

"Deserve?" she mused almost to herself. She shook her head. "I don't agree with that. While I do believe in the truth and that people have the right to be aware of events that affect their welfare and lives, they aren't owed pieces of a person's security, peace or soul. Each of us should have the right to privacy, and we don't need anyone's permission to covet it or request it. And this is from a reporter." She lightly snorted, again shaking her head. Pausing, she took another swipe of the ice cream, and her tone became more thoughtful than irritated. "My parents divorced when I was almost thirteen, and it was... Well, *unpleasant* would be an understatement. The nasty arguing and name-calling had been bad enough. But they saw me as an ally to be wooed, a prize to be won in a contest. And they attempted this by competing in who could tell me the foulest, most humiliating things about the other. How my father cheated or how my mother had sent them to the poorhouse with her spending. So many things a child shouldn't be privy to, especially about her parents.

"But they twisted the truth about each other in this acrimonious and desperate need to make the other appear as horrible as possible. Never realizing how they were slowly picking me apart ugly word by ugly word. Because all I heard was how it was my fault they were divorcing. My father cheated. That just meant he was so unhappy at home with me for not doing better in school or being a pest at home that he went somewhere else to find happiness. Or if my mother spent too much money, it was on me because I asked for too much."

She inhaled a breath, and he caught the slight tightening of her hold on the cone. After several seconds, she released a trembling but self-deprecating chuckle.

"Sophie…"

But she interrupted him with a wave of her hand. "No, I know none of that is true. Now, anyway. But back then…" Her voice trailed off, but seconds later, she lifted a slim shoulder in a half shrug. "They made my teenage years hell, but I should thank them. Because of all that, plus the shuffling back and forth to different homes, never feeling truly rooted or secure, I made sure that I would be able to stand on my own two feet as an adult. That no one would ever have the power or ability to ever rip the rug out from under me again. They also directed me on the path to my career. They fueled my desire to filter facts from half-truths or fiction. And, when it was called for, to shield the innocent from it."

He digested that in silence. "Which is why you didn't print the rumors about me having a daughter in the article," he added.

She nodded, not looking at him. "Yes. I know what you think of me, Joshua, but I wouldn't deliberately smear someone's name or hurt them. Not without all the facts that can be backed up and confirmed beyond doubt. Am I perfect? No. But I try to be."

He licked the melting ice cream in his hand, warring within himself about how much he could share with Sophie. Why he *shouldn't* share. But after her baring some of her chaotic childhood, he owed her. Still…

"Off the record?" he murmured.

She jerked her gaze to him, and in the dove-gray depths he easily caught the surprise. And the flicker of irritation. As if annoyed that he'd ask. But as lovely as she was, as honest as she'd been with him, he couldn't forget who she was. *What* she was.

"Of course," she said, none of the contrasting emotions in her eyes reflected in her voice.

"Of course," he repeated softly, staring down at her. *What the hell are you doing?* he silently questioned his sanity, but then said, "I deserve their censure because of my life before my father decided to screw us all six ways to Sunday. Mine was charmed. I won't say perfect, because in hindsight, it wasn't. Nothing is. But for me, it was close. My brothers and I—we didn't have to want for anything. Not material, financial or emotional. Dad was always busy building Black Crescent into one of the foremost hedge funds, but Mom? She'd been there, attentive, supportive, loving. We weren't raised by an army of servants, even though we did have them. But Mom—and even Dad to an extent—had been involved. We attended one of the most exclusive and premier prep schools in the country and, later, Ivy League universities. I knew who I was and what I wanted to be. I never had doubts back then. I held the world in my palm and harbored no insecurities or fears that I could have it all."

"I always wondered about that," Sophie said, that intuitive and insightful gaze roaming his face. "If you faced any backlash or disapproval from your father for choosing art over the family business."

Why the hell am I talking about this? He never discussed his art or his career ambitions. A pit gaped in his chest, stretching and threatening to swallow him whole with the grief, disillusionment and sense of failure that poured out. Those dreams were dead and buried with a headstone to mark the grave.

Forcing the memories and the words past his tightening throat, he barely paused next to a garbage can and pitched his cone into it. He couldn't talk about this and even consider eating. Not with his gut forming a rebellion at just the unlocking of the past.

"From my mother, no. Like I said, she supported me from the very first. When I was a child, she enrolled me in art classes, encouraged me to continue even when my father scoffed at it or dismissed my interest as a passing fancy. But art was…my passion. My true friend, in ways. Growing up in Falling Brook, we had to be careful about image, about never forgetting we were Vernon Lowell's sons and Eve Evans-Janson's sons. There was a trade-off for the life of privilege we led, and that was perfection. But with art? I never had to be perfect. Or careful. I just had to be me. I didn't have to curtail my opinions to make sure I didn't offend anyone or reflect on my father. I could be unfailingly and unapologetically honest. I could trust it more than anything or anyone else."

A vise squeezed his chest so hard, so tight, his ribs screamed for relief. Just talking about that part of him he'd willingly—but without choice—amputated brought ghostly echoes of the joy, the freedom he'd once experienced every time he took a picture, picked up a piece of metal, lifted a paintbrush...

He shook them off, shoving them in the vault of his past and locking the door. If he were going to discuss that part of him, of his life, he had to separate himself from the emotion behind it. Besides, that was who he'd been. That man had ceased to exist the moment his father had gone on the lam, leaving his family and ten others broke and broken.

"But to answer your question, there wasn't any strife. More so because I believe Dad thought I would indulge in art, get it out of my system and then come work for Black Crescent. Even when I scored my first gallery show the summer after I graduated from college, Dad was pleased for me, but he also told me I had a choice to make and he hoped I chose wisely. 'Wisely' being coming into the business with him."

Had his father known even then that he would be going on the run? Had he already planned his escape plan? Because only two months after that conversation, he'd disappeared.

"While researching the article, I always thought that was amazing. Do you know how many artists are capable of getting their own gallery shows so soon in their careers? But then again, I saw pictures of your work. God, you were phenomenal," she breathed.

The unadulterated awe in her voice snagged on something inside him, jerking and tugging as if trying to bring that ephemeral and elusive "thing" to the surface to be acknowledged and analyzed. He shrank from it. Not in the least bit ready to do that.

He never would be.

"Can I ask you something? And disclaimer—it's going to be intrusive," she said, dumping her cone into a nearby trash can before slipping a sidelong glance at him. When he dipped his chin in agreement, she murmured, "How could you step away from it? I'm just thinking of how I would feel if I suddenly lost my career. Or if I couldn't do it anymore. And not just reporting, but my purpose. Empty. And lost. How could you give it up so easily?"

"Easily?" His harsh burst of laughter scraped his throat raw. "There was nothing easy about it, Sophie. I had a choice to make. Family or a career in art." Leave, move to New York to escape the judgment and condemnation and pursue his passion, or stay and save his family and the business. Try to repair what his father had torn apart. Even when Jake had done just that, Josh had stayed. And there'd been nothing simple or easy about that decision. "In the end my father had been right. I would have to choose, and I did. Not that it'd been much of one. I couldn't abandon my family."

Not like him remained unspoken but deafening in the silence that followed his words.

"I'm sorry," she whispered.

He slipped his tightly curled fists into the pockets of his slacks. "For what?" he rasped.

"For assuming it'd been an easy decision. That you had to make it in the first place."

He drew to an abrupt halt, absently thankful they'd made it to the parking lot at the far end of Main where his car waited. Thankful no one loitered in the area, and that for once, they were away from prying eyes.

No one—no *fucking* one—had ever said that to him. Had ever thought to consider the cost of his sacrifice, the effect of it on him. And no one had ever thanked him or sympathized that he'd given up the best part of him to take care of family. A family in which two of its members resented him for making that choice.

Alone. Here, in this parking lot, partially insulated from the public that had judged him so harshly, the remnants of the past clinging to him like skeletal fingers, he could admit that for fifteen years, he'd been so damn alone.

That choice had cost him the closeness he'd once shared with his brothers. It'd stolen the plugged-in mother from his youth. The so-called friends he'd believed he had. Most of all, it'd left him bereft of his dreams and—how had she described it?—empty.

Yes. Empty.

But in this space, in this fleeting moment, he didn't. With this woman, with her silken skin, molten eyes and temptress mouth, he felt…seen. And it sent heat rushing through him like air caught in a wind tunnel—loud, powerful and threatening to rip him apart. He edged his feet apart, slightly widening his stance as if bracing himself against the overwhelming longing to touch, to hold, to *connect*.

He lifted his hand to brush his fingertips over her

delicate jaw, waiting, no, expecting, her to wrench away from him to avoid his caress.

She didn't. Sophie stood still, her headed tilted back, gaze centered on him. She didn't flinch from him. Didn't question what the hell he was doing. No, those sweet lips parted on a soft gasp that went straight to his dick, grazing it.

Locking down a groan behind clenched teeth, he shifted closer, turning slightly to shield her from any curious spectators. A thick cocoon of desire might be enfolding them, but it didn't erase the fact that they stood off Main Street. But where minutes ago that would've prevented him from lowering his head over hers, moving nearer still until his chest pressed against hers and his thighs cradled the slim length of hers, more than ever, he was aware of the disparity in their heights and frames. His body nearly covered her, and the top of her head just barely skimmed his chin. The surge of lust sweeping through his veins, lighting them like an SOS flare, competed with the urge to protect. The impulse to conquer warred with the need to shelter. But instead of being torn in two by the opposing instincts, they melded, mating. Assuring him he could do both. That, by God, he *should* do both.

His fingers continued to explore her jaw, her cheek, the thinner skin over her temple, the slope of her nose in spite of the lust baying in his head like howling dogs. He followed the graceful arches of her eyebrows before traveling back down to trace the upper curve of her mouth, linger in the shallow dip in the middle. Then, he moved to that plumper bottom lip, savoring the soft give of it under his fingertips. He didn't offer just his thumb the treat of it. All his fingertips got in on the pleasure of the caress.

Her breath hitched, and again he fought back a moan at the gentle gust of air against his suddenly overly sensitive skin. Words crowded at the back of his throat.

Tell me I can have this temptation of a mouth that has woken me up, hard and hurting, for days now.

Will you let me fuck this mouth, Sophie? Will you let me defile it so you can taste the dirtiness of my kiss for days? Weeks?

But he didn't utter them. Instinct warned him that breaking this lust-drenched and pulsing silence with any sound would rip this opportunity away from him. Shatter the cords that held them here in this moment—cords that shimmered with heat but were as fragile as glass.

He'd hungered for this chance for too long. Battled himself over it too hard to abdicate it.

So, instead, he planted his thumb in the middle of the bottom curve, pressed until the tip of his finger grazed the edges of her teeth. When she didn't draw away from him but tilted her head forward to lean into the pressure, he shuddered.

And when she parted those beautiful lips and flicked her tongue over his flesh, he had his answer.

Not bothering to trap his groan in this time, he dipped his head and took her. Releasing the greedy sound into her mouth, replacing his thumb with the slick glide of his tongue.

God, the taste of her.

Sweet like the butter-pecan ice cream she'd been eating. Sultry like air thick and perfumed after a spring rain. Heady like a shot of whiskey. Deliciously wicked. Like sex.

With hands going rough with greed, he burrowed one into her hair, fisting the strands and tugging. Tugging until her mouth was right where he wanted it... needed it. Her swallowed her small whimper, giving her a growl in return as she opened wider for him. Granting him entrance to her. To heaven.

He thrust between those beautiful lips, tangling his tongue with hers, dancing, dueling. Because Sophie wasn't a passive participant. Just as she challenged him in his office, in a newspaper conference room or a gym, she gave as good as she got here, as well. She sucked and licked, stroking into his mouth to demand and take.

His grip on her hair and hip tightened, dragging her closer, impossibly closer. His hips punched forward, grounding his erection against the softness of her belly. Fire ripped a scorching path up his spine, then back down to his dick. Jesus, she was about to set him off like a teenager copping his first feel behind the gym bleachers. Cocking his head, he delved deeper, a desperate hunger for more digging into him. One nip of her lips, one sample of her taste, and he was hooked, ravenous for more.

"Josh," she breathed against his damp lips. Hearing the abbreviated version of his name had his flesh hardening further, had him aching. And he couldn't not reward her—hell, thank her—with another drugging kiss and roll of his hips.

The ring of a phone shattered the thick haze of lust that enclosed them.

He lifted his head, the air in his lungs ragged and harsh. She stared up at him, those storm-gray eyes clouded with the same desire coursing through him like electrified currents. Her swollen mouth, wet from his tongue, glistened, and he'd lowered his head, submitting to the sensual beckoning of them when the peal of the phone jangled again.

Dammit.

Disentangling his hands from her hair and releasing the sweet curve of her hip, he stepped back, reaching in his pocket for his silent cell phone. At the same time, Sophie retrieved hers from the front pocket of her bag. Tapping the screen, she held the cell to her ear.

"Hi, Althea," she said, her gaze meeting his for a second before she turned away. Althea Granger, the editor in chief of the *Falling Brook Chronicle*. Her boss. "Yes, that's not a problem. Has anyone else picked up the story yet?"

A frigid deluge of water crashed over him in a wave.

For moments, he'd felt young again. Free again. He'd allowed himself to forget who Sophie was. Who he was. But reality had a way of slapping the hell out of a person and reminding him that life wasn't hand-holding and ice-cream cones or kissing a beautiful woman. It was hard, sometimes grueling work, disappointment and constantly brushing off scraped knees and bruised hands to get up and face it again.

He could still taste the unique and addictive flavor of her on his lips, his tongue. But he couldn't let Sophie Armstrong in. And her being a reporter was just one reason. A very good reason to keep his distance from her, but not the only one.

When Vernon had left, he'd broken his ability to trust. And his brothers had trampled on the pieces on their way out of Falling Brook. Even his mother had abandoned him. Not physically, but definitely emotionally. When he loved people, when he let them in, they left. They eventually abandoned him.

They eventually devastated him.

No, he couldn't trust Sophie. Leaving himself vulnerable again came at too high a price. And he had nothing left to pay it with.

"Okay, I'll head to the office now. See you in a few." Sophie ended the call and faced him again. "Sorry about that." She cleared her throat, twin flags of pink staining the slants of her cheekbones. Left over from their kiss—if that was what that clash of mouths, tongues and teeth could be labeled—or from the phone call. "I need to go into work for a few hours."

"I heard," he said, deliberately infusing a sheet of ice into his voice. As if just seconds ago it hadn't been razed to hell by lust. He glanced down at his watch. "That's fine. I have to leave, too." While he'd been taking her mouth, time had raced by, and he was due to pick up his mother in five minutes. But the errand was just a handy excuse to put distance between him and Sophie. Because in spite of his resolve and the reminder of why he couldn't become involved with her, he still had to threaten himself with self-harm to avoid staring at her mouth like a marauding beast. "Have a good weekend, Sophie."

Not waiting on her reply, he pivoted on his heel and strode back in the direction they'd come. And if that cloak of loneliness settled across his shoulders again, well, it was preferable to pain.

Preferable to betrayal.

And Sophie smacked of both.

Chapter 6

Sophie wove a path among the many businessmen, socialites, philanthropists and even a handful of celebrities crowded into the Ronald O. Perelman Rotunda of the Guggenheim Museum in Manhattan. The annual Tender Shoots Art Gala brought all the tristate area's glitterati out in support of the New York–based arts program.

Taking a sip of her cocktail, she dipped her head in a shallow nod at a woman whose diamond necklace and ruby-red strapless gown could probably pay off the entirety of Sophie's student loans. She held her head up, meeting the assessing gaze of every person she had eye contact with. Or maybe it just felt assessing to her. As if they were attempting to peer beneath the expertly applied makeup and strapless, glittery, floor-length dress that she'd needed a crowbar and a prayer to squeeze into in order to determine if she belonged.

Well, at an invite-only event that required fifteen
thousand a plate fee plus a hefty donation for entrance,
she didn't belong. She'd grown up in Falling Brook, one
of the most exclusive, wealthiest communities along
the Eastern Seaboard, but her family had been among
the few middle-class residents who either owned businesses in town or worked for Falling Brook Prep, the
independent K–twelve school. The kind of excess and
luxury represented in the grand, open space surrounded
by the spiral-ramped architecture capped by a gorgeous
skylight exceeded her imagination and bank account.
Thank God, Althea's partner was a stylist who had let
Sophie borrow a designer gown for the night. And didn't
that just increase the surreal feeling of Cinderella attending the ball before her carriage turned back into a
pumkin that had filled her since stepping onto the curb
outside the famous museum?

If not for Althea receiving an invitation because of
the paper's piece about the event, the organization and
the underprivileged youth it benefited, Sophie would be
home, catching up on season two of *The Handmaid's
Tale*. But since it'd been Sophie's article that had gar-
nered the invite, Althea had convinced her to accept
and attend. She should be grateful and flattered. But
while she had no problem reporting on the country's
wealthy elite, she drew a line at socializing with them.
It reminded her too much of a time in her life when
she'd been blinded by their world and the man she'd
once loved who'd belonged to it.

Too bad she hadn't remembered not to cross that line
that morning with Joshua Lowell.

A convoluted mixture of embarrassment, self-di-
rected anger and a relentless, aching need jumbled

and twisted deep inside her. Just thinking of how he'd cupped her jaw, gently caressed her face and then claimed her mouth had her shouting obscenity-laced reprimands at herself...even as she pressed her thighs together to fruitlessly attempt to stifle the throbbing ache in her sex. And all that led to her embarrassment. The man had sexed her mouth, then walked away from her without a backward glance. As if that devastation of a kiss hadn't affected him at all. If not for the insistent, commanding grind of his thick erection against her belly, she would've believed he hadn't been.

But no matter that he'd moaned into her mouth and had granted her a clear premonition of what it would be like to be controlled and branded by that big, wide-shouldered body, he *had* transformed from the approachable, almost vulnerable man who'd strolled down Main Street with her, licking ice cream in a way that had her sex ready to throw itself at his feet, to an iceberg who'd dismissed her as if their connection had been of no consequence. As if *she* were of no consequence. And hell, maybe to him, she wasn't.

Staring down into the glass, she didn't see the pale gold champagne but his shuttered expression and flat stare as she'd ended her phone call. A shiver ran through her, as if the ice that had entered that measured inspection skated over her exposed skin now. She didn't believe in deluding herself; she acknowledged that it'd been Althea's call that had changed him. He'd no doubt suddenly been reminded of what they were to one another. She was the woman who had dragged the darkest, most scandalous parts of his history back out, dusted them off and planted them on the front page of the newspaper for public consumption. Again.

Half of her was surprised he hadn't asked her if that kiss was off the record. Despite her best efforts, her lips twisted into a slight sneer. As if she'd treat him to an ice-cream cone just to butter him up for a scoop—no pun intended. Screw it. That pun was totally intended.

Smothering a sigh, she lifted her fluted glass to her lips and sipped. At least this gala provided one purpose. Distract her from thoughts of—

Joshua.

Her gaze locked with a beautiful and all too familiar pair of hazel eyes. Lust gut-punched her like a prize-fighter with a penchant for ear biting. If not for her locked knees and sheer grit not to humiliate herself in the four-inch stilettos, the blow would've knocked her on her ass. Beneath the bandage-style bodice of her dress, her nipples drew into taut, pebbled points begging for just a whisper of a caress from those long, blunt-tipped fingers. Pinpricks of electricity rippled up and down her exposed spine, sizzling in the base of her spine. And her feminine flesh... She stifled a needy and shameful moan. Her flesh swelled, damp and sensitive from just a hooded glance from those green-and-gold and way too perceptive eyes.

Good God, had she conjured him with her own wayward thoughts?

"Ms. Armstrong?" a low, cultured voice called her name, and Sophie yanked her scrutiny away from Joshua. A tall, powerfully built and handsome man stood next to her. Black hair waved back from a high forehead, emphasizing a face with strong facial features, a full, sensual mouth and intense blue eyes. He smiled, flashing perfect white teeth. "You are Sophie

Armstrong, correct?" he asked, extending a large hand toward her.

"Yes," she replied, accepting the hand. He squeezed it lightly before releasing it. "I'm sorry, do we know one another?"

"No, we haven't officially met. But I've followed your career these past few years from Chicago to the *Falling Brook Chronicle*. I'm a fan of your journalistic style. Most recently, I enjoyed the pieces you wrote on the Tender Shoots Arts Council as well as the one on the Black Crescent scandal. Considering the topic and the many times it's been reported on, I thought you wrote an objective, well-researched article. Especially about Joshua Lowell and his former art career. I don't think many people remember the accomplished artist he was and the potential career he once had."

Accomplished artist he is.

The words burned on her tongue. No one with the kind of talent she'd seen in his work or whose voice contained the passion his had while describing what art had meant to him could turn off the God-given gift he'd been blessed with. Joshua might be the CEO of his father's company, but now more than ever after this morning's conversation with him, she was convinced the artist who'd created such awe-inspiring, magnificent pieces of art still existed beneath those expensive, perfectly tailored suits.

"Thank you. I appreciate the compliment, Mr...." She trailed off. The man still hadn't given her his name.

A half smile quirked one corner of his mouth. "Christopher Harrison. I'm one of the organizers of the gala and on the board of trustees for the Tender Shoots Arts Council."

"Mr. Harrison." She nodded. "It's a pleasure to meet you."

"Christopher, please. The pleasure is mine." He crooked an arm and held it out to her. "Can I escort you into dinner? I believe we're sitting at the same table."

A little bemused, she settled her hand in the bend of his elbow. "I'm sitting at your table?" she repeated, unable to keep out the edge of incredulity.

He chuckled. "I confess to using my position with the organization to finagle a favor and moving your seat." He shrugged, but nothing about him said *repentant*. "It's one of the perks of the job."

"Do I need to be worried about why you want my company at your table?" she mused, part of her amused, but the other part wary. Years ago, another sophisticated, handsome man had approached her at a function. And his motives had been anything but pure. Too bad that by the time she'd figured that out, he'd nearly devastated her heart and her integrity. Old suspicions died hard.

Speaking of suspicions...

The charged tingle dancing across the nape of her neck informed her where Joshua stood. And she directed her glance in that direction. Immediately, his hazel gaze snared hers. Burning into hers. For a second, it released her to flicker to the man guiding her through the throng of people. Even across the distance, she caught the firming of his full lips, the darkening of his eyes. And when he returned his narrowed scrutiny to her, the fire in them seared over her exposed skin.

She sucked in a breath, jerking her head forward. Because she needed to pay attention to where her feet and the man next to her were taking her.

Not because she could no longer stand meeting that slightly ominous stare that had heat spiking in her body like she'd transformed into a thermometer.

At least that was what she told herself. As she settled at one of the tables closest to the dais erected at the far end of the rotunda, she continued to remind herself of that. And even as the electrified crackle hummed under her skin, she refused to allow her attention to slip toward the table to her right. Joshua Lowell was just a man. Yes, a beautiful, imposing man who wore a tuxedo as if it'd been created with the sole purpose of adorning that tall, powerful body. A complicated man who was like a puzzle missing several pieces. Pieces she wanted to hunt down and fit into the empty spaces so she could determine who he really was. The arrogant, commanding CEO with the icy reserve? Or the passionate artist who revealed tantalizing glimpses of vulnerability and kissed like he could consume a woman whole and make her beg him to take more?

He's a man who wants revenge because of the story you wrote on him and his family. A man who denies the existence of his child and is using you to control if you reveal it or not.

Or maybe one who just desperately sought to discover if he truly had a daughter that he'd known nothing about?

Jesus, she was arguing with herself. It was official. Joshua—or this unwarranted and dangerous fascination with him—was driving her nuts.

That same fascination had her casting a glance to the neighboring table. She was a masochist. There was no other explanation. And yet, she found herself once more helplessly ensnared by a copper-and-emerald stare as she'd been in the reception area.

Flayed. That was what that intense, gorgeous and entirely too-perceptive scrutiny did to her. Leave her flayed, open and exposed. Did he see the dueling emotions he stirred in her—the desire for distance, to borrow some of that renowned aloofness, and the desire to feel the intimidating thick length of him again. Not against her stomach this time, but inside her. Stretching her. Marking her.

The woman next to Joshua, a stunning redhead in a black sequined dress that screamed couture, leaned into him, whispering in his ear. He turned to her, releasing Sophie from their visual showdown.

A shaft of…something hot and ugly pierced her chest. She couldn't identify it. *Wouldn't* identify it. Because it wasn't jealousy. The woman, with the onyx jewels dripping from her ears and encircling her neck, belonged to his world. They were perfect for each other.

"Do you know Joshua?" Christopher's question yanked her from the rabbit hole that she'd been in the process of tumbling down. She met his curious gaze. Saw when it flickered toward the other table and Joshua and returned to her. "Are you two acquainted?"

"God, no," she denied with a small deprecating chuckle. Not a lie, exactly. She doubted anyone really *knew* Joshua Lowell. And something whispered that he preferred it that way. "I just wrote an article on one of the darkest periods in his and his family's lives. I'm sure he's not a fan of mine."

"Hmm." Christopher studied her, and she refused to fidget beneath that assessing regard. "I can understand that, I guess. Although, like I mentioned earlier, all things considered, it was a fair piece." He lifted a glass of wine and sipped from it, continuing to study her over the rim. "He's one of our major contributors to the nonprofit. Not surprising, really, with his own background in art."

Yes, she could see that. He might not create pieces anymore but imagining him pouring financial support into the lives of underprivileged youth so they might have the advantages of following the path he'd walked away from wasn't hard.

Still… She glanced over at one of the walls where numerous canvases, pen-and-ink drawings and framed photographs hung. The oversize, mixed-media collages that used to be Joshua's trademark would seamlessly fit in here. Did he ever wish they were? Did he ever dream of walking into this famed museum and seeing his pieces adorning these off-white walls?

Did it cause him pain to attend a gala celebrating art knowing he couldn't have this? Knowing others were doing what he'd been created to do?

She forced herself not to look at Joshua this time. Afraid she would see what she wanted to instead of who he really was. Maya Angelou had said, "When someone shows you who they are, believe them the first time." That day she'd barged into his office, he'd shown her the ruthless, dismissive and cold businessman. She needed to remember that, brand that image into her mind so when she started to visualize more—a sensitive, burdened man who grieved all that he'd lost—she'd shut that down.

And if that didn't work, remember Laurence Danvers. Remember how she'd spectacularly crashed and burned by almost choosing a man over her career, over her ethics. She'd paid for those errors in judgment, for her willing blindness.

Never again, though.

Returning her attention to Christopher, she finished dinner with a smile and surprisingly entertaining conversation. Charismatic and funny, he effortlessly charmed her, and when the dishes were cleared and the guests headed back toward the reception area for dancing and more cocktails, she accepted his invitation to join him out on the dance floor.

Tilting her head back, she smiled up at him. "Not that I doubt you could enjoy my company, but, call it a reporter's intuition, I just have the sense you didn't seek me out because of my smile. Or this dress. As gorgeous as it may be."

He grinned, his fingers tightening around her fingers. "It is that, but not as beautiful as the woman wearing it." When she arched an eyebrow, he tipped his head back, laughing. And drawing the attention of the couples swaying to the jazz music along with them. "Your reputation for a no-nonsense investigative journalist is well earned, Sophie Armstrong. I did have an ulterior motive when I approached you this evening."

"I'm waiting."

"Our nonprofit is always seeking out new ways to bring in donations and media coverage that will result in even more donations. Funding and philanthropic gifts are this organization's lifeblood," he said, the humor evaporating from his voice and the intensity that had radiated from him since their initial meeting intensified. "I read your article on the Lowell family and Black Crescent. But my particular interest in the piece was the attention placed on Joshua Lowell. The artist submerged, if I remember correctly. It started me thinking. What if the artist reemerged? Returned to the world where he once stood on the cusp of a promising career? Can you imagine the stir and the money that would bring to Tender Shoots?"

Against her will, excitement kindled in her chest. Yes, she could imagine this. All too easily. Maybe not if she hadn't walked along a sidewalk with him and caught the embers of a deliberately banked passion in his eyes, in his words. But Christopher was correct on all accounts. Joshua returning to the art world would be huge—for both the nonprofit and him.

"I agree it would benefit all involved," she replied vaguely. "But what does it have to do with me?"

"I have an admission to make, Sophie," he said, and unlike his playful confession earlier about the seating arrangements, this one caused an unsettling dip in her stomach. "After the article in the *Falling Brook Chronicle*, I researched you. I believe you, more than anyone, can appreciate the need to protect my sources, but despite telling me earlier that you didn't know him, I discovered you were spotted in Joshua Lowell's company several times."

She remained silent, not confirming or denying. But her heart thundered against her rib cage. Though there'd been nothing untoward or illicit about their meetings— *don't even* think *about the kiss!*—just the perception of conflict of interest could be detrimental to her reputation and career. Her original instinct to be wary around Christopher deepened, and she schooled her features into a polite but distant mask.

"I can guess what you're assuming, Sophie, and you're wrong," he murmured, voice gentling. "I don't intend to accuse you of anything or use my information against you or him."

"Then what are your intentions?" she demanded.

"I need your help in convincing him to consider a showing next year. Just because of who he is—the CEO of Black Crescent Hedge Fund—but also because of how he walked away from what critics had predicted to be an important art career."

Before he finished speaking, Sophie was already shaking her head. "I don't know why you'd think I possess the influence to convince Joshua Lowell to do anything, but—"

"Because I've seen how he hasn't been able to tear his gaze off you all evening. And how you've pretended not to notice—when you haven't been staring back at him," he interrupted. "Tell me I'm wrong."

Her pulse was a deafening beat in her ears, in her blood. "You're wrong," she rasped. And hated that her voice held the consistency of fresh-out-the-package sandpaper. "We barely know each other. And even if we were…more acquainted, Joshua Lowell has buried that side of himself. And it would take much more than a few words from me to resurrect it." *But what if there was a chance for him to discover his passion again?* She waved the hand that'd been resting on Christopher's shoulder. To dismiss his request or her own thoughts? Both applied. And anyway, it wasn't her business. Joshua wasn't her business. "I'm sorry, Christopher. I've enjoyed your company tonight, but your efforts on me were wasted. What you're looking for is a miracle, and unfortunately, I'm not in that market."

A sardonic smile curved a corner of his mouth, although his gaze on her remained sharp. Too sharp. "Okay, Sophie. But, if you please, just think about what I'm asking. And if one day you do find yourself in the position to carry influence with him, I and my organization would appreciate it if you would broach the possibility of a show with him. It would help so many students and could very well affect lives."

"Really?" she drawled. "The change-lives card? You're pulling out the big guns."

He chuckled, squeezing her fingers. "I'm nothing if not persistent and shameless."

Thankfully, he dropped the subject. But after their dance ended and she strolled off the crowded floor, a weariness crept over her. She was ready to call it an evening and moved across the room, removing her cell from her purse to place a call to the car service that had picked her up and dropped her off here hours ago. Accepting her thin wrap from the coat check minutes later, she stepped out into the warm May evening. Sounds and scents of the City That Never Sleeps echoed around her—honks, voices carried in the night, exhaust from the passing traffic and the frenetic energy that popped and crackled in the air. There'd been a time when she'd believed her future lay in New York or a busy city like it. But Falling Brook, with its slower pace and smaller population, was home, and she wouldn't want to live anywhere else.

"Leaving so early?"

She shivered as the deep, dark timbre of the voice that held a hint of gravel rolled over her. Vibrated within her. Tightening the wrap around her shoulders, she glanced at Joshua. Several inches separated them, but the distance meant nothing with that stare blazing down at her. Lighting her up. Pebbling her nipples. Wetting the insides of her thighs. Another tremble worked its way through her, and those narrowed eyes didn't miss her reaction.

"Are you cold?" he asked, already slipping out of his tuxedo jacket. The relief coursing through her that he'd misperceived the source of that shiver stripped her of her voice. But Joshua didn't need her answer. He shifted closer and draped the garment over her shoulders. Immediately, his delicious sandalwood-and-rain scent enveloped her, surrounded her as effectively as if it were his arms warming her instead of his jacket.

"Thank you," she finally said, mentally wincing at the hoarseness of her tone.

He nodded. A valet approached them, and Joshua handed him a slip of paper. After the young man strode away, Joshua returned his regard to her, sliding his hands into his pants pockets. "You're ending the evening before it's over?" he rumbled. "Did Christopher Harrison say or do something to make you uncomfortable enough to leave?"

"No," she said, adding a sharp head shake for emphasis. "He was fine. I'm just…tired. And I have a forty-five-minute ride ahead of me. So I'm getting a head start."

"You're driving?"

"Althea arranged a car service for me."

He didn't reply, but the full, sensual curves of his mouth tightened at the corners. He'd had a similar reaction to her editor in chief's name earlier today. As if he resented the sound of it.

"What are you doing out here?" she asked, glancing over her shoulder in the direction of the museum. "From what I saw, you seemed to be having a good time."

And by "good time" she meant the statuesque, gorgeous redhead he'd been seated next to at dinner. The ear whisperer. When she'd left the reception area for the coat check, Sophie had been unable to not take note of Joshua. And he'd stood on the rim of the dance floor, the other woman plastered to his side closer than ninety-nine was to a hundred. God, she sounded bitchy to her own self.

"Were you watching me, Sophie?" he murmured, that dark-as-sin voice dipping lower, stroking her skin in a smoky caress.

"Were you watching me, Joshua?" she volleyed back, just as quietly.

They stared at one another, the challenge they'd lobbied between them vibrating. The air thickened, taut with the tension emanating from their bodies.

"Come home with me."

The request edged with demand struck her in the chest. She locked her knees, but that only prevented her from falling onto her ass. It didn't prevent her mentally wheeling and sprawling in shock. She blinked up at him, felt her eyes widening, and her lips parted on a gasp she couldn't contain.

"What?" she breathed.

"Come home with me," he repeated in that slightly impatient tone that hummed with notes of frustration, anger and even surprise. But not directed at her. Through her rapidly ebbing surprise, she suspected all that emotion was aimed at himself. "I'll take you back to Falling Brook, but come home with me first. We need a place where we can talk openly...privately."

"About what?" she questioned, her heart racing for and nestling in her throat.

"About business that is just between us," he replied,

purposefully vague, she suspected. Here, in front of the Guggenheim and anyone walking the Manhattan streets, he wouldn't be more specific than that.

She studied him, her grip tight on her sequined clutch. Alone with Joshua. For possibly hours. Her mind—and common sense—balked. Absolutely not. The last time they'd been together, within feet of Main Street, he'd shown her the real purpose of her mouth. To mate with his. What would happen without the chance of prying eyes catching them? Without the constraints of being in public? He would probably be able to maintain his intimidating control, but her? She wouldn't advise any Vegas high rollers place bets on her. This man was proving to be her weakness, the chink in her professional and personal armor, and getting close enough to let him chip away more was lunacy.

Yet… She stared into his eyes. And almost glanced away from the coolness there. But at the last second, she looked deeper. And caught the shadows of need, of…loneliness. Both echoed within her, and something inside her reacted to them. Reached for them. For him.

Instinctively, she stepped back and away from him. To protect herself. But not from him. Herself. It'd been this same longing to soothe, to please, to be loved that had led her down the wrong path before. With Laurence, she'd been blind. But now, her eyes were wide-open to who and what Joshua was. And if she traveled this road, she would have only herself to blame for the catastrophic results to her career, her integrity, her heart. And God, she harbored zero doubts he would decimate her heart, leaving not even ashes behind.

"Come with me, Sophie," he murmured, holding out a hand to her as the valet pulled to the curb in a sleek black sports car that even her limited knowledge identified as an Aston Martin.

She stared at that palm with fascination, yearning and trepidation. Yes, she wanted him—what was the point in lying about the plain, bald-faced truth? But her body didn't rule her. Not anymore. If he intended to discuss her help on the paternity issue, they definitely couldn't do it out here on the sidewalk where anyone could overhear. And, her inner reporter chimed in, if he went off the record with her before, maybe he would agree to going back on and be willing to let her get that interview he'd denied her for the original story. Her deadline for the follow-up article was fast approaching.

And maybe she was just trying to justify her reasons for unwisely accepting his invite.

"Okay," she said quietly, slipping her hand over his and locking down the shiver that wanted to ripple through her as his fingers wrapped around hers. "But just for a couple of hours."

He nodded, his intense perusal scanning her face, then dipping down her body before returning to her eyes. Without a word, he escorted her to his waiting car. Within moments, she was tucked against the sinfully luxurious leather seat with Joshua behind the wheel. When he pulled away from the curb and merged with the moderate traffic, she couldn't help but admire the expert manner in how he handled the vehicle. A begrudging but warm throb settled just under her navel. If the man wielded such control over this four-thousand-pound rocket, how much would he exert in other places? Or... What would he look like if he loosened the reins on it?

Not my business, she informed herself with a mental sneer. Turning her attention to her phone, she called the car service back and canceled her ride. Then she settled back against the seat for the forty-five-minute ride back to Falling Brook. Other than asking her if the air was too cold and if she was comfortable, they barely uttered a word. But it didn't matter. The screaming tension crowded into the car with them did most of the speaking.

By the time he guided the car into the underground parking lot of a tall brick apartment building, she practically vibrated with the strain of fighting the desire coiled so tight within her and pretending as if he didn't affect her. Business. This was about the article. About their side investigation. She could keep it professional, because that was who she was.

Pep talk delivered, she didn't wait for him to round the car and open the door, but pushed it open herself and exited. He wouldn't open doors for his colleagues at Black Crescent, so he shouldn't for her, either.

Coward. You just don't want him any closer than necessary.

She flipped her inner know-it-all the finger.

And if she stiffened but didn't shift away from the broad hand he settled at the small of her back, well… She just didn't want to be rude.

Joshua led her to an elevator, and soon they were alighting from it into a huge apartment that could've fit her whole childhood home inside. She couldn't trap the gasp that escaped from her. Just as the charity event had exposed her to another level of wealth and luxury, so did his place.

Gleaming and pristine floor-to-ceiling windows that offered an unhindered and gorgeous view of Falling

Brook and beyond. A king surveying his kingdom. The impression whispered through her head, and she had to agree. Shaking her head, she moved farther into the foyer, taking in the rest of his space. An open floor plan that allowed each room to flow seamlessly into the next. A sunken living room, freestanding fireplace, dining room with a table large enough to fit a large family with no trouble, a large kitchen with a floating island, beautiful oak cabinets and what appeared to be stainless steel, state-of-the-art appliances. Because why not? Although, something told her he most likely used the double-door refrigerator for takeout instead of cooking with the wide six-burner stove and oven.

Beyond her stretched a dim but deep hallway, and just off the living room stretched a railless staircase to an upper level. Expensive-looking but comfortable furniture filled the vast space, but there was something missing.

Art.

No paintings decorating the cream-colored, freestanding walls. No sculptures that people often staged on tables or in the wide foyer. Not even a knickknack on an end table. The absence glared at her, and she glanced sharply at Joshua, who remained standing next to her, watching her survey his private sanctuary.

"Let me take this for you." He settled his hands on her shoulders and his jacket that she still wore. Though it was undoubtedly made of the finest wool, it should've disintegrated under the heat from his palms. Grinding her teeth against the inappropriate response, she nodded. "Would you like a drink?" he asked, opening a door behind them and hanging up the jacket and her wrap.

"Sure." She headed toward the living room, where

a large and fully stocked bar stood next to the dark fireplace.

"What would you—" His phone rang, cutting him off. He removed it from his pants pocket and glanced at the screen. "I need to take this. Help yourself, and I'll be right back." Pivoting, he headed toward the hallway, pressing the cell to his ear. "Joshua Lowell."

She stared after him for several moments as he disappeared into a room, shutting it quietly behind him. Only then did she move into the living room, releasing a heavy sigh.

A scotch sounded really good right about now.

Before long, she had a finger of the amber alcohol in a squat tumbler, and she raised it to her mouth for a slow, small sip. She hummed in appreciation at the full-bodied, smooth taste as it burned a path over her tongue and down her throat, settling a ball of warmth in her chest.

"Wow, that's good," she muttered, taking and savoring another mouthful.

Grasping the glass between her hands, she headed toward one of the windows and the magnificent and tranquil view. But there was a scattering of papers on the low chrome-and-glass table in front of the couch. How hadn't she noticed it before? The haphazard pile contrasted so sharply with the pristine order of everything else in the room. Hell, the apartment.

Unable to resist the lure it presented, she approached the table. Guilt crept inside her. Joshua hadn't invited her here to snoop. Yet, she still peered down at the papers.

A printout of names and notes written beside each in his heavy scrawl. Women's names. Now, even if God himself came down and admonished her for breaking the eleventh commandment—thou shall not poke thy nose into thy neighbor's business—she still wouldn't have been able not to look.

She recognized some of the names. A high-powered attorney who lived there in Falling Brook. A society darling known for her parties and benevolent efforts. A B-list actress one blockbuster away from catapulting onto the A-list. And about three other names she didn't recognize. But each one had dates typed next to them. Then a handwritten note about whether Joshua had called, made contact and the result.

No baby.

Child but two years old. Not the right age.

Has a little boy. Same age, wrong sex.

Her grip on the glass of scotch tightened until her fingers twinged in protest. Joshua hadn't been idle. This list bore that out. A list that apparently included the names of women he'd been intimate with in the last four years, if the earliest date was an indication. She wrestled down the hot flare of dark and unpleasant emotion that flashed to life in her chest and twisted her belly. Six women wasn't a lot, but damn, she resented each one because they'd experienced the passion he'd very briefly unleashed on her. With grim effort, she refocused on the paper in front of her. Joshua had clearly been working on finding the woman who was supposed to have birthed his child.

Shock and a softer, far more precarious emotion stirred behind her breastbone, melting into her veins like warm butter. Lifting her free hand, she rubbed the heel of her palm over her heart. Since her offer to Joshua on Wednesday to help research more about the

DNA report, she'd done some digging. But she kept hitting dead ends.

She wouldn't stop investigating but... Could the DNA results have been mistaken? Either that or Joshua's outrage at her accusation of being an absentee father had been genuine, and he really didn't know he had a child out there. He hadn't left these papers out for her benefit, because he couldn't have predicted they would meet tonight. Briefly closing her eyes, she ran his past reactions in her head like a movie reel. The pain, anger and, yes, grief. Viewed in a different, more objective lens, she had only one conclusion.

She believed him.

"Snooping, Sophie?"

Body jerking in surprise, she tugged her scrutiny from the table to meet Joshua's hooded gaze. So absorbed in what she'd discovered, she hadn't heard him enter the room. But he stood several feet away, head cocked to the side, studying her with an impenetrable expression. Didn't matter, though. The anger emanated from him, sending the guilt in her belly into a tighter, faster tailspin.

"Yes," she admitted quietly. If her honesty startled him, he didn't reveal it. That shuttered mask didn't alter. "I'm sorry. I shouldn't have invaded your privacy."

He didn't reply, his eyes narrowing further. Finally, he closed the short distance between them. But he didn't approach her but headed to the bar and fixed a drink. Turning to face her moments later with a tumbler in hand, he continued to study her, slowly sipping.

"Go ahead and ask," he said, his tone as dark and smooth as the alcohol in his hand. "Don't hold back.

Isn't that—" he waved the glass in the direction of the table and papers "—what you're here for?"

"Yes," she replied. It was the reason. At least the least complicated and safer reason. And the only one she wanted to admit to. "From your notes, I'm assuming you didn't find a woman with a child or if she did have one, not a child who was the correct age or gender."

He shook his head, tipping his drink up for another swallow. "No. None of them are behind the email you received or the DNA report. I'm not any closer to finding out the truth about whether or not I have a daughter."

"Is this list…complete?" She hated to ask—part of her didn't want to know the answer. No. More specifically, didn't want to know if there were more names. Not when a kernel of resentment and envy lodged just under her breastbone. But the question needed to be posed.

Joshua stared at her for several seconds before tipping his head back and loosing a hard and loud crack of laughter. But no hilarity laced the jagged edges of it.

"You're asking if I have more pages with a longer list of names hidden somewhere?" he drawled.

"Six women. Four years." She shrugged. And fought back the hot blast of embarrassment from staining her cheeks. "It does seem a little on the thin side."

"When you're a man in my position, you can't afford to be reckless with women. Especially when your father was a whore." He chuckled. "Come now, Sophie," he mocked. "You didn't come across that bit of information in all of your research?" Oh yes, she had. But her poker face must've been woefully inadequate because he arched a dark brow and downed the rest of the alcohol in his glass in one gulp. Setting the glass

on the bar behind him, he cocked his head to the side,
a razor-sharp half smile tilting the corner of his mouth.
"Of course you did," he murmured. "Well, don't leave
me in suspense. Tell me what you dug up on Vernon
Lowell's propensity for adultery."

"Joshua," she whispered, her mind, her traitorous
heart rebelling at engaging in this.

Not for his father's sake? No, Vernon had been the
whore his son had called him. She didn't want to go
there for Joshua's sake. Because underneath that taunt-
ing, I-don't-give-a-damn tone, his pain echoed like a
distant foghorn warning of upcoming danger.

"Don't stop now." The smile sharpened. "Do tell."

Inhaling a breath, she held it. Then slowly released
it. He wasn't going to let this go. For some reason, he
appeared in a masochistic mood, and was using her as
his weapon of choice.

"Vernon was known to have a…" She hesitated,
searching those gold-flecked hazel eyes. "Roving eye,"
she finished. Lamely.

"He fucked anything in a skirt." The bald, flat statement crashed between them like shattered glass. "That
is what you were so diplomatically trying to say, correct? He was an unfaithful bastard who betrayed his
marriage vows on a regular basis and didn't care if his
wife found out. And she did find out. My mother always knew when he found a new mistress. And we—
Jake, Oliver and I—all knew because they weren't quiet
about arguing over it."

Surprise rippled through her. Vernon had married up
when he'd wed his wife. Eve Evans-Janson had been a
society daughter with a pedigree that dated past colo-
nial times. Her connections had opened many doors for

him. Most people would consider her rather plain in the beauty department, but Sophie had always thought her loveliness exceeded mere looks. From pictures and her own memories, she remembered the other woman carrying herself like a queen. Dignified. Proud. So why would a woman like her accept a husband who cheated so openly without care for her feelings?

"Why would she—"

"Put up with a man who not only couldn't, but wouldn't, keep it in his pants?" he finished in a derisive drawl. "Simple. Comfort. Money. Even though my father did whatever he wanted and refused to give her the one thing she desperately wanted—a daughter—she stayed with him because divorce was embarrassing. Reputation and the image of a perfect marriage and family were vital to her. So she looked the other way in public and cried and raged in private. And… Despite all his selfishness, she loved him. Desperately."

Sadness coiled around her heart and squeezed hard. She should be outraged on his mother's behalf—even angry with her for settling. For not demanding more for herself, for her children. But… Hadn't she been Eve at one time? Hadn't she loved a man so completely she'd been willing to ignore her instincts, look the other way, almost ignore her ethics? The only difference between her and Joshua's mother was she finally walked away and refused to lose her independence to another man again.

Another of those serrated barks of laughter echoed in the room, and Joshua raked a hand through his hair, disheveling the thick blond strands.

"God, why in the hell am I telling you this?" he

snarled, turning away from her and stalking across the floor to the window.

The "of all people" didn't need to be said. It bounced off the glass walls, deafening in its silence.

She tried not to flinch. Tried not to allow the hurt to filter through. Tried…and failed.

"I'm not your enemy," she said to his wide back.

His shoulders tensed, but he didn't face her. "And I'm sorry if I implied that you were like your father. I didn't intend to." How to explain it'd just shocked her that such a virile, intense man who oozed power and sexuality had been intimate with only six women in four years? Hell, that didn't even average out to two a year. But given his history, the depths of which she hadn't known until this moment, she understood.

Sighing, she traced his steps and paused beside him, staring out over the beautiful view of Falling Brook at night. Houses, large and small, sprinkled among the trees and interconnecting map of streets, glittering like fairy lights. From this height, the town appeared almost magical. Serene. Made it seem as if they were hundreds of miles away instead of just several floors up.

"What do you see when you look out there?" she asked softly.

Tension and a cauldron of emotion continued to emanate from him, but when he replied, it was just as quietly. "A reminder."

"Of what?" It required everything in her not to glance at him, but to keep her gaze trained on the vista stretched out before them.

"Of why I do this." *Do what? What's* this? The questions bombarded her mind, but she forcibly held her tongue. And her patience was rewarded. "Why I continue to run a company I didn't ask for in the first place. Live this life that was my father's and not my own. For the last fifteen years, I've given it and Black Crescent everything—my dedication, my time, my loyalty, my goddamn soul. And in return? In return, I have a shade of a mother who I am powerless to help. My brothers don't speak to me because they hate who I've become a reflection of. My father is still MIA, and I have no idea whether he is dead or alive. And no matter how hard I work, how many hours I put in, how much money I bring in to repay those robbed and devastated by my father, it's never enough. I'll always be looked at with suspicion, judged for having the same blood in my veins as a criminal."

Her palms itched to touch him. To slide between him and the glass, smooth her hands up his hard chest and strong neck to cup his jaw between them. To, in some way, assume the pain that he wouldn't allow himself to show. But she caught herself, nonetheless. The sheer magnetism of this man dominated any room he stood in. Yet… How could anyone, after spending time with him, not see the emotions that roiled beneath that austere surface like water just under a boil?

"There's this gaping hole in my life," he continued in that gravel-and-midnight-silk voice. "And it doesn't matter what I do, I can't fill it. I don't know *how* to fill it." He shook his head, and he scoffed. "And the funniest, most pathetic part? When you first told me I might have a daughter, a part of me was thrilled. Because it meant that my life hadn't been a waste. That I had a purpose other than rebuilding the legacy my father nearly destroyed. That I would be more than Vernon Lowell's son. I would be someone's father."

"You're not your father," she contradicted him, taken aback at her own vehemence. Even more so at the knell of truth that bloomed in her chest...deeper. Somewhere between the meeting where he agreed to take her help and finding that list of names, she came to believe him about not knowing he had a child out there. Or even if the child from the DNA report was his. She released a trembling breath, spreading her hand over her suddenly tumbling stomach. "You're not Vernon," she repeated, stronger, firmer.

And maybe he heard the belief in her voice. Because he finally looked at her, his green-and-gold eyes burning down into her. Straight through her.

"You're sure about that?" he ground out. But before she could answer, he turned fully toward her, his palm flattening on the glass above her head. "You were the one who accused me of denying my illegitimate child's existence. Of carrying on and not caring that I had fathered a baby and left it out there somewhere for her and her mother to cope on their own."

Yes, she had. Regret eddied inside her, and she briefly closed her eyes against the oily, slick slide of it. Her article had dragged the scandal out of the past, buffed it up and placed it out all shiny and new for people to feast on again. She had a direct hand in him standing here, surrounded by a darkness that seemed ravenous and ready to swallow him whole.

Her fault. So at least, she owed him the truth. Her truth. Even if he could give two shits about it.

"It's true," she murmured, tipping her head back and meeting his piercing gaze. "I did believe that. But that was before I knew you—"

"You don't know me," he growled.

"That's where you're wrong," she objected, shifting into his space. Surprise flared in his eyes, flecks of gold brightening. But then his lids lowered, gaze becoming hooded and hiding his thoughts. His reaction. But it didn't stop her from claiming another inch. If she took a deep breath, her breasts would brush the wide, solid wall of his chest. The tips of her shoes nudged his, and his scent, so earthy, so virile, so delicious, enveloped her, and she battled the pull of it. For now. "You might be several things—ruthless, proud, arrogant, rude and at times so cold I'm afraid you'll leave burn marks on my skin—but you aren't a deadbeat father. You would never force a child to suffer what you have. Much less one who belonged to you."

He didn't move; his chest didn't even rise and fall on ragged breaths. Like hers did.

"So you're wrong," she said, surrendering to her earlier need and reaching for him. His hand shot out, quick as a snake, and encircled her wrist, his grip firm but not bruising. The dominance of his hold throbbed low in her belly. Her heart thudded against her sternum, but not in fear. Excitement. Need. They both streamed through her, one a sizzling current, the other fierce and liquid hot.

Testing him—pushing him—she lifted her other hand, cupping his face and half expecting him to evade her. But he didn't. He remained still, rigid. Yet, he let her hand mold to the blade of his jaw and the hollow of his cheek. The bristle of his five o'clock shadow abraded her skin, and she logged it as another sensory memory to hoard and savor.

"I know you better than anyone else. More than the people who only see what you permit them to. More than the brothers who left you to fix what was so broken. More than the women you've allowed to touch your body." She traced the curve of his bottom lip with her fingertips. "Does that scare you, Josh?"

She deliberately used the shortened version of his name, increasing the charged intimacy snapping between them like a loose live wire.

With a low rumble, he cuffed her other hand, trapping it against his mouth. His teeth sank into the fleshy heel of her palm, and her groan rolled out of her, unbidden and unrestrained. The flick of his tongue against the same flesh, as if soothing it of the tiny sting, drew another moan from her, this one softer...hungrier.

"No, you don't scare me, Sophie," he said, nipping again at her. "Because that would mean you had the power to hurt me. And I don't trust you enough to give you that power." Tugging on her wrist, he eliminated the negligent amount of space separating them, and she shivered as her breasts crushed his chest, her thighs pressed against his. His erection nestled against her belly. Whatever air remained in her lungs evaporated into vapor at the evidence of his arousal. For her. All for her. "But I want you. As much of a goddamn idiot it makes me, I want to fuck you until your voice is raw from screaming my name. Until you come around me, squeezing me so hard that my dick is bruised. Until my body aches from giving both of us what we need."

Oh. God. Each erotic word stuck her like tiny blows, her sex clenching over and over. Begging for the carnal image he drew. Pleading to be filled, taken, branded. She trembled, harder this time, thankful for the hard body and grips on her hands that held her up.

But doubts and threads of fear wound their way

through the fiercely pounding desire. If she were smart, if she'd truly learned from the past, she would halt this…this thing with Joshua before it went any further. At the very least, she could be in danger of losing her job for a serious conflict of interest if anyone found out about this. But not even her career trumped the very real terror of being that woman she'd been with Laurence. Her love for him had turned her into someone she hadn't known, dependent on his approval, his affection, his attention. She'd almost lost everything over him—her career, her future, herself.

She wasn't in love with Joshua, though. The lust turning her into this clawing, biting sexual creature demanding to be satisfied was unprecedented, but that was physical. Chemical. Not emotional.

As long as she kept her fickle, hardheaded heart out of this, she could give her body what it craved and protect herself.

"One night," she said, almost wincing at the note of desperation in her voice. And how he, again, went still, that multihued stare boring into her. But neither made her rescind the condition. "One night," she repeated. "No strings. No expectations. Just two people beating back their demons together."

God, why had she said that last part? It revealed too much.

And Joshua didn't ignore it. Releasing her wrists, he cupped the nape of her neck with one hand and cradled her hip with the other. Holding her. Steadying her. And because it would be only for the night, she allowed herself to lean into his strength. To depend on it.

"You have demons, Sophie?" he murmured, his gaze roaming her face as if already searching out the answer for himself rather than trust her to give an honest answer to him.

Smart man.

"Don't we all?" she countered, and it would've been flippant if not for the rasp betraying the power of hers.

"I'll exorcise them," he growled, pulling her impossibly closer. "We'll exorcise them together."

His mouth crushed hers.

On a whimper, she willingly, eagerly parted her lips for the sweet and wild invasion of his tongue. Impatiently twisted hers around his, dueling, parrying, meeting him thrust for thrust, stroke for stroke. With her hands free, she fisted the lapels of his tuxedo jacket, not caring that she was wrinkling the clothes that no doubt had cost thousands. Nothing mattered except the taste of him, the power of him, the raw passion he whipped to a frenzy in her.

Greedy for more, she rose to her tiptoes, the stilettos she still wore aiding in the endeavor. She opened wider for him, silently demanding he take more, give her more. The hand on her nape shifted upward, tunneling through her hair, twisting, tugging. Tiny pinpricks danced across her scalp, and every one of them echoed in a path down her spine, settling in the small of her back. Restless, she slid her hands up his chest, over his shoulders and into his shorter hair. Clutching the strands, she held him to her, drowning in this kiss that should be either illegalized or memorialized.

Joshua tore his mouth from hers, trailing a scorching path over her chin and down her throat, licking and sucking. She slicked the tip of her tongue over her kiss-swollen lips, savoring the flavor of him on her. Teeth scraped over her collarbone, and she tipped her head to the side, granting him easier access. Her lashes fluttered, lowering, and she basked in each gloriously wicked sensation.

And yet, it wasn't enough.

An urgent need to touch bare skin—his bare skin— riding her, she released him to dive her hands beneath his tuxedo jacket and shove it over his shoulders and down his arms. He straightened, staring down at her from beneath a hooded gaze, letting her strip him. Unable to meet it, she dipped her head, focusing on loosening the buttons down the front of his dress shirt. And as she revealed inch after inch of taut golden skin, all traces of awkwardness vanished. She sighed, fingers slightly shaking, anticipation soaring through her. When she pushed the last button through its corresponding hole, she placed her palms on his corrugated abs, her sigh transforming into a dark, low moan at first contact of skin to skin.

Jesus, did the man harbor a furnace in his big body? Heat simmered underneath her hands, skating up her arms, over her chest and tightening her nipples beneath her dress before flowing farther south to culminate between her wet, trembling thighs. She squeezed them together and shuddered as it only increased the aching emptiness. The desperate need.

"You're so beautiful," she breathed, stroking up his chest and under the open sides of the shirt, slowly peeling it, too, from his body so it tumbled to the floor with his jacket. "Like a work of art."

She stiffened as soon as the words tumbled from her lips and jerked her gaze from his magnificent form to his face. But if her slip caused him any pain, he didn't show it. Or maybe, in this place where they were baring the bodies and just a little bit of themselves, the thought of his former passion didn't bother him.

Or maybe she was assigning more importance, more intimacy to this night of sex than it warranted.

Regardless, he deserved to be admired. To be worshipped. Smooth, tight skin stretched across wide shoulders and chest and down over a flat, ridged stomach. Brown hair dusted across his pecs and narrowed to a silken line that bisected the ladder of abs. Twin grooves lined both hips, disappearing beneath the waistband of his pants. Heeding the call and invitation of that delineated arrow, she followed the lines with her fingertips, dipping beneath the band...

"Slow down," Joshua ordered in a sharp voice that carried a bit of a snap. He emphasized the command by grabbing her wrists and, turning her with his body, pressed her back against the window. Transferring both of her wrists to one hand, he lifted her arms above her head, caging them against the cool glass, as well. It didn't stop her from twisting in his grip, arching toward him. Rolling her hips over the prominent thickness tenting the front of his slacks. "Dammit, Sophie," he growled.

Then, with a jerk that left her breathless, he yanked down her dress, exposing her breasts to the air, his glittering gaze and, *oh God*, his mouth.

She cried out, her knees close to collapsing as he sucked so hard on her, the pull of it resonated high and deep in her sex. Could she orgasm just from this? Before Joshua, she would've scoffed at the idea of it, but with his tongue curling around her nipple, flicking it, drawing on it—she was a convert. Especially with her feminine flesh spasming, her hips bucking, seeking to grind that same flesh over him…

"Josh," she pleaded, tugging against his hold. "Please. Let me touch you." Yes, she was begging. And didn't care.

He loosened his grip, and she immediately took advantage, clutching his shoulders, digging her nails into the dense muscle. His grunt of pleasure fueled her on, and she raked a path down his back, then surrendered to the need to just…hold him.

Wrapping an arm around his shoulders and the other around his head, she embraced him, savoring the heat of him, the power of him even as he continued to sensually torment her flesh. Tipping her head back against the glass, she released another cry when he switched breasts, treating it to the same attention as its twin. Big, clever fingers plucked at and pinched the damp tip his lips didn't surround. He was driving her crazy. And damn if she wasn't enjoying the trip.

"No, don't stop." The plea escaped her along with a whimper when he dragged his mouth from her breasts down her stomach. She burrowed her fingers through his hair, cradling his head, attempting to pull him back.

"Not done, sweetheart," he murmured, straightening to swing her up in his arms. Once more rendering her lungs incapable of taking in air with both the show of strength and the softly spoken endearment.

They didn't go far. Just across the room to the dark freestanding fireplace. He lowered her back to the floor and, in seconds, had her side zipper down, the dress gone, and leaving her clothed in a skimpy black thong and silver heels. Her toes curled inside her shoes. For several long, charged moments, he stared down at her, his eyes more brown than green. Lust burned in them, throwing more kindling on the same fire razing her to the ground.

"Why do you hide this gorgeous body under those clothes," he ground out, his fingers flexing next to his thighs. "But if I'd known those conservative shirts covered these perfect breasts and lovely nipples… Or had a clue those knee-length skirts slid over these sweet little curves—" he slid a hand over her hip "—and legs created for squeezing a man's hips tight… Or how pretty and wet you would be—" he cupped her, and she swallowed a small scream at the possessive touch "—I would've had you up on my desk the first day you walked into my office, pretty much telling me to go screw myself. Did you know I wanted you then, Sophie? That I was picturing you laid out on top of my files and spreadsheets, your thighs wide, letting me pound inside you until everyone on the other side of that door knew that I was taking you, owning every scream and cry? Owning you?"

Shock rippled through her. At his explicit words and that he'd wanted her as far back as when she'd charged into his office. A tenderness that had no place between them tried to infiltrate the lust, but she battled it back. Self-preservation. She had to keep this about the sex.

Joshua didn't give her an opportunity to respond—if she'd been able to anyway—because he knelt between her legs. After whisking off her shoes, he stroked his hands up her calves, over her knees and palmed her inner thighs. Her breath, loud in her own ears, soughed in and out of her chest as she waited for him to graze the swollen, damp flesh covered by black lace. Air whispered over her but did nothing to cool the heat building inside her, stoked by his words and caresses.

His fingertips danced over her, and with a mewl that would probably embarrass her later, she rocked into the too-light but too-much touch. Sensitive and so deprived, her sex clenched hard, sending a spasm through her. She was ready to beg, to write a freaking formal entreaty, if he would only give her what her body literally wept for when he tugged aside the soaked panel of her panties and plunged a thick, long finger inside her.

She screamed.

And shattered. The release swept through her, over her, the pinched quality of it bordering on pain. It was good. So good. But still not enough. Even as the final waves of orgasm ebbed, the need returned, brewing underneath the blissed-out lethargy.

With a snarl curling his lips, Joshua yanked her panties down her useless legs and spread her wide for him. He dived into her, his mouth covering her still-quivering flesh, his tongue curling around the pulsing button of nerves cresting her mound. He growled against her, the sound vibrating against her, shoving her closer to sensory overload. He lapped at her, sucked, feasted on her in a way that should've been lewd, but instead was hot as hell.

"Josh." His name burst from her, a half shout, half whimper. Pleasure ratcheted from simmering to full-out conflagration. Her fingers drove into his hair, gripping his head, holding him to her. Pushing him away.

Too much.

Oh God, not enough.

He had to stop.

She'd kill him if he dared to stop.

If her mind was conflicted, her body knew what it wanted. What it craved. Her hips bucked and rolled under his mouth, urging him on. Demanding he give her everything he had. And as her lower back tightened and tingled in that telltale sign of impending orgasm, she gasped. Never, as in *never*, had she come more than once. She didn't think it possible for her. But the jerking of her hips, the shaking of her limbs, belied that belief, proving that she just needed the right partner to bring her to the brink of pleasure—and surpass it.

No. Not the right partner.

Joshua.

Another scream built in her throat, scratching its way up when he pulled away. Leaving her aching, throbbing, *hurting* on the edge of release.

"What?" she rasped. "Please." The two words were all she could manage, lust and an aborted orgasm confusing her.

Above her, Joshua surged to his feet. He snatched his wallet from his pants and tossed it on the floor next to her shoulder. In seconds, he wrenched his pants, shoes and socks from his big body, leaving him standing extraordinarily, unbearably beautiful before her. Joshua clothed in suits and tuxedos was gorgeous. Naked, stripped of all signs of civility, was...devastating.

As if drawn to him by an invisible thread, she sat up, rising to her knees, settling her palms on lean, powerfully muscled thighs that flexed under her palms. She sighed, sliding them up the defined columns...reaching for the thick, heavy, long length of him.

"No." His long fingers caught her hand before she could touch him. He knelt between her legs again, pressing her palm to his mouth and placing a searing openmouthed kiss there. "If I let you get your hand on me, this would be over quick. And, sweetheart, when I come, I plan to do it buried balls deep inside you, not on these pretty fingers."

He leaned over her, grabbing his wallet and removing a square foil packet. Quickly, he ripped it open and sheathed himself, then, *thank God*, he was over her, his erection nudging her entrance. Slowly pressing into her. Stretching her. Burning her.

Branding her.

Pain and pleasure mixed in a wicked, confusing blend that sent quakes rippling through her.

"Shh," Joshua crooned, brushing a kiss over her cheekbone, temple and, finally, lips. "Easy, sweetheart. You can take me. All of me." Until his reassurances, she hadn't been aware of the whimpers spilling from her or the restless shifting to get closer, to back away... She didn't know. The pressure of his possession... It filled her almost to overflowing. It overwhelmed her.

For a stark second, panic seized her. In this moment, she felt owned. Not just herself anymore. With him planted so deep inside her, she didn't belong to herself—she belonged to him. To them.

"Look at me, Sophie," he murmured, the soft tone carrying an underlying vein of steel. She couldn't help but obey and opened her eyes to meet his. Golden flames burned in a nearly dark brown field, scorching her. "Do you have any idea how you feel to me? So wet, tight like the most brutal fist but utterly fucking perfect surrounding me, squeezing me. Holding me. It's the sweetest hell. I might be covering you... I might be so goddamn deep I don't know if I can find my way out... But you have the control here. The power. So what are you going to do with me, Sophie? What are you going to do with us?"

His corded arms bracketed her head, and he held his large frame suspended above her, a very fine tremor running through him and belying the gentleness of his voice. And his words. God, they seeped into her, heating her, relaxing her tense muscles, dulling the edges of pain until only the pleasure of his dominance, his possession remained.

She released her grip on his upper arms and, sliding her hands up and over his shoulders, wound her arms around his neck, pulling him down for a slow, raw kiss.

"I'm going to take you. I'm going to wreck us," she whispered against his lips.

Hunger, dark and fierce, flashed in his gaze, but also delight flared bright and quick. Claiming control of the kiss, he pulled free from her body, then sank back inside, dragging a soft cry from her. Lifting her legs, she wrapped them around his waist, and he hissed, surging deeper. Filling her more. Thrust for thrust, she met him, taking him just as she promised. Wrecking them with each roll of her hips, each wet, voracious kiss, each scratch of her nails and whispered demand for "more, harder."

Carnal. Wild. Hot.

Joshua rode her hard, granting her no mercy. He buried himself inside her over and over, setting off sizzling currents with each drag of his cock through her channel. She cried out with the intensity of the pleasure, from the onslaught of it. Twisting and writhing beneath him, she chased the orgasm that loomed so close.

"Josh," she pleaded, desperate, greedy.

"Give it to me, Sophie," he ground out. "Come for me."

He palmed one of her thighs, spreading her wider, lifting her into his thrusting body. Sliding the other hand down between her breasts, he didn't stop until he circled the nerve-packed nub nestled between her folds. Thrust. Circle. Thrust. Circle.

The scream ripped from her throat as she exploded. For a moment, she fought against the release, afraid of the sheer ferocity and wildness of it. But it swelled stronger, swamping her, threatening to break her. Then reshape her into someone she was afraid she'd no longer recognize.

Closing her eyes, she surrendered.

Chapter 7

Joshua stared at his computer monitor, but just like the previous hour, the report from his chief financial officer remained a blurred jumble of numbers.

"Dammit." Disgusted, he threw his pen down on his desk and shot to his feet. His chair rolled back, bumping against the bookcase behind it.

He scrubbed a hand down his face, then wrapped it around the back of his neck. Massaging the tense muscles there, he strode to the floor-to-ceiling window and stared out. Usually, the sight of the parking lot full of his employees' cars sent a surge of satisfaction spiraling through him. There'd been a time after he'd taken over Black Crescent when the lot had been almost empty. Only he, Haley and a few other loyal staff members had remained when the company fell apart. Those days had been…grim. Though he'd kept up a stalwart front for everyone, he'd been terrified. Of failing to rebuild the company and paying back the families his father had devastated. Of letting down those few who'd still believed in and trusted him when his father hadn't given them a reason to.

Of proving those who'd condemned him with "like father, like son" right.

His father. It always came back to him.

But it wasn't Vernon who had him distracted and unable to concentrate this Monday morning. How easy it would be to place the blame on him instead of *her*.

Sophie.

As if just the thought of her name jammed open a door he'd padlocked shut, images from Saturday night rushed through his head, a ceaseless stream of erotic snapshots.

Sophie, hips rolling and bucking to meet his devouring mouth as he held her thighs spread wide for him.

Sophie, twisting and undulating beneath him, voice cracking as she begged him to possess her harder.

Sophie, body arched tight, beautiful breasts pointed toward the ceiling, eyes glazed with pleasure as she came so hard it required every bit of his tattered control to prevent immediately following her.

Sophie, curled up against his side, her head resting on his shoulder, her soft, even breath caressing his damp skin. Her small, delicate hand splayed wide on his chest.

If the mental flashes of her uninhibited passion had his body hardening and arousal clenching his gut, then it was the memory of her cuddled into his body, sleeping so trustingly, that had a vise grip squeezing his heart.

And that grip unnerved him.

One night. No strings. That had been their agreement. The reasons for it—for him, at least—hadn't changed come the morning when they dressed in silence and he drove her home.

She was a reporter who had just done a story on him and his family. How he'd let his guard down Saturday night and confessed his unhappiness about his life and the jacked-up state of his family even before the scandal still astonished him. That—his penchant to reveal things he'd never told another soul—was her superpower. And his downfall. He'd basically handed her information for her follow-up on him, and if she did write it, he had no one to blame but himself.

What was it about this woman that made him so vulnerable? That had him ignoring every self-protective instinct?

He couldn't do that again. Couldn't afford to. Couldn't afford to open Black Crescent up to any more controversy and couldn't afford to let her in. To open his heart.

Everyone he'd ever loved had abandoned him. His father with going on the lam. His mother by mentally leaving him. His brothers by withdrawing from him, then icing him out of their lives.

No, if she hadn't set the limits on their one night of the hottest sex he'd ever had or believed possible, then he would've.

"Joshua, I've been buzzing you," Haley announced from behind him. He pivoted sharply, bemused. He'd been so deep in thought he hadn't heard the phone intercom or his assistant enter his office. "Where were you just now?"

He shook his head, slicing a hand through the air to wave away her question. "Just going over my eleven o'clock appointment with Clark Reynolds from Venture Investments. What'd you need?"

Haley tilted her head, studying him through a narrowed gaze. She didn't outright accuse him of lying, but the speculation in her hazel eyes did. "Nice try. But deflection has never worked with me. Are you sure you weren't just mooning over Sophie Armstrong?"

He snorted, striding back toward his desk. "I've never mooned a day in my life."

"I know. And that's your problem."

"My problem?" He sank into his chair. "I wasn't aware I had one. Well, other than a bossy executive assistant who doesn't know when to let stuff go."

"Oh, you have one," she drawled, folding into the armchair across from his desk. Leaning forward, her dark blond eyebrows drew together in a frown. "When was the last time your life didn't revolve around this company, the employees or paying back the families affected by the scandal?"

"Haley," Joshua said, stiffening. "I don't—"

"I know you don't want to talk about it. You never do," she cut him off. "That's another problem. You might be the savior of Black Crescent, Josh, but that's not all you are. You deserve more. You deserve to have time to yourself, take a vacation. Leave this place at a decent hour. Have a private life. Yes, you've had relationships in the past, but when was the last time you just let yourself fall for someone? Let them interfere with your carefully regimented schedule and order? Let them make your life messy with laughter and love? I know the answer to all those questions. Never."

Joshua clenched his jaw, trapping the heated words that threatened to burst free. He didn't want to hurt her feelings. Haley might be his assistant, but she was also family. Like his younger sister. But this topic was off-limits. "Haley, I don't want to hurt your feelings. But this is—"

"None of my business, I know. But this—" she stood and set down the tablet she held on the desk, sliding it toward him "—makes it everyone's business."

He stared at her for several moments before dropping his gaze to the screen. His irritation evaporated, dissolved by shock.

Pictures from Saturday night's art gala. Some depicted him and other partygoers, including the redhead he'd been seated next to at dinner, who'd propositioned him with a nightcap after the event. Those images didn't ensnare his attention or had his heart pounding like an anvil against his chest. Didn't have desire flaming bright and hot inside him.

The photograph of Sophie, so beautiful in the silver strapless gown that had molded to her slim figure and highlighted every curve, and him standing outside the museum had him battling back the surge of lust brewing low in his stomach.

Unlike with the redhead, he'd lost the polite but aloof mask he usually donned at those occasions. Though a small distance separated them, he stared down at her with an intensity—a hunger—that was anything but polite. And Sophie, head tipped back, exhibited a vulnerability that he immediately hated the photographer for capturing.

He tore his gaze away from the image and scanned the caption underneath.

Black Crescent Hedge Fund CEO Joshua Lowell

*and mystery guest...or date? Could it be the famous—
or infamous—businessman is finally settling down?*

Flicking a glance to the top of the page, he glimpsed
the name of the site. And fisted his fingers next to the
tablet. A notorious gossip website that focused on dish-
ing dirty on high society. If he had a dollar for every
time his or his family's names had been mentioned in
this column, he'd have been able to compensate the
bankrupted families years ago, and with interest.

Dammit. Had Sophie seen this? Possibly not. She
might be a reporter, but she was also an investigative
journalist. Not some gossipmonger.

"What's going on between you and Sophie Armstrong?" Haley asked softly.

He jerked his head up, having momentarily forgotten
she stood across from him. "Nothing. She happened to
attend the same gala as I did, and we were leaving at
the same time. She wasn't my date."

"The columnist mentioned you two left together.
That she got into your car," Haley persisted.

Dammit. Anger pulled hard and tight inside him.
Fucking media. "I gave her a ride home since we were
both headed back to Falling Brook. End of story." If the
end of the story included his driving into Sophie's sweet
body on a rug that he wouldn't ever be able to walk by
again without seeing her coming apart on it.

Haley silently studied him again, her scrutiny too
seeing, too knowing. "Neither of your faces say 'casual
acquaintance' or 'friendly ride home.'" Before he could
snarl a reply, she continued, voice soft, "And I'm glad."

He frowned, taken aback. "You're glad my privacy
was invaded and I'm now a topic of speculation and
gossip? Again."

Haley straightened, a flicker of emotion rippling across her face. But before he could decipher it, she arched an eyebrow, her eyes direct and unwavering. "No, I'm positively delighted that someone has managed to get through that thick layer of 'back the hell off' that you've wrapped yourself in these past fifteen years. I'm happy that you've found someone that you would let down your guard long enough to be captured by some random photographer. Because whether or not you want to admit it—or are ready to admit it—she *is* important to you. Now I'm just praying that you don't mess it up by pushing her away."

She turned away and strode across his office and left, closing the door behind her with a quick snick. But her warning reverberated in the room like a report of a gunshot.

I'm just praying that you don't mess it up by pushing her away.

Mess it up? Push her away?

He'd have to let her in first.

And that wasn't happening. Ever.

Chapter 8

What the hell am I doing here?

The question ricocheted off Joshua's skull as he sat in the back seat of his Lincoln town car outside Sophie's apartment building. Showing up here after the photo of them on the gossip site didn't rank among his smartest decisions. If anyone saw him here, it would only feed the fires of speculation. But he'd tried to call her to see if she'd seen it and give her a heads-up if she hadn't. Either she hadn't seen his phone call or she'd refused to answer, because he hadn't been able to reach her.

Logic argued that he leave it alone—leave her alone. But the thought of her being blindsided... Well, here he was sitting outside her home like some kind of goddamn stalker. Growling a curse, he shoved open the back door.

"John, I'll give you a call when I'm finished here," he instructed his driver.

The younger man behind the wheel nodded. "Yes, sir."

Closing the door shut, he stalked across the street and up to the two-story brick building with its neat side lawns and sidewalk bordered by honeysuckle. Just as he approached the door, a couple with a small child pushed through the entrance.

"Oops, sorry 'bout that," the man apologized with a grin. "This one's a little anxious to hit the park."

"No, no, it's fine," Joshua said, stepping out of the way and catching the door before it could close.

But his gaze remained ensnared by the little girl who couldn't have been older than four years old. The same age the child Sophie accused him of having was supposed to be. A sudden longing jerked hard in his chest, catching him by surprise. Years ago, when the world had been his to conquer, he'd wanted what this husband and father had—family.

Now? Now, a wife, a child... They just meant a person had more to lose.

Shaking his head, he moved into the large lobby, letting the door close behind him. An elevator ride later, he stood in front of Sophie's apartment. Before he could again question the wisdom of being here, he knocked. And waited. And knocked again.

Hell. He glanced down at his watch: 6:48 p.m. She should've been home by now, but then again, Sophie had the same work ethic as he did. It was one of the things he admired about her despite her choice of career. So she very well could still be at the office.

He had turned and taken a step away from her door when it opened.

"Sophie," he greeted, running his gaze from the brown-and-gold wavy strands that fell over the shoulders of a purple slouchy T-shirt that hung off one shoulder, down the black leggings to her bare feet with pink-painted toes. Dragging his perusal back up, he couldn't look at her—not those slender, toned thighs, high, firm breasts or lovely dove-gray eyes—without thinking of how she'd looked, naked and damp from sweat, under him.

"Joshua, what are you doing here?" Joshua, not Josh, as she'd called him for most of those hot, dark hours they'd spent together.

Part of him wanted to demand she call him the shortened version again. And in that sex-drenched, husky voice. Instead, he slid his hands in his pants pockets and kept a careful distance between them.

"I needed to talk with you about something. I'm sorry for dropping by unannounced, but you weren't answering your phone today."

"Yes." She thrust a hand through her hair, drawing the strands away from her face. "I saw the missed calls. I intended to call you back but just got really busy."

He cocked his head. "You make a shitty liar, Sophie."

She dropped her arm, heaving a sigh. "What are you doing here, Joshua?" she repeated.

"I need to talk to you. And not out here in the hallway."

"I—" Indecision flicked in her eyes, her full lips flattening. Finally, after a brief hesitation, she nodded and stepped back. "Fine. Only for a minute, though. I'm working."

Suspicion flared quick and hot in his chest. Was she writing the follow-up article on him? On what he'd revealed to her? He hadn't stipulated that Saturday night had been off the record. Would she…?

He snuffed the thoughts out as he entered her apartment and closed the door behind him. But the embers of doubt... He couldn't extinguish them. How messed up was it that he harbored reservations about her trustworthiness, but he still wanted her with a hunger that gave him stomach pains?

"Can I get you something? I was about to fix a cup of coffee. But I have wine or a bottle of water," Sophie said.

The reluctance in her offer had a corner of his mouth quirking into a humorless half smile. Good manners probably had her extending the courtesy instead of truly wanting him to stick around and enjoy a drink.

So he accepted.

"Coffee is fine."

Again, her lips tightened, but she headed to the kitchen that was separated from the living room by a breakfast bar. Taking the opportunity, he surveyed the apartment. Though on the small side, the living room with its overstuffed couches, wood coffee and end tables and big arched windows appeared cozy rather than cramped. Lived in. Compared with his condo, her place was a home, not a place to just crash instead of the office sofa.

The room flowed into a space that could've been a dining area but Sophie had jammed with filled-to-overflowing bookcases, a tiny love seat and lamps. A reading nook. Easily he could imagine her curled up on those cushions, book in hand.

He tore his gaze away, returning it to her as she finished up the second coffee in the one-cup brewer. Though irritation practically vibrated off her petite frame, her movements were fluid, graceful.

"What are you working on?" he asked, needing to

remind himself of who she was. What she did. What she was capable of.

"The follow-up article from my visit to Black Crescent. I need to have it in by the end of the week."

There it was. The reminder. Ice trickled through his veins. Yes, he'd invited her into the inner sanctum of his company and revealed the programs that were close to his heart, but now, tiny pinpricks of doubts stabbed at him over that decision.

"What?" Sophie propped a hip against the counter and crossed her arms over her chest. "Having second thoughts? *You* asked *me* to Black Crescent, remember? This time I didn't force my way in," she drawled.

"I don't need any help remembering...anything," he said, and yes, it made him an asshole to feel hot satisfaction well in him as slashes of red painted her high cheekbones. But he didn't care. Not when she couldn't hide the gleam of arousal in her eyes before abruptly turning back to the counter and the coffee cups.

"Do you take sugar or cream?" she rasped. And the sound of the slightly hoarse tone...

He barely stopped himself from stalking across the space separating them and pressing his chest to her ramrod-straight spine. From notching his hard dick just above the tempting curve of her perfect ass.

"Black," he ground out.

Seconds later, she handed him the mug with Shouldn't You Be Writing? emblazoned along the side along with a picture of a shirtless Thor and his hammer. He would've assumed the choice in cup was by accident if a smirk didn't ride the corner of her mouth.

"Cute," he drawled.

"It's one of my favorites. Nothing but the best for

you," she purred, strolling past him with her own plain
black mug back into the living room, where her laptop
sat propped on the coffee table in front of the couch.
"Not that I don't doubt my coffee is wonderful, but what
are you really doing here, Joshua?"

The pointed question shoved away any vestiges of
humor, and he took a sip of the steaming-hot, fragrant
brew before replying. "Pictures of us together from the
art gala were posted online in a society gossip column. I
didn't know if you were aware. But in case you weren't,
I wanted to give you a heads-up. Although you weren't
named, the columnist included some speculation about
our relationship to one another."

She huffed out a dry laugh. "Oh yes, I already know
about it. Althea called me into her office today and
asked if anything was going on between us. She's worried about the conflict of interest for the paper if the reporter of the story on Black Crescent is involved with
the CEO."

"What did you tell her?"

"I told her no, of course."

"So you lied," Joshua drawled.

If he hadn't been watching her so closely, he might've
missed the slight tremble in her hand as she set her mug
on the coffee table. But he didn't. And he had to battle
back the urge to cross the floor, take that hand, lift it
and still the shivering with his mouth.

"It wasn't a lie. There isn't anything between us.
Saturday was one night. One time. That was our deal."

"And if I want to renegotiate the deal?" he murmured.

The same shock that widened her eyes reverberated
through him. Where had that come from? Asking for

another night—another taste of her lips, another chance to drive into that sweet little body—hadn't been his intention when he'd pulled up outside her building. *Warn her, get out.* That had been the plan. But lust had overridden common sense and hijacked his mouth. But he couldn't exist within four feet of her and not crave her. Not want a repeat of the night that was branded into his memory with startling and unnerving clarity. Maybe he just needed to convince himself that his brain had exaggerated the pleasure he experienced. That nothing could be that good in reality.

And maybe he was just seeking an excuse to get her under him again.

He still didn't trust her. Didn't 100 percent believe that she wasn't using him for another story. But none of that stopped his dick from throbbing like a toothache—insistent, hurting and needing relief.

"Joshua…" She shook her head, ducking her head as she pinched the bridge of her nose. "I don't think—"

"Look at me, Sophie," he ordered, setting his cup on the breakfast bar behind him. He moved farther into the living room, not stopping until only inches separated them. She lifted her gaze to his, and her obedience in this when she refused to give it to him anywhere else had excitement and arousal plowing through him. "Look at me and tell me that you're not already feeling my hands on you. Tell me your nipples aren't already hardening, begging for my fingers, my tongue. Tell me you're not already hot and wet for me, desperate to have me stretching you again, filling you." He grasped her chin between his thumb and forefinger, tilting her head farther back. "You can tell me all of that, Sophie, and I'll walk out of here."

Her moist, warm breath broke on her parted lips, echoing in the room. For several long moments, she stared up at him with those molten silver eyes, her slender body swaying toward his, as if seeking his warmth, his possession.

A shudder worked through her, and, lowering her lashes, she stepped back, breaking his hold on her.

Rubbing her hands up and down her arms, she turned away from him. *Give me those eyes. Look at me*, battered his tongue, needing to get out. But he clenched his teeth, trapping the command. Pride imprisoned what sounded too damn close to a plea.

"Is it so easy for you?" she whispered.

He frowned, shifting forward, reclaiming a little of the distance she'd inserted. It was an unconscious movement, as if his body couldn't stand not feeling her warmth or being wrapped in her scent.

"Is what easy for me?" he pressed.

"This." Pivoting to face him again, she waved a hand between them. "You don't trust me," she said flatly.

"No," he replied, just as blunt. "I don't."

Hurt spasmed across her face, but in the next instant her expression hardened into a cool mask that somehow appeared so wrong on her. Like an ill-fitting dress.

"Then why would you want to be with someone you believe would possibly sell you out for a story?" she scoffed, but a thin line of anger edged the question.

"A relationship with you and fucking are two different things," he said, voice hard, matter-of-fact. "And if that's what you're looking for from me, then we can end this now. I don't do long-term commitments. I'm not the man who can give you the happy home with a perfect, smiling family and well-behaved dog. But I am the man who can make you come so hard it hurts. Yes, Sophie. I'll make it hurt in the very best way," he murmured, lust gripping him so hard, so tight, he could barely draw in a breath. "I don't need to trust you for that."

Her thick fringe of lashes lowered, and her hooded silver gaze razed his skin. Red stained her cheeks and that lush mouth appeared even plumper, bitable. The aloof coldness had evaporated from her expression, leaving this one behind. And he recognized it. This face, stamped with arousal, had haunted his every waking and sleeping hour since Saturday night.

Yet, he couldn't deny glimpsing the flicker of pain beneath the lust.

Before his mind could check him, he took a step toward her to…what? Ease it? Order her to tell him how to make it disappear?

She shot a hand up, palm out, and he halted.

Thank God.

"I have my own stipulations. I don't have your trust, fine. But I will have your fidelity. While we're doing… this arrangement, you don't sleep with anyone else. Just me."

"Of course," he growled. "And the same with you. I'm the only man inside you."

"Of course," she said, throwing his words back at him with a snap. "And at any time either of us wants out, it's over." He nodded, but she continued, "One last thing. This stays here. No one else knows. Anyone finding out could cost me my job. I might be losing some of my pride entering into this with you, but I refuse to lose my career."

She murmured the last part of that almost to herself, and he scowled. What the hell did that mean? Before he could demand an explanation, though, she stuck out her hand toward him, the fingertips nudging his chest.

"Deal?" she asked.

He stared down at it, anger and wild, raw need crowding into him. Pride? Being with him stripped her of pride? What else could he strip her of?

Grasping her wrist, he tugged her hand up to his mouth. And licked the center of her palm, swirling his tongue over the soft flesh. Her gasp reverberated around them, and she tried to curl her fingers into her palm, but he stayed the motion with his other hand, holding her spread wide for him. He flicked a wet caress in between each finger before sinking his teeth into the heel of her palm.

A shudder racked her body, followed by a throaty moan that had his dick twitching.

"Joshua," she whimpered.

"Josh," he corrected, voice harsh, roughened by the hunger that gnawed at him like a voracious beast. "Say it." He trailed a finger down the elegant line of her throat, tracing the shallow dip in the middle of her collarbone.

"Josh," she whispered, and her swift capitulation was a stroke over his thick, pulsing flesh. And a caress to his pounding heart. She moved forward until her thighs bumped his and her breasts plumped against his chest. He fought to lock down the urge that howled at him to take her down to the floor and claim. Rising to the tips of her bare toes, she brought her mouth a breath away. He slid his tongue out, brushing that temptation of a full bottom lip. "Josh," she repeated, softer, huskier.

In answer, in reward, he took her mouth.

Releasing her hand, he cradled her jaw, pressing his

thumb on her chin and tugging down to open her more to him. She tilted her head, complying. Breathing a snarl into her, he thrust his tongue past her lips, rubbing and twisting, coaxing her to play with him. Not that she needed any persuading. She met him, danced with him. Dared him. Nails digging into his shoulders through his suit jacket, she coiled her tongue with his, sucking hard, and the pull arrowed straight to his dick.

A savage, almost animalist burst of lust exploded within him, and he bent his knees to cup her ass in both hands and straightened, hauling her up his body. Her legs wound around his waist, her arms around his neck, settling her sex right over his erection. *Goddamn.* He clenched his molars together, reaching for his rapidly dwindling control. Still, nothing could stop him from punching his hips forward and stroking her up and down his dick. Her thin yoga pants and his slacks might as well as have been created of air. Her folds slipped over him, shooting electric pulses down his spine.

"Bedroom?" he ground out.

"Down the hall," she rasped. "Last door on the right."

In the small apartment, it didn't take long to find her room. With long, impatient strides, he entered and headed straight for the bed. Carefully, he lowered her to the floor, sliding his hands up over her hips, the indents of her waist, the sides of her breasts until he held her face in his hands. Tipping her head back, he stared into her eyes. And though desire rode him like a jockey hell-bent on leather, he paused, seeking any flicker of hesitation, of second thoughts.

"I need to hear you say it, Sophie," he said, his voice seeming to boom in the tense quiet of the bedroom.

"Say you want this. You want me to touch you. You want me inside you."

He waited. And he would continue to wait. Because a part of him—the stubborn part that grief, pain and betrayal hadn't managed to amputate—*had* to hear her utter those words. Craved it like a drowning man seeking that life-giving gulp of air.

"I want this. I want you," she whispered, threading her fingers through his hair and pulling his head down until their noses bumped and her lips grazed his. "I want you to touch me. Want you so deep inside me I'll feel you tomorrow. Will you give it to me, Josh?"

He didn't answer her. At least not with words. But with his mouth, his tongue, his hands? God, yes. He dug his fingers into her hips, jerking her closer so she would have no doubts of her effect on him. Unable to help himself, he ground his cock into the softness of her belly, even as he devoured her mouth. And she held nothing back from him. Not her response, not her sexy little whimpers and cries. Had a woman ever fully let herself be so uninhibited, so vulnerable with him before?

No.

And he'd never been that way with another woman.

But with Sophie? Regardless of his claims of not trusting her, he couldn't throw up his protective shields with her. Not in this.

Here, they could be fully honest with each other. Naked in more than the baring of bodies.

Naked. As soon as the word entered his head, the longing, the greed in him intensified until it became a chant in his head.

Tearing his mouth from hers, he fisted the bottom of her T-shirt and yanked it over her head. And *oh God.*

"All that time you were offering me coffee and arguing with me, you didn't have a bra on?" he snarled, palming her pretty, firm breasts and thumbing the pink nipples. Already tight, they pebbled further, and Jesus himself couldn't have stopped him from dipping his head and having a taste. And when she tugged on his hair, her groan accompanying the pricks across his scalp, he indulged himself and sucked her into his mouth, lashing the tip. Pulling free, he rubbed his lips across the beaded flesh. "If I'd known you were bare underneath that top, you would've been against the wall with my mouth on you as soon as I closed that door."

He grazed her with his teeth, wringing another cry from her. It became his mission to drag them from her, to earn a shudder from her slender frame. His mission and his pleasure.

While he switched from one breast to the other, Sophie removed his jacket, pushing it off his shoulders and arms, casting it to the floor. His shirt followed. Her nails raked down his bare back, trailing fire in their wake, and it was his turn to shiver.

Releasing her with a soft pop, he straightened, shifting forward and moving her backward until the backs of her knees hit the edge of the mattress. But at the last second, she twisted and, grabbing his upper arms, turned him. They switched positions, and she pressed her palms to his chest, her touch like live coals on his skin.

"My turn," she said, eyes so bright he swept a thumb underneath one. Then brushed his lips over the same spot. "Can't distract me," she breathed, and pushed.

He sank to the bed, his palms slapping down beside his thighs. She didn't hesitate, but knelt in front of him,

and his thighs automatically spread, making room for
her. His breath hitched in his lungs, and his body froze.
Anticipation, lust and excitement hurtled through him,
and he could only stare down at this beautiful, sensual
creature as she fumbled with his thin leather belt and
the closure to his pants.

The metallic grind of the zipper ricocheted through
the room, deafening in his ears. She pushed the edges
apart, exposing his black boxer briefs. Together, they
studied the almost obscene bulge of his thick, long erection. Was she remembering the same thing as he? How
he fit inside that too-tight and too-perfect sex? How
he'd had to work his way inside her, claiming her bit
by bit as she softened around him, strangling his dick
even as she embraced it?

Because, God, he remembered. Remembered and
wanted it so bad he'd become one huge walking ache.

Finally, when she snagged the waistband, his paral-
ysis broke. He covered her hand with his, squeezing.

"You don't have to do this, sweetheart," he rumbled,
offering her an out. Even though the thought of her
tongue sliding down his column nearly had him coming without one touch.

"I know I don't *have* to," she said, lifting her gaze
from his cloth-covered dick to meet his. "I *want* to."

Then she was gripping him. Stroking him.

Pleasure so sharp it danced on the edge of pain seized
him, and, head thrown back, palms flattened on the
mattress, he strained against it.

Nothing, *fucking nothing*, had ever felt as good as
this woman's hand on his cock.

Oh damn.

He stood corrected. Hot, wet warmth bathed the

head, followed by gentle swipes of a tongue. His head jacked forward, *needing* to take in the sight of Sophie with her mouth full of his flesh.

Locking his muscles, he fought down the ball of fire coalescing and swirling at the base of his spine and lower. God, he was going to come. Right down her throat from just the swipe of her tongue. He closed his eyes but, seconds later, snapped them open, unable to not look. To stare. To behold this picture of knee-shaking carnality and brand it on his brain.

Lashes lowered, color painted her sharp cheekbones and one of those hungry whimpers escaped her as she swallowed him down, tongue rubbing, mouth sucking. Her fist pumped the bottom half of his pounding column, and her damp lips bumped her fingers each time she bobbed over him. Up and down, she tortured him, loving him, making him her slave.

Because right now he would do anything for her if she. Just. Didn't. Stop.

"Sweetheart," he growled, and the endearment was churned-up gravel in his throat. "You're trying to break me with your greedy little mouth. And I'm going to let you do it. I'm going to let you take me apart."

His words seemed to galvanize her, to fuel her passion. Tunneling both hands in her hair and tangling them in the thick strands, he didn't try to control her, just allowed himself to be swept along in the ride.

She took him deeper and deeper until the tip of him nudged the back of her throat.

She let him slip into that narrow passage, swallowed around him.

She elicited shudder after shudder, curse after curse from him.

And when the telltale sizzle snapped and popped down his spine, legs to the soles of his feet and then back up to the base of his dick, he didn't hold back. Didn't pull her off him.

He gave her everything. Every last bit of him.

Chest heaving, he waited for the dark edges crowding his vision to retreat. Only then did he loosen his grasp on Sophie's head and suck in a much-needed breath into his screaming lungs. That orgasm should've destroyed him, laid him out. Instead, it fed the desire that still flowed through him like an open pipe.

He clutched her shoulders and, surging to his feet, dragged her up with him. In seconds, he had her naked on the bed and under him. He attacked her mouth, voracious. The taste of him on her tongue only inflamed him more. Snarling against her lips, he nipped the full bottom one, then treated her chin and throat to the same erotic bites.

Once more he feasted on her breasts, licking, lapping and tweaking until she writhed beneath him, those kitten mewls spilling from her. God, he loved them. Hoarded them in his head so he could replay them later when he was alone in his bed.

He shook his head, dislodging the thoughts and the sharp stab of loneliness they lugged along with them. Skimming his lips down the center of her chest, he paused to flick his tongue in the bowl of her navel, then continued until he reached his goal.

Inhaling, he trapped the musky sweet-and-tart scent of her. He jerked awake last night with this scent teasing him, tormenting him. Unable to resist the lure, he dipped his head and dived into her sex. One hand splayed wide on her lower belly to hold her down, he palmed her inner thigh with the other, granting him easy access to the flesh that he couldn't get enough of. Her scream danced around his ears as he slid his tongue through her swollen, soaked folds, circling the bud of nerves at the top of her mound. Over and over he returned to gorge on her like the delicious, addictive feast she was.

Her thighs clamped around his head, and her fingers dug into his hair, grasping tight, and he didn't let up. Not until he pushed her right to the edge of release—and over it.

And as she still shook and gasped on the waves of pleasure, he shoved from the bed and stripped. Removing his wallet and then a condom from the billfold, he tossed his pants to the floor and climbed back onto the mattress, crawling over her. Quickly, he sheathed his rock-hard flesh in the protection, then maneuvered her until she straddled his hips. His erection surged up between them, and he swore he could feel her labored gusts of breath on the tip.

"Ride me, sweetheart," he grated, cupping her hip and fisting his dick. "Take me."

Her eyes found his, and, without breaking their visual mating, she rose over him. Then sank down on him.

He was the first to break their locked gazes. Closing his, he released a hiss as she enveloped him, slowly accepting him. Both hands gripped her hips, steadying her. She fell forward, her palms slapping his pecs. Head bent, she pulsed up and down his flesh, taking more and more of him until, finally, she was seated on top of him. And he was so deep inside her, he had to, once more, battle back the rising of his orgasm.

"Sophie," he growled, bucking his hips as if he could

screw just a little bit more of himself inside her, when there was nothing left of him to give. "So tight. So wet. So damn hot. I didn't—" He cut himself off before he could utter the rest of the too-revealing sentence. He hadn't imagined how perfect she took him. How she undid him. "You good, sweetheart?" he asked, flexing again, unable to help himself.

"Yes," she breathed, crushing a kiss to his lips. "God, *yes.*"

"Take me, then," he ordered. "Take us both."

Lifting off him until only the head of his dick remained, she hovered for only a second before slamming back down on him.

Moments ago, he'd thought nothing had felt as good as Sophie's mouth on him. So wrong. Watching her rise and fall above him, face saturated with lust… Having her lush, muscular core sucking at him, fluttering around him—nothing could compare to this.

Jackknifing off the bed, he sat up, burrowed his fingers in her hair and captured her mouth, swallowing each sob, each whine. Wrapping her arms around his shoulders and head, she rode him, jerking on him, hips swiveling like the most carnal of dances. She wrenched her mouth from his, tipping her head back on her shoulders, lost in the pleasure she chased. The pleasure bearing down on him like a freight train with greased wheels.

Not without her, though. He wouldn't go without her.

Reaching between them, he slid his fingers down her quivering belly to the small, swollen bundle of nerves cresting her sex. One stroke. Two. Three, and he pressed down hard.

Her core clamped down hard on him like a vise grip,

feminine muscles milking him. Grabbing her hips, he held her aloft as he thrust up into her, granting her every measure of the release that shook her like a leaf in a passion-whipped storm. Only after her screams ebbed to muted whimpers did he let go, hurtling into the dark, shattering abyss of release.

As he fell, slender arms encircled him.

And he held on.

Chapter 9

Sophie rested her head on Joshua's chest, his steady heartbeat a reassuring thud under her ear. She should move. Should order him to leave since the sex was over, and her senses had winked back online. But her limbs, weighted down by postorgasmic lethargy and wrapped around his torso and thigh, wouldn't obey. Besides, when he'd left the bed to get rid of the condom, he'd returned with a warm, wet bath cloth to clean her. After that tender and thoughtful consideration, it would be rude of her to kick him out.

Okay, and that sounded weak even to her own ears.

She might as well just admit it; she wanted him here in her bed. His weight next to hers. His heartbeat echoing in her ear.

So dangerous. She was entering such treacherous, risky territory.

Saturday night, she'd been so certain that she would be able to contain the passion between them to one night. That she could walk away unscathed.

God, she'd been so arrogant.

He'd left her singed to her soul. And days later, she still felt the burn. So much that when he'd shown up on her doorstep, she'd tried to convince herself again that she could separate physical from emotional. That she didn't need his trust. Didn't need anything but another release that left her feeling like a postapocalyptic refugee.

Closing her eyes, she tried to block out the direction of her wayward thoughts, but that only caused a livestream of how she'd spent the last hour with Joshua. Of their own volition, her fingertips brushed her lips. And she shivered, experiencing again the fierceness of his possession.

He was the first man she'd gone down on. Had he been able to tell? No other had stirred the need to share that intimacy, to make herself so vulnerable. To give so much—her mouth, her throat…her control.

But Joshua wasn't just any man.

Somehow, he'd sneaked beneath her carefully constructed armor and touched more than her body. He'd infiltrated her heart.

Terror barreled through her as she admitted the truth to herself.

And this time, when she squeezed her eyes shut, it wasn't the erotic reel that played over the backs of her lids. It was her, alone, curled up on her couch, hurting. Her, staring at her computer screen staring at an image of Joshua with another woman on his arm. Her, crushed and lost, gazing at her apartment door, willing a knock to sound. For him to be standing on the other side.

Pain cascaded through her in a crimson shower. Pain and fear.

He'd warned her about not wanting a relationship. Straight up told her he didn't want to be in one with her or any woman. But especially not her. He might not have voiced that, but the words had been there, ringing in the room. Not a woman who might betray him or use him for a story. He would never be able to disassociate her from her job. So once more, she faced the decision—love or her career.

Well, she would be faced with that decision if he wanted her for more than sex.

Which he didn't.

But the fear went deeper than his rejection. It reached down to the core of her that dreaded becoming dependent on a man for her happiness, her security. Because when he left, where would she be?

A shell.

"That's the second sigh in as many minutes," Joshua said, his voice rumbling under her ear. He traced a meandering trail up and down her arm, and she savored his touch. Committed this relaxed version of him to memory. "What're you thinking about?"

Of how I'm foolishly falling for you even though I know you will shatter me.

"Actually, I was thinking about you." Not exactly a lie. But sharing the truth wasn't an option.

Tension invaded his body, and she hated it. "What about me?" he asked, the same stiffness coating his question.

Heaving a sigh—her third—she sat up, her hip pressed

to his, drawing her knees to her chest and wrapping her arms around them. "While I was working on my follow-up article, it struck me again how much you do for those who are in your employ and this community. All without any expectation of credit or acknowledgment. It's so admirable, and if I could put all of that in bold, font size eighteen, I would. People should know that you're not just a CEO consumed with making money. You're not just another businessman with the 'rich getting richer' mentality. You actually care about people and their welfare and their success."

Joshua rose, resting his back against her headboard, the sheet he'd pulled over them pooling around his lean waist. "I don't do it for accolades or recognition, Sophie. None of that is important to me."

"Isn't it?" she whispered. His hazel gaze sharpened, narrowing on her. Though her heart lodged in the base of her throat, she pushed on. "You might not do it for public consumption, but I suspect personal acknowledgment drives you even more."

A frown creased his forehead, and anger, as well as another unidentifiable emotion, flashed in his eyes. "You have no idea what you're talking about," he snapped.

She should let it go. He obviously didn't appreciate her playing armchair therapist. Especially not from the woman he was just fucking. But she couldn't. Joshua might not want her outside this bedroom, but God, he deserved so much more than this half life he lived. He was too good a man, had sacrificed so much for family and those who had been devastated by the Black Crescent scandal. And if no one else cared enough to tell him so, to let him off the hook he'd leaped on himself, then she would.

"Maybe not. But I know what I've seen. And as I told you before, I know you." Lowering her legs, she curled them under her hips and fully faced him. "Every time you set up a new program assisting those less fortunate than you... Every time you donate to a worthy cause... Every time you make another payment in reparation to the families bankrupted by your father's actions, you attempt to erase a black mark you believe mars your name. A black mark that you didn't put there and isn't yours anyway."

"Sophie, stop," he growled, throwing the sheet back and swinging his legs over the side of the bed.

But she shot her hand out, grabbing his wrist. He could've easily shaken her grip free, but he didn't. Maybe he didn't want to hurt her, and she had no problem taking shameless advantage of that display of thoughtfulness.

She rose to her knees and crossed the small space of the bed until she knelt at his side. Tentatively, she reached for him, her hand hovering above his shoulder. Not willing to back down now, she gently touched him. He didn't jerk away, but he remained stiff, unyielding. A slash of pain lacerated her heart, but she refused to back down.

Not when his happiness could be the casualty.

"You've lived in your father's toxic shadow all these years. When do you come out of it?" she asked softly. "When do you get the chance to live in the sun in your own light?"

"That sounds like a pretty fairy tale, but there is no

coming out of it for me. Not as long as my last name is Lowell."

"But what if there is? You have nothing left to prove—you've rebuilt what Vernon almost destroyed. You've repaired your family's reputation with your hard work, dedication and loyalty. You've reimbursed the families your father stole from. What more can you give? Your life...your soul?"

He scoffed, but she didn't let him accuse her of being dramatic, which she was certain had been his next comment. Before he could reply, she slid off the bed and scooped up her discarded shirt from the floor with a "Be right back. Don't move."

By the time she returned moments later with a black binder in her arms, she half expected him to be already dressed and ready to leave her apartment. He had pulled his pants on, but they remained unbuttoned, and he sat in the same place she'd left him.

Relief flooded her, even as fear trickled underneath. Would she be revealing too much when she handed him the binder? Would he see what she so desperately tried to keep hidden?

Inhaling a breath, she crossed the few feet separating them and perched on the mattress next to him. "Here," she whispered, handing him the thick folder.

He glanced at her, his gaze steady and unwavering on her face. Searching. Though everything in her demanded she protect herself from that too-knowing, too-perceptive stare, she met it.

"What is it?" he asked, voice low, intense.

"Look," she instructed instead of answering. "Please."

After another long second, he finally nodded and accepted the binder. Her heart slammed against her rib cage like a wild thing, reverberating in her head and deafening her to everything but the incessant pounding.

Slowly, he flipped the top open.

And froze.

Afraid to lift her gaze to his face—afraid of what she'd glimpse there—she, too, studied the image of one of his mixed-media collages. This one reflected the tragedies of war. With haunting photographs, pieces of metal that appeared to be machinery, newspaper and paint, he'd created a powerful work that, even though it was a black-and-white copy, thrust into her chest and seized every organ. She *felt* when she looked at his art. Anger, grief, fear but also hope and joy. Jesus, how could one man create such raw, wild beauty? How could he walk away from it? Had it been like cauterizing a part of himself? She couldn't imagine...

Silent, Joshua flipped to the next page. A black-and-white copy of a piece commentating on homelessness. Another page. A work celebrating women, their struggle, their suffering, their strength, their beauty. Page after page of his art that both criticized and celebrated the human condition.

When he reached the last copy, he sat there, unmoving, peering down at it, unblinking.

"Why?" he rasped, the first word he'd spoken in the last ten minutes as he perused his past and what had once been his future.

She didn't pretend to misunderstand his question. "When I was researching you and your family for the first article, I came across several stories about you as an artist. From your college and local newspapers as well as several art columns. They carried pictures of your art. And they were so... *Good* is such an inadequate choice. They were visceral. And to think you, Joshua Lowell, had created them…" She shrugged a shoulder. "I guess it became kind of an obsession. I hunted down any image of your work I could find. Finding out about this man who could drag this from his soul and share it with the world? I needed to talk to him, to discover how he'd become a CEO instead of an artist. And that's why I wanted the article to include that side of you. Because I was struggling with reconciling the two."

"That man doesn't exist anymore," Joshua stated flatly. "You're searching for a ghost. He was buried fifteen years ago."

"I don't believe that," she countered. He glanced sharply at her, but she didn't tone down her vehemence. "You might have tried, but he trickles through when you help others follow their own dreams about art. When you support them and give your time and money toward them. If you'd truly put that man aside, he wouldn't help others who need him. That passion to educate people about this world may not have been exhibited in artwork these past years, but you still reveal it in your actions."

He shook his head, and despite the grim line of his full mouth, a tenderness entered his gaze. "You see what and who you want to, Sophie."

"No, I see you. This." She smoothed a hand over the image of his artwork. "This is you. A visionary. An activist and change agent in your own way. An *artist*." She tilted her head, studied his face. "What if your life doesn't end with Black Crescent? What if, after all these years, it's your time to live your own life, the one you left behind for family? A family that you owe nothing to but love and loyalty. You once said you couldn't

abandon your family. But then you abandoned yourself.
What's the worst that could happen if you followed your
own delayed dreams, your own passions? Your mother
will be okay and taken care of. And your brothers? If
they choose to cut you out of their lives, then that's
their problem and issues, not yours. Now's your time.
And you never know. Maybe if given no other chance
but to step up and assume the mantle of responsibility
that you've worn for so long, your brothers might surprise you and do it."

She hesitated. Did she tell him all of it? In for a penny
and all that... Inhaling a deep breath, she held it, then
exhaled. And leaped.

"I didn't tell you before now, but Christopher Harrison with the Tender Shoots nonprofit approached me
about you at the gala. He read my article, saw the pictures of your art included in it. He wants to offer you
your own show in Manhattan, at the Guggenheim. Not
only to bring in money for the organization, but he
would be excited about seeing you reemerge as the artist you were. Are."

For a moment—a quick, heart-stopping moment—
a light glittered in his eyes. A light that could've been
hope or joy. But then, in the very next, his hazel eyes
dimmed. And disappointment squeezed her chest, her
heart. He glanced away from her, staring at the far wall
as if it revealed precious answers.

"That's not possible, and I'm not interested. You have
no clue how it is to live under the weight of society's
expectations," he murmured. His fingers curled into a
fist atop the binder. But deliberately, he stretched them
out, splaying them across the page—covering the image
of his art. "You don't understand the burden of always

knowing someone's waiting for you to misstep to prove that bad blood will out. It doesn't matter whether I continue to run Black Crescent or pick up a camera or paintbrush again. I can't escape, because I can't evade who I am. Joshua Lowell, Vernon Lowell's son."

She swallowed the silent sob of frustration, anger and grief. Grief for the man who believed he was forever tainted by the actions of his father. Who believed the only road available to him was the one he trod—even if it led to a future that wasn't his.

"Maybe not," she murmured, cupping his cheek and turning his face toward her. "But maybe I can help you bear the burden. Just a little."

Leaning forward, she brushed her lips across his, then covered his mouth with hers. His groan vibrated between them, before he turned, letting the binder fall to the floor, and hauled her up the bed. He took control of the kiss, crawling over her, finding his place between her thighs.

And as he consumed them both with his burning passion, she wept inside for him.

For the both of them.

Chapter 10

"Josh, I'm heading home now," Haley announced from the doorway of his office. "Do you need anything before I leave?"

Joshua looked up from his computer. "No, I'm good."

Nodding, she stepped back, then paused, tilting her head to the side. "Everything okay with you?"

He leaned back in his chair, frowning. Other than a busy schedule and meetings all day, he was fine. He also had plans to meet Sophie at her apartment, so he was actually more than fine. But that, he kept to himself. "Yes, why do you ask?"

"You seem, I don't know—" her hazel eyes narrowed on him "—relaxed this past week. Something up I should know about?"

He snorted. "No, Haley. I'm good, like I said."

"Okay, if you say so."

"I say so."

"Well, not saying I don't believe you, but whatever—or whoever—has turned you into the Zen version of Joshua Lowell, give them—or her—my thanks." With an impish smile and arched eyebrow, she stepped back and shut the door behind her before he could reply.

"Brat," he muttered, but after a moment, chuckled. Yes, she was definitely the annoying younger sister he never asked for. But he didn't know what he'd do without her, either.

Glancing at the clock at the bottom of his monitor, he nodded. Six ten. Finishing a review of the report his CFO had sent him would take only about fifteen more minutes, twenty tops. Then he could head out.

When was the last time he'd looked forward to leaving his office that had become his second—hell, first—home? Not until Sophie. A lot of things in his life could be separated into two eras. Before the Scandal and, now, After Sophie.

God, when had she become that significant in his life?

The answer blazed bright and sure. From the moment she barged into his office, demanding and so beautiful.

From the release of the article, to her revelation about his supposed child, to her ice-thawing passion and kindness… She'd changed his world.

She'd changed him.

A kernel of fear rooted inside him, and try as he might, he couldn't dislodge it. It'd been there since Monday night after she'd shocked him with the binder full of his previous artwork, and damn near taken him out with her body and the abandoned pleasure she'd offered him.

No one had ever taken the time to look further than

the persona he presented. No one had bothered. Except for Sophie. She'd challenged him, as she'd been doing since their first meeting. Daring him to grab ahold of the dreams, the future he'd aborted when his father had disappeared. For a moment, he'd glimpsed what he could have, who he could be through her eyes. And the joy that had spread through him like the brightest and warmest of lights had been stunning. And terrifying.

Stunning because he hadn't felt such happiness in years—fifteen to be exact.

And terrified because he wanted it so badly. His old life back. The opportunity to work in his passion again. The possibility of his own show.

Sophie.

But he couldn't have any of them.

None of them were meant for him.

All he could do was be satisfied with the here and now, because it, too, would eventually end. Sophie would eventually leave him when she became discontented with what he could offer her. What he couldn't give her.

But he knew that going in. Everything ended. Everyone left.

Shaking his head, he frowned, refocusing on the work he had left to finish. But then a notification for an email popped up on the bottom of his screen.

The frown deepened, as did an unnerving sense of dread.

He hesitated, his cursor hovering over the notice. Dammit, what was he doing? It could be anyone. His clients and some of his employees worked longer hours than him. The message could be from any one of them.

Clenching his jaw, he resolutely clicked on the notification.

Anonymous.

Just like the name on the message that had arrived in his inbox yesterday.

Congratulations, Papa! Your daughter can't wait to meet you!

He'd passed it off as some kind of joke. Since no one had contacted him about a possible child, and Sophie hadn't found anything more concrete yet, he'd assumed the DNA test had been a mistake. Or a way to just mess with him by inserting his name at the top. Wouldn't he know, somehow *feel*, if he had a child out there? Though it'd thrown him, he'd ignored the email yesterday…and hadn't told Sophie about it.

But now, he stared at another email from the same person. Disquiet settled over him like a suffocating weight. Trepidation churned in his gut, and his grip on his mouse tightened until the casing squeaked a threatening crack.

He didn't want to open it.

So he did.

Don't know why you're denying it. I paid good money to make sure you'd get the proof.

The words blurred, jumbled together, then leaped into startling clarity. They glared up at him, almost blinding him. Tearing his gaze from the message, he pushed from his chair and stalked across the room, thrusting his fingers through his hair. But he couldn't escape the image branded into his head.

I paid good money to make sure you'd get the proof.

There was only one person who'd brought an illegitimate child to his attention.

One person who'd provided him with the so-called proof.

Sophie.

Anger rolled through him like an ominous storm cloud spiked with bolts of lightning. Hot, heavy, sizzling.

He'd been so stupid. So goddamn blind.

What had been her endgame? Send him on this wild-goose chase, pretend to help him just to get close and what? Write a story on the whole journey? Paint him as some deadbeat? Or a pathetic father on the search for a child who wasn't his? That maybe didn't even exist?

Pain tried to course through him, but he blocked it. Allowed the fury to capsize it.

Fury was better. It razed everything to the ground. Including the fact that he'd started to trust this woman, and he'd been betrayed.

Again.

Sophie stepped off the elevator onto the second floor of the Black Crescent building. Anticipation danced a quick step inside her, and she smiled. Joshua would be surprised to see her there, since they'd planned to meet at her apartment later. But she couldn't wait. She'd finished the follow-up article and wanted to give him the first look at it before Althea saw it Friday morning.

God, this trod so close to her experience with Laurence. She'd made the mistake of granting him the opportunity to read her articles first. But unlike her ex, Joshua wouldn't use this as a chance to sabotage the story or have her change it to fit his needs or agenda. One, Joshua didn't have an agenda. But two, and most important, he wasn't Laurence.

Nerves trotted in her belly, but they didn't trump the happiness spilling through her veins. This week had revealed even more of the man she'd fallen so hard for.

Yes, she could admit it to herself.

She loved Joshua Lowell.

And no, he hadn't rescinded his "no relationships" condition, but he felt more for her than someone to warm his—or her—bed. She sensed it in his every small but genuine smile, the casual affection, the endearments, in the time he asked to spend with her.

God, did it make her pathetic that she was another woman believing she could change a man?

Probably.

But the knowledge didn't dim her smile as she knocked on his door, then pushed it open.

"Josh," she greeted, entering his inner sanctum. "I know we were supposed to meet at..." She trailed off, taking in the guarded, aloof expression she hadn't seen in a week. "What's wrong? Did something happen?"

She rushed forward to his desk, but drew to an abrupt halt when he rose, that glacial stare not melting or wavering from her face. No, it hardened, and dread curdled in her stomach. What the hell was going on here?

"Josh?" she whispered.

"Joshua," he corrected in an arctic voice that matched his gaze.

Only her hands flattened on his desk kept her from crumbling to the floor. But it couldn't prevent her heart from cracking down the middle and screams wailing from every jagged break.

"What's going on?" she rasped. "Why—"

Without shifting his contemptuous regard from her face, he slowly spun the monitor on his desk around to face her. She dragged her eyes from the stark lines and sharp angles that she'd just traced with her lips the night before and shifted them to the computer screen.

A thread of emails. From an address named Anonymous.

She skimmed them, her horror growing, the slick, grimy strands twisting around the happiness that had filled her only moments earlier, strangling it until only sickness remained. Bile surged up from her stomach, past her chest and raced for her throat. Convulsively, she swallowed it down.

Not because of what the emails stated; she had no idea who had sent them or what they were implying by paying to make sure Joshua had received the DNA test. Because she hadn't received any money. But obviously, just one glance at the anger and disdain in his green-and-gold eyes, and she knew—*she knew*—he believed she had.

The nausea swelled again with a vengeance.

"I don't know what this is supposed to mean," she said, reaching for a calm that had abandoned her the moment she'd stepped into this office. "No one gave me money to give you the DNA results. But you don't believe me," she added, voice curiously flat.

"What, Sophie? I'm supposed to believe you over my lying eyes?" he drawled, eyes snapping fire. "I wondered why you would show me the test when you were so adamant about protecting your research and sources." He loosed a harsh, serrated bark of ugly laughter. "Now I have my answer."

"You really think I would do this? Accept a bribe to trick you into believing you had a daughter?" she demanded, her own rage kindling, burning away the pain. For now. "For what? Why would I do that?"

"You're a reporter, Sophie. I don't know. An editorial piece that could grace the front of your paper might be a very good reason." A terrible half smile curved the corner of his mouth. "How would your editor in chief feel if she knew her star reporter resorted to underhanded tactics just to get a story?"

So much for the anger. Pain, red-hot and consuming, blazed a path through her. She could barely draw in a breath that didn't hurt. But she wouldn't allow him to see it. She'd given him everything—her trust, her faith…her love. And he'd shit over all of it.

No, he'd get nothing else. Most definitely not her tears or her pride. Fuck him.

"I don't know why I'm so surprised," she said, jerking her chin higher. "This is what you wanted. What you were waiting on. And that email is just the convenient excuse."

"Should I know what you're referring to?" he asked, the man who'd made her laugh, made her cry out in the most unimaginable pleasure, gone. And in his place stood the man of ice she'd originally met those weeks ago.

"You're so transparent, Joshua," she murmured, shaking her head. "You've just been waiting for me to screw up. To disappoint you. To leave you. Just like everyone else. But the sad part of it is I wouldn't have. I would've stayed by your side for as long as you asked. Longer. But you can't trust that. You can't possibly believe someone would put you first, would love you enough to never abandon or hurt you."

"Sophie," he growled, but she cut him off with a slash of her hand.

"No. You would rather self-sabotage and destroy what we had, what we could've had if you'd just let me love you and let yourself love. Instead, you would accuse me of something so horrible, so cruel that it's beneath me and definitely beneath you. You're nothing but a coward, Joshua Lowell." She shoved off the desk, silently promising her legs they could crumble later once she was in her car and away from this place, this man. But not now. "You've been running scared for so long that you can't even recognize when someone is running toward you and with you, not from you."

Pivoting, she focused on putting one foot in front of the other and not stumbling. Concentrated on just getting away. Even as part of her hoped, prayed he would call her name. Apologize. Take back the ugliness that had breathed in this office.

But he didn't. And another part of her broke.

As she reached the door, she paused.

Without looking back over her shoulder, she grabbed the doorjamb and stared straight ahead into the dim outer office.

"I love you, Joshua. When I didn't believe in it anymore, you showed me it could exist again for me. I don't regret that. But I do regret that you would rather hold on to the past than my heart. And for that, I pity you."

She pulled the door closed behind her.

Closing it on him…and who they could've been.

Chapter 11

"Well, if it isn't Joshua Lowell. Slumming it." Joshua glanced up from his whiskey to see a tall, lean but muscular man with dark brown hair and blue eyes sink down onto the stool next to his. "To what do we owe this honor?"

Ignoring the man and his irritating smirk, Joshua returned to his drink and stared blindly at the flat-screen television overhead, where a basketball game he couldn't care less about played. But anything was better than his empty, lonely apartment. Everywhere he looked, memories of Sophie bombarded him. In his living room. On his rug. In his kitchen. In his bed. It'd been only four hours since she'd left his office, her words ringing in the air long after she'd left.

I love you, Joshua... I do regret that you would rather hold on to the past than my heart. And for that, I pity you.

She loved him. How could she? He'd warned her he didn't do relationships. Didn't do happily-ever-afters. She'd called him a coward, but he had his reasons. And they were good reasons. They were...

Damn. He rubbed the bridge of his nose, pinching it, before lifting the tumbler to his mouth for another sip.

Yeah, even boring games, the din of conversation and subpar alcohol was better than the memories as his only company. Still, he thought while he glanced at the guy next to him as he called the bartender by name and ordered a beer, that didn't mean he wanted to be chatted up by a stranger with a chip on his shoulder. That smart-ass greeting had clued Joshua in that this man with his hard eyes and harder smile wasn't a fan of his.

Fuck. He'd come to this bar in the neighboring town for some peace, not more judgment from a drunken asshole.

"I heard the rumor you were here drinking, but I didn't believe it. Daryl, get another round for Mr. Lowell," he called to the bartender. "He looks like he could use it."

"No, thank you," Joshua told Daryl. "I'm good with what I have here."

"What? My money isn't good enough for a Lowell?" he drawled, a steel edge to his question. No, not a question. A gauntlet thrown down on the bar top between them.

Too bad for him, Joshua didn't feel like picking it up. That required too much effort, and he was just too tired.

"Do I know you?" Joshua turned, facing the other man, who seemed vaguely familiar, but his mind couldn't place him. "Because if not, then can you just tell me what your problem is with me so I can go back to my drink?"

A faint snarl curled the corner of his mouth. "Why am I not surprised that you don't recognize me? Why would you? From that lofty tower you rule from, it would be difficult to distinguish between the peasants. Even the ones you had a hand in destroying." Before Joshua could reply, the guy stuck his hand out. "Zane Patterson. Maybe you know the last name, if not me."

Patterson. The whiskey turned to swill in his stomach, roiling. God, yes, he knew that name. It'd been the name of one of the families that had been his father's clients.

"Oh, so I see you do remember." Zane nodded. "I guess that makes you somewhat better than your father, who screwed us over and never looked back."

"Yes, I do, and yes, he did," Joshua agreed, earning an eyebrow arch from Zane. Had the other man expected him to deny the accusation? To defend Vernon. He silently snorted. Not in this lifetime. Or the next, if his father was indeed there instead of lying around some beach surrounded by younger women and mai tais.

"What are you doing here, Lowell?" Zane asked, picking up the beer the bartender set in front of him. Sipping from the mug, he studied Joshua over the rim. "Drowning your woes, maybe?"

"Listen, I understand why you of all people can't stand the sight of me. But I'm here, just trying to have a drink. You can hate me from across the room."

"Still so high and mighty," Zane murmured. "Even after finding out you're no better than the rest of us. Worse, I'd say. You wouldn't catch me abandoning a kid of mine. But like father, like son, I guess."

Shock slammed into him, nearly toppling him from the stool. "What the hell did you just say to me?" he rasped.

A sardonic smile darkened Zane's face. "You heard me. Don't tell me the reporter didn't give you the DNA test results? I specifically chose Sophie Armstrong to share that with."

The shock continued to resonate through him like the drone of a thousand bees, but anger started to rush in like a tide, swallowing it. "You paid Sophie to make sure I received it?" he ground out.

"Paid her? Hell no. It was free of charge. And my pleasure." He again smiled, but it nowhere near reached his icy blue eyes. No, that wasn't correct. They weren't icy. Something volatile and...bleak darkened those eyes. Pain. If Joshua wasn't mired in it, he might not have been able to identify it. "Someone anonymously emailed the results to me," Zane continued, his level voice not reflecting the turmoil he would probably deny existed in his gaze. "And I just passed them along. The test spoke for itself, so I really didn't give a damn who sent them. But whoever it was must've known I wouldn't mind paying it forward. Your father and family destroyed my world, my family." Gravel roughened his tone, and Zane jerked his head away from Joshua. A muscle ticked along his jaw as he visibly battled some emotion he no doubt hated that Joshua glimpsed. After several seconds, the other man returned his regard to Joshua, his expression carefully composed. Too blank. "I was only too happy to return the favor. Everyone believes you're this perfect guy when you have a child out there that you won't even take care of. I can't wait for people to find out just who you really are."

Oh God.

He'd fucked up.

Numb, Joshua turned back to face the bar, Zane's hurt scraping Joshua's skin, his bitter words buzzing in his ears. He'd sent the DNA tests. Free of charge. Sophie had been telling the truth. No one had paid her to show him the results. She hadn't lied to him.

But… He'd known that, hadn't he?

Deep down, where that terrified, lonely and angry twenty-two-year-old still existed, he'd known she wouldn't have been capable of betraying him. She'd been right about him; he was a coward. So scared she would leave him like everyone else he'd loved, he'd jumped on the first obstacle that had presented itself to push her out the door. Save himself the pain of her rejecting him and walking away from him.

Even though he'd known she could never do what he'd accused her of. Not sweet, honorable, honest, strong Sophie. She said that she knew him better than anyone else, but he also knew her. Fear had kept him from acknowledging it in his office, but the truth couldn't be denied. He did know her.

And he loved her.

He *loved* her.

She'd seen beyond his tainted past and who his father was and had accepted him, believed in him, when he hadn't even been able to do the same for himself. She'd seen him as blameless, as a hero for so many people, as an artist with a passion and a dream. Sophie had never given up on him.

Now it was time he didn't. Time he believed in himself. In them.

Setting the drink on the bar, Josh reached into his jacket and removed his wallet. He threw down several bills that covered his drinks and a healthy tip before turning back to Zane.

"I'm sorry my father caused you and your family so much pain. He was greedy and selfish and had no thought whatsoever for who he would hurt. But I was every bit as much of a victim as you were. I lost my family, too. But I refuse to apologize or take on his guilt and shame anymore, though. I've tried to make amends for his sins. But I'm tired of it. I'm done."

Without pausing or waiting to hear what Zane Patterson had to say to that, he pivoted and strode out of the bar.

For the first time in a decade and a half, feeling…free.

"Dammit," Sophie muttered, jerking the strap of her laptop bag from the car door where it'd snagged. Huffing out a breath, she let it slip to the ground and reached in the back seat for the cardboard box that contained some of her personal items from her desk.

Tears stung her eyes as she scanned the framed photo of her and her mom on vacation at Myrtle Beach a couple of years ago, her favorite "only the strongest women become writers" coffee mug and several other knickknacks. She'd waited until almost everyone on her floor had left for the evening before she packed up most of the items and carried them to her car. Fewer questions that way. Especially since she hadn't yet informed her boss that she was leaving her job with the *Falling Brook Chronicle*.

It'd been her decision, and not one she made lightly.

And not because she feared Joshua would follow through with his subtle threat about informing Althea of being paid to pass on the DNA test. And also not because she was afraid her editor in chief would fire her after finding out she and Joshua had slept together.

No, she was leaving the paper and Falling Brook for herself.

Start over fresh.

Free of memories of Joshua and her own foolishness.

Maybe she'd return to Chicago. Or even go somewhere totally new, like Seattle. She'd visited once in college and had loved the eclectic and vibrant energy of the city...

"Sophie."

No. It couldn't be. Her stubborn, starved brain had conjured up his voice. She squeezed her eyes close, trying to banish it. The last thing she needed was to start imagining him when she was trying to let him go.

"Sophie, please. Can I have just a minute?"

Okay, this was no dream. Even her mind couldn't envision Joshua Lowell saying "please."

She carefully set her box back onto the seat, then pivoted.

And she really should've taken several more minutes to prepare herself for coming face-to-face with him after yesterday. God, it was so unfair. He'd stomped all over her heart. That should wear on a man. He should at least have new wrinkles. Bags under his eyes. Gray hair.

Horns.

But no, he was as beautiful as ever.

Damn him.

"What are you doing here, Joshua?"

"What is that?" he asked instead of answering, his gaze focused on the cardboard box before jumping to her face. "Are you planning on going somewhere, Sophie?"

"That isn't any of your business." Not anymore. Sighing, she shut the rear door and picked up her laptop bag. She'd just come back for the rest of her stuff later. "Now, please answer my question. What are you doing here?"

"I came to see you," he said.

She shrugged a shoulder, moving past him toward her apartment building. "Well, you've achieved that objective, so if you'll excuse me…"

A firm but gentle grip encircled her elbow, and she briefly closed her eyes, thankful her back was to him. He couldn't witness the pain and longing that streaked through her at his touch. She vacillated between ordering him to never put his hands on her again and throwing herself into his arms, begging him to hold her… to love her.

Why, yes. She was pathetic.

Deliberately, she stepped back, out of his hold. Then shifted back even farther so even his scent couldn't tease her.

Pride notched her chin up high as she forced herself to meet his gaze. A gaze that wasn't cold like the last time they'd been together. No, it was softer, even… tender.

She hardened her heart, made herself remember how he'd accused her of lying to him, betraying him. Made herself remember that he'd cracked her heart in so many fragments, she still hadn't been able to find all the pieces.

"Sophie, one minute. That's all I'm asking, and then if you want me to, I'll walk away and never bother you again."

"Thirty seconds," she shot back. That was what he'd given her the first time she'd bulldozed her way into his office.

As if he, too, recalled the significance, a small smile curved his mouth. "I'll take it." He rubbed a hand across the nape of his neck and moved forward, but at the last second, halted. Respecting the distance she'd placed between them. "Sophie, I'm sorry. I'm so sorry for not believing in you. For accusing you of selling me out. For jumping to conclusions and painting you as the villain. For looking at you through the lens of my past instead of seeing who you really are. You were right about me. I was so scared you would leave me so I used whatever excuse I could to push you away first. I would rather be alone than risk the chance of someone hurting me again, betraying me again. And I punished you for my fears, my shortcomings. I'll never forgive myself for letting you walk out that door believing that I thought you capable of that. I know words are inadequate, but, sweetheart, I'm so fucking sorry."

Her lungs hurt from her suspended breath. His apology reached beneath skin and bone to her bruised and wounded heart, cupped it. Soothed it.

But the words were a little too late. The damage had been done. And she couldn't undo the hurt, the humiliation. The rejection of her love.

Her rejection of herself.

"Joshua, a few years ago, I met a man. Fell in love with him," she whispered. "I didn't know it at the time, but he was using me for his own ends. Not that you've ever done that," she hurriedly added, because of all he'd done to her, Joshua was incapable of that kind of perfidy. It just wasn't in him. "But I almost lost my career—I almost lost myself—because I loved the wrong man. A man who didn't love me in return. I did lose my way, though. And I promised myself I would never give up my job, my independence, my integrity, my soul for another man. The cost was too high, and I wasn't— I'm not—willing to pay it. But standing in your office last night, I found myself on the precipice of doing just that. I may not have betrayed you, but I almost betrayed myself. I won't put myself in that position again. I refuse to." She shook her head, a heavy grief of what could've been for them an albatross around her shoulders. "Thank you for coming here, but I don't need your apology. I know who I am. I know what I deserve. A man who loves and trusts me. Who won't ask me to be less so he can be secure. A life where I can have it all and not feel guilty because I compromised myself to get it."

"You do deserve all of that, Sophie," he rasped, the fierceness in his voice widening her eyes, leaving her shaken. "All of it and more. I—" He took that step toward her that he'd hesitated over moments ago. "I am that man who loves and trusts you. I'd never ask you to be less so I can be secure, because the greater you are, the happier you are, the more successful you are, the better I am as a man. The man who loves and supports you. Compromise? If you compromised who you are, I would never know the joy of having all of you, just as you are. Brilliant, strong, determined, driven, beautiful. Sweetheart—" he tunneled a hand through his hair, disheveling the short, dark blond strands "— you've shown me that I don't have to bear my father's burdens any longer. You've taught me that I'm not forgotten, that I am so much more than I ever believed possible. I thought what happened with my father fifteen years ago was the worst thing that could ever happen to me. But if it hadn't occurred, you wouldn't have written an article on it. You wouldn't have come crashing into my life. And, sweetheart, all the pain, all the fear, all the loss—I'd go through it all again in a heartbeat if it meant meeting you, touching you...loving you." He closed the distance between them and cradled her cheek. "If that box means you're leaving your job, please don't do it. That's a compromise you should never make."

Tears stung her eyes, and she choked on the hope that insisted on rising in her chest. She'd called him a coward yesterday, but now it was her who was terrified. Of being crushed again. Because unlike Laurence, he could destroy her, and though she would find a way to cobble herself together again, she wouldn't be whole.

No, she couldn't.

Not again.

As much as she loved him, she just...couldn't.

"Joshua, I'm sorry. I can't. I love you—I probably always will—but I'm not that strong. I...can't."

She couldn't contain her sob as she cupped his hand and turned her face into it. Kissed it.

Then fled into her apartment building.

Chapter 12

Joshua stood near the bank of elevators, the animated and excited hum of chatter from Black Crescent's lobby reaching him. Beyond the wall he stood behind congregated reporters and cameramen from the tristate area. All hungry and anticipating the announcement that Joshua had promised to deliver. Anything concerning Black Crescent Hedge Fund would've stirred their interest, but on a Saturday morning, coming from Joshua himself, who never did press conferences, they would've jumped on this tidbit. Just as he'd hoped.

The media expected a business-related statement. And they would receive that.

But so much more.

Joshua's future rode on this press conference.

"Ready, Josh?" Haley asked, laying a hand on his upper arm. Concern and just a bit of sadness darkened her hazel eyes. "Are you sure about this?"

He nodded. "I've never been more certain about anything in my life." He covered her hand with his and clasped it. "And just in case I've never said so before, thank you for everything you've been to this company and to me. Those first few years, I don't know if I would've been able to make it without you."

Tears glistened in her eyes, but, Haley being Haley, she tipped her chin up and cleared her throat. "You're right. You wouldn't have," she drawled.

He chuckled and, giving her hand one last squeeze, moved forward into the throng of media.

At his appearance, the noise reached a fever pitch as questions were lobbed at him from overeager journalists. But he ignored them as he stepped to the podium and microphone, scanning the crowded lobby for one person...

There.

Sophie stood in the middle, lovely and composed.

Relief barreled into him. He'd been afraid she wouldn't show up—had even placed a call to Althea to request Sophie's presence. But that hadn't guaranteed she would've agreed. Seeing her here, though, the anxiety that he'd fought off all morning kicked in the door of his calm. This was the most important moment of his life. Hell, he was fighting for his life—his future.

I love you—I probably always will—but I'm not that strong.

Her words, so final but so weary, echoed in his head. The resolve in her voice had set his heart pounding, terrified he'd lost her. But hope, his love for her and, yes, desperation refused to let him give up. He would go to war for her. He just had to hold on to her declaration of love. And his belief that she was stronger than both of them put together.

"Thank you for coming here today on such short notice," he said into the mic. Immediately, the voices hushed, but the excitement and tension crackled in the air. "I'm going to share my announcement and will take only a few questions at the end."

He inhaled, his eyes once more finding and locking onto Sophie. Her silver gaze met his, and he found the strength to continue there.

"Fifteen years ago, I took the helm of Black Crescent Hedge Fund after my father embezzled money from the company, nearly bankrupting it and devastating his clients and their families. Since that time, I've rebuilt the business and have tried to make reparations for his crimes. But today, I will be stepping down as CEO of Black Crescent."

A roar of disbelief filled the lobby and camera flashes nearly blinded him. Still, he kept his attention on Sophie, spying the shock and confusion that widened her eyes and parted her lips. Questions bombarded him, and he held up his hands, warding them off. Again, silence descended.

"Over the next few months there will be a search for my successor. He or she will be carefully handpicked to replace me as CEO. I'm sure you're all wondering why I'm resigning. I plan to go back to my first love, my art. I gave it up to run Black Crescent, but I've decided to return to it. And possibly—if the woman I'm in love with will agree to marry me—to plan a wedding."

Again, the room erupted. But he cared only about Sophie's reaction, and his heart seized at the shock and tears and…and love. *Please, God, let that be love glistening in her gray eyes.*

"I let my pride and fear blind me and hold me hostage for far too long. And I'm praying that it doesn't cost me her love. I've spent too many years in my father's shadow, worrying what other people thought. If I was worthy enough. But she brought me out of the dark and into the light with her love. And because she loves me, I am worthy. And I want to spend the rest of my life proving that she didn't make a mistake by taking a chance on me. If she'll have me."

He stared at her, silently willing her to let him tell the world her identity. But more, silently asking her again for her forgiveness and her love. Her hand in marriage.

It seemed like an eternity passed as he stood behind that podium, reporters yelling at him, cameras flashing again and again. But still, he caught her nod. Caught that beautiful smile that lit up her face, her eyes and his heart.

"Sophie, will you come up here with me?"

She didn't hesitate, but wound a path through the throng, and like Moses with the Red Sea, they parted, letting her pass. He didn't pay attention to anyone but her. His heart swelling larger than his chest as she neared. And when his hand finally enfolded hers, something inside him that had been hollow, filled. That lost puzzle piece slotted into its place, and he was whole. Complete.

He drew her close, and closer still until she walked into his arms. Bending his head over hers, he pressed a kiss to her hair. A shiver worked through him and he didn't care who saw it. She was in his embrace again.

Her scent enveloped him. She warmed him. And God, he'd been cold for so long.

Leaning back, he cupped her face, tipping her head back. The tears he'd glimpsed seconds ago tracked down her face, and he wiped them away with his thumbs, brushing his lips across her cheekbones, the bridge of her nose, her lips.

"Sophie Armstrong, I'm who I was meant to be with you. I was created to love you, and I not only cannot imagine a future without you, I don't want one without you in it. Would you do me the honor of being my wife?"

"Yes, Josh," she said without hesitation and with a certainty and confidence that erased the hurt, shame and pain that had dogged him for fifteen years. "I love you, and there's nothing I want more than to live by your side."

With reporters exploding into chaos around them, he claimed her mouth.

And his future.

* * * * *

HARLEQUIN
PLUS

Try the best multimedia subscription service for romance readers like you!

Read, Watch and Play.

Experience the easiest way to get the romance content you crave.

Start your **FREE TRIAL** at
www.harlequinplus.com/freetrial.